To Tom
Thank you for all your support.
My greatest fan.
Anthony Hulse

CUPIDS POISON ARROW

ANTHONY HULSE

D1428488

Copyright @ Anthony Hulse 2014

ISBN: 978-1-291-08342-2

Chapter One

The white-robed man with the long, flowing locks and beard stood amid his kneeling flock, his hands outstretched, his deep voice reassuring. In another era, this could have been the Messiah addressing his many followers, but this was not the Messiah. Gideon the chosen one, more commonly known as Paul Robbins, mingled with his devotees and touched each one on the head as he chanted strange, mystical words to them.

Two men watched the ceremony from the safety of a dry, stonewall, their salary not worth dying for. The sun beat down on the normally tranquil countryside known as the Cotswolds, but today the serenity would be disturbed.

Vincent Slattery cleaned his spectacles, before he dried his tacky hands on his denim jeans. He understood how fortunate he was to have located Gideon and his normally inaccessible cult. He selfishly looked about him, and begrudged any intrusion on his discovery. Distant sirens carried by the gentle breeze drowned out the singing birds, and deemed their chorus unnecessary.

"Sam! How much more film is there?"

"Enough, Vince."

"make sure you save some for when the law arrives. Things could get very interesting around here."

Gideon was passed a large plastic container from one of his purple-robed worshippers and proceeded to dowse each one. He chanted as he did so. The odour of petrol reached the nostrils of the two men, who looked at each another.

"Shit! He's not going to do what I think he's going to do is he?"

Slattery appeared excited. "Just keep filming, Sam. There's nothing we can do to save those poor souls."

The sound of the sirens grew louder, which confirmed the presence of police vehicles on the brow of the hill.

Slattery afforded another peep over the wall to see that Gideon was holding a lighted torch. "Fuck! They're not going to make it," he yelled. He watched the Armed Response Unit leave their vehicles and scramble towards the wall.

A red-faced officer led the charge and squatted besides Slattery. He was clearly out of breath. "What's the score, Vince?"

"You must act fast, Joe. He's going to torch them."

"What?"

The police officer peered over the wall to hear Gideon command his disciples to join hands. The cult-leader looked to the heavens and chanted loudly, before he put the torch to one of his followers and stepped back. He spread his arms and watched the circle of fire spread rapidly, as it engulfed the fifty or so fanatics in an orange inferno.

Numerous police officers ran forward, but they were powerless, due to the intensity of the heat. The stench of burning flesh merged with the fumes of the petrol. The onlookers watched helplessly.

Gideon laughed loudly, before he dowsed himself and placed the torch against his gown.

The tall reporter showed no emotion when the elderly police officer stared disapprovingly towards him. No words were needed.

******

If a beauty contest was an Olympic event, then Rosie Cochrane would have won enough gold to put Fort Knox to shame. Sadly, the young redhead had only to utter a few words for the ideal girl dream image to be shattered. Rosie was not the brightest star in the sky, but wealth is a great compensator for intelligence. She sat at the bar of the luxurious Dorchester Hotel and sipped champagne, as if the world would end tomorrow. She was elegantly attired in a silk, emerald-green gown; the strap that hung down her arm testament to her condition. Her raven-haired companion was in danger of falling from her barstool as she giggled childlike, and welcomed the attention lauded on them by the two apparently well-educated hooray Henrys.

If they noticed the suave, handsome stranger seated at the other end of the bar, they did not show it. His Italian tailored suit, black slicked-back hair and goatee beard, gave him the appearance of someone who had just stepped out of a scene from *The Godfather*. He shaped his mouth into a *Humphrey Bogart* like grimace, swallowed the dregs of his Jack Daniels, before he ordered another.

Canned classical music filtered from the giant speakers, which befitted the lavish surroundings of the hotel. Only a handful of people had opted for a nightcap at this late hour, and it was apparent that the sombre looking barman would rather be somewhere else. He checked his wristwatch for the umpteenth time, even though a large clock faced him.

The lone stranger observed the boisterous behaviour of the other four drinkers. He frowned when the hand of one of the men climbed the slender leg of Rosie, to reveal her suspender belt. The ginger-haired man received a slap, the hand mark evident on his red face.

"Ferk off, you sleazy bastard," came the strong Irish accent from Rosie's red lips. Her eyes drooped jadedly as she clutched the bar and attempted to keep her balance.

"Come on, Rosie, he was only having fun," slurred her dark-haired companion, her hand around the back of the other man.

The tall man stooped to kiss her, and she vomited, much to the amusement of Rosie.

"Shit!" moaned the tall man. "You've fucking ruined my jacket, you silly cow."

She dismissed him with a wave of the hand and staggered towards the exit.

"Looks like we're doubling up, darling," suggested Ginger.

Rosie sneered. "I'd rather have a leg off. Now run along, I'm sure your mammy will be looking for you." She sipped the remainder of her champagne and wavered on her feet.

Ginger seized her by the wrist, while his partner squeezed her face, distorting her pretty features.

"Leave her alone, arseholes!"

The tormentors looked around in unison to see the stranger loom over them. The barman had sensibly made himself conspicuous and wiped down the tables at the other end of the bar.

"Who the fuck are you?" asked Ginger.

"I'm the man who's going to shove your head up your arse if you don't leave… Your choice, you little shit."

The bulge in Ginger's throat was perceptible. His companion grabbed his arm. "Come on, Bradley… she's only a whore anyway."

Rosie stared at her saviour as the duo retreated into the warm night air. "Why, thank you very much, er..."

"Charlie. Charlie Bojangles."

She giggled and covered her mouth with her hand. Her long painted fingernails appeared more like talons.

"What's so funny?" he quizzed.

"Mr Bojangles, eh? Just like the song…? I'm sorry. I'm Rosie. Here, let me buy you a drink. It's the least I can do?"

The returning barman rolled his eyes towards the ceiling and abandoned any hope he had of an early finish.

Bojangles smiled. "Jack Daniels will be fine."

Rosie nodded to the barman.

Bojangles stared into the blue narrow eyes of Rosie and could not help but feel an attraction for her. She reached into her handbag for her silver cigarette case, and her companion inhaled the aroma of expensive perfume. He lit her cigarette from the book of matches on the bar and she blew out the smoke towards the ceiling.

"So, Mr Bojangles… are you staying here?"

"In this hotel? No. I was just passing and heard the wonderful music."

Rosie studied his handsome face. "You like Beethoven?"

"Right up my street, darling."

She took another pull on her cigarette and gazed up into his dark eyes. "What do you do for a living? No! Let me guess… A stockbroker?"

He shook his head, and wry smile covered his face.

She tried again. "I've got it… You own a string of nightclubs?"

Again, he shook his head.

"Okay, I give up. What do you do?"

"You really want to know?"

"Of course… Come on, Mr Bojangles. Don't leave me in suspense?"

"All right… I'm a hit man."

She giggled and spilt some of her champagne down her gown. "You're not serious?"

He shrugged his shoulders and swallowed a mouthful of his Jack Daniels.

She playfully punched his arm. "That's not funny."

Bojangles glanced at the clock. "A young lady like you shouldn't be walking home alone at this late hour."

"I don't have to. I'm staying here at the hotel."

"Really? What about your friend?"

Rosie shrugged. "She lives in Shepherd's Bush. No doubt she'll have taken a cab."

The dark man probed further. "I don't understand. Are you staying here alone?"

"I certainly am… You see, I often stay here, although I've a house in Kensington… I adore this place."

Bojangles stared down at her diamond wedding ring. "What about your husband?"

"Ralph? He died a month ago."

"I'm sorry."

"I'm not. I never loved him; and besides, he left me the house and so much money."

Bojangles swallowed another mouthful of his Jack Daniels. "How long were you married?"

"Three months."

"You fell out of love in such a short time?"

Rosie scowled. "I was never in love with the old bastard… That's another story, and I'll tell it to you one day… How about a nightcap in my room, Mr Bojangles?"

He looked down to see her slender hand on his leg.

"But, surely you're still in mourning?"

She licked her lips provocatively. "Are you turning me down?"

He smiled. "Lead the way, lady."

She ground out her cigarette and linked his arm. The barman winked at Bojangles, relieved to see them ascend the marble staircase.

They eventually arrived at her room and she passed him the key. The exquisite room was in darkness, and as he reached for the light switch, she pulled him close to her. Their lips met and her long, warm tongue explored the inside of his mouth. Her hand went down to his crotch, and she felt for the zip, as he pulled the dress over her head. She fell back onto the bed and felt the pink silk sheets cool her buttocks.

Bojangles stared down at the girl, who was clad in only black stockings and suspenders. Her breasts he guessed had been enhanced by silicone, and the erect nipples begged to be caressed. She sat up, reached inside his trousers and teasingly massaged his half-erect penis. She then lay back on the bed, her legs wide apart.

"Come on, big boy, take me."

He never removed his jacket. He straddled her and reached for the pillow. Rosie fought for breath when the darkness engulfed her. She kicking out her legs and groped for his strong arms.

Bojangles reached inside his jacket and held the pistol against the pillow. He pulled the trigger once, content that the silencer had done its job. Her body was now still. Bojangles moved to the dressing table, looked into the mirror and straightened his tie. He brushed back his hair and entered the bathroom. A blob of toothpaste was squeezed onto his finger and he proceeded to clean his teeth.

The killer returned to the room and wiped the door handle clean, before he left. He strolled leisurely towards the staircase and whistled a Beethoven tune as he did so.

The hotel clerk nodded and wished Bojangles a good morning, before he left the hotel and mingled with the late night pedestrians.

"I told her," he mumbled quietly to himself. "Why didn't she believe me?"

******

Vince Slattery grimaced at the unwelcome rain that had gate crashed the funeral. He shuffled to one side and attempted to shelter beneath the umbrella of a black-veiled, weeping woman. He hunched slightly as he did so.

"Bloody weather, eh? Wouldn't think it was June would you?"

The speechless woman turned away, and seemingly regarded the journalist as if he was something on the bottom of her shoe. Hundreds of people had assembled to pay their respects to the great comedian, Gus Sherwood.

Slattery had once interviewed Gus some three years ago when he was at his prime, and had struck up a relationship with the comic. Gus was partial to throwing the most lavish of parties, and Slattery always ensured his name was on the invitation list. That was until he met Gus's young bride, Elizabeth Todd.

Gus's career was effectively over when he married Elizabeth. His performances were now sub standard and his critics lambasted him. That she had worn him out had been the gag doing the rounds in celebrity circles, and who could have blamed him for his supposed condition?

Elizabeth Todd was twenty-five years of age, and her husband almost seventy. She was despised by Gus's two sons and assumed to be a gold digger. Why else would she marry someone old enough to be her grandfather? That he died in bed, apparently from a heart attack, fuelled more hate onto the blonde beauty. It was rumoured he had been bonked to death, and Elizabeth it's said had boasted of this to her hanger-on friends when under the influence of alcohol.

Slattery looked over to see the apparent distraught widow toss a large bouquet of flowers onto the coffin, and wondered if indeed the crocodile tears were sincere. Several of the mourners it appears had attended the funeral as a means of celebrity spotting. Slattery half-wished he had brought his photographer with him, but Sam had opted for the afternoon off, stating that The Echo could manage without him for a few hours.

Slattery felt the eyes burning into his head. He afforded a glance to his right through his misted up spectacles. The middle-aged woman scowled at him, obviously none too pleased that he had taken it on himself to share her umbrella.

Vince Slattery was a fresh-faced thirty-four year old and had been a journalist since he had left school. He had worked his way through the ranks from a meagre tea boy to his current position. Though likeable, especially to the fairer sex who adored his magnetic grey eyes and fair wavy hair, his work always came first, and he did not care who got in the way. He was of average build and stood at five-ten in his stocking feet. Slattery was obsessed with getting that elusive scoop, and had several contacts, each who owed him a favour or two. He liked to wheel and deal as he liked to call it; grease the odd palm here and there. He had even resorted to a little blackmail. His most major scoop to date was when he unveiled the foreign secretary as a user of high society call girls. The politician had been ousted from office and Slattery had taken another rung on the ladder to success. Slattery's ambition was to work on murder stories, a post occupied at the moment by Harry Orton, a colleague he despised.

He felt the raindrops run down his hot face and realised that the woman in black had deliberately manoeuvred her umbrella to her other hand. He ran for his car and decided he would make an appearance at the wake; after all, Gus would have wanted him there. He sat at the wheel of his Mondeo and reached for his mobile phone.

"Cheryl, hi it's Vince. Listen, I'm at Gus's funeral and will be late home. His family has invited me to the wake."

"Orgy more like it, if I know you! So, it's pointless me doing your dinner yet again?"

"Come on, Chez," he said in a strong south London accent. "I could hardly refuse could I?"

"Why don't you just join the bloody Foreign Legion? In fact I'd probably see more of you."

"Kiss the girls for me, sugar. I shouldn't be too late. I'll make it up to you, Chez… honest."

"Yeah yeah, I've heard it all before."

"Love you."

She hung up without reply. He checked his mirror and adjusted his tie before he drove off.

Chapter Two

Detective Sergeant Danny Jenson had one more look at the dead girl before she was taken away in a body bag. Jenson, an intimidating figure of a man was six feet four in his stocking feet. With his shaved head and broken nose, he looked more like a thug than a detective in CID. He unwrapped a piece of chewing gum before he ambled over to a bald man, who sported a Van Dyke beard.

Detective Chief Inspector Brian Entwistle was deep in conversation with a member of the forensic team. He listened attentively and jotted down the details in his pad.

"Looks like an execution, guv," suggested Jenson.

"It looks that way. No sign of sexual interference, even though she was undressed. She still has a couple of hundred quid in her handbag, which rules out robbery."

DS Jenson continued. "Do we know who she is?"

"Rosie Cochrane. Twenty-four years of age. What a waste. She apparently was staying in the hotel and was a regular guest. Her old man died three months ago and it seems she's been living it up."

Jenson chewed vigorously on his gum as he pondered. "Is there a connection, guv?"

"Not that we can see. Her husband died of a heart attack."

"Have we any witnesses?"

Chief Inspector Entwistle checked his notes. "The barman downstairs claims she went to her room with some geezer late last night, around midnight. Jamie's questioning him… You'd think that a place like this would have security cameras."

Jenson left the room and trotted towards the staircase, taking them two at a time. DC Jamie Benton, a tall thin detective with a seventy's perm did not look too happy to see him as he approached. The detective sensibly decided not to upset the big man.

"Jamie, is this the barman?" asked Jenson

The detective nodded reluctantly.

Jenson turned towards the barman. "This man who was with Rosie. Have you ever seen him before?"

"I've already asked..."

The daunting stare from Jenson terminated the chief constable's response.

"Jamie, go and take a hike will you."

Jenson watched the sulking detective depart, like a child who had been rebuked.

"Now, Mr..."

"Pete, just call me Pete."

"Okay, Pete. Had you seen this man before?"

The thinning, middle-aged man shook his head and stroked his ample chin. "No. He wasn't a regular."

"Can you describe him?"

"Flashy. Looked like he was loaded... Had one of those shiny blue suits... like a gangster."

"What about his looks?"

"Handsome bloke, goatee beard, dark hair, combed back like. Dark eyes. Yes, I remember the eyes. Like pieces of coal they were."

DS Jenson continued. "Was he big... small?"

"About five nine, five ten. Average build, but it was the way he stared at you that told you he wasn't a man you'd want to upset. In fact, two blokes were chatting up Rosie and her friend, making a nuisance of themselves, when this bloke walked over and told them to leave in so many words. And they did, believe me, they did."

"Do you know these men?"

"Not by name, but they come in here regular... The girl is called Sandy. She works at the Wig and Pen around the corner."

"How did he pay for his drinks?" asked the detective.

"Cash."

Jenson rolled the gum around on his tongue before he continued. "The glasses from last night. Have they been washed?"

"Of course. I always wash them before going home."

"Okay, Pete. I'd like you to go with our artist if that's okay? Also, can you give DC Benton the details of the girl? Thanks, you've been a great help."

DS Jenson left the hotel, glad of the fresh air. His eyes focused on the short, weasel-faced man who smoked a cigarette. "Hello, do you work here?"

"I do. I'm the desk clerk."

"Were you on the desk last night around midnight?"

"Yes, but I've already told the detective."

"Tell me," insisted Jenson.

The desk clerk puffed on his cigarette. "It was about twelve fifteen. I know, because the news had just finished… A gentleman left the hotel and I wished him a good morning."

"How was he? I mean, was he flustered?"

"No, he appeared very calm."

"Think carefully. Did you see him drive away?"

"No, and I never heard an engine. I've already told the other officer."

"Okay, thanks… Incidentally, you don't have security cameras installed. Why is that?"

"Oh, we have them installed all right, but they're not working right now, due to technical problems."

Jenson re-entered the hotel in time to see DCI Entwistle heading towards him. "Guv, we ought to contact the taxi offices."

"It's already being done, Danny. Speak to the girl's friends and family. Find out if she has any male friends and question them."

"What's the motive, guv? There has to be a motive."

The older man shrugged. "It appears she's loaded, but who stands to gain from her death? We'll look into it."

Jenson strode purposefully towards his car: his destination, the Wig and Pen.

******

Goldie Lamour attracted only the occasional glance as she paced proudly through the streets of Soho. Any other part of the world, she would have been ridiculed about her gender, but Londoners just shrug aside the spectacle, as they do homosexuals, lesbians and all ethnic minorities. It would take something of exceptional proportions to turn a Londoner's head.

Goldie wiggled her hips purposefully and walked expertly on her newly purchased high heels. Her bushy, blonde wig and proficiently applied make-up portrayed Goldie as a beautiful woman, but to her friends in the Ship Inn she was a harmless transvestite. Her eyes were the colour of the deepest ocean, which added to the allure of the confident Londoner.

Occasional conversations with admirers, not all knowing her secret, usually resulted in saucy banter and nothing more. Goldie, as she often stipulated was not a homosexual, and therefore did not attend the usual gay haunts of Soho. She preferred instead to flaunt her majesty in straight bars.

Goldie was a new favourite with the tipplers of Soho, and often captivated her audience with a saucy joke or two. In fact, if anything, Goldie was respected, mainly because she never imposed herself on the punters and was seen as one of the lads. She was more of an exhibitionist than a sexual participant, and her exquisite and stylish dresses bore testament to this.

She made her grand entrance into the smoke-filled lounge of the Ship Inn and was greeted by numerous offers of a drink, some from strapping hunks, unashamedly happy to be seen in her company. Goldie blew a kiss to one such admirer and accepted the glass of red wine, her usual tipple, unless she was celebrating, and then it was bubbly.

"How's it going, Goldie?" asked the short, plump proprietor with the red face.

"Oh you know, Cyril, I'm holding my own," she said saucily in a husky voice.

"Nice dress, Goldie. Must have cost a fortune?"

"Do you like it? I got it on special offer from Franny in Carnaby Street. He's so sweet."

Two denim-clad youths involved in a game of pool turned their attention to Goldie. They giggled loudly, obviously the worse for alcohol.

Goldie pouted at them, mounted the barstool, then ensured her ruby red dress rode up her thigh to reveal a slender leg. "Who's the young blood, Cyril?"

"A couple of airheads up from Scotland for the weekend... Do you want me to turf em out?"

"Come come, Cyril. Have you forgotten southern hospitality?"

Goldie removed a cigarillo from her handbag and Cyril leant over the bar and strained to light it. Like many supposedly straight men, the portly proprietor was intrigued by Goldie's mesmerising beauty, and harboured shameful fantasies about her.

"What do you think about my tits, Cyril?" she asked, as she blew out a plume of blue smoke.

His face reddened even more by the candid question, even though you could expect it from Goldie.

"They're perfect."

"Ooh, you fibber. I'm saving up to get real tits. This padding is irritating me."

"What about...You know?" quizzed Cyril, who motioned with his eyes to Goldie's groin.

"One thing at a time, darling... I'm not made of money you know."

Cyril probed further. "So how will you get the money? I mean, you don't work now do you?"

Goldie checked her face in her compact mirror. "One of my two fellow tenants is absolutely loaded. I'm tempted to ask for a loan, but he's not very approachable. I'm working on it though, and by the way, did I tell you? He's absolutely gorgeous, or so I've been told."

"How come he never comes in here, Goldie?"

The transvestite fluttered her long, false eyelashes. "Charlie would not be seen dead in a place like this. No disrespect, darling, but he moves in classier circles."

"And the other tenant?" asked Cyril.

"I loathe him… Duncan Brady is a no good bum. I wish I had a pound for every time he's missed his rent." Goldie adjusted her padding. "I could get the lot done, and maybe have a little left over for a tuck."

"You don't need cosmetic surgery, girl. You're gorgeous, besides, how old are you? Thirty… thirty-one?"

"Ooh, Cyril. You should know better than to ask a girl her age."

The conversation was interrupted by the loud laughter of the youths, who made fun of Goldie. They rubbed their groins and wiggled their tongues at her.

"Right, that's it," insisted Cyril, as he tossed his tea towel onto the bar.

He was restrained by Goldie, who winked at him. "Relax, Cyril. Perhaps it's time I introduced myself."

She took a sip of wine and stubbed out her cigarillo, before she approached the jukebox that was situated close to the pool table. Her walk was leisurely, and she ensured that the wiggle of her bottom captured the attention of her watching audience. The expectant onlookers nudged each other eagerly and anticipated a classical performance from the transvestite.

Goldie leant over the jukebox and cast a glance towards the smirking duo. She winked at them and was met with a barrage of obscenities. Goldie made her selection and waited for the music to start before she made her move.

"Oh, oh, wee-eel-now, relax, don't do it, when you want to go to it, relax don't do it, when you want to come!"

She approached the curious youths gracefully, before she rocked her head back and forth and wiggled her body suggestively to the music. Her necklace of imitation pearls moved in rhythm.

The amusement was etched on the faces of the numerous revelers.

The youths looked to one another, unsure how to react.

"Fucking queer!" yelled one, who grasped his pool cue threateningly.

"Cock sucker!" snarled the other.

"Relax, don't do it, when you want to go to it, relax don't do it, when you want to come!"

Goldie ran her tongue provocatively across her lips and continued to gyrate sexily, now only inches from her mockers.

Relax, don't do it, when you want to suck on it, relax don't do it, when you want to come!"

Goldie had been given her cue and each of her finely manicured hands reached down for the groins of the two Scotsmen. She squeezed forcefully and threw her head back in laughter, as the embarrassed youths grimaced.

"Tut, tut, not much to brag about have you, boys?"

She released her grip and they hesitated, uncertain if to react with aggression. The numerous scowls directed at them from the customers made up their minds. They tossed their pool cues onto the ground and left the Ship Inn, their confidence diminished and the applause and wolf whistles ringing in their ears.

Goldie ambled to the bar, smiled contently and milked the applause, before she reached for her fresh glass of wine.

******

Slattery heard the familiar clatter of keyboards and the incessant ringing of the telephones when he entered the enormous Echo newspaper building in Canary Wharf. The occasional nod of the head or wave of the hand was exchanged when he made his way to his desk. Standing directly in his way with a smug smile emblazoned across his face was Harry Orton. The bald journalist with a lazy eye was only too eager to pass on the worrying news to his colleague.

"Madison wants to see you in his office straight away, Slattery."

The fair-haired journalist ignored him, sat at his desk and sparked his computer into life. Out of the side of his eye, he saw the editor's door open and feared the worst. A personal visit from Roland Madison, the editor of The Echo, usually meant trouble. Numerous thoughts went through Slattery's mind, as he tried to determine what he had done to upset the great man.

Roland Madison was a short man, almost as wide as he was in height. His silver, combed back hair and ever-present pipe clenched between his teeth was his trademark. He made up for his lack of stature with his infamous temper. Many an ambitious young journalist had dared to challenge Madison, and found themselves reporting on the Chelsea flower show or the grand opening of a supermarket.

Slattery continued to browse at his computer screen. The last thing he needed on a Monday morning was hassle from the editor.

"Vince, in my office straight away." It was not a request but an order, delivered with all the charm of a regimental sergeant major.

Orton stood arms folded, and smirked, as Slattery followed his employer to his office. The journalist observed the petite girl who was stood by the window. She had long black hair that went down to her waist and a figure that suggested she visited the gym regularly. Unsmiling, she turned her head towards him, and he noticed her large, brown saucer shaped eyes, and oh, so long eyelashes. With her tanned face and sculptured high cheekbones, she looked like a fashion model. Her tight jeans seemed as though they had been painted on, and the odour of leather offered proof that her grey bomber jacket was newly purchased.

"Have a seat, both of you… Christ, Vince; have you been with a tart? You reek of cheap perfume…This is Sophie Wilson, your new photographer. Sophie, meet Vince Slattery."

"Now wait a minute, Roland. Sam's my photographer."

"He was. He's quit, and who can blame him after working with you for so long?"

"He's quit? I don't understand."

Madison looked minuscule, as he sat behind his desk and lit his beloved pipe. "The Gideon cult story was too much for him, Vince… Congratulations on the story by the way, but how you arrived there before anyone else, I'll never know."

Slattery nodded. "Right…you'll never know."

The editor continued. "You pleased a lot of people high up, as you and Sam were the only journalists present at the time of the mass suicide… Some really awesome pictures, Vince."

"Where is Sam?" asked Slattery, who tried hard to ignore the beauty.

"I heard he's taken a job at some wildlife magazine. The animals there are probably tamer. Anyway, I've been authorised to offer you the post of crime reporter. You made the right noises upstairs it seems."

Slattery grinned. "Shit, no kidding." He pointed towards Sophie. "What's the history on the chick?"

Madison turned towards the girl. "Sophie? Well why don't you tell him yourself?"

She cleared her throat. "I studied photography at college and worked two years for a fashion magazine."

"That figures," muttered Slattery.

Sophie ignored the slur. "Although I enjoyed my position, I felt I needed a more stimulating challenge. I applied for this post, and here I am. I have a sample of my work if you want to take a look?"

Her voice possessed a tinge of dignity; a highly educated voice without being over posh.

Slattery responded. "No, that won't be necessary. I'm sure Roland has given you the once over or you wouldn't be here… If you work with me, there's no compromise. You do as I say and take pictures. You do not question my methods, which may seem a little unsavoury for a lady of your standing."

Sophie clicked her heels together and saluted. "And I suppose I report for drill every morning at dawn do I?"

Madison could not but help a wry smirk before he spoke. "Vince, a girl was found murdered at the Dorchester Hotel in Mayfair on Saturday night. Harry Orton was covering the story, but I want you to take over. Get the relevant information from him and get onto it immediately. I'm sure you have a contact or two in CID."

"Was it robbery?"

"Apparently not. It appears she'd been shot in the head, execution style. Let's see how this goes, Vince. An opportunity has presented itself to you. Make the most of it."

"And Orton?"

"He's taken your old job. They're not too pleased with his work recently. Send him in on your way out will you?"

The broad smile on his face reflected his triumph. "With pleasure, Roland. With pleasure."

Chapter Three

Duncan Brady lit yet another cigarette and foraged through the shabby room. He cursed when yet another drawer was emptied without reward. He, along with Goldie and Charlie Bojangles shared the rented accommodation in Gower Street, central London. The apartments were cheap, hence his being there. He had never met the other tenants, but felt as if he knew them well, after the details of them had been relayed to him by the chattering Mrs Parish. Brady detested both of them for different reasons. Goldie, because he despised transvestites or homosexuals, and Charlie, because he oozed wealth, thus his reason for rummaging through the mysterious man's belongings.

Yes, Charlie Bojangles was indeed a strange fish. He dressed elegantly and his appearance was of someone of opulence, but why then was he staying in such a hovel?

Duncan Brady was not a likeable fellow. In fact, he was a foul-mouthed, uncouth man. His greasy, dishevelled blonde hair and thick spectacles, along with his straggly beard, gave him the appearance of a paedophile; but children were not what interested him. His infatuation was with money, something he had a hard time finding. Brady was work shy, and instead had turned to a life of crime in order to sustain his passion for cash.

Every suit of Bojangles had been searched and offered no financial gain. The white-vested thief replaced the drawers and ensured he put everything back exactly as it was. Brady was not an intelligent man, but the last thing he wanted was to upset his enigmatic fellow tenant.

The faraway knock of a door rattled him. His heart pounded rapidly as he frantically replaced the clothing, before he exited the room of Charlie Bojangles. He walked hastily along the dank, paint-shy corridor and edged towards the middle-aged woman, who rapped on his equally paint-shy door.

"Ah, the elusive Mr Brady. You owe me two month's rent in case you've forgotten?"

The thin woman with her hair in curlers stood with her arms folded.

"Mrs Parish, you'll have your rent by the end of the week. "

"Ha! How many times have I heard that? I agreed to let you and your friends rent this exclusive establishment on the understanding that the rent would be paid in full on the first of every month. You still owe me for May, Mr Brady."

Brady placed his hands together in prayer. "Listen to me. I swear I'll pay you the two month's rent on Saturday. I'm going through a hard time at the moment."

"I could rent your room out to anyone you know. Accommodation is in great demand around here."

"Please, Mrs Parish... Saturday?"

"Very well, but not a day later or you'll be out on your ear... I've had no trouble off that queer or the charming Mr Bojangles... Saturday, and don't you forget."

He closed the door on her and headed for his room. His need for money was now even greater, which left him no choice. His mind was made up. Tonight he would have his reward.

******

Many a head turned when Slattery and Sophie strode intently through the wave of detectives in Charing Cross police station. Slattery halted and peered through the smoke screen. He sought one man in particular. DS Danny Jenson thumped the coffee machine when the journalists approached.

"Easy, Danny, you'll do yourself an injury."

The giant of a man turned to face Slattery. His eyes settled on Sophie. "Vince, long time no see. Who is this vision?"

"Sophie, my new photographer... Listen, can we talk?"

"Sure. Hey, that was some scoop getting the pictures of the looney cult torching themselves. Must have made you a packet, eh?"

"I'm afraid not, Danny. I receive the same salary come what may."

The detective turned back towards the coffee machine. "Haven't seen you at the Valley for a while."

"I gave up my season ticket. I still go and watch the Charlton occasionally, but I usually have to work on Saturdays."

The two journalists followed the imposing detective to the canteen. DS Jenson had more success at this coffee machine and offered to buy the visitors one, which they politely declined. They settled at an isolated table and once more Jenson's eyes devoured Sophie.

"Some people have all the luck, Vince. The women I work with are either butt ugly or dykes."

Sophie blushed as he continued.

"So what brings you to the nick?"

"A girl was murdered at the Dorchester on Saturday night. Rosie Cochrane, right?"

"Yeah, that's right. What's it to you?"

"What's the story on her?"

DS Jenson tasted his coffee and grimaced. "Shit! You're working on murders now?"

"Not before time… Was she raped?"

Jenson cautiously scanned the canteen. "You trying to get me fired? You know I'm not allowed to talk to you about the case."

"Give me a break, Danny? You owe me a favour or two."

"Okay, but you never heard this from me… She took a bullet in her head, fired through a pillow. No apparent motive as she had money on her and it wasn't touched. She was topless and was wearing sussies, but the killer never shagged her."

"Any leads?" asked Slattery.

"Don't push it, Vince… All I can tell you is she was married to Ralph Cochrane, a multi-millionaire, Irish businessman. He died just over a month ago of a heart attack. They'd been married for some three months only."

"Ralph Cochrane the racehorse owner?"

"Yeah, that's him."

"Who stands to gain from their deaths?" probed Slattery.

Sergeant Jenson scowled. "Are you fucking with me? I've told you enough… Okay, Rosie was with a girlfriend on the night she was murdered. Sandy's her name, and she works as a barmaid at the Wig and Pen in Mayfair. Now piss off before you drop me in it." He flashed his most charming smile at Sophie and winked. "How about a date?"

"I don't date coppers."

"Ooh, posh as well… You lucky bastard, Slattery."

They shook hands and the journalists departed the police station. Once outside they felt the warm rays of the sun caress their faces. The fresh air was most welcome.

"How do you know him?" asked Sophie, who lit up a cigarette.

"Danny? He's a Croydon boy like me. We grew up together and went in different directions."

They climbed into his black Mondeo and he looked across at her, as she wound down the window.

"Rule number one, baby, you don't smoke in my car."

She frowned at him, before she flicked the cigarette through the window. "Let's get one thing straight; I'm not your baby."

Slattery turned off the engine. "Listen to me. You may think you're some lady of the manor, but it holds no credence with me. I don't care how many cocks you sucked to get this job, but I'm stuck with you no matter how much I dislike the idea. You take pictures and we'll get on just fine."

He started the engine and the uncomfortable silence on their journey was broken only by the music from the stereo.

******

The darkness of the shop doorway offered him a satisfactory view of the bookmakers without detection. It was nine-forty five and the last of punters had long since gone home after the night racing had finished. Duncan Brady checked his wristwatch and felt the beads of perspiration run down his face. His mouth was arid and his palms sweaty, as he waited for the right moment.

For a week now, he had watched the routine when night racing took place. He waited patiently for the manageress to arrive. He was aware that only two young girls were inside the shop, and his plan was based on them not willing to risk their health for a greedy bookie. The manageress was a different proposition though. She was probably the husband of the bookie and with a personal interest in the takings.

He cupped his shaking hand over his cigarette, drew deeply and heard the approach of the car. A track-suited, fair-haired woman alighted from the sports car and headed for the betting shop.

Brady tossed his cigarette to the ground, gripped his holdall with one hand and removed his spectacles. He waited until the bus had passed before he advanced across the road. He had another casual look around as he stood in the betting shop doorway, before he nervously put on his ski mask. He reached inside his holdall when the door opened and he faced a young plump girl. He shoved her inside the shop and waved his baseball bat menacingly.

"Back up against the wall or I'll fucking do you!"

The manageress retreated behind the counter, applied the lock on the solid door and left the two young girls outside.

"You, come out now or I'll do em!" barked Brady.

The manageress shouted back. "There's an alarm behind here and the police are on their way. They'll be here at any moment."

Brady advanced with one finger pointed towards the trembling girls. "Open the fucking door, cow or I'll swear, I'll top em?"

The tearful manageress weighed up her options. "I'm sorry, but I cannot. Go while you can before it's too late."

Brady thumped the counter with his bat. "I'm going to count to five. If that fucking door isn't unlocked, you'll be responsible for those girls. Do you hear me?"

"No, please. Open the door, Wendy," begged one of the girls who wore spectacles.

"Five... four, "

"He's bluffing, Judy," insisted the manageress. "The police are on their way."

"Three... two."

Brady edged over towards the cowering girls. The plump one wet herself when she slid down the wall.

"One... Open the fucking door!"

The manageress shook her head.

Brady swung the baseball bat powerfully and connected with the head of the bespectacled girl, the deafening crack evidence that the skull had split. The blood splattered against the wall when she collapsed at the feet of the screaming plump girl.

Brady trod on the discarded spectacles and grabbed the hair of the pleading clerk. See what you've made me do? Now, will you open up or do I have to do her as well?"

The sobbing manageress fumbled with the keys, the sound of sirens now audible.

"Come on, you fuck. Open the poxy door!" snarled Brady.

The sirens grew louder and the manageress protested she could not locate the key. Brady swung the bat once more, and narrowly missed the plump girl's head. He tossed the baseball bat into his holdall and ran for the door, amid the screams. His victim lay motionless on the ground, and a stream of blood oozed from her wound.

Brady dashed blindly across the road and pulled at his ski mask, which caused an oncoming black cab to brake violently. The air was disturbed by a chorus of tooting car horns. Brady sprinted towards Tottenham Court Road subway and fumbled for his spectacles as he did so.

The other commuters were used to seeing passengers running for their trains, and so his haste warranted no suspicion. With trembling hands, he purchased his ticket from the machine and waited three minutes for his train. He checked over his shoulder constantly. By the time he had reached his destination, he had calmed down sufficiently for him to call into his local for a much-needed pint of beer. The ordeal of Judy Sullivan was long forgotten.

******

Tuesday afternoon brought a change of climate. The blue skies had been replaced with greyness, as the streets of London were awash with torrential rain. Slattery and Sophie dashed across the busy road into the sanctuary of the Wig and Pen. Only a few punters had braved the weather, and business was quiet when they approached the bar.

"Hi, is Sandy working this afternoon?" asked Slattery.

The large-breasted, blonde barmaid looked them up and down cautiously. "It depends. You're not her husband are you?"

"No, I'm a reporter."

"Oh, well, in that case, that's Sandy over there."

The raven-haired girl with the heavy mascara on her eyes leant on the bar, reading a magazine.

"Sandy."

"Not you lot again," she moaned. "I've told you everything I know."

Slattery smiled. "We're not from the police… we're journalists. Have you got a moment?"

"I'm not sure I want to talk with you."

"I'll buy you a drink," offered the journalist.

The barmaid conceded. "Kathy, cover for me a few minutes will you?"

Slattery tossed three-pound coins onto the bar and Sandy poured herself a gin and tonic. She pointed to a table in the corner and the sodden journalists followed her.

"Okay, fire away."

"Do you mind if I tape our conversation?" asked Slattery.

Sandy accepted a cigarette from Sophie. "No, why should I?"

"You were with Rosie the night she was murdered?"

Sandy blew out the smoke. "Yeah, that's right… Two blokes were hitting on us. One of them was cute, but the one heckling Rosie was a right pain in the arse."

"So what happened, Sandy?"

The thirsty barmaid drained her glass and waved the empty glass in front of Slattery's face. He removed his wallet from his pocket and passed a five-pound note to Sophie. "Be a good girl and get Sandy another will you?"

"Make it a double."

Slattery continued to probe.. "Well, Sandy?"

"Oh, yes… We were absolutely sozzled and I threw up over the dishy one. He wasn't too pleased as you can imagine, and so I pissed off."

"You went home?"

"Yeah."

"These two men. Can you describe them?"

"Sure I can, but the police were more interested in the other geezer."

"What other geezer?" quizzed Slattery.

Sandy tapped her cigarette against the ashtray. "Apparently, this bloke chased the two Romeos off and moved in on Rosie."

"Did you see this man?"

Sophie returned with the gin and tonic.

Sandy winked. "Thanks, honey. I don't usually drink so early, but what the heck."

"The man?" asked Slattery.

Sandy was deep in thought. "I didn't take much notice of him. He was standing at the other end of the bar… I recall he was smartly dressed in an expensive whistle and flute."

"So, you never spoke to him?"

She shook her head and took another sip of her drink.

The journalist was adamant. "I have no intention of offending you, Sandy, but Rosie was married to a multi-millionaire, right?"

"She was before he kicked the bucket… What's your point?"

"How did Rosie know you? I mean, her being married to a multi-millionaire… and you..."

Sandy glared at her interrogator. "A common barmaid you mean? Rosie lived in Kentish Town when she met Ralph Cochrane. In fact, we shared a flat together."

Slattery sat back, as the smoke from the cigarette obviously irritated him. "How did she meet Cochrane?"

"Through the escort agency... Cochrane was besotted by her, but the only thing they had in common was they were both Irish... What Rosie saw in him, I haven't a clue?"

"A big fat pay cheque perhaps?" offered Sophie.

Slattery glowered at her.

Sandy continued. "Rosie was not like that... Sure, she slept around, but she was fond of the old geezer at first, then later despised him."

An elderly man sat in the corner alone began to play the spoons, and croaked out a rendition of, *"Maybe it's because I'm a Londoner."*

"Rosie used escort agencies?" asked Slattery.

"No, you silly bugger. She could have any man she wanted. She worked for the agency. They had a few dates, and before you could say fiddlesticks, they were married. Right posh do it was; no jellied eels and pork pies, I can tell you."

"What was the name of the agency, Sandy?"

The barmaid ground out her cigarette and squinted. "Cupid's Arrow. It's on Portobello Road. I went for an interview there once, but nothing came of it. Didn't have the looks I suppose... Now Rosie, she was something else."

"How long did she work there?"

"About a month... In fact, Cochrane was her first date."

Slattery pondered. "Sandy, can you think of anyone who would want to harm Rosie?"

"The cops have already asked me this, and I'll tell you exactly what I told them. Cochrane's son was all against the wedding, and he was absolutely bubbling when his father left everything to Rosie. If that isn't a motive for murder, then I don't know what is."

"His son, Sean, the horse trainer, right?" suggested Slattery.

"That's him, the greedy bastard... He detested Rosie and told her so."

Half a dozen saturated customers entered the pub and Sandy rose to her feet. She swallowed the remains of her gin and tonic. "I have to go. Thanks for the drink."

"Thank you, Sandy," said Slattery, who switched off his miniature tape recorder.

The journalists stood in the doorway of the Wig and Pen and looked up towards the forlorn sky. "Sophie, when I question someone, I don't want you butting in. You almost blew the interview there."

"Well jiggle my tits. What am I here for? Two days I've been with you and I haven't taken one bloody photograph."

"You'll get your chance, don't worry."

"So what now?" asked Sophie.

"Now, my fair maiden, we make a dash for the car."

Chapter Four

The loud rapping on the door disturbed Mrs Parish from her sleep. She checked her alarm clock to see it was just after midnight. She put on her nightgown and slippers and mumbled to herself as she shuffled towards the door. She opened it as far as the safety chain would allow and faced an agitated looking Goldie, her eyes tarnished by the running mascara.

"Oh, it's you. Do you know what time it is?"

"I'm sorry to disturb you, Mrs Parish, but that nasty man has been through my things," sobbed the transvestite, her breath reeking of alcohol.

"What do you expect me to do about it?"

"Evict him. That Duncan Brady is nothing but trouble."

"He couldn't possibly have been in your room," insisted the tired landlady.

"He has, I tell you. I can smell his awful body odour in my room."

The middle-aged woman yawned. "Well, you know the saying; coughs and sneezes spread diseases."

"Meaning what, Mrs Parish?"

"You chose your sordid life and you deserve everything that you get. If I didn't need the money so much, I'd evict you tomorrow."

Goldie was livid. "What sordid life is that, Mrs Parish?"

"It's late and I'm tired."

"What sordid life is that?"

Mrs Parish folded her arms. "Whatever you do outside is of no concern to me, but if I ever suspect you're bringing filth in here, I'll turn you onto the streets before you can bat an eyelid. Do I make myself clear?"

"You're living in the Stone Age. This is the twenty-first century in case you've forgotten, and a girl's free to do as she pleases."

The landlady sneered. "But you're not a girl, are you? You're sick and need help. It's disgusting what you do."

Goldie realised this was one argument she could not win. "What are you going to do about Brady?"

"I'm going to collect my rent off him on Saturday and I'll be happy. I don't need this you know. I can easily fill those rooms. There's plenty of people without a roof over their heads."

"Nobody will be stupid enough to live in this hovel… If I had the money, do you think I'd be living here?"

The door was slammed in Goldie's face and she retreated to her room. She wept as she rearranged her clothes in an orderly fashion, knowing without doubt that the unruly Brady had been through her things. She had a special way of arranging her clothes by colours, and they had definitely been disturbed.

"A girl can only take so much," she cried. She placed her ear against the wall and listened for any movement from her flatmate. There was only silence.

******

The house was in darkness when Slattery pulled into his drive at midnight. The flick of the light switch revealed his slumbering wife, curled up on the sofa, her curly, red hair cascading over her pretty features. He kissed her on the head and she stirred. She screwed her blue eyes up to observe her husband.

"Sorry to wake you, Chez. I thought you'd be in bed."

She glanced at her wristwatch and sat upright. "It's after midnight. Where've you been?"

"I've been working late."

Cheryl narrowed her eyes. "Don't you lie to me. I passed the office earlier this evening and it was in darkness."

"I went for a little drink afterwards… Listen, what is this? Are you spying on me?"

Cheryl softened. "What's happening to us, Vince? The last three months we've hardly seen anything of each other. We say good morning at the breakfast table, and then that's it until after midnight... You see the girls for ten minutes in the morning. Can't you see what's happening?"

"No, I can't see what's happening, but I'm sure you're going to tell me," he said, as he popped open a can of beer.

"Don't you think you've had enough alcohol?"

Slattery slammed the can down on the coffee table. "Just what the fuck do you want, Cheryl? I give you a good home, two lovely daughters and beautiful clothes. I have to work overtime to keep you and the children, but do I moan?"

"So what's changed in the last three months, Vince? We were getting along fine before... without the overtime."

"I don't need this. I'm going to bed!"

Cheryl followed him to the foot of the staircase. "You come in here stinking of cheap perfume and booze and you expect me to take this? I've heard she's pretty, this new photographer of yours."

"Jesus Christ! So that's what this is all about. You're bloody jealous."

"Mum, why is Daddy yelling at you?" came the cry from the top of the staircase.

Slattery ascended the flight of stairs and hugged his ten-year old daughter. "I wasn't shouting, honey. Adults just talk loudly, that's all. Now you go back to bed like a good girl, okay?"

She nodded, climbed into bed and accepted a kiss on the forehead. "Daddy, can we go to Disneyworld this year like you promised?"

"Of course we can, my cherub. Go to sleep or you'll waken your little sister."

Cheryl had poured herself a glass of brandy and was now sat staring into the fire. She squirmed when she felt his reassuring arm around her.

"Chez, Sophie's a photographer and nothing more. Shit, we don't even get on. She thinks she's royalty does that one. Sam left and I'm lumbered with her."

"And she wears cheap perfume?"

"If you say so. Chez, I love you and would never ever consider going with another woman. You have to believe me."

The forgiving woman embraced him and kissed him on the lips. "I miss you so much, Vince. We spend so little time together, even at weekends."

Slattery reached for his beer. "It won't be for much longer. I've been promoted to head crime reporter. It's not much more money, but it helps."

Cheryl reached for his hand. "Do you know the last time we made love?"

"Has it been that long?"

"April fool's day. Over two months ago."

The journalist sipped his beer. "No kidding? We'll have to do something about that won't we?"

He picked her up and carried her up the staircase, kissing her as he went. He collapsed onto the bed and his wife removed her clothes. She climbed into bed and hooked a leg over him, before she cupped his face in her hands. She kissed him lightly and no response was forthcoming, only the gentle snoring from his lips. She turned on her back and wept.

******

Ross Tyreman looked down from his exquisite office onto the bustling River Thames. Carlton House was a magnificent new building in the heart of the dockland, not too distant from Canary Wharf.

The pony-tailed director puffed on his Cuban cigar as he watched his visitors arrive. With his all over tan and daily saunas, Ross Tyreman looked ten years younger than his forty-five years. His fingers were covered with expensive rings, and only the finest threads would do for the immaculately dressed businessman. He removed his mirror from his drawer, vainly checked his image, and awaited the arrival of the detectives.

Ross Tyreman was losing his hair, and all the money in the world could not disguise his anxiety, as he tried treatment after treatment. Nevertheless, his misfortune did not refrain from his prowess with women

He rose from his desk as the two men marched across the polished hardwood floor towards him.

"Good afternoon, Mr Tyreman," said the bald man with the Van Dyke beard, offering his hand. "Thank you for taking the time to see us. I'm Detective Chief Inspector Entwistle of CID and this is Detective Sergeant Jenson. "

"Please have a seat," offered Tyreman. "What can I do for you gentlemen?"

The chief inspector led the questioning. "You are I believe the director of Jade Export Services Ltd?"

"I'm the executive director."

"Mr Tyreman; are you acquainted with a Mrs Rosie Cochrane?"

"No, I don't think so… Should I be?"

"You see, it appears Mrs Cochrane invested a large sum of money in your company a short time ago."

Tyreman pondered. "Cochrane! Of course, how could I have forgotten?"

The senior detective continued. "Jade Export is a new company, Mr Tyreman, is it not?"

"It's relatively new, yes."

"You see, I just can't seem to fathom out why a young girl would invest four million pounds in such a new and uncharted company?"

Tyreman fiddled with his rings. "This company has enormous potential, Chief Inspector, and Mrs Cochrane no doubt had some inside information."

"Rather a huge gamble though, wouldn't you say?"

"But just think of the benefits she could reap, Chief Inspector."

"You've met Mrs Cochrane of course?"

"Yes. She was rather charming."

"So now you do remember her?" The detective was clearly irate.

"Chief Inspector, I do not like your tone of voice. What exactly are you implying?"

"Implying? I'm simply trying to make some sense out of this. You see, Rosie Cochrane was murdered four days ago, just three days after she invested in your company. Her outlay by our calculations would have left her with just £100,000, and the house of course."

Tyreman covered his mouth with his hand. "Murdered! My word, the poor girl... To answer your question, Chief Inspector, it's a free country, and as I've already said, she obviously saw the company had potential"

"Can you provide evidence of the transaction, Mr Tyreman?"

"Of course, but you'll have to call at my solicitors. This is his card. I'll ring him and tell him to expect you."

"Thank you, Mr Tyreman. We'll find our own way out."

The detectives bypassed their car, leaned on the embankment railing and looked at a rainbow that straddled the river.

Chief Inspector Entwistle turned to his younger colleague. "Do you know, Danny, when I was a boy I used to play down here? It was all wasteland then. Just look at it now. You wouldn't believe it was the same place." There was a lengthy silence before Entwistle continued. "Danny, what do you make of Tyreman?"

"He's a smug bastard. Filthy rich no doubt, and he likes everyone to know it."

"Four million, Danny... why? You could understand Rosie playing the stock market with a few grand, but four million fucking pounds!"

"I know what you mean, guv. If Rosie is anything like her friend, Sandy, then a large investment would be out of character. She'd be more likely to travel the world than to blow it on some dodgy deal."

"Unless she did have a tip-off, like Tyreman suggested... Did you notice anything about the building?"

"Only that it must have cost a packet."

The older man shook his head. "All those other offices we passed were leased out to various companies. Also, there weren't any staff present."

"What are you getting at, guv?"

"Only the one office belonged to Jade Export. Where does the administration work go on?"

"They must have a warehouse and other offices somewhere. Do you want me to check it out?"

"No, forget it; besides, why would Tyreman want Rosie killed if she had already parted with her money? No, I have a mate in Customs and Excise. I'll see what he knows about Jade Export. Come on, I'll let you buy me a pie and a pint."

******

The red Mini looking so out of place, parked between the Bentley and the Jaguar. The decision had been made to use Sophie's car, as Slattery had conceded the Mondeo to Cheryl for the day as a peace offering. They gazed in awe at the mansion of the late Gus Sherwood in Earls Court before they approached. The door was answered by a sombre-faced butler who requested them to follow him.

They marvelled at the works of art, which adorned the corridor and led to the parlour. The sound of piano playing greeted them, the performer a middle-aged man in a red silk dressing gown, which surprised them, as it was mid-afternoon. He swivelled around on his stool, smiled broadly and exhibited a full set of radiant teeth that seemed too large for his mouth. His wavy, grey hair was direly in need of a comb. He slapped his hands down on his knees and stared manically at the journalists. "Before we begin, what would you like to drink?"

"Nothing for me thanks," said Slattery.

"Just a coffee please, no sugar," followed Sophie.

The pianist nodded to the butler, who left the parlour.

"You must wonder why I've asked you to come here."

He motioned for them to sit on the black leather couch.

"Something to do with your father?" quizzed Slattery.

"Correct! First of all, Mr Slattery, I want to thank you for attending my father's funeral. He spoke fondly of you before he died."

"He was a great man and a brilliant comedian."

"Indeed… Oh, how uncivil of me. I'm Max. And who is this delightful creature, Vince? You don't mind me calling you Vince do you?"

"No, of course not."

"I'm Sophie. Oops! He doesn't like me talking."

Max seemed bemused. "Really? I love to hear a woman speak. If I was that way inclined, I would whisk you away and marry you my dear; but I prefer someone a little taller with hairs on his chest, if you get my meaning."

"So what is it you want, Max?" asked Slattery impatiently.

"My brother and I, who incidentally could not be here today as he is in Bangkok of all places, believe that my father was murdered."

"Are you serious?"

"Oh, I'm always serious, Vince. I think that bitch of a wife of his had him killed."

"So why don't you go to the police?"

"Because, they wouldn't believe me. Do you?"

"Where's your proof? Gus died of a heart attack."

"Did he? That whore had him killed I tell you."

The butler returned with Sophie's coffee and she thanked him.

Slattery continued. "Max, I can understand your resentment of her. It's only natural. Also, I don't want to sound crass, but isn't it true that your father left everything to Elizabeth?"

"Yes, it's true, and I would be lying if I said I wasn't bitter, but the money is of little consequence to me… My father in his lifetime gave me more than enough for me to live comfortably. His career went downhill when he met that bitch, and she milked him for every penny he had."

"How long were they married?" asked Sophie, who checked for Slattery's expected, displeasing reaction.

"Three frightful months… I'm convinced that if my father had not met that woman, he would still be alive today. I mean, what sort of a woman works in an escort agency."

"Escort agency? Your father met Elizabeth in an escort agency?"

Max nodded. "Yes, you see he was lonely after my mother's death. It was kept quiet of course. My father would have been a laughing stock."

"Do you know the name of this agency?" quizzed Slattery.

"No, does it matter?"

Slattery pondered and looked towards Sophie. "Cupid's Arrow?"

"What's that?" asked Max.

"Nothing. Max, when your father died, surely a doctor must have examined his body?"

"True, but not his doctor... She could have paid him."

The journalist tried to conceal his excitement. "Come on, Max, let's be realistic here. You're trying to say that Elizabeth murdered your father and then paid the doctor to fake the death certificate?"

"Precisely. I was with my father that morning and he showed no signs of being ill. You knew him, Vince. He was as strong as an ox."

"So what do you want me to do? Not that I believe you?"

"Reveal that woman for what she is. Prove she murdered my father."

"I'm a journalist, not a detective. If you really believe to be true what you've told me, hire a private detective."

"Don't you think I haven't thought of that? My father respected you, and I thought that..."

"Now hold on a bloody minute," insisted Slattery. "Don't put this sentimental crap on my shoulders. Yes, I admired your father, but let him rest in peace and drop your absurd claims."

Max appeared disappointed. "I'm sorry I've wasted your time, Mr Slattery... George will show you to the door... A good day to you both."

The loud music of Chopin accompanied them out of the mansion.

"You were a bit hard on him," suggested Sophie.

"He's cuckoo. Gaga... That man is obsessed with ruining Elizabeth Todd."

"What if he's right?"

"Sophie, it's not our war. We're supposed to be reporting on the

Rosie Cochrane murder, and Madison won't be too pleased if we don't come up with something soon."

Sophie continued. "What about the escort agency? Rosie meets Cochrane and he dies after three months of marriage. Elizabeth meets Gus and he also dies after three months of marriage. Both women are left a huge amount of money."

Slattery smiled at his colleague. "Clever girl. What a scoop that would be, but we don't even know if it was the same agency."

"But, if it was the same agency?"

There was a mischievous glint in the eye of the reporter. "There's only one way to find out isn't there? Now get into your rust bucket and let's get out of here."

Chapter Five

Portobello Road hosts the world's largest antique market. The bustling crowds basked in the sweltering heat as they sought that elusive bargain. Slattery and Sophie meandered their way through the crowds, mingled with the street musicians and listened to the steel band playing loudly. The fragrance of fresh fruit and flowers was appropriate on this fine summer's day, and the cockney cries of the traders accompanied them on their way.

They had opted to park the car and save driving through the heavy traffic, not an appealing prospect on such a scorching morning. They emerged from the hustle and bustle of the market and searched the row of offices and shops for the familiar sign.

The bureau door was painted a tawdry pink colour and red hearts embellished the windows. They looked up in unison at the sign above the door, to see a cherub with a bow and arrow, and the bold lettering, Cupid's Arrow Escort Agency.

"You'd better make yourself scarce, Sophie," ordered Slattery. "It wouldn't look right if you went in there with me now would it?"

She shrugged her shoulders and walked away briskly towards an ice cream van that was parked nearby. She purchased a cone, settled on a bench and watched her colleague entered the bureau.

The pretty, fair-haired girl was painting her nails when Slattery approached. He cleared his throat and she peered over the top of her spectacles. "Can I help you?" she asked, with a sarcastic smile that made him feel uncomfortable.

"Yes, well I hope you can… I'm looking for a date."

"Sorry, I'm tied up tonight." She laughed hysterically. "Only kidding! Well, that's what we're here for. Take a seat, Mr er..."

"Sullivan."

"Okay, Mr Sullivan, we require you to fill out an application form first of all, and to accept our terms. Then we'll see what type of girl you prefer. I must remind you that this agency will be discrete and a date will mean a date, not like some tacky establishments you read about in the newspapers. Some people have the wrong impression of an escort agency, but we pride ourselves on our service."

"This fee is rather steep isn't it?" asked Slattery, when he browsed through the form.

"Mr Sluman, our girls are special, which is reflected in the fee. I'm sure you'll agree, once you've seen them for yourself."

"It's Sullivan… It says here, occupation. Why do you need to know that?"

"Simply to access what type of girl we think you're suited to."

Slattery was now fishing. "A friend of mine recommended this place to me. He couldn't stop talking about this girl who works here."

The blonde eyed him suspiciously. "Really… who is she?"

"Er, Elizabeth, I believe they call her."

The girl frowned.

"That's it, Elizabeth Todd."

"I think you're mistaken, Mr Sullivan."

Slattery detected the uneasiness in the girl. "Yes, she married the comedian, Gus Sherwood."

"I'm sorry. I know all our girls and you're mistaken."

Slattery continued to fill in the form and the girl excused herself and left the room. Two minutes later, a ginger-haired man in his thirties with numerous freckles and huge bags beneath his eyes entered the office. His white, perspiration-stained shirt was evidence of the soaring temperature.

"Mr Sullivan, welcome to Cupid's Arrow. I'm Ross Chivers, the general manager."

They shook hands and Slattery regretted it, as the manager's paw was clammy.

"I believe you're looking for a particular girl?"

"Yes. Elizabeth Todd."

"Sorry, I haven't heard of her. If she worked here I would know."

"I must have been misinformed."

"You must have been."

Slattery could feel Chivers's eyes burn a hole in him.

"Could I see your application form please?" Chivers smiled and nodded his head as he read the form. "Ah, a Croydon man, eh? You state your occupation as a bus driver. Very unusual, I don't believe we've had a bus driver before… Well, that's that. If you apply again in say six months, we'll see if we can accommodate you."

"Six months?"

"Yes, didn't Hilary tell you? We're fully booked up until then."

"I find that hard to believe," challenged Slattery.

"Sorry, we're very busy. Besides, if you don't mind me saying; I doubt you'll be able to afford our fee on a bus driver's salary. Good morning, sir."

Chivers was up and out of the door before Slattery could protest. The journalist resigned himself to the fact he was wasting his time and exited the building. He joined a hot looking Sophie on the bench and tried not to notice she was not wearing a bra. Her camera dangled between her ample breasts.

"Well?" she quizzed.

"I rattled them, Sophie. They say they've never heard of Elizabeth, but they're lying. The manager couldn't get rid of me quick enough… Big mistake pretending to be a bloody bus driver. Perhaps if I said I was a solicitor…"

Sophie removed her sunglasses. "Where do we go from here?"

"Take a few shots of the bureau and come with me," ordered Slattery.

Slattery entered the premises again and smiled at the unhappy looking receptionist, who had resumed painting her nails. "Can you tell Mr Chivers I'd like to see him a moment please?"

When she left the room, Sophie joined Slattery, her camera at the ready. The office door opened and a startled Chivers faced a barrage of flashes.

"Say cheese, Chivers," laughed Slattery.

"Who are you?" yelled the irate man, who covered his face with his hands.

"The bus driver, remember."

******

The pretty, blonde, blue-eyed girl glided through the crowded mansion, a glass of champagne in her hand. She delivered a wave of a hand to her minions as she progressed towards the drawing room, like a Queen would her subjects.

Elizabeth Todd ignored the naked bodies that writhed on the floor and the staircase; an everyday spectacle nowadays that warranted no attention. The guests were not the highborn characters one would usually associate with such a grand establishment, but Elizabeth's friends from the days when she was penniless. It was just after seven in the evening, but the revellers had been drinking for most of the day, taking speed and other illegal stimulants to keep up their exertions.

Elizabeth swallowed another mouthful of champagne and approached the long polished table.

"Hey, leave some of that for me!" she slurred.

She reached for one of the many twenty-pound notes and rolled it up, before she followed the trail of the white powder. She snorted loudly and her eyes watered. She repeated the process.

A tall, dark man approached her from behind and kissed her neck. Her disappointment at seeing who it was urged the words, "Fuck off, Cally."

Elizabeth giggled at a standing black man, who pumped away vigorously. The naked, blonde girl moaned with delight as she lay back on the table.

Elizabeth bumped into a drinks trolley when she left the room and cursed, when she watched a decanter of whiskey fall to the ground. The booming music of *Blur* echoed around the mansion and serenaded every room. The inhabitants were either in the throes of passion or intoxicated. She snatched another bottle of champagne from the bar and endeavoured to find solitude, in which she could experience the effects of the cocaine. The conservatory was her preference, as nobody had thought to fornicate amongst the various rubber plants and other exotic delights.

Elizabeth slumped in the wicker chair, bored with the human leeches that were bleeding her dry. Since Gus had died, she had bonked her way through umpteen lovers, none who had satisfied her. Cocaine and champagne were her lovers, as they fulfilled her like no man had.

She sang along to the music that reached her ears. " *All the people. So many people. They all go hand in hand.* "

"Hello, all alone?"

She screwed her eyes up to see the blurred outline of a man. "Who is it?"

"You can call me Charlie."

"Charlie, I don't think I know you? Who did you come with…? Oh, it matters not… Pass me that bottle will you?"

"Lovely place you have here," complimented the stranger.

"I hate it."

"Oh, really. Why is that?"

"Because, it's his place, and always will be. Even in death, the odour of the old bastard still lingers."

Elizabeth focused on the stranger and liked what she saw. His slicked back hair and goatee beard gave him the appearance of the devil, and Elizabeth Todd had always been intrigued by the satanic powers. "Nice suit, Charlie."

He took a swig of champagne from the bottle.

"It's so warm. How about a swim?" she asked.

"Now? Are you serious?"

"Why not? Good a time as ever."

She held out her hand and they left the conservatory, thankful for the refreshing cool air. Elizabeth proceeded to remove her clothes, and danced teasingly to the muted music.

"What's the matter? Shy…? Strip, Charlie."

He smiled and removed his tie and then his jacket. He placed them carefully on the chair. Elizabeth giggled boisterously when she stripped to her bra and knickers. She continued to undress and tossed her bra towards Charlie, before she ran unsteadily towards the pool.

Charlie watched the drunken, semi-naked girl disappear beneath the blue water before she submerged, twirling her knickers in the air.

"Come on, Charlie. Off with your shorts."

He stood naked and her eyes devoured him. He dived into the pool and she squirmed when the water splashed her face.

She rubbed her eyes and looked around for him. "Where are you, Charlie?"

"Right behind you, Elizabeth."

She felt her legs being pulled from beneath her and slid under, gasping for air. Charlie's hand pushed on her head as she struggled frantically and kicked out her legs in vain. His dark eyes scanned the surroundings, happy that nobody had ventured outside.

Elizabeth's frightened eyes threatened to explode from their sockets when her lungs filled with water. He puckered his lips at her, smiled, and watched the bubbles escape from her mouth. Her body relaxed and he released her, allowing the corpse to float to the surface.

Charlie Bojangles climbed out of the pool and dried himself before he casually dressed. He looked to the drowned girl and saluted before he straightened his tie. He returned to the conservatory and picked up the half full champagne bottle, before he ambled leisurely towards the gate.

Chapter Six

The slim girl in the blue headband stared open-mouthed at the blonde newcomer, who strode gracefully across the polished floor. The entire class of overweight women turned their heads towards Goldie, whispering to one another as she jogged towards the group.

Goldie wore a red headband and leotard, along with pink training shoes. The instructor stood arms folded; searching for the hidden cameras, and suspected this must be some sort of wind-up.

"Sorry I'm late. Bloody underground, never on time. I'm Goldie; we talked on the phone earlier."

"Goldie? Yes, I remember, but I was expecting..."

"Someone with more meat? I understand, girl. Even though I'm in good shape, or so I've been told, I need to keep in trim and saw your advertisement in the local paper. Have I missed anything?"

"No. Okay, ladies; let's continue with some light running on the spot. That's it, keep those knees up."

Goldie smiled at the plump, red-faced woman who ran next to her. She slowly edged away from the transvestite. The instructor played music and the class were put through some routine exercises.

Goldie was an enthusiastic pupil, but the other fitness seekers, judging by their stares felt uncomfortable. She caught the instructor staring at her crutch and winked, which caused the embarrassed girl to cut short the session.

"Right, ladies, that's enough for today. Stick to those diet sheets I gave you and shed those pounds for our next meeting, which will be on Wednesday evening. Off to the showers with you."

The women's facial expressions as they trotted off to the changing room were comical. They looked over their shoulders to see Goldie trailing them.

"I don't fucking believe it. If that's not a fella, then I'm *Brigit*

Bardot," complained a peroxide blonde.

"We have to have a word with Lynn. I'm no prude, but this is a woman's fitness club and trannys are not welcome," complained the woman who had edged away from Goldie earlier.

"We don't know for certain. Maybe she is a woman."

Peroxide glanced over her shoulder. "We'll soon know when we get in the shower."

The gazing eyes watched attentively when Goldie wiped her face down with a towel. One by one, they stripped and covered themselves coyly. They eyed Goldie, who seemed to have no apparent interest in them.

Goldie reluctantly approached the showers. She listened to the giggling and the whispers that were audible above the hissing of the water. The steam inhibited the vision of the women as they cleansed their bodies. They cracked jokes about the strange new member of their club.

Goldie stepped into the shower, her head covered with a cap. The women looked down to her waist and screamed. They grappled with each other and scrambled for the exit.

The din had alerted Lynn, the fitness instructor, who now stood before the alarmed women. "Problems, girls?"

"In there," pointed the peroxide blonde.

Lynn hesitated before she headed for the showers. She squinted as she made out Goldie, who was stood lathering herself, her back to the instructor. "Goldie, can we talk?"

The transvestite faced her and Lynn's lips quivered. Her eyes involuntarily focused on the intrusive penis.

"Oh, my god, get out! Get out and don't come back, do you hear?"

"What's the problem, dearie?" Goldie looked down and fingered her flaccid member. "Oh, this little thing. Don't let that bother you. I'm in the process of getting it removed. Sometimes I just forget about it."

"Out now!"

Goldie strolled naked through the screaming women and proceeded to dress. She applied her make-up in the mirror before she left.

******

DS Jenson crouched down and inspected the shrivelled body of Elizabeth Todd. The forensics team was in the process of placing the corpse into a body bag.

Jenson straightened up and applied a stick of gum to his dry mouth. "Any sign of a struggle, Jimbo?"

The silver-haired head of forensics faced the giant of a man. "None whatsoever, Danny. Judging by her pupils, she was as high as a kite, and she reeks of alcohol. Looks like the drugged up girl fell into the pool. She wouldn't have been in any state to save herself."

Jensen stared past the leaf-covered swimming pool towards the security gates in the distance, to see several reporters attempt to gain entry.

He never heard Chief Inspector Entwistle approach from behind. "Makes you want to puke doesn't it?"

"Yeah, I know what you mean, guv. Flashy place like this and another wasted girl, claimed by the ravages of drugs. Do we know who she is?"

"Elizabeth Todd, also known as Elizabeth Sherwood."

"Not Gus Sherwood's daughter?"

"Not daughter Danny, but wife."

Jenson recalled the young body. "The dirty old bastard. She can't have been more than twenty."

"Twenty-five actually," corrected the chief inspector. "Apparently, she held a party last night, and we're still questioning some of the guests who dossed down here. The rest are being traced by the plods."

"Who found the body, guv?"

"The skinny girl over there. She went for an early morning swim and almost dived on the body."

"That should have sobered her up," joked Jenson.

DCI Entwistle remained straight-faced. "We found no traces of drugs in the house, but they obviously cleaned things up before contacting us."

"Jimbo reckons she was stoned and probably fell into the pool."

"Probably… Well, let's get out of here and get on with the murder of Rosie. I've found out some interesting facts about Jade Exports from my friend in Customs and Excise. Apparently, they were formed some three months ago, but have not commenced trading yet. In fact, he's unable find any trace of them having a depot or having any employees."

"A bogus company, guv?"

"It's a possibility, Danny. They set up a company not intending to trade, and the girl invests four million pounds. What I can't understand is why?"

DS Jenson pondered deeply. "She could be Tyreman's lover and they planned this from the start. She marries Cochrane, and when he snuffs it, she invests in his company."

The chief inspector was not so sure. "Why, Danny? If that was the case, the money was hers anyway. She would be free to marry Tyreman and they would still have the money… Why the company?"

"Jamie did some spade work for me, guv. He couldn't find any romantic link between Tyreman and Rosie, but did find out some history on him. He's had a string of dodgy companies, mainly on the Internet. The punters send in the cash for bogus goods and he doesn't deliver, ensuring the company always goes into liquidation before he's traced. He then puts the money into another company and the chain begins again."

"So why don't we nick him?" asked the chief inspector, who helped himself to a handful of peanuts from the table.

"Tyreman's a shrewd customer, guv. He knows every loophole in the law and uses it to his advantage. He has the best briefs and we can't touch him."

"So we can expect Jade Exports to fold at any time now?"

"That's just about the gist of it, guv."

The older detective deliberated. Mmm, Tyreman must have either threatened Rosie or he was blackmailing her."

They strolled around the grounds of the manor and avoided the many witnesses being interviewed. Jenson looked towards the gate to see Vince Slattery wave at him.

"Excuse me, guv."

DS Jenson nodded at the constable to let Slattery and Sophie through, much to the annoyance of the other baying reporters. The detective smiled at Sophie, who was attired in figure hugging jeans and a white vest.

"This is as far as you go, Vince. I thought I told you to piss off. You'll have me walking the beat in no time."

"Rumour has it that Elizabeth Todd is dead."

"What of it? It was an accident, Vince. She was found in the swimming pool... I thought you were working crime nowadays?"

"Are you certain it was an accident?" asked Slattery.

"It looks that way... Why, do you know something I don't?"

"Maybe. Listen; meet me in the Rat and Parrot tonight at eight."

Sophie took several photographs inside the mansion and paid special attention to the pool.

"Will she be there?" asked Jenson hopefully.

Slattery shrugged his shoulders. "Perhaps."

"Okay, eight 'o'clock it is... This had better be good. Now move your butt back behind that gate."

******

Two hours later, a scruffy man with a grubby beard and greasy hair was given a wide berth by the other shoppers in *Tesco.* His knee length, soiled parka would have warranted no special attention had this been winter, but it was not.

Duncan Brady pushed his empty trolley from aisle to aisle. He examined the goods before he replaced them back on the shelf. He hummed along to the gentle music of *Greensleeves,* unaware of the inquisitive eyes of the store detective. It had not been a bad day at all for him. The news that Judy Sullivan had not fractured her skull after all, coupled with the five-pound note he had managed to steal from Goldie made him feel good about himself. He now aspired to continue his good fortune, notably finding something to flog in order to pay his rent.

Brady removed a packet of custard creams from a shelf and inspected them. He held the thick lenses of his spectacles against the product, before he carefully placed them in his trolley. A packet of gingersnaps was added to his shopping, before he moved on.

Bob Durcan pretended to read a magazine. His expert eyes watched every move from the undesirable customer. At sixty years of age, Bob just wanted to melt away gradually. The job as store detective offered him pocket money without the hassle, or so he thought. With his pristine black blazer and white slacks, Bob certainly looked the part. His military manner had stayed with him all of these years, and he was always well turned out. His thinning hair was immaculate, his parting precise and just the right dosage of Brylcreem had been applied.

Brady moved on and still hummed his tune. He looked around when he heard the loud squeak.

Bob cursed his new shoes and turned towards the shelf again, pretending to examine a cornflake box.

Brady's eyes narrowed when he suspected he was being followed. He turned the corner and waited a few seconds, before he re-emerged in the aisle.

Bob was taken by surprise and bent down to fasten his shoelace, a spontaneous reaction that pleased him. Yes, old Bob still had his reflexes.

"Excuse me, can you tell me where the bog rolls are?"

Bob straightened up. "Pardon me."

"The shit paper… loo roll; where is it?" asked Brady.

"I'm sorry. I'm sure I don't know."

"Just browsing are you?"

"As a matter of fact, I'm looking for my wife. I appear to have lost her," said Bob, who stood on his tiptoes. His shoes squeaked as he feigned to scan the supermarket.

"Maybe she lost you on purpose, eh?"

Brady went on his way, crooning. *"Alas my love you do me wrong, to cast me off discourteously, and I have loved you so long, delighting in your company."*

Brady turned down another aisle, picked up a packet of disposable razors, and swiftly shifted them into his inside pocket.

Bob craned his head around the corner, unaware that Brady had already registered his presence. The irritating squeak was evidence that the thief was still being pursued.

Brady increased his pace and turned down another aisle. He scooped up three ballpoint pens rapidly, and expertly ensured they joined the razor blades. He manoeuvred around two chatting women and put on a spurt, crouching over the handle of the trolley. The spirits aisle was his destination. He parked his chariot close to the whiskey section. A half bottle of *Bells* was slipped into his inside pocket of his parka and he moved on towards the checkout. He registered surprise when he saw the elderly store detective waiting. A smug grin covered his rugged features.

Brady joined the queue behind a plump woman, and tried to ignore the glares of his adversary. He removed his biscuits from the trolley, placed them on the table, and received a disgusted look from the young shop assistant.

"Is that it, sir?"

"That's it, girl. I'm on a diet."

"Haven't we forgotten something, sir?" came the voice from behind.

Brady turned to face the store detective. "No, I don't think so... Found your wife did you?"

"Do you mind emptying your pockets please?"

"As a matter of fact I do, Granddad."

Bob glared at the insolent man. "Will you step into the office please?"

Brady vaulted over the turnstile, sprinted for the exit and knocked a youth to the floor in the process.

"What the fuck!"

He regained his footing and meandered briskly through the crowd of customers. Once more, he heard the squeaky shoes behind him. He reached the safety of the car park and turned around to see the red-faced store detective stooped over, his hands on his knees.

Brady stuck up his middle finger before he merged with the shoppers. There were plenty more shops for the taking.

Chapter Seven

Sophie sat at the bar, smoked a cigarette and watched the toothless woman whine an appalling version of *I Will Survive* on the Karaoke machine. The slender journalist was dressed casually in a light blouse and jeans. Slattery had requested her presence, partly to lure Jenson and partly because his feelings for her had surpassed loathing. He realised she was not responsible for Sam quitting, and supposed it was no garden party for her either, having to partner a seemingly cold-blooded colleague.

He tapped her on the shoulder. "Drink, Sophie?"

"No thanks; I still have this one... Where've you been all afternoon? Madison's been screaming blue murder."

"I had some business to attend to."

"He's not too happy, Vince. He insists we get something in print for tomorrow morning."

"Let me worry about him, he's putty in my hands. Besides, he'll have the scoop of the year if this is as big as we think it is... Where's Jenson?"

"He hasn't turned up yet... Must be catching."

Slattery ordered his beer, his face contorted as he looked towards the badly out of tune crooner.

"This business. Did it concern Elizabeth Todd?" asked Sophie.

Slattery ignored her and gazed towards the door to see the familiar sight of Danny Jenson, who awkwardly shuffled through the crowd of tipplers. Some made to complain, but had second thoughts when they viewed this colossus of a man. The wave of customers parted when he approached the bar and ordered a lager, before he joined the journalists. He puckered his lips at Sophie, who shook her head slowly, repulsed by the sex mad detective's behaviour.

"Vince, I hope this is good. I turned down a date with an eighteen-year-old nymphomaniac to be here."

"Yeah, yeah, of course you did. Don't forget, I've seen your dates,

Danny."

Jenson looked over the heads of his companions towards the dance floor. "Christ, who's strangling the cat? I can fart better than she can sing."

Slattery nodded. "You know, for once I agree. Let's go in the bar. It's quieter there."

The smoke-filled room housed a handful of elderly people, who enjoyed a game of dominoes. In the corner sat a sad-looking man in a flat cap and raincoat. His faithful mongrel sat at his feet and lapped beer from an ashtray. He nodded to the trio and Sophie acknowledged his greeting with a "hello."

They relaxed into their seats and Sergeant Jenson opened up. "Okay, spit it out, Vince."

"I think I know who killed Elizabeth Todd."

"So do I. The person who supplied her with the coke... She fell into the pool and was too stoned to save herself."

Slattery continued. "Listen, I received a phone call from Max Sherwood on Thursday, requesting I meet him... and man is he cuckoo? He, along with his brother suspects that Elizabeth Todd had her husband Gus murdered."

"Gus! The comedian? He died of natural causes didn't he?"

"Heart attack. He claims she hired the doctor to fake the death certificate."

"Where's this leading?" asked DS Jenson. He wiped the froth from his lip and winked at Sophie.

"They hated Elizabeth. Enough to have had her murdered."

"Slow down, Vince. So what you're saying is there are two murders here?"

"There's more."

"Continue; I'm all ears."

"We're investigating the murder of Rosie Cochrane as you know. It transpires that she met her husband through an escort agency, Cupid's Arrow. Have you heard of them?"

"Nope, can't say I have."

"Well lend me your ears, Danny, because Gus Sherwood also met his wife Elizabeth through an escort agency."

"So? Was it the same agency?"

"I don't know, but we called at their bureau on Portobello Road on Friday and they denied all knowledge of knowing Elizabeth Todd."

The detective swigged his beer and seemed uninterested. "There could be a simple explanation for that. Maybe they haven't heard of her."

"Danny, they were lying; I know they were. I applied for an escort and they were only too willing to oblige until I asked for Elizabeth Todd, and then things changed. The general manager was called for; a bloke called Ross Chivers. My application form was torn up and he couldn't get rid of me quick enough."

"I don't think I'm following this, Vince."

"Two rich old men meet two escorts and marry them. The husbands die after three months and the wives inherit the money… Come on, *Columbo*; even you must admit there are similarities."

"What do you want me to do?"

Slattery nodded towards Sophie, who reached into her handbag. She passed over a photograph to the detective.

"Who is this?"

"This, my friend is Ross Chivers."

"You want me to run a check on him, eh?"

"This could be something-big, Danny, really big."

"And what do you get out of this?"

"I want to be there when you bust these people. I want a twenty-four hours start ahead of our rivals."

Sergeant Jenson grinned. "Where have I heard this before? Ah yes, Gideon and his cuckoo nest. You're getting greedy, Vince."

"I came to you remember."

The detective considered his options. "If Max Sherwood is involved, then why tell you about his father meeting Elizabeth through an escort agency? It doesn't make sense."

Slattery was adamant. "Who stands to gain from the deaths of the girls? You could find out."

The detective nodded. "We're a step ahead of you on that one… We have a suspect… I'll tell you what I'll do. I'll do some checking into this agency and also try to find out who inherits Elizabeth's money. Don't attempt to contact me. I know where to find you."

DS Jenson swallowed the remains of his lager and slammed his glass down on the table before he stood up. He crouched down, stroked the dog and turned his back to the journalists. "It's still early. Perhaps I will make my date after all."

******

The bell tolled for last orders and Sophie clung onto the arm of her colleague, hoping not to fall from her stool. She giggled when Slattery's hand accidentally stroked her breast.

"Go on, Vince, ish your round," she slurred, as her eyes rotated in their sockets.

"Shit, you drink like a bloody fish. Haven't you had enough?"

"Come on, you old git. One more vodka and I'll make you breakfast."

"Are you serious? You hated my guts this morning."

"Can't a girl change her mind?"

Slattery composed himself. "You're pissed and I'm happily married," he said. He then ordered two more vodkas. He gazed upon the swaying Sophie and laughed when she tried to light the filtered end of her cigarette.

She staggered backwards into a large black man, who caught hold of her. "Sorry, hic! My, you are a hunk aren't you?"

Slattery took her by the hand and escorted her outside. He held her up as she threatened to kiss the concrete. He flagged down a taxi and laid her on the back seat, before he reached for his wallet.

"Take her home to Harrow on the Hill, mate. This should be more than enough, so don't rip her off as I have your number. You'll have to wake her up when you get there. I'm not sure of the address." He stared at the slumbering girl, content that he had not taken advantage of her.

Slattery could not help but smile, and imagined her with a king-size hangover in the morning. Tonight, they had connected; felt more at ease with each other. It had taken a large amount of alcohol to break the ice, but Slattery now realised what an intelligent and humorous girl Sophie was. He pondered over his missed opportunity, but perhaps it was for the best; besides, he would not have fancied waking up next to Sophie in the morning, with her throwing accusations of rape at him.

His thoughts turned to his wife. He checked his wristwatch and cursed, knowing what to expect when arriving home. Perhaps Cheryl was right. They had seen so little of each other recently, and he had to admit his feelings for his wife had gradually diminished. He felt so fatigued nowadays and put that down to his obsession with his work. He mentally promised himself he would take his family to Disneyworld, just as soon as he had edited his story.

The taxi pulled into the kerb and Slattery gritted his teeth. He listened to the driver rant on incessantly about nothing in particular. The Asian man repeatedly peered at his passenger through his mirror.

"What the fuck are you doing?" groaned Slattery.

"Pardon me, sir?"

"Where are you going? I may be pissed, but I'm not stupid. You should've taken a right back there."

"You did say Addington Road didn't you, sir?"

"Are you taking the piss? Drop me off here!"

The taxi pulled up and Slattery clambered out of the cab. He slammed the door noisily behind him.

"That will be six pounds and thirty-five pence, sir."

"Piss off!"

"I'll call the police."

Slattery turned towards the cowering man, who wound up his

window. He searched his wallet and threw a five-pound note at the vehicle, before he staggered away. The loud protests gradually faded away.

Slattery stood opposite his home. He was shrouded in darkness, like a burglar stalking his next victim. Cheryl always left the front light on if she was up, and the absence of light gratified him, for the last thing he needed was a quarrel.

He turned the key quietly and put his index finger to his lips as he fell into the hallway. The light switch was located after much fumbling in the darkness and his eyes focused on the large piece of paper that rested against their wedding portrait. The words at first did not register with his addled mind, until he re-read them.

Vince, you have pushed me too far this time and left me with no option but to leave you. I had to take this step, as you no doubt would have talked me into staying if I confronted you. I have suspected for a long time that you were seeing someone else, and my fears I'm sure have been vindicated. Do I still love you? I have searched my heart, hoping the answer would be yes, but I would be deluding myself if I told you what you wanted to hear. We are staying at my mothers, as I need some time to think. We both do. I will contact you just as soon as we're settled, so please do not com*e here, as it will upset the girls.

CHEZ.

Slattery removed his spectacles and rubbed his tired eyes. The shock sobered him more adequately than any amount of black coffee could. He lay on the sofa and stared up at the framed photograph of him and his family that was clutched between his clammy hands. He closed his eyes and felt the beginnings of a migraine, a regular visitor nowadays to his troubled mind. He relaxed his grip on the photograph, it hit the carpet and shattered the frame. The impending sleep he welcomed.

Chapter Eight

Conversation that Monday morning was uncomfortable, for the two journalists each in their own way had regretted Saturday evening. Sophie had noticed the apparent ignorance from Slattery towards her, and searched her ambiguous memory cells, attempting to fathom the reason for his lack of acknowledgment. Little did she know that their boisterous frolicking was not the cause of her colleague's mood.

They were ushered to Madison's office and marched down the aisle, like two murderers approaching the gallows. The knock on the door was followed by an authoritative, "Enter!"

Slattery espied Harry Orton out of the side of his eye, who brought his finger across his throat with a smug smile on his face.

Madison sat at his desk and filled his pipe. His face did not betray his mood. He beckoned for them to sit. He sat for a minute, stared at his employees and sucked vigorously on his pipe. "Well, Vince, what have you come up with?"

Slattery, who was thankful that his editor seemed in an amicable mood, passed over his presentation to the diminutive man and watched for a reaction. The scowl on Madison's face did not fill Slattery with the feel good factor.

"Do you expect me to print this?"

"What's the problem, Roland?"

"The problem? I'll tell you what the problem is shall I? If I run this story, we'll be out of business. We'll have at least two lawsuits to face from Max Sherwood and Cupid's Arrow, not forgetting the families of the girls who you accuse… What grounds have you for such an onslaught, Vince?"

"We've done some sniffing around and everything in my report points to a massive conspiracy by the escort agency."

The response did not satisfy the editor. "Where's your proof, god damn it? Did Elizabeth Todd ever work for Cupid's Arrow?"

"I think she..."

"Think! Hell, Vince. We're in the newspaper business and are sitting targets from the headhunters waiting to sue the arses off us. We need concrete proof before I can even start to consider your story... Does this Max Sherwood have any ties with Cupid's Arrow?"

"Not that we can find, but he hated Elizabeth enough to have her killed."

"And Rosie Cochrane? Pray tell me why he would have her killed?"

Slattery pleaded his case. "We need a few more days, Roland. This is big, I can feel it."

Madison tossed the folder onto his desk. "Harry Orton's already ran the story of Elizabeth Todd's death. The coroner says it was accidental death, caused by excessive drink and drugs."

"Let me delve into the agency's past. There may be others."

"And how do you propose to do that, Vince? Are they going to give you a dossier of their former employees?"

"There are other ways, Roland."

"What other ways? Never mind, I don't want to know... You have your methods and they usually produce results, hence your advancement to your present post... I'll tell you what I'll do. I'll give you until the weekend to come up with something, but do not put yourself in a position that threatens The Echo with a lawsuit. The shareholders are already outraged and there are rumours of job cuts to balance the books... Nothing illegal eh, Vince?"

"Of course not. What do you take me for?"

Madison turned towards Sophie. "That will be all for now. I need to talk to Vince alone. Oh, and you can take your photographs with you. We won't be running them. Not yet anyway."

He waited until she had left the room before he continued. "How are you finding her, Vince?"

"She's okay. Not had much opportunity to see her work as yet, apart from the snaps inside the agency."

"You've changed your tune haven't you?"

"It's just that I was so used to Sam."

Madison could see that his employee was troubled. "You look like shit. How are things at home?"

Slattery stared hard at his editor and wondered if he knew that Cheryl had left him. "So, so."

"Where were you Saturday afternoon, Vince?"

"Saturday? You know where I was. Investigating the case."

"Without your photographer? Is there something you want to tell me? You're not screwing around in work's time are you, because if you are?"

"Have you been talking to my wife? Have you?"

"So there is something wrong... No, Vince, I've not been talking to Cheryl... Numerous times now, you have gone missing. What I want to know is why?"

Slattery slumped in his chair. "Everything I do is job related. If you're not happy with my work, then fire me."

"Whoa boy. Take a chill pill. Nobody's suggesting your work is bad. It's just...Well, I don't want you to compromise Sophie's position."

"Meaning?"

"Meaning don't put her in the position of having to lie for you. She is highly regarded by some quarters."

"Oh, now I see. She didn't get this job on merit. As I thought, she was born with a silver spoon up her arse... Who's her sugar daddy, Roland?"

"Greg Finch, our majority shareholder. He's her uncle."

Slattery laughed. "Well sorry, but I'm not going to change the way I work to suit Lady Penelope."

"Remember, Vince, I'll give you Sunday to come up with something. Now get your life together and sort your head out."

******

The tall, fair-haired man and the younger pretty girl were accepted as an item. They sat at the fibreglass table, sipped cappuccino and talked quietly. Slattery peered through the soiled cafe window on Tottenham Court Road and watched the various characters going about their business. Some of them hurried, as the bleak, ominous sky threatened to dispense its nasty contents onto the grey urban jungle.

The middle-aged gum-chewing waitress topped up their cups and Sophie checked her wristwatch. Nothing had been mentioned of Saturday evening, and both seemed comfortable with the situation. However, they were inwardly embarrassed by their juvenile behaviour.

Slattery broke the silence. "You never told me Greg Finch was your uncle."

Sophie grasped her waist long hair and tied it into a ponytail. She studied his face as she did so. "What difference does it make?"

"You gave me the impression you applied for the job independently."

"Oh, so that's it? You think my uncle influenced me getting this post?"

"Well, did he?"

"No! He most certainly did not... He knew nothing of me applying for this job until I had actually been appointed. I would have it no other way."

Slattery grimaced. "Don't flatter yourself, Sophie. He knew all right."

"What the hell are you saying? That's bullshit and you know it."

"Forget it."

She slammed her cup down on the table. "No, let's not forget it. I'm telling you I got this job on merit."

"If you say so."

"Yes, I bloody well do say so."

The smirking waitress approached, eager not to miss anything.

"Go away!" yelled Sophie.

The wind chimes jingled with the opening of the door and the giant of a detective entered.

The waitress backed off, expecting a robbery when she eyed the man with the shaved head. "Can I help you?"

"Yes, you can, darling," said DS Jenson. "Give me an orange juice will you... with a straw."

"With a straw," the waitress mumbled. She scowled as she bit her tongue.

Jenson sought out the journalists and sat besides Sophie, ensuring his leg was flush against hers.

"Why don't you buy a watch, Danny?" moaned Slattery.

Jenson ignored him and faced the angry-looking photographer, who struggled to light her cigarette. He removed the lighter from his pocket and obliged.

"Have you had any more thoughts about our date?" he asked, as he winked at her.

He coughed when she blew the smoke in his face. "You're just not my type, Detective." She moved her leg away from his.

"Well, Danny; did you find out anything?" quizzed Slattery.

"This doesn't get printed, okay?"

"In case you've forgotten, I'm a reporter and that is what reporters do... report."

The peeved detective was adamant. "You can't print this. They'll know it was me. I want your word, Vince."

"Okay, you have my word."

They waited until the waitress brought Jenson his orange juice and placed it on the table. "One orange juice with a straw." She retreated behind the counter and shook her head.

Jenson opened up. "Rosie Cochrane was left over four and a half million pounds by her husband. Shortly before she was murdered, she invested four million in a company calling itself Jade Exports Services Ltd. The executive director of the company is a man by the name of Lance Tyreman, who incidentally has a history of setting up bogus companies, only for them to go into liquidation. He then sets up another and the chain goes on. Rosie had approximately £100,000 when she died."

Slattery was curious. "Why invest so much?"

"Good question, especially as the company was newly formed and hadn't even commenced trading... We could find no prior connection between Rosie and Tyreman."

"Was he blackmailing her?" asked Sophie.

"We found no reason why she should invest in the company, but there's more. Elizabeth Sherwood, or Todd as she likes to be known, invested in a company just days before her death. She put three million pounds into a company calling itself Emerald Bloodstock Agency. Wait for it; the company was formed some three months ago, and nobody in Newmarket appears to have heard of the owner, George Mikhos. He took over some stables, but as yet, no racehorses have been seen in his yard."

"You went to Newmarket?"

"No, Vince, of course not. I have a friend in the Suffolk police force and he owed me a favour."

"So are you investigating this George..."

"Mikhos... Evidentially, he's a Greek businessman. No, we're not investigating him, as Elizabeth Todd's death was not suspicious... We do have Lance Tyreman under surveillance though, but he's laughing at us. I expect his company to fold at any time now."

Sophie stubbed out her cigarette. "What about Cupid's Arrow?"

Jenson shrugged. "It's been difficult to check them out, seeing as I've been too busy working on the Rosie Cochrane case. I ran a check through the computer and they seem to be a legitimate company, established some three years ago by a Matthew Torrance."

Slattery butted in. "Did you get a list of past and present employees?"

"Sorry, my guvnor's not buying this. He's told me to rely on the man last seen having a drink with Rosie in the Dorchester. You're on your own I'm afraid. If you do find anything interesting, then get back to me and I'll see what I can do... DCI Entwistle is a stubborn man, who bases his investigations on facts, not maybes."

"Surely you can see a connection here, Danny? I cannot believe CID isn't interested."

"Like I said, Vince, Cupid's Arrow is not under investigation."

"I'll apply for a job there."

The two men turned to Sophie.

"Out of the question," insisted Slattery.

"Why not? What better way is there to investigate the agency than to have someone on the inside?"

"Sophie, aren't you forgetting something? Ross Chivers has seen your face."

"Maybe not. My face was concealed behind a camera, and he didn't wait around long enough to have a good look at me. Besides, I can wear a wig."

Slattery objected. "No way. You're a photographer, not a detective… But there's nothing to stop CID putting someone undercover."

Jensen shook his head as he sucked his straw. "Sorry, you're on your own here. Vince is right; it would be foolish to try to pull off something like that. It could get dangerous."

"So you do admit they could be involved?" asked Slattery.

"Forget Cupid's Arrow… I'll try to reason with Entwistle, but don't put your mortgage on him listening… Look, I have to go now. I'll be in touch."

The waitress scurried after Jenson.

The detective motioned towards the journalists. "The gentleman in the spectacles is paying."

Chapter Nine

The sun lay low in the orange sky as Duncan Brady strolled along Gower Street. The protesting screams of an obese woman were aimed at a dozen children. She objected to them kicking a ball in front of her house. They were met with chants of obscenity from the ignorant footballers.

"Keep that fucking ball away from my house, you little shits. My Ernie's in bed."

The ball landed at Brady's feet. He looked up and grinned at the boys, who stood hands on hips and waited for their football to be returned. He put his foot on the ball, folded his arms and posed. His behaviour failed to not please the mumbling teenagers.

"Come on, Specky. Pass the ball."

"On my head, yer tramp," screamed another.

Brady smirked at the boys. His eyes peered insanely from behind his thick lenses. "Take it from me if you think you're good enough."

"Put a knife in the bloody thing!" yelled the fat woman.

One of the youths approached, crouched and prepared to tackle the scruffy, bearded man. He lunged with his foot, and Brady, with the expertise of a Brazilian soccer player, dragged the ball back with a deft flick, which caused the boy to lose his balance. Another boy came at him, and he set off dribbling through the closing pack, until he was clear of them.

"Giz our ball back, mister."

Brady winked at them, took a run up and blasted the football over their heads towards the nagging woman. She screamed and held her hands out in front of her, as the football slammed against the wall of her house, amid the giggles of the boys.

Brady walked on and the smile vanished, for he dreaded the inevitable confrontation with another battleaxe, Mrs Parish. The two weeks rent he had promised her on Saturday was not forthcoming. He had sold the razors and the whiskey he had stolen for a fiver, not nearly enough to satisfy the demanding landlady.

He paused outside the front door, his ear pressed against the woodwork. He listened for any sign of Mrs Parish. She was prone to retiring early and he hoped tonight would be no different. He turned the key and opened the door carefully, before he tiptoed towards the staircase. He cursed when the staircase squeaked, and waited.

"Mr Bojangles, is that you?"

Brady closed his eyes when the door opened behind him. The aroma of a fry-up escaped from the landlady's room.

"Well, well, if it isn't Mr Brady. I'd have more luck finding Lord bloody Lucan than finding you… Well, do you have my rent?"

He turned to face her, and put on his lost child look. "My, you are looking radiant this evening… It's like this, Mrs P; I did have it, but..."

"I want you out of here first thing in the morning, do you hear me? You've had more than enough chances and I don't need this. That nice Mr Bojangles and even that tranny from room three pay me on time, so why can't you?"

"Give me more time, Mrs P, I beg of you?"

"I'm not listening to you. If you aren't gone first thing in the morning, I'll call the law and they'll lock you up."

The door was slammed and Brady gritted his teeth and put two fingers up at the absent landlady. He climbed the staircase and ambled miserably towards his room. His eyes focused on the room at the end of the hall. Brady was desperate and his need for cash predetermined his desperate deed. He had in his mind just what he would say to the reclusive Charlie Bojangles. He rapped on the door quietly and waited. Again, he knocked, but this time louder. The last thing he needed was for him to enter the room and find the strange man asleep.

Brady removed the wallet from his pocket and selected the appropriate key. His dishonest artistry had come in handy when he had visited Mrs Parish's room and had acquired the spare keys. The landlady suspected nothing, and believed she had simply misplaced the keys.

His last search of the room had proved fruitless, but this time he would steal anything that was not nailed down. If he could acquire the rent by the morning, perhaps he would be reprieved.

The odour inside the room was stale, the heat intense as the windows were closed. Yet again, he rifled through the collection of elegant suits without success, before he turned his attention towards the chest of drawers. The squeak of the floorboard alerted him, and his eyes swivelled towards the displaced edge of the carpet. He noticed that the carpet was not sitting flush against the skirting board.

Brady knelt down and pulled the carpet back, which revealed a niche in the floorboard. He pulled at the section of timber and smiled as a gaping hole faced him. His hand plunged inside the hole and he made contact with something cold. He rattled the green tin and heard nothing. With his greedy hands, he prized the lid off and stared down at a huge wad of notes and some notepaper. He counted out the twenty-pound notes and stopped when he reached three thousand pounds. There was, he estimated at least twenty-thousand pounds in the tin. He felt the perspiration on his beard, as he stroked his face, his mouth as dry as the Sahara Desert.

With shaking hands, he unfolded one of the sheets of paper and read the contents. There was a photograph of a pretty redheaded girl and the name Rosie Cochrane printed below it. An address accompanied the photograph, along with a list of hotels and pubs. He fumbled with the next sheet of paper and this time a blonde girl faced him, Elizabeth Todd. Again, the address and a list of locations were jotted down.

Brady fingered the money and kissed it, before he giggling childishly. Something caught his eye in the void of the floorboard and he groped for the object. His eyes bulged when he stared at the polythene bag that held the pistol and silencer.

"Mr Bojangles, whatever have you been up to?"

He pondered over the situation before he counted out a thousand pounds. He returned the rest of the money and the dossiers on the girls to the hole, along with the pistol. It went against his gluttonous nature to return the money, but Duncan Brady was a coward at heart, and the thought of a killer coming after him did not appeal to him. Perhaps Bojangles would not miss such a paltry amount as one thousand pounds, and he could always come back for more.

Brady replaced the piece of floorboard three times before he was satisfied, and covered it with the carpet. He hastily walked towards the door and checked the corridor, before he dashed to his room. He lay on his bed with the notes in his hands and sniffed their texture. He chuckled contently, before he approached his door and secured the lock. He would pay Mrs Parish first thing in the morning and his troubles will be over; or so he thought.

******

The wolf-whistles directed at the shapely blonde, drowned out the noise of the heavy traffic. The orange-vested council workers made some sexist comments, which were ignored by the girl, before they continued to dig the road.

She peered over her designer sunglasses at her destination before she entered the bureau. The woman seated behind the desk was reading a novel and did not look too pleased with the intrusion of the girl in the purple dress.

"Can I help you?"The secretary looked her visitor over, as a farmer would with his prize bull.

"I hope so. I'm looking for work."

The novel was placed on the table, and the blonde sat opposite without invitation. The aroma of expensive perfume lingered in the air-conditioned office, and negated the odour of stale tobacco.

"What makes you think we're taking people on, Miss..."

"Dougal…, Clare Dougal. I've tried a few places and need the work desperately. I saw your office so thought, what the heck. Why not?"

"Have you done this sort of work before, Miss Dougal?"

"It depends what the job entails… if you know what I mean?" said the jobseeker mischievously, with a twinkle in her eye.

"This is a high-class establishment and our clientele are normally people of high standing, who wish to retain their anonymity for various reasons."

"Would I be expected to sleep with them?"

"Miss Dougal! You would be paid to escort them to dinner or some sort of function. What you do in your own time is not our concern."

"So you mean I date them, and if I want to make a little extra, you don't want to know?"

"Miss Dougal, at this present time, we're not taking anyone on, but if you leave a contact number, we'll bear you in mind."

"You mean you're giving me the cold shoulder?"

The secretary scowled at the job applicant. "I don't believe you'd fit in around here. I'm sure you're used to something more adventurous, should we say?"

The door swung open and Ross Chivers approached the secretary, a folder tucked under his arm. "Hilary, here is a list of new clients. File them will you, that's a good girl?"

His eyes were attracted to the blonde girl with her sunglasses resting on the top of her head. He projected his most charming smile, which was returned.

"And who is this delicious creature, Hilary?"

"Oh, she's just leaving, Mr Chivers."

"I need work," uttered Clare.

The secretary protested. "I've told her we have nothing at present, Mr..."

The raised hand stopped her completing her sentence. The ginger-haired manager was obviously impressed with what he saw. "Could you step into my office, Miss..."

"Dougal, but you can call me Clare."

Hilary gawped at the blonde, livid that she had been granted an interview.

Clare winked at the irked secretary before she left the office.

A list of awards and framed photographs adorned the panelled walls. Several familiar celebrities stared down at Clare.

"Very nice. I assumed your clients would wish to remain discreet?"

Chivers flashed his polished teeth. "Not all of them. It's good for their image, you understand, being seen on a date with a beautiful woman. When visiting London, celebrities often call us, after being recommended by their showbiz friends... Yes, we're one big happy family here at Cupid's Arrow."

"So are there any vacancies?"

"Don't be so hasty, Clare. First things first. Have you done this type of work before?"

"No, I can't say I have."

Chivers offered Clare a cigarette, which she accepted. He lit it for her with an impressive silver lighter. "So what type of work have you done?"

"Modelling, waitress, barmaid... You name it, I've done it."

"You were a model?" quizzed Chivers.

"Yes, I've done some modelling."

"Where?"

"Gemini Studios. Langleys..."

"You've modelled at Langleys?"

"Yes, a couple of years ago."

Chivers jotted down some notes and Clare noticed the bags beneath his eyes, which made him appear older than his age of thirty-three. He rose from his desk, approached a filing cabinet and selected a form before he returned to his seat. "Would you like some tea, coffee perhaps?"

"No thank you, I'm fine. Besides, too much caffeine is bad for you."

"My very words... Now, Clare, I have here an application form, which you're required to fill out. Usually, the girls complete it at home, but I think we can do it here. Rush it through, if you get my meaning... Your full name please?"

"Clare Louise Dougal."

"Your address?"

"Aat the moment I'm staying with a friend. I've not long since returned from Rome."

"Really? No problem. We'll skip that part."

Clare smiled a false smile. If the galling manager's tongue protruded any further, he would be licking dust mites off the carpet.

"Age? Sorry, I have to ask."

"Twenty-four."

"Blonde, brown eyes," he said, when he inspected her features. "Of course we'll require a few snaps of you for the dossier, you understand? Our clients usually need to know what the girl looks like before he makes his or her decision."

"Her?"

Chivers grinned. "Occasionally, there are one or two actresses that prefer the company of women. If you're uncomfortable with that of course..."

"No! I'll have a date with a baboon if it means me getting a job."

Chivers laughed and showed off his gold tooth. "Hobbies?"

"Aerobics, dancing, golf..."

"You play golf?"

"I love playing a round."

Chivers scowled at her, unsure if she was mocking him. "Do you know your National Insurance number?"

She delved into her handbag and passed over the document.

"Thank you, that's fine. Now, if you'll jot down your former employers from the last say five years, I'll get this processed as soon as possible."

She racked her brains and attempted to recall previous jobs. She felt the eyes of Chivers rape her.

The irksome man continued. "Before we do consider offering you employment, you'll be required to go out to dinner with me. Just so I can give you some advice of course on etiquette, and to see how you come across as a date. A sort of screen test if you get my meaning... Should we say tomorrow evening?"

"But, I haven't even got the job yet."

"Oh, I think we can say with a fair deal of certainty that you'll be part of our family, unless you're lying of course. I will need to check your details. We've had some unsavoury characters applying brfore, including ladies of the night. Of course, they were dismissed... I'll pick you up at seven 'o'clock if that's okay? What's the address of your friend?"

Clare hesitated. "It's a bit delicate at the moment. It wouldn't look too good if you turned up at the flat."

"Oh, I see, a jealous boyfriend, eh? Fine, I'll pick you up outside here then."

"Seven 'o'clock, you said?"

She stubbed out her cigarette and they shook hands. Clare could not help but glare at Hilary, who had turned back to her novel.

Once outside, she welcomed the fresh air, leant against the wall and breathed a sigh of relief. Sophie had come through the first part successfully. It was what lay ahead that bothered her.

Chapter Ten

"Shepherd's Pie or Lasagne?" asked the butch-looking woman, with her face set in a permanent scowl.

"Is there a difference?" moaned Jenson, who opted for a salad instead.

DCI Entwistle rubbed his hands together. "Shepherd's Pie, Betty and don't scrimp on the chips.

The detectives found a vacant table close to an open window and settled down for their lunch. The police canteen was hardly bustling, as the majority of the staff sensibly opted for the nearby pub.

"So when are we moving on Tyreman, guv?"

"Forget it, Danny. Tyreman's out of bounds."

"Come again?"

"We've nothing on him. He's complained to his MP and we've been told to cool it."

"You're not serious! He can complain to the bloody Queen if he wants, but his arse is mine."

"Relax. Forget about Tyreman."

DS Jenson stared disgustingly at the older man, who shovelledthe stale looking Shepherd's Pie into his mouth. "He had Rosie Cochrane killed to shut her up. If you can't see that, you ought to be carrying a white stick."

DCI Entwistle raised his voice. "Danny, enough! I in case you've forgotten, I'm your senior officer… Forget Tyreman…What progress have you made with the search for the geezer in the Dorchester?"

Jenson threw down his knife and fork and pushed away the salad. "Sweet fuck all. It's as though he's disappeared off the face of the earth. We've issued photo-fits and have had calls suggesting him to be a local window cleaner to him being *Al Pacino.* We have toto lean on Tyreman, guv. He's our only link with Rosie Cochrane."

The senior detective put down his knife and fork. "Am I talking in Chinese or what? Okay, so she invested some cash in a dodgy company.

Why then would he have her killed? After all, she couldn't exactly have taken it back now could she?"

DS Jenson was eager to put over his point. "What if he wanted to keep her quiet? He could be involved with Cupid's Arrow."

"That's shit and you know it. Just because Rosie Cochrane met her husband through the agency doesn't mean a thing. Concentrate on the man from the Dorchester, Danny."

"Who's got to you, guv? You've soon changed your tune. You were convinced Tyreman was involved in the death of Rosie."

DCI Entwistle dabbed at his mouth with his napkin. "Okay, between you and me you stubborn bastard, there's pressure from upstairs. Lance Tyreman has been under surveillance for some time from Special Branch. Something to do with exporting illegal arms. They evidently don't want us stepping on their toes."

"Why didn't you tell me this earlier, guv?"

The chief inspector resumed devouring his meal. "Because, I'm putting my balls in the grinder here. If this gets out, we'll be directing traffic on Oxford Street."

"I understand, but what can be more serious than murder?"

DCI Entwistle pointed his fork at Jenson and spoke with his mouth full of chips. "Multiple murder, that's what. Have I made myself clear?"

"So we lay off Tyreman, but we can still investigate Cupid's Arrow, right?" asked Jenson.

"Give me fucking strength! You're a good copper, Danny, but an obstinate bastard."

The younger man spoke reluctantly. "A friend of mine may take it upon himself to infiltrate the agency. Don't you see why we have to act now before someone is killed?"

"What friend?"

"You know I can't tell you that, guv."

"Listen, you tell this so-called friend of yours to back off."

"So you admit he could be in danger?"

"You said yourself, Cupid's Arrow is a legitimate company. Do yourself a favour and take a holiday. Your brain is scrambled."

DS Jenson pushed away his plate. "I'll do everything I can to catch the bastard who killed Rosie Cochrane, and possibly Elizabeth Todd. Special Branch or no Special Branch."

Chief Inspector Entwistle stood up, his face flushed. "Danny, I'll fucking suspend you if that's what it takes. By god I will."

"You're going to have to, guv."

"You're off the case!"

"How convenient."

"Meaning what?" growled the chief inspector.

"You work it out... guv!"

Jenson strode briskly towards the exit, his fists clenched and the devil in his eye.

******

Slattery almost bumped into his photographer when he exited the premises of The Echo. Sophie, after her interview with the unsavoury Ross Chivers was now dressed casually. The scowl on Slattery's face told her she was about to be chastised for her unauthorised absence.

"Where the hell have you been, Sophie?"

"You wouldn't believe me if I told you."

"I was about to call at your place… Where's your camera?"

"In my car."

"Okay, let's go."

"Where?"

"Carlton House. The home of Jade Export Services Ltd. It's just a little further along the river."

"Vince! You promised Danny."

"Don't worry. I just want Tyreman's picture, that's all."

"And what if he's not in his office?"

"Oh, he's there all right. I telephoned the reception at Carlton House earlier."

Sophie was confused. "So we're going to just waltz into his office and ask for a photograph?"

"Don't be stupid. We're going to wait until he makes an appearance. He must leave the premises at some time."

Sophie clambered into the driver's seat and the red Mini pulled away. Slattery directed her the short distance to Carlton House. She felt his eyes scrutinising her, as she pulled up opposite the impressive building.

"What?" she asked.

"Where have you been?"

"Promise you won't shout?"

He held his hands up. "Promise."

"I've applied for a job at Cupid's Arrow."

"What! You stupid little cow!"

"You said you wouldn't shout."

"I lied… What goes on in that small mind of yours, Sophie?"

She grinned mischievously. "I'm meeting Ross Chivers tomorrow evening for dinner."

"Like shit you are. Are you crazy?"

"He's more or less promised me the job… I gave them my friend's name, who has done a bit of modelling in her time. I was convincing, and if he does check me out, he'll find nothing to link me with The Echo."

Slattery calmed down. "I hope your friend appreciates what you've done."

"Clare? She didn't mind me using her details."

"And pray tell me what you intend to do?" asked Slattery. "This is not some bloody game."

"I intend to have dinner with Ross Chivers, and who knows what I'll find out?"

"Chivers is only taking you for dinner for one thing. Can't you see that?"

"Oh lord, you're jealous, aren't you?"

"What? You're talking out of your arse. Jealous of what?"

"Listen, Vince; I'm a big girl now. I'll plug him for information, and afterwards refuse the job. What have we to lose?"

"I don't know. It's too dangerous."

"What's he going to do… strangle me in the restaurant? Come on, Vince; don't say you never took a risk or two to get where you are today?"

Slattery considered her appeal. "Okay, but after dinner you refuse the job. Promise?"

"Of course."

Sophie reached for a cigarette and noticed the disapproving glare on Slattery's face. She left the vehicle and leaned against her pride and joy to enjoy her smoke.

Slattery rifled through her music collection, with one eye on the entrance of Carlton House. He screwed up his face, as he rejected tape after tape, before he leaned through the window. "Haven't you any proper music?"

Sophie opened the door, selected a tape and inserted it into the deck. The music of *Eminem* did not appeal to the appalled journalist, and he made his escape, ambling towards the fast food van that was parked nearby. He nibbled on his hot dog, looked out onto the river and felt the cooling breeze.

Sophie was now sat behind the wheel. Her head nodded in time to the music.

He tossed his hot dog into the litterbin and his eyes focused on two smartly dressed men, who left the building and chatted intensely. They paused opposite the red mini, shook hands, and held their friendly grip for longer than expected.

One of the men sported a chic ponytail, obviously attempting to make up for the lack of hair elsewhere. The sun reflected off his impressive collection of jewellery worn on his well-manicured fingers. His perfect tan was evidence of his globetrotting trips. The other man was taller and thickset with a broad nose, his skin much darker, as if he hailed from the

Mediterranean.

Slattery looked anxiously towards the Mini and hoped Sophie had captured the two businessmen on film. The darker man walked towards his vehicle, a silver Mercedes. The shorter man clambered into his green Jaguar.

As they pulled away, Slattery jogged towards the Mini and jotted down the license plates. "Well, did you get the shots?"

Sophie nodded proudly. "Of course, but they could have been anyone. That's one hell of a large building."

"Wait here," ordered Slattery. "I'll be back shortly."

She watched as he bounded up the steps and entered the building. He loped across the tiled floor, impressed by the decor of the new structure. He was glad of the air conditioning, as the temperature outside was intense. Slattery approached the Asian girl who sat behind the desk at reception. He put on his charming smile.

"Good afternoon. Could you tell me if Mr Lance Tyreman from Jade Export Services is in please?"

"I'm afraid you've just missed him. He left a couple of minutes ago."

"Just my luck… Tell me, that wasn't him with the dark looking gentleman was it?"

"Yes, as a matter of fact it was… Did you have an appointment?"

"No… Where is Mr Tyreman's secretary?"

"Mr Tyreman does not have a secretary. I direct all of his incoming calls to his office on the eight floor."

"No secretary?"

The receptionist continued. "Jade Exports is currently in the preliminary stages of development. As yet, no staff has been recruited."

"Really? How many offices does the company lease?"

"Just the one upstairs… As I've already told you, they've just started out… Why are you asking all these questions?"

"Thank you. You've been most helpful."

Slattery joined Sophie, who waited outside her car and smoked another cigarette.

"Well?"

He turned off the offending music and he took his place in the passenger seat. "That was indeed Tyreman. Jade Export Services consists as far as I can see of one man. Lance Tyreman… It doesn't make sense, Rosie Cochrane investing so much money in a company that hasn't even been established yet."

"Not unless of course she knew Lance Tyreman," suggested Sophie.

"Even so, there's something not right about the transaction."

"So where do we go from here?"

Slattery considered. "We'll do some delving into Tyreman's background and see what we come up with."

Chapter Eleven

Mrs Parish scrambled out of her room when she heard the lock being turned in the front door. Her make-up had been applied in the hope of confronting her esteemed tenant, whom she had affection for. Her hair had been cut in preparation and she wore her best low-cut beige dress. The last time she had dolled herself up had been some five years ago, when her Harry had still been alive. Now at the age of fifty, Dorothy Parish harboured fantasies of seducing the delectable lodger; after all, she was long overdue some affection herself.

Bojangles closed the door quietly and turned to face his landlady. The aroma of cheap perfume lingered in the hallway. He smiled half-heartedly and put up his hand as a greeting, before he made to ascend the staircase.

"Mr Bojangles!"

He turned slowly, unhappy with the irritating woman's intrusion.

"Mr Bojangles, I see so little of you nowadays. Won't you join me for a drink? I've a nice bottle of claret chilling in the fridge."

"Sorry, maybe another time. I'm feeling very tired."

She reached out and he felt her ice-cold hands against his. "Oh, come on, Mr Bojangles. One drink can't do any harm?"

He checked his wristwatch… "Well, just the one then."

He followed the fervent landlady into her room and his eyes scanned the tasteless surroundings. The drab, green-flowered wallpaper and matching carpet reminded him of puke. She invited him to sit down beside her on the tan coloured couch. The odour of baking was evident when she sprang from the couch and walked briskly towards the kitchen.

Bojangles racked his mind for a means of escape. He had been in some scrapes before, but none as scary as this.

She returned from the kitchen, clutching a bottle of claret and two glasses. She set them on the coffee table before she once more retreated to the kitchen. This time she returned with a tray of sausage rolls.

"You must try one of my sausage rolls, Mr Bojangles."

"No thank you."

"But you must. I made them especially."

The dark-eyed man relented and selected the smallest one he could see. Mrs Parish poured out the wine and handed him a glass.

"Thank you, Mrs Parish."

"Dorothy. Call me Dorothy; after all, we are living under the same roof aren't we?"

Bojangles felt increasingly uncomfortable, and sensed the middle-aged vamp was undressing him with her eyes. "Nice room, Dorothy."

"I like to keep a clean house... I've redecorated this room since Harry passed away, you know."

He chewed on his sausage roll. "Nice room."

"I say I like to keep a clean house, but I'm not too sure about that horrible Duncan Brady... What do you think of him?"

"I'm sorry, but I've never had the pleasure," said Bojangles.

"You haven't? Surely, you must have bumped into him. He only lives down the corridor from you... Thick spectacles, dirty beard."

"We appear not have met."

Mrs Parish sat on the sofa opposite her lodger and ensured that her skirt rode up her leg to reveal a suspender. "Like passing ships in the night, eh? You're lucky; he's not the most pleasant of characters. In fact, I was about to throw him out, but he came up with a month's rent. The weasel's probably nicked it, but I'm not the type of person to pry... Anyway, here we are, Mr Bojangles. Don't you have a first name?"

"Charlie."

"Cheers, Charlie."

He tasted the claret and attempted to hide his dissatisfaction when he swallowed the cheap plonk. He noticed Mrs Parish's sudden movement as her skirt intentionally rode even further up her leg. He reddened when she fluttered her eyelashes at him, and drank down his wine greedily.

"Thank you for the claret, Dorothy... I must go."

The frustrated woman sat beside him and placed her hand on his leg. "But, Charlie, you've just got here. Please, just one more glass?"

"I really should be..."

"Nonsense," she remarked, and refilled his glass. "Tell me; what do you do for a living?"

"I'm a stockbroker."

"Really...? There's something I don't understand... Given your immaculate clothes and intellectual manner, you're obviously not short of a bob or two. Why then do you choose to stay here?"

He felt her hand stroke his leg rhythmically.

"It's only temporary, Dorothy. I'm looking for a house."

"Really? That explains why I see so little of you... Are you sure there's nothing else holding you here, Charlie?"

"Such as?" He realised he had come up with the wrong response when she snuggled up close to him.

"Me."

"He sprung up and placed his half-empty glass on the coffee table. "Thank you, but I really must go now. I have to be up early in the morning."

Her protests were unheard as the rattled man headed for the door.

"Charlie, we're two lonely people. We can find solace in each other."

"Goodnight, Mrs Parish."

The door slammed and Bojangles took the stairs three at a time, checking behind him for the sex-mad widow. He strolled towards his room and chuckled to himself, more from relief than amusement. He flicked the light switch and jingled his keys, before he selected the appropriate one. He crouched down and his face turned ashen when he noticed the strand of cotton was absent. It was an old habit of the assassin, that he always placed the thread across his door, thus alerting him of any unwelcome intrusion. Mrs Parish cleaned the room on Wednesday, so he searched his troubled mind for another solution. Somebody had been in his room.

Bojangles slammed the door behind him and flicked the light switch. He darted over to the window, fell to his knees and dragged back the carpet.

The floorboard was hastily removed and he groped in the chasm, smiling slightly as he felt the pistol and the tin. He removed the lid of the tin and counted out the cash, just in case. His eyes bulged wildly as he recounted. Bojangles was a precise man of habit, and he acknowledged that he was one thousand pounds short.

The irate lodger marched back downstairs and pounded loudly on the landlady's door. Her eyes lit up when she saw who was responsible for the intrusion. She pouted her lips at the angry man. "Why, Charlie. Changed your mind have you?"

"No, I bloody well haven't... Someone's been in my room and stolen some money from me."

"You as well? Are you sure?"

"Of course I'm sure... What do you mean, you as well?"

Mrs Parish scanned the corridor before she lowered her voice. "That tranny next door to you came to me three days ago, saying someone had been in her room. She thinks it's that Brady."

Bojangles pondered. "How could he get into the rooms? He would have to have a key, wouldn't he?"

"Funny you should say that," whispered the landlady. "I lost a set of keys a couple of weeks ago and had to have them replaced... I'll call the police."

"No! I mean, we'll sort this out ourselves. I want a word with this Brady."

Mrs Parish clambered up the staircase after the angry Bojangles. If she cared about him pounding on Brady's door, she never showed it. The unscrupulous man was either not in, or he was not answering his door.

"When is the last time you saw him?" asked Bojangles.

"Er, let me think. It was last night. We had rather an intense argument about him not paying his rent, and I told him he'd have to leave this morning. Only, he came to my room later and paid me a month's rent... Oh my god, it makes sense doesn't it? Do you want me to open his room?"

Bojangles shook his head. "No. I don't imagine he'd leave the money in there. I'll catch up with this Brady in my own time... Do you know where he goes?"

"No, I only see him in the evening... Are you sure you don't want me to call the law, Charlie?"

"If you do that, I won't get my money back. No, leave him to me."

She watched the man in the Italian suit retreat to his room, and hoped for the look over his shoulder to invite her in. It never came.

******

Wednesday evening was overcast and rain threatened. Sophie felt ill at ease when she waited standing outside the premises of Cupid's Arrow. She received several looks of disdain from the pedestrians. One motorist even had the audacity to stop. The driver questioned her about the range of her services, but he quickly realised his error after being on the receiving end of her verbal onslaught.

With her blonde wig and turquoise dress, complete with a split almost up to her waist, it was no surprise she had been mistaken for a call girl. Sophie was disappointed. She imagined she looked better than that, and had made an audacious attempt with her appearance this evening. Her make-up was expertly applied. Her eye shadow matched the colour of her dress, and her lips were a subtle shade of pink. A white handbag hung from her slender shoulder, which matched her high-heeled shoes, a luxury she usually shunned. Leather jackets and denims, she felt more comfortable in. Only occasionally, if the function warranted it would she make an effort to look effeminate.

She watched the approach of the black BMW and saw the ginger-haired manager lean over and unlock the passenger door for her. Ross Chivers may have been perceived as a charming, polite gentleman, but his ignorance of not opening the door for Sophie proved otherwise.

"Clare, sorry I'm a teeny bit late, but better late than never, eh?" he said, as he displayed that awful gold tooth on his top row of molars.

"That's okay; I like being goaded by leering perverts thinking I'm on the game."

"Ha, ha. I like a girl with a sense of humour… You look absolutely gorgeous by the way."

"Where are we going, Mr Chivers?"

"Please, call me Ross. I have a formal relationship with all my girls."

I bet you do, thought Sophie.

Chivers glanced at Sophie's slender legs. "I thought we'd venture to The Greenhouse in Mayfair, a favourite of mine."

Not too far from The Dorchester, mused Sophie. She wondered if there was a connection.

"Incidentally, Clare, I thought you'd be pleased to know that your application has been accepted. Granted of course that you pass the initiation test this evening."

"Initiation?"

"Just kidding. I'm sure everything's going to turn out just fine. I'm certain you'll make a charming escort."

They pulled into the car park and Sophie waited in vain for her date to open the door. He instead lit a cigar before being approached by the delighted looking manager of The Greenhouse.

"Mr Chivers, it's so nice to see you again… Drinks in the garden perhaps before your dinner?"

"Splendid idea." Chivers looked around to see Sophie making an exhibition of herself, as she tried to alight from the BMW gracefully. She only succeeded in allowing her dress to ride up her thighs, and relieved herself of what decency she had managed to preserve. She linked Chivers and they proceeded to a table in the garden. Her date nodded to various opulent acquaintances as they did so.

Sophie took in the wonderful scenery of the garden, the fragrance of the colourful blossoms evident in the air. The dark, menacing clouds still threatened, but the humidity had been the deciding factor in their decision to take drinks in the open air.

The smiling waiter approached and Chivers shared a joke with the grey-haired man. Sophie smiled politely and noticed the not too pleasant stares directed at her. It was as if she had intruded on a select club, and the leers as well as the clammy atmosphere made her feel uncomfortable. She removed a menu from the table and fanned herself rapidly.

Chivers noticed her discomfort. "Yes, it is a trifle warm my dear, but the rain will clear the air… Now what's your tipple, Clare?"

"A cool glass of white wine will do fine thanks."

"Two glasses of your finest Chardonnay, Horace, that's a good chap."

Chivers puffed vigorously on his cigar, his black blazer, white slacks and cream turtle-necked sweater giving him the appearance of someone from the Roaring Twenties. "Clare, how are you fixed for Friday evening?"

"Why do you ask?"

The cigar smoke was directed from the side of his mouth. "I think I may have your first assignment."

He made it sound like she was about to embark on a secret mission rather than a date.

"Friday is fine with me."

"Splendid."

"Any clues to who he is?" probed Sophie.

"You assume it's a he?"

"Well, is it?"

Chivers smiled teasingly. "Relax. Henry Goldsmith is one of our best customers… Single, in his forties and stinking rich after he inherited a fortune from his father. He's rather shy, and often employs our services for functions, feigning to his friends and associates that he's courting the girl."

"So his friends must know it's a sham if he turns up with a different girl on his arm each time?"

"Probably, but that is not our concern… Just keep him happy."

The waiter arrived with their drinks and they clinked glasses and toasted her success.

"Ross, Hilary said there would be an opportunity to make extras."

Chivers looked embarrassed as he checked the other tables for unwanted listeners. "Not with dear Henry. He just likes our girls to escort him to parties."

"Oh."

"You look disappointed, Clare."

"Let's just say, I'm not exactly rolling in money right now."

He studied her face unnaturally, as if looking for a telltale sign. "First things first. After Henry, perhaps we can fix you up with a more generous client, if you get my meaning… One thing I must clarify though; your sexual frolicking has nothing to do with Cupid's Arrow. In no way can you smear the name of the company… Mr Torrance of course absolutely forbids such goings on, but I know it happens and do not deny the girls a little pocket money."

"It's more than a little pocket money that I need," hinted Sophie.

Chivers regarded her curiously. "You're really that desperate are you?"

"You bet I am."

"I'll bear that in mind… Perhaps I may have something for you, but let's not rush things, dear… Damn rain! Shall we retire into the restaurant?"

The complaining customers made a dash for it, as the rain came down forcefully. A flash of lightning illuminated the surroundings.

The hand-painted walls were of blades of grass in delicate shades of silver and cream. The large, jade-fabric tablecloths and luxurious leather seats blended in well with the surroundings. Gentle music swept the room, classical offerings from the great composers.

Chivers this time did pull out Sophie's chair for her, before he handed her a menu. "I hope you're hungry, Clare?"

"Starving, but there's such a selection."

"Let me choose for you… Tell me you're not one those vegetarian types are you?"

"No way."

"Splendid. Horace, we're ready for our order."

"Of course, Mr Chivers."

Chivers studied the menu. "I think we'll plump for the assiette of salmon for starters, followed by the grilled pave of beef on garlic. Also, creamed potatoes with the sauce chasseur... For dessert, the red berry soup with basil sorbet sounds delicious. What do you think, Clare?"

"Sounds yummy."

"Good, then that's settled. And a bottle of Dom Perignon, Horace, to wash it down with."

Sophie deserved an Oscar for her performance that evening, as she listened to numerous bad jokes and tasteless sexist comments. Several times, the clammy hand of her new employer rested on her leg, and his leering gaze was directed at her inviting bosom.

Sophie had decided to take drastic measures to wriggle out of his intended finale to the evening. As the black BMW waited at the traffic lights in Knightsbridge, Chivers fiddled with his stereo. Sophie thrust her fingers down her throat and vomited violently onto the leather-fitted dashboard.

"Good lord, girl! Not in my fucking car!"

"I'm sorry, Mr Chivers, but I feel awful. It must be the champagne." Sophie covered her mouth with her hand and belched loudly.

"Listen, Clare. Something has cropped up that I almost forgot about," lied Chivers. "Here is twenty pounds. Take a cab home."

"But, I thought you were taking me to see your home?" moaned Sophie.

"Some other time... Now please go before you make any mess of my car."

"Is my date with Henry still on?"

"Yes, yes. Give me a ring tomorrow and I'll give you the details... One more thing; if he offers you champagne, refuse it."

Sophie stood in the drizzle, watched the car depart, and could not help feeling smug. The evening had worked out rather well. She wiped the remnants of vomit from her face and flagged down a cab. She realised that at some time in the near future, she may have to sleep with the repulsive man, but for tonight, she had escaped his clutches.

Chapter Twelve

The chanting of. "Get your tits out," was directed towards Goldie Lamour as she walked gracefully along Gower Street on Thursday evening. She glanced at the crowd of juveniles gathered around a lamppost and smiled satisfactorily, their comments most welcome. They appeared to her like moths swarming around a light bulb. Their remarks were evidence of her transformation becoming successful, and she felt more like a woman every day.

Her elegant, sky-blue gown fluttered in the breeze, a garment enhanced by her matching stilettos and mascara. A string of imitation pearls adorned her long neck, and a white-mock Gucci handbag hung from her shoulder. The repulsive odour of the Chinese take-away marred the fantasy, and erased the catwalks of Paris from her confused mind.

Mrs Parish waited arms folded when Goldie entered the premises she detested. Someday, she would live in Paris, parade past the numerous cafes, and attract the attention of an agent, who would put her on the road to renown and riches. She faced the scowling landlady and offered an artificial smile.

"Well, well, If it isn't the lady of the night," mocked Mrs Parish.

"To what do I owe the pleasure of this confrontation, Mrs Parish? My rent is paid in full is it not?" Goldie peered over the shoulder of her inquisitor. The television screen was what held Goldie's attention. A photo-fit of a man with a goatie beard, black slicked back hair and dark eyes stared back at her.

"Miss Lamour, did you hear what I said?"

"Sorry, Mrs Parish."

"I said, have you noticed anything missing from your room lately?"

"No…Why do you ask?"

"That despicable Mr Brady has stolen some money from Mr Bojangles."

Goldie tutted. "I related to you a week ago that he'd been through my things, but nothing is missing as far as I can tell."

"Probably had nothing worth stealing; not like that nice Mr Bojangles."

"How did he get into our rooms?" enquired Goldie. "I always ensure my door is locked."

"It appears he stole my spare keys... There's a locksmith coming in the morning to change the locks. In the meantime, Miss Lamour, I recommend that you keep the chain on your door."

"Have you called the police?"

"No. Mr Bojangles insisted I did not. He said he was going to sort Brady out."

"That's very irregular, Mrs Parish... Why on earth you rented out a room to such an undesirable character is beyond me."

The landlady smirked. "A thief and a queer. I don't know which is the worst?"

"Sticks and stones," said Goldie. "I'll have my operation one-day, and I'll be every bit a woman as you are. Then I'll show you... When I parade the catwalks of Paris and Rome, you'll boast to all of your friends that I once lodged in this squalor. That's if you have any friends, which I somehow doubt."

"Dream on, fairy."

The door was slammed in her face and Goldie ascended the staircase, more determined than ever to accomplish her dream.

Mrs Parish grinned contently and changed channels when the news had finished. *Eastenders* was just starting, but her eyes focused instead to the evening newspaper, which lay unread on the coffee table. She reached for the tabloid and her hands trembled when she looked at the face that adorned the front page.

HAVE YOU SEEN THIS MAN?

The startled landlady's eyes left the familiar face momentarily and browsed the headlines. The cold tea refreshed her dry throat as she took in the full horror of the story. The newspaper fluttered to the ground and the face of Mr Bojangles stared up at her.

"No, it couldn't' be," she muttered to herself. *It certainly looked like him with those so dark eyes, but it could have been anyone.* The fact that he wore smart designer suits played on her mind, as she watched the soap half-heartedly. *No, it wasn't possible. Not her nice Mr Bojangles.*

******

The black Mondeo came to a halt and Slattery looked across at his partner. "Thanks, Sophie. This shouldn't take too long."

"Take all the time you need, Vince," she answered, and reached for her pack of cigarettes. She could not fail to notice just how fatigued her colleague looked, but with his matrimonial troubles, it was not surprising.

Slattery removed his jacket and ambled along the pavement towards the pleasant-looking, white-painted house with the well-groomed garden. His decision to not park outside the house was prompted by Sophie's presence. He was in enough trouble with his marriage as it was.

The pleasant aroma of the rose bushes and carnations mingled with the odour of fresh grass cuttings. He rang the doorbell twice, but the sound of the lawnmower told him the occupiers were in the back garden.

Slattery entered the premises and wiped his feet on the doormat. He was aware that his mother-in-law was a stickler for cleanliness. He strolled across the pristine, white-pile carpet towards the patio doors, and his eyes watered when he saw his two daughters, Mandy and Debbie playing on the lawn with their dolls. Cheryl, dressed in her bikini, moved her sun lounger when the lawnmower driven by her father manoeuvred across the spacious lawn.

The movement of the doors alerted the girls, and they sprinted towards the patio to greet their father. The lawnmower was switched off and Cheryl removed her sunglasses. She watched her daughters smother their father with kisses.

Cheryl's mother, Jean, who was on her knees planting some shrubs, turned her head to see what the commotion was.

Slattery picked up his daughters and walked towards his wife. "How are you, Chez?"

She flicked back her red locks. "I'm doing fine."

I'll put the kettle on," offered Jean, who motioned for her husband to go indoors. "Come on, girls, I'll treat you to a banana split."

Slattery smiled and watched his daughters sprint indoors. "Ten years has certainty flown by?"

Cheryl nodded. "It has, hasn't it? Do you remember when Mandy was born, and you passed out when you mopped my brow?"

"Well, it was warm in the maternity ward."

"Bullshit, you softie."

"I miss you, Chez."

"I miss you too, but I've been missing you for some time now."

"Come home."

"To what? You're a stranger, Vince. I'm tired of making excuses to the girls... Christ, everything used to be so wonderful. We went on trips at the weekend to the country and the coast, but they fizzled out...You've become a stranger in your own home."

"I'll try to make more time. I swear I will."

"Your family comes second, Vince, and that can't be right."

"So what do I have to do to win you back?"

"Find another job. One where you can come home after work and see your family."

"I can't just walk out on my job like that."

"There are hundreds of jobs you could take with your talent. We're financially comfortable, and you could take a pay cut no problem."

"What if I knocked the overtime on the head?"

"For how long? You need time to think; we both do. Seeing you for a couple of hours in the evening and an hour in the morning is no way to live... Shit, sometimes you don't even come home at all... Think of the girls. You owe them that much."

"I'll see Madison and ask him if he'll consider cutting my hours."

"You do that, Vince, and when you can make time for your family, then I'll come back… You've lost weight. What have you been eating?"

Slattery ignored the question. "I love you, Chez." He leaned over to kiss her, but she turned her head and his lips connected with her warm cheek.

"Tea's up, you two."

"Not for me, Jean, I have to dash," insisted Slattery. He noticed Cheryl shaking her head as she returned to her lounger. He bent down to kiss his daughters and left reluctantly.

Sophie leaned against the Mondeo and smoked when Slattery marched towards her.

"Well?" she pried.

"Chez wants me to pack my job in."

"And?"

Slattery changed the subject. "Are you sure about this date tonight, Sophie?"

"According to Chivers, Henry Goldsmith just uses the girls from the agency to impress his friends. Chivers is going to offer me something big, I just know he is."

"He almost offered it to you on Wednesday night remember… I don't like this, Sophie. You can't puke up every night; besides, you're a photographer, not some undercover cop."

Sophie flicked away her cigarette. "Don't worry. You can take the credit for the story."

"That's not what I meant and you know it!"

"I'm sorry, Vince. That wasn't fair of me. I have so much on my mind at the moment."

"Exactly…I don't like you going in there blind. Maybe you should wear a wire."

"And how pray would you acquire a wire?"

"Danny. He still owes me a favour or two."

"He's made it clear he wants nothing to do with Cupid's Arrow."

"Leave it to me."

"And where am I supposed to wear this wire?" smiled Sophie.

"Meaning what?"

"Listen, Vince; to get close to Chivers, I may have to sleep with him. Any suggestions for the wire?"

"Shit, you're serious aren't you? Just how far are you prepared to go?"

"All the way, boss. All the way."

Chapter Thirteen

Mr Bojangles straightened his tie and entered the premises of the safe deposit company in Belgravia. The loud clicking of his smart leather shoes against the polished wooden floor, prompted the small, balding clerk to look up from his paperwork. A quick glance at the wall clock confirmed there were only fifteen minutes to closing time, and a customer at this time was not what he had hoped for, as it was his bridge night.

"Can I help you, sir?"

Mr Bojangles returned the smile and glanced at the uninterested security guard, who attempted to stifle a yawn.

"Yes, I have a postal box I'd like to check. I realise I'm rather late, but I'll be brief."

"Can I see your swipe card please?"

"Of course."

Bojangles was led to the postal boxes and used his swipe card to access the room. The clerk left him alone and he opened up the box. He reached for the two large envelopes. The first contained a large wad of money, which he inserted into his inside pocket. The other contained a document and a photograph of his next victim.

Bojangles liked it this way. No contact with his client, just a secure postal box. He had a phone number of course, but chose to receive his information and payment through the safe deposit company.

The reason for the increase in his salary was evident, as he scanned the dossier on his victim. It was a detective with CID. A little more difficult perhaps, but one victim was much the same as another for the hired killer. The message requested that the detective be terminated as soon as possible, and made to look like an accident.

Bojangles folded the envelope and added it to his inside pocket, before he called for the clerk, who replaced the box in its rightful slot.

"If you'll follow me, Mr Benson," said the clerk, happy in the knowledge he could now close up.

Bojangles exited the building and waved down a black cab.

"Where to, guv?"

"Gower Street."

******

Sophie dressed a little more conservatively in a cream trouser suit for her date with Henry Goldsmith. Her orders were to wait inside a Portuguese cafe on Charing Cross Road until he turned up. She lit her second cigarette, sipped her cappuccino, and her eyes took in the surroundings.

A large, heavily tattooed man with large sideburns, and wearing a white vest and faded jeans ogled the blonde woman. He winked at her and she tried to avoid his leer, feeling uncomfortable with the situation.

"Shit," she murmured, as the Teddy boy made his move.

"Hi, baby, you look like you need some company?"

"No thank you. My boyfriend will be here at any time now."

"Not much of a gentleman is he, leaving a beautiful lady in a place like this?"

"Please leave me alone."

He ignored her and sat opposite. "So what's yer name, baby?"

Sophie smiled thankfully, when she noticed the silver Rolls Royce pull up outside the cafe. She did not need to ask to know the driver was Henry Goldsmith. The tattooed man grunted when Sophie dashed out of the cafe and towards the grand car.

Goldsmith, a tall, dark man, had a prominent hawkish nose and piercing blue eyes. He was attired in a tuxedo and held a large cigar between his manicured fingers. He closed the door for Sophie, before he clambered into the driving seat.

"Sorry for the choice of venue, but I have to be careful... Henry Goldsmith at your service." He offered his hand.

"Clare Dougal."

She held his gaze for a few moments, and she could not help but notice that he was handsome in a sort of way. Perhaps she craved the wealth, as she never failed to be impressed by a man of prominence. He drove away and the music of *Frank Sinatra* serenaded her from the smart stereo system.

"Do you like *Sinatra,* Clare?"

"Not really. A little before my time."

"And mine, but I adore him… I like a girl who is honest."

"How do you know I'm honest?" she asked.

"Because, my dear, I've asked the same question to other girls, and they all swear they love old blue eyes just to impress me. You can learn a lot about a person from such little information."

"So where are we going, Henry?"

"To a friend's party in Holland Park… You do like parties don't you, dear?"

"As a matter of fact I do."

The armada of cars that graced the forecourt of the mansion was impressive. Goldsmith parked the Rolls Royce and invited Sophie to link his arm, before they sauntered along the gravel pathway. The mounted security camera followed their every move, and the loud click told them they had been granted admittance to the elegant structure.

A toothy, middle-aged man who wore the garb of someone from the eighteenth century greeted them, his curly white wig, ruffed shirt and brown tights giving him the appearance of a modern day Casanova. He inspected Sophie through his hand held spectacles. "My, you have excelled yourself this evening, Henry. A vision of utter beauty."

"Clare, this is Oscar. He owns the mansion… Oscar, meet Clare."

He took her hand and kissed it, but lingered a little too long over it for Sophie's liking. She could not help but notice the odour of baby powder that permeated from the leering man. The couple followed Oscar as they meandered through numerous impressive rooms, nodding to guests who were also attired in similar costumes. The sweet fragrance of cannabis swept through the mansion, a substance so out of place in this historic setting.

Gentle medieval music reached them from the ballroom. The door was ajar, and a giggling woman fluttered a fan rapidly and held the hand of her escort. They passed the trio fleetingly and proceeded up the long, sweeping, marble staircase.

Oscar turned towards his guests. "Before we join the ball, perhaps you'd feel more comfortable in costume? You know the way by now, Henry?"

"Of course."

Henry nudged Sophie, and she followed her escort through the kitchen into a large, dimmed room.

"What kind of party is this, Henry?"

"Oh, Oscar's a bit eccentric. He likes to hold these theme parties now and again. You're lucky; it was a toga party last week."

"You expect me to dress up like someone out of *Dangerous Liaisons?*"

"It's only a bit of fun, Clare… The lady's changing room is in there."

She reluctantly entered the room and was impressed by the array of costumes that were displayed on the rack. A bank of dressing tables with dozens of bottles of perfumes and various items of make-up were beyond the racks. Numerous shelves displayed wigs of various styles, and even the countless pairs of shoes looked so authentic.

Sophie selected a wine-coloured pleated frock and a pair of shoes to match. The tall wig was a worry, as she had to somehow apply it over her own blonde disguise without fear of detection. She added a beauty spot and smiled at the outcome. A decorative fan completed the transformation into an eighteenth century, high society lady, and she left the room.

She laughed when she set eyes on Henry, who looked absurd in his wig and gold braided tunic. He also had opted for a beauty spot, a fashion accessory in its time.

"You look ravishing, Clare, and by your reaction, I must look a complete ass."

"No, Henry, it's just that you look different."

"How Casanova could attract so many lovers in this outfit, I'll never know," moaned Henry.

She took his arm and he led her to the splendid ballroom. Magnificent crystal chandeliers and valuable portraits gave the room a touch of elegance, which befitted the occasion. A waiter approached them with a tray and they helped themselves to a glass of champagne, before they filled their plates with offerings from the marvellous buffet. They took their seats and watched the colourful, costumed guests dance to the medieval melody.

"Henry, haven't you ever considered marriage?" asked Sophie, who nibbled on a chicken leg.

"Is that a proposal?"

Sophie blushed. "I mean, you're rich and handsome."

"I don't want a wife to complicate matters."

"So you use girls from the agency?"

"Have you a problem with that?"

"Of course not, but..."

A raised hand ended the conversation.

"Would you like to dance, Henry?"

"No, I hate dancing."

Sophie probed further. "So where are your friends?"

"Friends? I have no friends, apart from Oscar."

"But Ross Chivers said you hired the girls to show us off to your friends."

"He told you that? The man is an imbecile."

The waiter approached and they accepted another glass of champagne.

Oscar strolled across the dance floor with a girl on each arm. "Henry, midnight approaches. Tonight we will entertain in the master bedroom."

Sophie scowled at the pretty girls.

Oscar directed his words at Sophie. "The eighteenth century must have been a fine time to live, don't you think? So much sexuality and promiscuous goings on."

Henry checked his pocket watch and Sophie noticed Oscar, his two companions and the other revellers look towards the large wall clock. The music ceased and the ballroom fell silent. Only the ticking of the clock could be heard as the second hand approached twelve. Sophie scanned the faces of the waiting masses, wondering what was to come. She did not have too long to wait.

The chiming of the clock acted as a detonator, as the male guests tore the dresses from their partners. A mass orgy followed and Sophie took a deep breath. Tongues lapped at nipples, and women reached for the groins of their lovers. Loud groans were audible, as an accumulation of bodies writhed and thrust; every position and every orifice being exhausted.

Sophie looked towards Henry, his face expressionless.

"Shall we proceed to the bedroom?" asked Oscar.

Sophie felt a hand in hers, and her mind was in turmoil. Henry led her past the ecstatic fornicators and she tried to blank them from her mind. One partygoer pumped away at his partner from behind. His hands groped her large breasts, oblivious that he obstructed the group's exit from the room. Oscar tapped him on the shoulder and they simply took a step to the right, before they continued with their lovemaking.

This was not real, thought Sophie, as she was ushered up the marble staircase towards the master bedroom. The two big-breasted girls muzzled the neck of Oscar, before they hastily made their way to the love nest.

The large double doors were opened, and a gigantic four-poster bed dominated the bedroom. Everything was red. The silk wallpaper, the deep pile carpet, and even the satin bedclothes. Sophie's eyes wandered to the mirrored ceiling, before she focused on one of the many graphic portraits that was displayed on the wall. The painting portrayed an orgy, such as the one she had become embroiled in.

Henry saw the hesitation in Sophie's eyes when Oscar and the girls proceeded to undress each other on the bed.

"Is something wrong, Clare?"

"Of course not. Give me a minute will you? I need the ladies room?"

"There's one at the end of the corridor... I'll be waiting."

She exited the room and dashed to the sanctuary of the toilet. She leant over the washbasin and stared into the mirror. A million thoughts entered her troubled mind. *What purpose could she possibly serve by going through with this debauchery? Why had Chivers lied about Henry?* She threw water on her face and took a couple of deep breaths before she made her decision. Chivers was testing her, that much was obvious. Slattery's words came back to her. *How far are you willing to go?"*

The naked quartet it seemed had not waited for her, when she re-entered the master bedroom. One of the girls fondled Oscar, and the other sucked at her friend's breast.

"Okay, Clare?" asked Henry.

She nodded, approached the four-poster and proceeded to strip. She fell into Henry's arms and blanked everything from her mind. This was part of the job she told herself.

Chapter Fourteen

Monday morning and Sophie entered the premises of The Echo to find Slattery working away on his computer. Her early morning arrival was intended, as she wished to avoid the flock of journalists. What she had to say was for his ears only. Slattery, she acknowledged, was always the first of the staff to arrive for work, and she was not to be disappointed this morning.

Slattery saw the intent approach of his colleague and turned to face her. "Sophie, how are you this fine morning?"

"Arsehole! You fucking arsehole! Where were you on Friday? So much for wearing a wire, eh?"

"Calm down. I've sorted it with Danny. The wire will be available when we need it. Nothing was going down Friday night. Henry Goldsmith is a pussycat. He just wanted a bit of company, right?"

Tears formed in Sophie's eyes. "Wrong… oh you're so bloody wrong, Slattery… Where have you been? I've been trying to contact you all weekend."

"I needed a break. I went to the Lakes for a spot of fishing."

Sophie rolled her eyes skyward. "Oh, that's just dandy isn't it? Here's me romping in a four-poster with four perverted strangers, and you're off fishing."

"You're serious?"

"Look at me! What do you think?"

He placed a consoling hand on her shoulder, which she shrugged off. "Shit, what have you done, Sophie?"

She reached for her cigarettes and lit one with trembling fingers. She watched some of the staff arrive.

"Come on, you could do with a coffee." suggested Slattery.

The canteen was deserted and they opted for a table towards the rear of the room. Slattery opened a window and welcomed the fresh air, as Sophie took a long draw on her cigarette. He foraged through his coins and deposited them into the machine, before he set his partner's cup on the table.

"What happened, Sophie?"

"That bastard, Chivers; he lied to me. He said Henry only used the girls to show off... I now know different."

"He hurt you?"

"No... well not exactly. He took me to a bloody orgy in Holland Park... A friend of his, someone called Oscar hosted a party. He was a weird fish if ever I saw one. Apparently, he throws one every week."

"Tell me you never joined in?"

Her angry eyes told him he had said the wrong thing. "Do you think I bloody enjoyed it? I had a decision to make and made it."

"But it served no purpose," insisted Slattery. "You should have made your excuses and left."

"And then what? Chivers would have dropped me before you could say boo... At least now he may trust me."

"Are you okay, Sophie?"

Her hands trembled. "A bit sore, but yes. I'll survive I suppose.... I've tried to contact Chivers, but he's not answering his phone."

"Maybe you should pull out... After what you've..."

"No fucking way, Jose. My tits are red raw and I've so many bruises and bites on my arse; you'd think I'd been in the ring with *Tyson*. No, I'm going to nail Chivers and his cronies."

"Do you think he's testing you?" asked Slattery.

"It makes sense, especially if he's lined me up for something special."

"Like marrying a wealthy old man perhaps?"

"Exactly... Maybe he just wanted to see how far I'd go."

"I think you should call at his office this morning."

Sophie ground out her cigarette. "My thoughts exactly... After this is all over, maybe we can run a story on those perverts, Goldsmith and Oscar."

"Consider it done, Sophie... Are you sure you're up for this?"

"One hundred percent, only don't ever go AWOL on me again, Vince."

"Scout's honour. The sooner we get that wire the better. I'm meeting Danny tonight."

"What the hell's going on here?" came a booming voice from behind. The irritating pipe smoke told them Madison was the inquisitor.

"Just having a coffee, Roland."

"Coffee? It's eight 'o' bloody clock. I don't pay you to drink coffee."

"Actually it's only seven forty five. You only pay us from eight," joked Slattery.

"Smart arse! Well, what do you have for me? I've been lenient and extended your deadline, but I don't see any story."

Slattery sipped his bitter coffee. "We're onto something big here, Roland. Give us another week?"

"Like shit I will. If you're onto something, then where's the story; and by the way, I haven't received a single photograph… What am I paying you for, young lady?"

She opened her mouth to speak but Slattery held up a hand. "Roland, have I ever let you down?"

"Yes."

"Listen, you'll have the biggest scoop this newspaper has ever had. We've infiltrated a corrupt company involved in murder on a large scale."

"Cupid's Arrow, I suppose?"

"Yes."

"I hope you've been careful. Remember what I said before?"

"They suspect nothing," said Slattery.

"So what do you have?"

"Give us a week, boss?"

"No deal. Tell me what you have and I'll consider it… Have you proof that Elizabeth Todd ever worked for Cupid's Arrow?"

"Not yet."

"Bloody hell, Vince! You're no further on than our last meeting."

"Sophie's infiltrated the agency."

"What?"

"Sophie is working as an escort in Cupid's Arrow."

The editor's face was a shade of crimson. "Jesus fucking Christ! Does it get any worse? What am I supposed to tell her uncle, our main shareholder? His niece is working part time as a prostitute?"

"Tell him nothing, Roland... Listen, I believe that Chivers is about to make Sophie an offer. We just need more time."

"What sort of an offer?"

Slattery checked the vicinity for any eavesdroppers. "Okay, this is how we think it works. One of the agency girls befriends a wealthy old man on the books of Cupid's Arrow. They eventually marry and then the sugar daddy dies of a supposed heart attack, leaving all of his money to his young wife. Then she's bumped off, but not before she invests a huge sum of money in a bogus company."

Madison seemed confused. "Hold on. So how do they know that the old man is going to have a coronary?"

"They don't. They murder him."

"Aren't you forgetting the death certificate?"

"So they bring in their own doctor."

"You're saying they hire a doctor to sign the death certificates?"

Slattery shrugged. "Why not?"

"Your proof?"

"We'll get it."

Madison pondered and clasped his teeth around the stem of his pipe. "The agency girls. Surely they must suspect something after two of them died so soon after their husband's deaths?"

"That's just it, Roland, the girls are isolated. They're discouraged from meeting their colleagues at the agency."

"But surely they must be in on this?"

"Yes. My guess is they're offered a sum of money for doing this. Once they agree, then they're too afraid to go back, so they donate the bulk of their inheritance to a bogus company as planned. They come out of it with a couple of hundred grand or so and are then killed off to keep them quiet. It makes sense, Roland."

Madison pointed the stem of his pipe at Slattery. "And you base all of this on your hunch that Elizabeth Todd worked for Cupid's Arrow?"

"Where would we be today without hunches?"

"So where does Max Sherwood come into this?"

Slattery crushed his coffee cup. "I don't think he's involved... He just wants revenge for his father's death."

"One more week you said?"

"One week."

Madison narrowed his eyes. "Okay, I'll agree on one condition. Sophie is not placed in a position that could jeopardise her."

"It's sorted. We're going to use a wire."

"Bloody hell, I won't ask where the wire's coming from... Tread carefully, Vince. We could face a massive lawsuit if you're wrong."

"We're not wrong. Lance Tyreman and some Greek geezer called George Mikhos own the bogus companies, and I did some checking. They were seen together outside Carlton House almost a week ago. We have the pictures, Roland."

"How do you know it was them?"

"I checked their license plates."

"Listen, Vince, maybe you do have something here, but with the evidence you now have, perhaps we should contact the police?"

Slattery was enraged by the proposal. "And lose the scoop of a lifetime? CID know about Tyreman and he's under investigation, but they want nothing to do with Cupid's Arrow or George Mikhos, because there's no proof that Elizabeth Todd ever worked for them."

"But you now have proof that Tyreman and Mikhos know each other."

"It's your call, boss... I'm sure that if I discovered about their relationship, CID will no doubt know of it too."

"One week, Vince... I must be mad, but one week's what you have."

Chapter Fifteen

Jenson sank his eighth pint of the evening before he bade his chums farewell. Since he had been taken off the case, he now spent more and more time down the pub, and a sympathetic barmaid acted as his mother confessor.

The wispy smoke followed him out of the Hogs Head in Croydon and merged with the humidity of the night air. Jenson paused by the deserted roadside, before he advanced towards the taxi rank. He lived just two miles away, but his intake of beer compelled him to take a cab.

He saw the glare of the headlamps first before he heard the motor turn over. The vehicle accelerated towards him and he now stood transfixed, pondering over his course of action. It all seemed to happen in a split second as the green Grenada sped towards him. His inquisitive eyes attempted to focus on the driver's features. He turned and ran when the engine grew louder. The car closed in on him and the screech of brakes intruded on this tranquil summer's evening.

An alleyway seemed Jenson's best option. His unsteady legs moved in slow motion as he awaited the impact. A glance over his shoulder told him he had to act quickly. He watched the headlights approach like a giant predator of the night.

He hurled himself sideways, upset a couple of dustbins and landed with a thud on the welcome bin bags. The rancid odour of the decaying food polluted the air as the Grenada skidded and knocked several dustbins to the ground, much to the dismay of the wailing cat.

The vehicle reversed and Jenson heard the grind of the gearbox as he looked around for salvation. The car now sped towards him and he again dived to avoid certain death. The car hit the wall and the driver lunged forward, only for the seatbelt to prevent him being catapulted through the windscreen. The experienced detective saw his opportunity and dashed towards the offending vehicle. His intended killer reacted swiftly, abandoned his car and bounded for the main road.

The burly taxi drivers who had witnessed the spectacle, attempted to block the driver's way, as Jenson closed in on his prey.

Bojangles whipped out his pistol and the drivers backed off, their interest in apprehending him waning. Jenson hesitated, then felt the wind from the bullet whiz past his face. He had no choice but to take cover behind one of the taxis. He watched the gunman pose menacingly, his frame silhouetted by the moonlight. Bojangles walked backward slowly and waved his weapon to and fro, before he made his escape. He replaced the pistol in his pocket and mingled with the late night revellers, an anonymous man in search of satisfaction.

******

"Well if it isn't the super model. Take a seat. Mr Chivers is busy at the moment."

Sophie ignored the secretary and entered the manager's office, amid the loud protests. Ross Chivers browsed through an adult magazine, his feet rested on his desk. "What is this?" he asked. He tossede his adult magazine into his drawer and appeared like a child who had been caught smoking behind the bike sheds.

"I told her you were busy, Mr Chivers."

"Never mind. Leave us alone, Hilary."

Sophie noticed the permanent sweat stains on the white shirt of the manager.

"Have a seat, Clare… How did your date go?"

"Bastard! You lied to me."

"Calm down. It's nothing you haven't done before."

Sophie grimaced. "Goldsmith never even offered me any money for the extras… shall we call them?"

"Listen, I'm sorry, but I had to see if you were genuine… Henry Goldsmith likes to hire a different girl every week, and you I'm afraid were the only girl he..."

"Hadn't had? Are those the words you're looking for, Ross?"

"I was going to be a little more subtle with my choice of vocabulary."

"I want double money for Friday night."

"What! Are you crazy?"

"Oh, you'll know just how crazy if you ever drop me in the shit again. You're lucky I'm only asking for double money… You see, Henry's chum got a freebee, not forgetting his two floosies."

Chivers grinned. "Like I said, I'm sorry, Clare." He abandoned his chair and walked towards the safe that was concealed behind a portrait of the Queen. Sophie noticed his erection, which did not seem to bother Chivers.

"You see, Clare, I had to be certain you were the right type of girl," he uttered. He tossed a wad of notes onto the table.

"You mean the type who'd sleep with anyone for money?"

"Okay, if you want to put it like that, then yes... Listen, our girls are all vetted and they have to be right for the job. You have the credentials we're looking for. Pretty, nice figure, intelligent and an ex-model... I have a proposal to put to you, Clare."

"Sorry, but I draw the line at marriage."

Chivers smiled. "Ah, add witty to your repertoire of credentials… Funny you should say that though, because what I'm about to tell you concerns marriage."

"You're not serious?"

"Clare, how would you like to become a rich woman?"

"Very much, but I also want to sleep with *Richard Gere,*" she joked, as she counted out the two hundred pounds."

"Richard Gere, I'm afraid will be most difficult."

"I'm listening."

Chivers approached her. "Will you please stand up?"

Before she could protest, Chivers frisked her.

"What the hell..."

"I'm sorry, Clare, but I have to be sure."

"Sure of what?"

"That you aren't wearing a wire," he said, before he browsed through her handbag.

"This is madness… Am I working for an escort agency or MI5?"

"There are people out there trying to destroy us. We have to be very careful."

"I don't follow," lied Sophie.

"How badly do you want money?"

"How badly do you want to give it to me?"

He smiled again and displayed his gold tooth. "The offer I'm about to make is between us, and us only. The consequences will be dire for you if what I'm about to tell you goes any further than these four walls. Do I make myself clear?"

"And if I refuse your offer?"

He shrugged his shoulders. "Then you continue to earn a paltry two hundred pounds for escorting perverts to dinner… It's up to you."

"What's the offer?"

Chivers moved closer. "An elderly client of ours has not long to live. I want you to befriend him and win his confidence. Make him the happiest man on the planet for the remainder of his life and the rewards will be great."

"How great?"

"After you're married, he'll die within three months and you'll inherit his fortune. He has no children, so the property and his nest egg will be yours. "

"That's gross… What's he dying of?"

"That at this moment in time is unimportant."

Sophie played along. "What do you get out of this?"

"After you've inherited the money, you'll invest the bulk of the money into a company that I'll disclose to you later. Your pay packet for doing this is two hundred grand."

"Wow! Hold on. How much exactly is this bloke worth?"

"At least ten million."

"Ten million and I get two hundred grand? What happened to the good old ten per cent?"

Chivers no longer smiled. "That's the offer. Take it or leave it."

Sophie hesitated. "How old is this man?"

"Sixty-seven."

"Bloody hell. What if he lives to be one hundred?"

"He won't."

"But, how can you be sure?"

"It's your decision, Clare."

"Can I think about it?"

"Sure you can, but don't take too long. He could kick the bucket at any time… Two hundred grand could pay off a lot of debts."

"Okay, I'll do it."

Chivers put up his thumb. "That's what I like, a decisive girl… No sympathetic misgivings, okay? It's important you don't get to like him too well."

"Didn't I tell you? Acting is in my blood."

"You won't regret this, Clare."

She noticed that his shirt was now saturated and his ginger hair was matted to his skull. "So when do I begin?"

"Ring me Thursday afternoon and I'll know more… The board will have to meet to decide if you're suitable… I'm sure they'll agree."

"Thursday it is then," she said. She rose from her chair and tucked her wad of money into her handbag.

Chivers waited until she was about to leave the office before he spoke again. "Oh, Clare, remember what I said. Not a soul must know about this… The agency does not take kindly to songbirds."

"My lips are sealed, Ross."

Chapter Sixteen

Lance Tyreman puffed eagerly on his huge Cuban cigar and leant on the railing, taking in the magnificent view of Hampton Court. He liked to think himself as a bit of an historian and a loyal subject to the Queen, hence his interest in the home of Henry VIII. It was no coincidence that he had called a meeting aboard his luxury cruiser. It was a chance to show off his pride and joy. He sipped his cognac and heard the approaching footsteps.

"Everyone's ready, Mr Tyreman."

Tyreman removed his designer sunglasses. "Splendid, Chivers... Will you just look at the grandeur of the palace? Can you just imagine Henry VIII being chaperoned down the river, barking out his orders to his oarsmen?"

"Mr Tyreman?"

"It matters not… How can I expect an imbecile like you to understand the historic significance of Hampton Court?"

Chivers watched his employer rearrange his thinning hair and attempt to cover his baldness. The rays of the sun reflected off his rings as he groomed himself.

"Cut the engines, Larry will you, that's a good fellow?" shouted Tyreman, who ran his hand through his ponytail. "We'll resume our cruise after the meeting."

George Mikhos helped himself to a glass of red wine, whilst a large, obese man with a well-groomed beard nibbled on a chicken drumstick. Matthew Torrance was the founder of Cupid's Arrow and the brainchild behind the corrupt company.

"I see you haven't given up your love of food, Matthew?" scoffed Tyreman, after he poured himself another glass of brandy.

"Lovely nosh this, Lance. You must compliment the cook."

"Tell him yourself. He's sailing this cruiser."

"Well, are we going to begin?" enquired Mikhos.

Torrance wiped his hands with a napkin. "Always in a rush aren't you, George?"

"We should not be seen together. You know how I feel about this."

Tyreman directed a plume of smoke towards the overhead fan. "Relax, George, we're safe here."

Chivers sat down hastily, and realized the others were waiting for him.

Tyreman opened up. "Well, Ross… have you found a girl?"

"Yes, she's perfect."

"I assume you've checked her out?" asked Mikhos.

"Of course… An ex model with money troubles. I checked her file and she's kosher."

"Can we trust her?"

"Mr Mikhos, I set her up with Henry Goldsmith."

"Ha ha, the poor girl," laughed Torrance. "So when are you going to introduce her to Candy?"

"I thought Friday. It'll give her time to think it over."

Torrance's expression changed as he tossed his napkin onto the table. "Think it over? I thought you said she was in?"

"She is, but we have to be sure… Remember that Cochrane girl. She almost pulled out, didn't she?"

"If she pulls out, she must be eliminated Chivers," demanded Torrance.

"Of course, Mr Torrance. That goes without saying."

"I think we should quit while we're ahead," moaned Mikhos. His thick eyebrows looked like a couple of caterpillars nested above his eyes.

Tyreman stubbed out his cigar and scowled at the Greek. "What are you twittering about, man? There are ten million reasons why we should go ahead."

"We are rich men. Perhaps this is once too many."

"Bullshit! We'll cool it for a while after this one."

"Maybe George is right, Lance," said Torrance, who stroked his beard. "We're taking a big risk every time we approach a girl… Incidentally, what the fuck happened Monday night?"

"Bojangles botched it, Matthew… Jenson was lucky."

"What are you two talking about?" asked Mikhos.

Tyreman was reluctant to answer. "It's nothing. A meddling detective needs to be taken out of the equation, that's all."

"Detective? What detective?"

Tyreman continued. "This detective from CID somehow traced the money from Rosie Cochrane back to me, but don't worry. Everything's in hand."

"Shit! Didn't I tell you? Didn't I say it was too good to be true?"

Torrance interrupted. "This Bojangles; I thought you said he was reliable, Ross?"

"He has been so far hasn't he?"

"Apparently not… Is this copper going to be a problem?"

"No, he's been taken off the case," interrupted Tyreman.

"So why have him killed?"

"It was a precautionary measure, Matthew."

"So now he knows we want him killed?"

Chivers fidgeted uncomfortably. "I told Bojangles to make it look like an accident, but there were witnesses."

Torrance thumped the table and caused Chivers to jump. "Perhaps we should have Bojangles eliminated. They already know what he looks like, and if he's pulled in, what's to stop him from talking?"

Chivers grinned. "You don't just have Bojangles killed. You haven't seen him have you?"

Mikhos composed himself. "This Bojangles; how did you meet him, Ross?"

"Shotgun Billy introduced him to me. He was a regular in his shop, and often purchased firearms from him. Bojangles apparently liked to boast that he was a hit man."

"Jesus Christ! He sounds like a psycho. Who in the right mind advertises he's a hired killer?" asked Torrance.

"We needed someone and I could hardly look in the Yellow Pages now could I? Or would you rather I put an ad in a shop window? Killer needed. No experience necessary, apply in writing to Cupid's Arrow with your CV."

"What do you suggest, Chivers?"

"Me, Mr Torrance?"

"Come on, Ross; you must know a few more seedy characters in the underworld. I need someone to eliminate Bojangles."

"Well, I could ask around. How much are you willing to pay?"

"Hold on. What if this backfires and Bojangles comes looking for us?" asked Mikhos, who trembled.

"Relax, George," assured Torrance. "Chivers is the only one who has met Bojangles. He doesn't even know you exist."

Torrance left his seat and walked over to refill his glass. "This DCI Entwistle. Can we trust him, Lance?"

"He'll keep CID at bay, don't you worry. He's more than happy with what we're paying him."

Mikhos was becoming increasingly worried. "This is becoming complicated. Too many people know about us?"

Tyreman shook his head. "George, do you want to go and check your Y-fronts? Relax. Entwistle has more to lose than us. He won't talk."

"And this other detective?"

"Like I said, he's off the case; and besides, Entwistle will keep us informed if he steps out of line."

Torrance drained his glass. "Well, that's settled then. Ross will hire someone to kill off Bojangles before he's caught. We could set him up."

"There's something I haven't told you, Matthew."

"Fucking hell, Ross. You're making this a shitty day."

"Jenson mentioned to Entwistle that a friend of his might try to infiltrate the agency."

Mikhos stood up and gripped the table. "My god."

"Sit down!" ordered Torrance… "How could he do this?"

"He couldn't. Not unless he used a girl."

Torrance stroked his beard. "Chivers, double check this girl. We can't afford to take any chances."

"She's sound. If she was a cop, she wouldn't have gone with Goldsmith now would she?"

"Maybe she's not a cop."

"Bloody hell," uttered Chivers, who took a swig of his cognac.

"Have you something to tell us, Ross?"

"I think I have, Mr Torrance… A couple of weeks ago, this geezer came into the office, saying he was interested in one of our girls. He claimed he was a bus driver."

"So? Bus drivers have fantasies too."

"No, Matthew. He asked about Elizabeth Todd."

"Fuck! Why didn't you tell me about this?"

"I wasn't sure if he was genuine or not. Anyway, he came back minutes later and some girl took my photograph."

"Bloody hells, bloody bells. And you didn't think this was important enough to merit telling me?"

"I think they were reporters."

"But nothing's been reported in the newspapers, right?"

"No, Mr Torrance."

"I wonder. Could this reporter be the friend Jensen mentioned to Entwistle?"

"More than likely."

Torrance was deep in thought. "We have to be extra vigilant. Vet all the girls who have joined the agency in the last fortnight. This reporter; would you recognise him again if you saw him?"

"I think so."

"Then perhaps your hired killer could be in for a bonus, Chivers."

******

The red Escort pulled up outside the enormous, wrought iron gates and DS Jenson turned off the engine. He approached the gate and peered through the railings, to see a short man in a flat cap and green wax jacket walking towards him and carrying a shotgun.

The man, who resembled a bulldog, looked the giant of a detective up and down suspiciously. "What's your business here?"

"This is Emerald Bloodstock Agency isn't it?"

"That's right."

"Is it possible to speak to Mr Mikhos? I may be interested in purchasing a couple of foals."

"Mr Mikhos is away on business."

"Oh, is that so? That's too bad, as I've travelled all the way from London."

"Like you said, it's too bad."

Jenson was not about to give up so easily. "Well, how about you showing me some of the bloodstock?"

"Sorry, no can do."

"When will Mr Mikhos return?"

"Who knows? It may be a week; it may be a month."

"Damn… Where are the horses incidentally? It's very quiet."

"Like I said, you'd have to speak to Mr Mikhos… Who shall I say called?"

Jenson whipped out his ID card. "DS Jenson, CID… Have you a license for that shotgun?"

"Of course… Now if you don't mind, I'm rather busy?"

"Please open the gate."

"Have you a warrant?"

"Have you something to hide?"

"No, but you're not coming in here without a warrant."

"What's your name?"

The man chuckled and turned his back on Jenson, before he retreated back towards the stables.

Jenson admitted defeat and drove away, ignorant of the picturesque countryside of Newmarket.

He drove along the High Street and parked outside The Crown. He opted to take in some liquid refreshment. Only a handful of customers inhabited the pub and Jenson offered a friendly nod, which was not returned. The interior of The Crown was decorated with horse brasses, and portraits of famous racehorses adorned the wood panelled walls.

Four elderly gentlemen eyed him suspiciously, then half-heartedly studied their dominoes. Jenson approached the bar and removed his tie.

"Aye, it's a warm one isn't it, sir?" greeted the landlord.

"It certainly is. A bit quiet this afternoon isn't it?"

"Aye, it livens up in the evening… What's your poison, sir?"

Jenson's eyes took in the numerous pumps and shrugged his shoulders. "What do you recommend?"

The portly landlord with the bushy sideburns poured a pint of the dark liquid.

"Here you are, sir; get that down your neck. It'll put hairs on your chest will that."

The ringing of Jenson's mobile phone interrupted the serenity of the countryside pub and the detective smiled apologetically. The four domino players eyed him in disgust.

Jenson stared at his mobile phone and switched it off when he saw who was calling. Chief Inspector Entwistle was not someone he wished to speak to at this time; besides, he ought to have been in North London working on a GBH case.

"The missus?" pried the landlord.

"No, a colleague actually… Do you know of the Emerald Bloodstock Agency down the road?"

The landlord rubbed his chin. "Not really. Albert's your man. There's nothing that old Albert doesn't know about horse racing."

The landlord pointed at the flat-capped man, who sat in the corner reading a newspaper. "I think he'll be more forthcoming if you buy him a pint, sir."

The big man nodded and he carried the fresh pint of bitter over towards Albert, who peered over his spectacles.

"Can I join you, Albert?"

"If that's for me you can."

Jenson placed the pint in front of the old man and he drank thirstily, before he wiped his mouth with his sleeve. "Here's to your good health, sir. So what brings you to Newmarket?"

"Business… Do you know of the Emerald Bloodstock Agency?"

"The Greek? Aye, I know of it. Why do you ask?"

"I was thinking of purchasing a couple of foals."

"You're an owner then?"

"Yes, well I mean… I hope to be."

"There are numerous bloodstock agencies around here. Why this one?"

"Why… is there something you want to tell me?"

Albert drained his glass, rattled his glass on the table and offered a toothless grin. Jenson nodded towards the landlord and he delivered another pint of foaming ale to the thirsty customer.

"I don't think he has any stock."

"Come again?" quizzed Jenson.

The old man moved closer. "If you ask me, I think the Greek's having second thoughts. Usually, you would see owners and trainers call at the yard, but the only visitors that he's had are from the big city."

"How can you tell, Albert?"

"I can tell a mile off… You for instance, you wouldn't know the front of a horse from the back."

Jenson smiled. "Okay, I confess. I don't suppose you caught a glimpse of the vehicles that have called at the yard?"

"Why would you want to know that? You're a copper aren't you?"

DCI Jenson gave him a glimpse of his ID.

"I knew it. As soon as you walked in, I said, there's a copper."

"Shh, I don't want to advertise it."

"What's the Greek done?" quizzed Albert.

"About the cars, Albert."

"Ah yes, the cars. Some real beauties I can tell you. A Ferrari, a Jag, a BMW, and of course, the Greek's silver Mercedes."

"You're very observant, Albert."

He tapped his nose before he finished his pint.

"Have you seen this Greek recently?"

"Naw, he wouldn't be seen dead in a shithole like this. You have to give him credit; he's got real class has the Greek."

"This Jaguar; can you recall the colour?"

"Aye, green."

"Thank you very much," said Jenson. He shook the man's hand and clambered to his feet. He approached the bar and tossed a five-pound note onto the counter. I think our friend's thirsty, landlord."

Chapter Seventeen

Several heads turned as the limousine coasted through the streets of London. Each one endeavoured to catch a glimpse of the celebrity behind the darkened window. Their disappointment would have been apparent, with their knowledge that no celebrity occupied the lush vehicle, but Sophie Wilson, alias Clare Dougal.

Sophie, much to her disappointment was forbidden from using the four-hundred pounds fee she had earned at Cupid's Arrow, and had purchased a new outfit with her own money, which Slattery insisted she could claim in expenses. The fee was handed to Roland Madison and placed in an envelope, which they intended to hand over to the police at the conclusion of their enquiries.

Sophie wore a strapless peach dress, complete with gloves and floppy hat, after Chivers had instructed her to wear something alluring.

The limousine arrived at Cupid's Arrow in Portobello Road exactly on time and now headed for the exclusive area of Belgravia. Sophie marvelled at the historic buildings and huge foreign embassies, whilst she sipped a glass of Dom Perignon.

It was early evening, but the black sky threatened to dampen the arid, urban landscape. The limousine came to a halt and the uniformed chauffer opened the door for Sophie. She gulped down the remainder of the champagne and gazed in awe at the magnificent Victorian building ahead. The door opened and a thin, grey-haired man attired in the garb of a butler invited her in.

"Mr Candy awaits you in the study, Madam. If you'll kindly follow me."

Sophie strolled slowly along the entrance hall and admired the splendid decor of the building. It was as if she had stepped back in time, when she took in the sight of the classical Roman statues and the black and white marble floor. The huge fountain was surrounded by finely sculptured lions. The entire structure was inspired by the ancient Roman Empire, which thrilled Sophie immensely.

The study was adorned with statues of gilded gods, supported on antique green marble columns. A huge white marble fireplace stood unlit in the centre of the room. The study looked so pristine, the walls also being white, along with the tiled floor.

Seated in a huge, white leather armchair, a tall, proud figure rose up to greet her. He extended his hand towards Sophie. His thick hairy forearms were the first things she noticed about the man, who was attired in a pink silk shirt.

"Good evening. Maurice Candy at your service." His voice was aristocratic and authoritative.

"Clare Dougal."

"You look positively radiant, child. Why haven't I had the pleasure of your company before now?"

"I've only been with the agency for one week."

"Philip, champagne for our guest please."

The butler nodded and left the room. Sophie's eyes inspected the wondrous surroundings.

"You like it?"

"That's an understatement, Mr Candy. This is breathtaking."

"I think so, and do call me Maurice. I was always mesmerised as a child by the Romans, and now I can afford it, I'm living my dream."

"This must have cost a fortune."

Candy welcomed his butler. "Ah, champagne. Place it on the table, Philip, that's a good chap."

The butler obeyed his master and left them alone.

"Make yourself comfortable, Clare. My home is your home."

She removed her hat, sat opposite her host and took in his handsome features. He certainly did not look sixty-seven years of age. Candy's tanned face-radiated kindness, his piercing blue eyes alert, and his apparently perfect white teeth belying his years. His silver hair was thick and swept back, which revealed a horseshoe-shaped scar above his right eye.

Candy opened his silver cigarette box. "Can I offer you a cigarette?"
"Thank you."

He lit her cigarette with an impressive gold lighter, before he ignited his own. "You look a trifle worried, Clare."

"Do I really?"

"I know what you're thinking. What does this dirty old man want with me?"

"No! No, Maurice, I wasn't thinking that at all."

"Really? Relax. This may sound corny, but my intentions are honourable. My dear wife died seven years ago and I've remained faithful since that day… I loved Rachel and would never dishonour her memory."

"Then, why…?"

"I like the company of beautiful women, hence your presence here. Yes, I'm a wealthy man, but opulence does not always bring happiness, my dear. I miss my wife and only crave women for conversation. I hope your mind is now at ease?"

"How did your wife die, Maurice?"

"She drowned off the coast of Corsica. As I sunbathed on my yacht, Rachel opted for a dip in the ocean. She was a marvellous swimmer; she won several medals. Do you know, she never even screamed. I wakened from my nap, but she was nowhere to be seen. She was found later that afternoon… You remind me of her a little. She also had long, blonde hair and large, brown eyes."

Sophie felt a little guilty, deceiving the pining man.

He poured out a glass of champagne and smiled. "Do you like classical music, Clare?"

"Some of it."

"Splendid. Come with me. I've a surprise for you."

She followed him to the end of the room and watched as he pushed a button on a panel. A segment of the wall rotated and a black grand piano appeared. He took his place on the stool and rested his cigarette and champagne glass on top of the piano. He flexed his hands like a great concert pianist and began.

Sophie leant on the piano and gazed at this extraordinary man. His fingers nimbly danced across the ivory keys, and the music of Bach echoed around the room. Tears formed in her eyes when she observed Candy, who was lost in his performance. He put so much energy and passion into his recital.

The room was silent and Candy bowed his head, before Sophie applauded loudly.

"That was wonderful, Maurice. Absolutely mind blowing," she said, as she wiped away the tears.

He looked up at her. "Rachel used to also cry whenever I played that piece."

"It's such an emotional piece. What's it called?"

"Bach's prelude & fugue 1 in C major… Any the wiser?"

"I'm afraid I'm not, but it really was beautiful. Play some more."

He closed the lid, sipped his champagne and ground his cigarette into the ashtray. He then headed towards to the panel. "Maybe later, Clare. Are you hungry?"

"Starving."

"Good. I'll get the cook to rustle something up."

Philip was called for and he headed for the kitchen to relay his instructions to the cook.

"Tell me a little about yourself," asked Candy.

"What do you want to know?"

"Everything."

"I'm twenty-four years of age, and before I worked for Cupid's Arrow I worked as a model for Langleys."

"You worked for Langleys?"

"Yes, it wasn't as glamorous as it sounds."

"What about your family?"

"My father is a solicitor and my mother a teacher… I have a brother in the army, serving overseas." Sophie felt better when she related some elements of the truth to her date.

"You seem to be an intelligent and educated girl. Why choose this profession?"

"It pays well."

"Do your parents know what you do for a living?"

"No way! They'd take a fit."

Candy laughed. "Tell me, how much are you being paid for being with me?"

"Two hundred pounds."

"Ah! The bloody thieves. I'm paying them a grand for your company."

"I suppose they have to make a profit."

"Get out of this business, Clare."

"Why are you so concerned?"

"Because, not all of your clients will be as frugal as I am. Prostitution does not befit you."

"I can look after myself, Maurice."

"I don't doubt, but get out before it's too late."

They ambled slowly to the impressive dining room and the cook confronted them.

Candy placed his hand on the shoulder of his employee. "Ah, what wonderful fare are we to be treated to this evening?"

"What you always request, Maurice. Smoked salmon followed by..."

"Splendid. He's a marvellous cook, but his manners are something else."

"Kelvin Spencer," he said, and offered his hand to Sophie.

"Soph...Clare Dougal," she corrected. She looked to Candy for his reaction.

As she sat down to dinner, she cursed herself for her clumsiness. She may have gotten away with it this time, but another error like this could be vital. Candy raised his glass to her and was apparently unperturbed by her slip up. Sophie was not so sure.

******

The Ship Inn was bustling that evening. The thirsty office workers mingled with the labourers and tradesmen to celebrate the impending weekend. Also present were the undesirables; the citizens who had no intention of seeking work. Duncan Brady was one such man. It was now eleven days since he had stolen the money from Bojangles, and he had sensibly stayed away from Gower Street.

He flaunted his wad of money, yelled through the crowd to Cyril the landlord, and received distasteful scowls for his intrusion. His funds were low, and the Dutch courage from his alcohol intake had prompted his decision to return to his lodgings first thing in the morning. Bojangles had probably not discovered his loss, and Brady was a greedy man. It was pointless him paying to stay in a bed and breakfast when he had settled Mrs Parish's rent until the end of the month.

He saw Cyril mouth something and he put his hand to his ear. The red-faced landlord motioned for him to go to the end of the bar, where it was quieter.

"What's up, Cyril?"

"I don't know why I'm telling you this after the trouble you've caused me recently, but there's this geezer been looking for you."

"Geezer, what geezer?" Brady felt the blood drain from his face.

"Some bloke in a swish suit, tough looking you know, like one of those gangsters."

"Oh, shit. When?"

"Earlier this evening, about eight."

"Did you tell him anything?"

"Of course not. What do you take me for, a grass?"

"Okay, cheers, Cyril."

"It's not that Bojangles character is it?" asked the landlord.

"What do you know about Bojangles?"

"Only what Goldie said… She said you stole some money from him."

"That cross-dressing cow. It's none of her business."

"She claims you've been through her things as well."

"She's got fuck all worth nicking, Cyril… Thanks again, mate. Get us a pint will you, and have one yourself."

A familiar noise from behind reached Brady's ears. He had heard that squeak somewhere before. He turned and saw the unmistakable, immaculately polished shoes of Bob Durcan, the store detective. Durcan wore a blazer, decorated with a medal, a reward for his heroics in Korea. The parting was still intact, the odour of Brylcreem rife.

"Well, well, if it isn't our resident tealeaf," stressed Durcan.

"Fuck off, pops and have a pint."

Durcan reached for Brady and twisted his arm high up his back, which caused the scruffy, bearded man to scream loudly.

"This is a citizen's arrest. Anything you say will be taken down and may be used in evidence against you."

"You're kidding me, aren't you, pops?"

Durcan tugged on the arm again.

"Argh! You're breaking my fucking arm."

A passing constable was beckoned, and Brady was taken to Charing Cross police station. Durcan peered into the interview room and smiled contently as Brady faced a female detective.

"You can go now, Mr Durcan. You did a grand job out there."

"Anything to keep the riff raff off our streets, Detective. " He saluted before he departed.

The big-boned detective shook her head. "Where were we? Ah, yes, I'm Detective Constable Hunter and you're nicked. You claim your name is Duncan Brady and you reside at a boarding house in Gower Street?"

"Yeah, that's right."

"Well, Mr Brady, it appears we can find no evidence of your existence. You don't even appear to have a National Insurance number. How on earth have you managed that?"

"Don't know."

"How do you claim dole money if there's no record of you?"

"I don't."

"I find that hard to believe, Duncan, if that's your name… You don't mind me calling you Duncan, do you?"

He shrugged his shoulders.

The detective continued. "You were found to have two hundred and fifteen pounds in your possession. How did you come by this money?"

"Saved up."

"Listen, you piece of shit. Don't fuck with me. What's your real name?"

"Duncan Brady."

"Two weeks ago, you stole a number of items from Tesco and were chased by Mr Durcan. Do you deny this?"

"I've never been in Tesco."

"Listen; you'll save a lot of time by telling the truth. You, according to Mr Durcan were caught on their security camera."

"Not me."

The detective checked her wristwatch. Her hopes of meeting her date diminished with every minute. A constable entered the room and DC Hunter followed him into the corridor.

"Well, Dave?"

"It's like he said; he's staying in a boarding house on Gower Street. I checked with his landlady."

"What's his angle? Why can't we find any record of this bum?"

"Because he's a bum… Maybe he's never claimed dole before."

"But, he'd still have a National Insurance number, surely?"

A bespectacled, bald man joined them. "Still here, Kate?"

"It's this bloke in the interview room, guv. We cannot find any record of him. An off duty store detective recognised him as someone who stole from his store, and he made a citizen's arrest."

"Good for him. What's he nicked?"

"Some disposable razor blades, some ballpoint pens, a half bottle of whisky and some custard creams."

"Bloody hell, hardly crime of the century, is it? Charge him, tell him to return to the station tomorrow and we'll give him his trial date… I'm gagging for a pint."

"I'm not so sure, guv," moaned DC Hunter. "There's something not right about him."

"Tomorrow, Detective. Tomorrow."

Chapter Eighteen

The drizzle and cool conditions were not enough to deter the sightseers from Trafalgar Square. One man who sat on a bench and tossed bread to the greedy pigeons was not a sightseer, but a resident of London. Slattery looked up to see Jenson walking across the square towards him. A black baseball cap protected the detective's shaved head, and the collar of his brown leather bomber jacket was pulled up.

"Vince."

"How's it going, Danny? What's so important that drags me out in this weather?"

DS Jenson joined him on the bench and his eyes scanned the crowd, looking for intruders. "I've been taken off the case."

"What? For what reason?"

"I keep asking myself that. Entwistle has told me to lay off Lance Tyreman and George Mikhos."

"But, why?"

"Special Branch is on Tyreman's tail... Evidently, he's involved with arms smuggling."

"So why's he taken you off the case. It doesn't make sense, Danny?"

"In his own words, I was ruffling too many feathers... That's not all. Someone tried to kill me."

"Shit! When?"

"Monday night. Someone tried to run me down."

"Are you sure? Maybe..."

"Of course I'm fucking sure. He took a shot at me, but either I was lucky or it was a warning."

"Did you see who it was?"

"No, the headlights blinded me, but when he done a runner a couple of the taxi drivers had a good look at him. It appears it was the same man who was with Rosie in the Dorchester."

"Bloody hell. Have you told Entwistle?"

"Of course I've told him."

"Maybe that's why he's taken you off the case, Danny? For your own safety."

Jenson unwrapped a stick of chewing gum. "No, he took me off the case before that… Something stinks about this investigation. I took a trip to Newmarket on Wednesday and did some sniffing around. George Mikhos was not at home, but some country bumpkin with a shotgun gave me a nasty welcome. There's more chance of a horse being seen in Leicester Square than at Emerald Bloodstock Agency. Also, I think Mikhos knows Tyreman. A green Jag was seen at his yard."

"Tell me something I don't know," boasted the journalist.

"What?"

"I have pictures of them leaving Carlton House together."

"So, they're definitely in this together? We now have the proof we need."

"What proof, Danny? You can't convict them just because they know each other; besides, whom can you trust at the station? You said yourself, they've already tried to have you killed."

"What do you suggest?" asked the detective

"Sophie's been approached with an offer. She's to marry Maurice Candy, a rich widower, and then inherit his money when he kicks the bucket. She gets two hundred grand and invests the bulk of the money into a bogus company."

"What are we waiting for?"

"We have no proof, Danny. You, more than me should know this… It'll be Sophie's word against Chivers; and besides, we want the whole nest, not just the drones."

"You're playing a dangerous game here, Vince… What do you want me to do?"

"I did contemplate a wire, but it'll be too dangerous. Chivers has already frisked her once. I think we should let Candy in on this."

"And what if he doesn't want to play?"

Slattery cleaned his spectacles. "We haveto convince him. It's our only chance of setting a trap."

Jenson clambered to his feet up and the pigeons scattered. "Incidentally, I checked out the doctors who signed the death certificates of the victims. Dr Graham Fleming signed the death certificates of Ralph Cochrane and Gus Sherwood. He was Cochrane's doctor, and apparently was just passing when Gus died. Heart attacks, both of them."

"How convenient."

"So what does Sophie feel about getting married?" asked the detective.

"He hasn't proposed yet, but if we tell Candy, I'm sure we can hurry things along."

"Aren't you forgetting something? They'll be legally married after this is all over."

Slattery shrugged. "What choice do we have? It's too risky trying to arrange a bogus marriage. Too many people would have to know about it."

The rain came down with more intensity and the couple ran for cover beneath a tree.

"Who can you trust, Danny? We may need help on this one."

"I'll have a word with our Dr Fleming and see if I can't exert a little pressure on him. If all else fails, we'll lie in wait for the killer. We can't afford to risk the life of Sophie, or Candy."

"I'll call you when the wedding is arranged, Danny. Take care."

The detective jogged for his car, and kept a vigilant watch as he went.

******

The fragrance of cheap perfume greeted Charlie Bojangles when he entered the boarding house. The door to Mrs Parish's room was ajar and the suave killer tiptoed towards the staircase, attempting to avoid the infuriating landlady. He would rather be faced with a deranged gunman any day, than face the prospect of another lustful assault from the woman. His relief was short-lived when he heard the squeak of the door hinge.

"Charlie, you're not trying to avoid me are you?"

Bojangles reluctantly turned his head towards the painted lady, who wore a see through nightdress. She fluttered her eyelashes at him.

"Of course not, Mrs Parish. I'm really tired and I have to be up early in the morning."

"Dorothy, remember? Nonsense; surely you can find time for one teeny weenie nightcap?"

"I'm sorry, Dorothy. Maybe some other time."

"Have you seen the newspapers recently?" She fanned herself with the tabloid and teased the object of her infatuation.

"No, why do you ask?"

She held up the photo-fit and slowly walked backwards into her room. Her joy was apparent with the appearance of Bojangles in her doorway.

He stroked his chin with his gloved hand and closed the door. He cast his dark eyes over the lustful woman and deliberated that she was not bad looking. With the application of war paint, she may even have warranted his attention, had he consumed a bottle of whiskey.

"Now, Dorothy, what's so interesting about that newspaper?"

She planted her ample behind on the couch and patted the vacant space next to her. Bojangles reluctantly joined her.

"Take a look at this picture, Charlie. Remind you of anyone?"

He showed no emotion as he studied the image. "No. Give me a clue."

"It's you, Charlie. Well, I say it's you, but of course it can't be. You must admit though, there's a striking resemblance?"

"That could be anyone."

"Okay, listen to the description, Charlie. This man is wanted in connection with a murder enquiry. He is not to be approached and if seen, contact the nearest police station. He is believed to be approximately six-feet tall with dark eyes, swept back black hair and a goatee beard. It is possible that the suspect may have a liking for classic Italian suits and shoes. We repeat, this man is not to be approached."

She folded the newspaper and studied his face, before a contented smirk adorned her features.

"You don't really think that is me do you, Dorothy?"

"You know it's my duty to contact the police?"

"If you really thought I was that man, you wouldn't be sitting alone with me now, would you?"

The man-eater licked her lips. "Charlie, it's so long since I had a man, and I realise how lonely you are. We could come to some sort of arrangement."

She shifted closer to him and revealed a naked thigh.

He felt nauseated and rose up from the couch. "Are you blackmailing me, Dorothy?"

She faced him, and her hands clasped his. "No, no of course not. I'd never betray you. I'm so fond of you and hoped we could... you know, have some sort of relationship?"

Bojangles smiled at her before he backed off. "You're right; perhaps I do need to let my hair down once in a while. Wait here, Dorothy; I need to fetch something from my room."

Her heart beat rapidly and a tingling sensation spread throughout her body. Not since she was a teenager had she felt like this. She reached for her spray and giggled when she felt the perfume chill her bare breasts. Dorothy faced the mirror and reapplied her lipstick, before she slumped once more onto the couch. Her nightdress was arranged expertly, and displayed just the right amount of leg. She heard the squeak of her door and pouted at her admirer, who clutched a bottle of wine.

"A special vintage for a special occasion, eh, Dorothy?"

He grasped her hand and she stood up.

The besotted woman melted against him when he kissed her forcefully. She reached down hesitantly and felt his flaccid member through the fabric of his trousers. "The wine can come later, Charlie. The bedroom's that way."

He picked her up and carried her. Their lips met and her hand still worked away ineffectively at his groin. He laid Dorothy on the bed and she removed her nightgown. She reclined on the bed in her stockings and suspenders, her breasts large and sagging.

"Aren't you even going to take off your gloves, Charlie?" she gasped.

He grinned, cupped her breasts in his gloved hands, and with her eyes closed, she let out a gentle moan. She opened her legs and the fully clothed Bojangles straddled her, whilst his hands still fondled her breasts.

The ecstatic woman reached out for his belt and proceeded to unbuckle it, as her lover let out a tirade of giggles.

"You're going to enjoy this, Charlie."

"You pitiful, ugly hag! Do you really think I would entertain such a grotesque gargoyle like you? How dare you attempt to blackmail me, you insignificant cow?"

She tried to raise herself, but Bojangles had her arms firmly pinned down with his knees. She screamed and he slapped her powerfully across the face, before he squeezed her cheeks together.

"Quiet, you slut. I'm about to do you a favour, Dorothy;" he uttered. He removed his pistol from his waistband. "You're about to join your tortured husband in heaven, God forgive me. He won't thank me for it, but you've brought this on yourself."

The pillow was pushed over her head. He smothered her and muffled her attempted cries for help. Bojangles held his weapon against the pillow and squeezed the trigger. The lifeless body relaxed and the killer rose from the bed, amid the cascade of feathers. He retrieved his bottle of wine and closed the door quietly behind him, before he climbed the staircase, ready for any interception from the thief or the transvestite. There was none. He had some packing to do.

Chapter Nineteen

The receptionist's knitting was discarded when she peered over the top of her spectacles at the tall, shaven-headed man in the leather bomber jacket. He was not the usual class of client Dr Fleming dealt with, and her repugnant stare told him so.

"Excuse me, sir, can I help you?"

"I'm here to see Dr Fleming."

"Have you an appointment?"

"Here's my appointment," sneered DS Jenson, who displayed his ID.

The receptionist scowled. "I'm afraid he's with a patient at the moment. He may be some time."

The lofty detective ignored her, entered the surgery and startled a half-naked woman who brought her arms up to cover her breasts.

The white-coated doctor's bottom lip trembled with rage at the intrusion. "How dare you? Who the hell are you?"

"Sorry, Doctor, but my time like yours is precious. DS Jenson, CID. Sorry luv, you'd better get covered up."

The doctor turned to his patient. "I apologise, Mrs Devers; I'll see you tomorrow at the same time."

The red-faced woman covered up quickly and left the two men alone.

"You're out of order, Detective."

"I see I interrupted you at a bad time, Doctor," said Jenson, with a mischievous look in his eye.

"Mrs Devers complained of a lump on her chest. Of course I don't expect someone of your intellect to understand that."

"You don't have to explain your actions to me, Doc, not unless you're telling me porkies."

"Your uncouth actions will be reported to your superiors, Detective. Now, if you'll state your business."

The doctor was a tall, gangly man with a huge quiff of black hair that almost covered one eye. His nose was long and pointed, his thick lips unable to hide his protruding teeth. His accent was highly polished, with no hint of an accent.

"Do you recall the death of Ralph Cochrane in May, Doctor?"

"Yes, of course. Why do you ask?"

Jenson's eyes took in the movement of the doctor's Adam's apple, a sure sign of his anxiety.

"How did Mr Cochrane die?"

"He had a heart attack, but I'm sure you already know this, as it's common knowledge."

"Was he dead when you arrived at the house in Kensington?"

"Yes, as a matter of fact he was."

"Who notified you of his condition?"

"His wife, Rosie. Yes, she telephoned me."

"And there were no suspicious circumstances?"

"Suspicious? Why of course not. Ralph Cochrane had a history of cardiac problems and I had no reason to be suspicious."

The doctor avoided eye contact and loosened his tie.

"What about Gus Sherwood?" probed DS Jenson.

"Gus Sherwood?"

"Yes, Doctor. How was it that you happened to call at his home shortly after his death? You were not his doctor, were you?"

"No, I was not… I was passing his home and Elizabeth Todd his wife waved me down. She related to me she could not wake her husband, and I of course responded to her pleas."

"Hold on, Doc. She waved you down in the middle of the road, and remarkably by coincidence, it just so happened you were a doctor?"

"Well, yes. I'd been playing chess with a friend and he lives close to Mr Cochrane. As I drove past, I saw the distraught woman."

"And how did Mr Sherwood die?"

"Heart attack."

"Pardon?"

"He had a heart attack... Listen, Mr Sherwood was not a young man, and his profession as a comedian must have put a great strain on his health. Apparently, he had been making love to his wife when he had the attack."

"And Rosie never thought to contact her own doctor? Don't you find that strange? Why didn't she just phone her own doctor?"

Dr Fleming reddened. "Shock, who knows? I cannot vouch for her actions. I though it pointless contacting another doctor when it was a straightforward case."

"Do you know Lance Tyreman, Doctor?"

"No!"

"You seem so sure. Think about it... Balding gentleman with a ponytail, mid forties."

"I've told you, I know of no such man... Anything else, Detective?"

"What about George Mikhos?"

"No, never heard of him."

"Matthew Torrance?"

"No! What is this? I've a very heavy schedule."

"Dab your forehead, Doctor. You look a little warm."

"DCI Entwistle will hear of this. This is an outrage!"

Jenson was surprised to hear the name of his senior officer mentioned. "So, you know good old Brian do you? How do you know he's my senior officer?"

"I-I've met him before at some party. He's an inspector in CID, right?" he stammered.

"He's a chief inspector actually...Yes, but there are many Inspectors in CID. Another coincidence, eh?"

"Please leave me alone. If you want to ask any more questions, then do so in the presence of my solicitor."

"How much were you paid?"

"Get out! I've never been so insulted in my life. Just what are you implying, Sergeant?"

"Implying? Why nothing, Doctor, nothing."

Jenson unwrapped another piece of chewing gum and smiled sarcastically at the frantic doctor before he left the surgery. Dr Fleming had admitted nothing, but Jenson's suspicions of DCI Entwistle were enhanced.

******

It was an unsettled, gloomy evening, and the ebony clouds ominous in their hostile presence, befitted the scene that welcomed Jenson. The yellow tape cordoned off the unwelcome spectators and journalists, who had hoped to catch a glimpse of the macabre discovery in Gower Street.

DS Jenson winked at the constable who was posted outside the boarding house. The policeman passed him some plastic shoe covers and gloves. The snubbed detective had been ordered to Gower Street, where the body of Dorothy Parish had laid undetected for almost forty-eight hours.

The detective entered the premises and wrinkled his nose when the rank odour reached him. The head of the forensics team greeted him.

"What's the score, Jimbo?"

The silver-haired man wiped his brow before he spoke. "Female, mid-forties, fifties. Been dead for at least twenty-four hours I'd guess, perhaps longer. She's been shot in the head through a pillow… Sound familiar, Danny?"

"No! Is it the same calibre bullet, Jimbo?"

"I'd say so, but I'll know more when we match them down at the lab."

"Is DCI Entwistle aware she was shot?"

"Not as far as I know. I was told you were in charge of the investigation, Danny, and had no reason to contact the inspector."

"Do me a favour, Jimbo; keep it that way for the time being."

"What's going on?"

"Nothing, just do as I say… Was there any sign of a break in?"

"No, her room door was open, but the outer door was locked."

"So how did the killer get in? Window?"

"If he did, he closed it after him. There was no sign of a struggle in the lounge where the window is located, so it makes sense that she knew her killer and invited him in."

"This is a boarding house, right?" asked Jenson.

"Yes. That woman over there is one of the tenants."

Jenson looked towards the weeping, blonde woman being questioned by DC Jamie Benton. There was something strange about the elegantly, attired woman, but he could not put his finger on it. He patted Jimbo on the back. "Let me know just as soon as you find out about the bullet, okay?"

"Of course."

DC Benton scowled at the approaching figure, and paused in his questioning of Goldie. "Sarge, are you on this case?"

"Come on, Jamie; everyone at the station knows I was taken off the Rosie Cochrane investigation... I'm afraid I've been lumbered with this."

DS Jenson nodded at the blonde and pulled Benton to one side. "Who's she?"

"Goldie Lamour. She's one of three tenants lodging at the boarding house. Actually, she was the one who found the landlady."

"Okay, Jamie, grab a cup of tea. I'll take over now."

"Wait a bloody minute! When are you going to start treating me with the respect I deserve? I'm sick of your interventions every time I'm questioning a suspect."

"Piss off, Jamie, that's a good boy. Go and report to your master."

The tall, thin detective glared at his teaser and relented when the scowl was returned. Jenson offered his most charming smile to the woman in the purple gown, who was in the process of lighting a cigarillo.

"Miss..."

"Lamour. Goldie Lamour."

"Mrs Lamour, I'm DS Jenson from CID. I understand you found the body?"

She blew out the smoke in a camp way and fluttered her eyelashes at the brawny detective, liking what she saw. "Miss, Detective, it's Miss. Yes, as I was telling that sweet detective, I knocked on Mrs Parish's door, intending to pay my rent. It was the third time this evening I tried and I was worried."

"Worried? Why?"

"Mrs Parish rarely left the house in the evenings, and most certainly would not have missed *Eastenders.* Anyway, my curiosity got the better of me and I entered her room. The bedroom door was ajar and I thought perhaps she was taking a nap. That poor woman. I must admit, we never saw eye to eye, but I wouldn't wish her ordeal on my worst enemy."

"So you didn't get on with Mrs Parish?" quizzed Jenson.

"No, she hates anything which she calls immoral. Homosexuals, lesbians, and of course, transvestites."

Jenson's suspicions were confirmed, and he felt a little aggrieved when he realised this cross-dresser had been eyeing him up. "What time did you find her?"

"Seven forty- five. Like I said, *Eastenders* had started."

"The other tenants. Where are they?"

"Up to no good, I imagine. That nasty man, Duncan Brady is a thief, and Mr Bojangles. Well, he's certainly a man of mystery."

"Meaning what, Miss Lamour?"

She took another long drag of her cigarillo and blew the smoke out of the side of her mouth. "He comes and goes… He's obviously a well-off man, so what he's doing here is beyond me."

"This Mr Bojangles. Can you describe him?"

"Sorry, I've never seen him before. Mrs Parish spoke of him often though."

"So how long have you been lodging here, Miss Lamour?"

"About three months… Yes, it was early April when I moved in."

"And Mr Bojangles? How long has he been staying here?"

"I'm not sure. He was staying here when I arrived."

"You've been here three months and haven't set eyes on your fellow lodger?"

"Bojangles is an elusive man, Detective. He's either in his room or out. He doesn't like to socialise, or so Mrs Parish told me."

"What about this thief as you called him?"

Goldie flexed her wrist and tutted. "That awful man has been through my things more than once. He also stole money from Mr Bojangles."

"How do you know this?"

"Poor Mrs Parish told me."

"So, were the police informed of..."?

"Duncan Brady," added Goldie. "Though I doubt that's his real name… No, Mr Bojangles talked Mrs Parish out of contacting the police, saying he would sort Brady out."

"Really? This Brady, can you describe him?"

"I've never met him, Detective."

Jenson looked up at the transvestite, unsure if he was being given the run-around. "Miss Lamour, you must leave a rather sheltered life."

"I don't understand."

"Either you're taking the piss out of me, or you're lying… You know so much about these people, yet claim you've never met them?"

"It's the truth, Detective. Arrest me if you must, but it's the truth."

"If I may be so bold as to ask, what is your real name?"

"Goldie Lamour!"

Jenson smiled. "Come on, Goldie, we both know that isn't true… Okay, let me try to be a bit more subtle. What was your name as a man?"

Goldie's eyes bulged and her breath came in spasms. "A man? A man? I've never been so insulted in my life."

"Calm down, Goldie; I'm not trying to ridicule you. I have to ask you these questions, you understand?"

Goldie cried loudly and attracted the attention of policemen and the forensics team.

The detective relented. "Okay, Goldie, that will be all for now. You can go."

DC Benton was in the lounge, talking to a pretty WPC when Jenson interrupted them.

"Jamie, check out the three tenants and find out Goldie's real name. Find out where they are and take statements off them. Has anyone notified the family of the deceased?"

"She has a sister living in the Lake District. Someone is on their way right now."

"Find out whom she socialised with, where she went. Bingo, club, pub, you know the routine, Jamie."

"Jimbo seems to think that the same man who murdered Rosie Cochrane may have killed the landlady, Sarge."

"Bullshit! Twenty sovs says he didn't.

"What's the motive?" asked DC Benton. "There's no apparent sign of sexual interference, even though she was naked, and no money was taken as far as we can see."

"Maybe he was disturbed," muttered DS Jenson. He cast a glance at the newspaper on the coffee table. He picked up the tabloid and noticed it was dated Thursday 14th June, making it eleven days old. He scanned the facing sports page before he turned it over. The photo-fit of Rosie Cochrane's killer stared back at him.

"What is it, Sarge?" asked DC Benton.

"Nothing, nothing at all." Jenson had found the motive.

Chapter Twenty

The thunder of hooves and the encouraging cheers from the generous crowd enhanced the atmosphere at the racecourse. Ever since Sophie was a child, there had been an infatuation with horses. Fond memories of visiting such grand places as Ascot, Goodwood and York with her family were still fresh in her mind. Maurice Candy had offered her the opportunity to revive her memories, an occasion too precious to turn down for the photographer.

The blustery weather had not deterred the bustling race-goers from attending Epsom races, an event highly regarded on the racing circuit. Maurice Candy had a special reason for his attendance. His filly, Rachel's Memory was scheduled to run in the third race.

Sophie had used the occasion for an excuse to visit the High Streets of London in her quest for a suitable costume. This act would probably not go down too well with Roland Madison, as she added the tally to her expense sheet.

A pale blue dress with matching hat was her choice, her date having opted for a smart grey suit and trilby. They smiled together, even in their disappointment, as the nag that carried their hopes passed the line in fifth place. Maurice dismissed the loss with a shrug of his shoulders.

The couple strolled hand in hand towards their private box for a refreshing glass of champagne and some strawberries and cream.

Candy whispered in her ear. "Not to worry, Clare, Rachel's Memory will make up for your disappointment. You'll love her, I'm sure."

Sophie felt humbled at the magnitude of high society race-goers, including the odd celebrity who knew Maurice. He was obviously a much-revered man in the circles of the upper echelon.

They climbed the steps to the private box and held onto their hats as the wind picked up. They took their place at their table next to the window and poured themselves another glass of the superb champagne, before the waiter brought their strawberries. There was one more race before Maurice's horse ran.

"This is wonderful, Maurice; I do so love racing."

"Really? There'll be many such occasions in the future; that I'm certain... How are the strawberries?"

"Mmm, delicious," giggled Sophie, with her mouth full. "How many racehorses do you own?"

"Eight, but Rachel's Memory is my favourite. She's special. Today she runs in a group one race for the first time, and the trainer informs me she has a very good chance, especially now the favourite has been withdrawn."

"Are you going to bet on her?"

"Of course. I enjoy a little flutter now and again. It keeps me on my toes and adds a little welcome stimulation to my life."

His voice reminded her of *Rex Harrison* in *My Fair Lady,* a film she adored. He caught her staring just a little too long at his handsome features.

"These friends you want me to meet this evening, Clare. Who are they?"

"If you don't mind, I'd rather wait until later?"

"A surprise, eh? Let me guess... a business proposal? I do so hate business. I'm retired now, and any offer tempting me to part with money will I'm afraid be snubbed. I'm financially comfortable and will refuse any such offer. I hope your friends will not be too offended?"

"No, it's nothing like that, Maurice. You must listen to what they say."

"I wait in anticipation, my dear... Eat up; they're mounting for the next race. "

******

Another loser followed, before the race they waited for beckoned. Sophie felt like royalty when she stood in the enclosure with all the other owners, who conversed with their trainers. A tall, smiling man in a trilby approached and shook Candy's hand.

"Clare, I want you to meet James Kettering, one of the finest trainers in the land. He's awfully expensive, but he's worth it."

"Pleased to meet you, Clare," he said, with a tinge of Irish in his voice.

"How is the old girl?" asked Candy. He eyed his horse up with pride, as a young girl led it around the paddock.

"She's fine, don't worry. We took her for a gallop this morning and she's never been better. She'll definitely make the first three, but if she'll win it or not may depend on the ground. The jockey reports it as being a bit tacky out there, so we'll wait and see."

The instructions for the jockeys to mount came from the intercom system and the magnificent beast was led across the turf towards them. Sophie patted the filly, and the shiny coat looked splendid. The odour of the animal failed to curb her enthusiasm. She stayed in the background when the trainer meted out his instructions to the jockey, who was attired in pink silks. The jockey mounted and the filly received encouraging pats, before it departed for the racecourse.

The trainer shouted after it. "I'll see you in the winner's enclosure, Seamus."

They reached the grandstand and climbed the steps, before they settled close to the top. The two men focused their binoculars on the start and Sophie stood on her tiptoes.

"I'm sorry, Clare," apologised Candy. "Here, these will help you."

She reluctantly accepted the binoculars and watched the horses down at the start.

The racehorse owned whispered in her ear. "Wait here, Clare, I must place my bet. I'll put a little something on for you, shall I?"

She watched Candy bound down the steps like a teenager. He manoeuvred his way through the crowd, before he arrived at his destination. She homed in on him with the binoculars and was surprised that no cash was exchanged between punter and bookie. She assumed that Maurice probably had an account with them.

Candy rejoined his companions and rubbed his hands together. "Three to one. The stingy bastards are only giving three to one. I've placed one hundred pounds on for you, Clare."

She opened her handbag and reached for her purse, but the powerful arm of Candy intercepted. "Now don't be silly… Enjoy the race."

"Maurice, you shouldn't have."

"Don't worry, girl, the old fool can afford it," offered Kettering.

The horses were loaded and the commentator's voice informed them they were off.

"Come on, Rachel!" screamed Sophie, as the horse approached the winning line in front. She jumped up and down and hugged Maurice, who informed the red-faced girl there was another circuit to run.

Rachel's Memory was still in front when the field approached the final furlong. The murmuring of both owner and trainer told her the horse was in with a big chance. A grey horse came out of the pack and the two principles drew clear of the field. Neck and neck they raced with fifty metres to go. The screams of Sophie merged with the urgings of Maurice and Kettering, as the two battling horses passed the line together.

"We've won, we've won," enthused Sophie, who jumped up and down excitingly.

The two men looked to each other when the racecourse announcer relayed that it was a photo finish.

Marice stroked his chin in nervousness. "Well?"

"It's close. I'm not sure," returned the trainer.

They waited an agonising five minutes before the intercom came to life.

"The result of the Savoy stakes for fillies. First, number four, Jinxed Lady; second, number two, Rachel's Memory."

"Oh no," moaned Sophie.

"Bad luck, Maurice," offered Kettering.

"Oh, well, she ran a marvellous race and the prize money for second place is nothing to be snubbed at."

They made their way to the winner's enclosure and applauded the winning horse as it was led in, followed by Rachel's Memory. They patted the filly for its brave effort, even though the sweat-drenched beast was not quite good enough on this occasion.

The racing journalists entered the paddock and spoke to the trainers about their hard luck stories, as the photographers snapped the unlikely heroes for the morning tabloids.

"Sophie, my word, it is you isn't it?"

She tried to usher Candy away, but the damage had already been done.

The young, blonde photographer approached. "How are you doing, Sophie?"

"You two know each other?" asked Candy, curiously.

The photographer nodded. "Yes, Sophie and I worked for Tobelmory fashion magazine. I heard you've joined the ranks of the paparazzi?"

"Sophie? You're a reporter?" quizzed Candy.

"I'm sorry. Have I dropped you in it, old girl?"

"It's okay, Stanley. It's been nice meeting you again."

Sophie lit a cigarette and faced Candy.

"So you're a reporter are you, Sophie?" He put the emphasis in her name.

"No, I'm a photographer working for The Echo, but let me explain."

"There's no need to. It's obvious to me your motive. Old rich man uses escort agency to live out his fantasies. Am I close?"

"No, you're bloody not… Listen to me, Maurice. I was going to tell you this evening; that's what the meeting was to be about."

"Do I whiff a hint of blackmail here? You're wasting your time, my dear, as I don't care what you print. I'm past caring."

She walked after him and flicked her cigarette to the ground. "It's not like that, Maurice, please listen to me?"

"Why should I? You've deceived me, so tell me, why should I listen to you?"

"Because, your life is in danger."

She looked around to ensure she had not been heard. The words had registered with Maurice and his face was ashen.

"My life is in danger? Tell me more?"

"Tonight, Maurice. Eight 'o'clock in the Dog and Bull."

"Do you work for Cupid's Arrow or not?"

"Yes, I mean no. Tonight, Maurice, please be there?"

His face was now etched with sadness. "I'm such an old fool, aren't I? Do you know, I actually thought that you genuinely liked me?"

She stood on her tiptoes and kissed his cheek. "I do,really I do. Tonight, Maurice?"

"I'll be there."

Sophie smiled at him and turned her back, before she walked briskly towards the exit. What Candy did not see, was the tears stream down the face of Sophie.

Chapter Twenty One

Slattery, Sophie and Jenson arrived one hour early at the Dog and Bull in Croydon. The latest unforeseen dilemma involving Maurice Candy had prompted their action. They sat isolated from the other customers in the corner of the bar, their table laden with their drinks.

Jenson opened up. "So, Candy knows who you are, Sophie. What was his reaction?"

"He wasn't too pleased, as you can imagine, but he'll turn up."

"I hope you're right. There have been more developments in the investigation. I think our killer has struck again."

Slattery wiped the froth from his mouth. "What? Are you sure?"

"A landlady was murdered in Gower Street. Identical method as Rosie Cochrane, and the bullets match… I found a newspaper lying on the coffee table with the killer's photo-fit. It looks like she confronted the killer, who must have been staying there. We think he calls himself Bojangles."

"Do you have a description?" asked Sophie.

"No. The other two tenants staying there are a bit of a mystery. There's a transvestite, who goes by the name of Goldie Lamour. She found the body and called the police. She refused to give me her real name and broke down when I implied she was a man. I left it at that and told DC Benton to check her out. Nobody seems to know anything about her, not even the punters in her local. She appeared on the scene about three months ago, and now she's disappeared."

"What does she have to do with the killer?"

"That's just it, Vince, I don't know. That's not all. The other tenant, a Duncan Brady is also missing, along with Bojangles. They all apparently have been staying at the boarding house since April. Three students we questioned bear this out. They were staying at Gower Street until April, and then rented a flat."

Sophie frowned. "Do you believe Bojangles killed Brady?"

"It's possible, but there's more. Duncan Brady was arrested last Friday evening on a shop lifting charge. The arresting officer could find no record of him, not even a National Insurance number. They released him and ordered him to return to Charing Cross nick the next day, but he never showed up."

"So he could have been murdered?" suggested Slattery.

"Maybe, but don't you think there's something not right about these people? The transvestite says she's never set eyes on the other two tenants. Also, we can find no record of this Bojangles. A local landlord of their pub informed us that a smartly dressed man did come looking for Brady on Friday evening, shortly before he was arrested. The description fits the photo-fit of Bojangles. Apparently, Brady had stolen some money from him."

"So how come you're back on the case?" quizzed Slattery.

"Entwistle was unaware the cases were connected, but now after discovering the bullets came from the same weapon, he's put me back on another investigation. The bullets came from a MK23 SOCOM, a weapon used mainly by the Special Forces in the States. We're checking our usual sources in an attempt to find out where the weapon was acquired, but these people are very secretive, and we don't hold out much hope."

Several of the curious customers assembled at the window and wondered who owned the silver Rolls Royce that had pulled into the car park. Maurice Candy ordered his driver to wait for him. He removed his gloves before he entered the premises. Sophie waved him over and he introduced himself to the others.

"What are you drinking, Mr Candy?" asked Slattery.

"Oh, thank you. I think I'll indulge in a pint of the local bitter."

Candy removed his overcoat, and his eyes scrutinised the large man with the shaved head. "So you're a detective with CID, young man? Have you any identification?"

Candy put on his reading glasses and inspected the card thoroughly. Slattery returned from the bar with the beer.

"Thank you. Now what is this about?"

DS Jenson was the first to speak. "Mr Candy, what I'm about to tell you must not go beyond these four walls. Whether you agree to participate or not, the same terms apply, as your betrayal could end in tragic consequences."

"I'm intrigued. Go on. You have my word, young man."

"We believe Cupid's Arrow is employing girls such as Sophie to win the hearts of prominent men like yourself. They eventually marry and he dies from a heart attack. The wife then inherits the estate... We think the heart attack is actually something more sinister. The same doctor has signed both death certificates and I questioned him yesterday. He was certainly rattled, and I'd be very surprised if he's used again... Where was I? Oh, yes. The girl then receives a healthy sum for her trouble and is later killed off, but only after she invests the bulk of her fortune to a bogus company."

Candy remained impassive and removed his silver cigarette box from his pocket. He lit the cigarette and pondered over what had been divulged to him. "I see, and you want me to act as bait to catch your prey?"

"That's about it, Mr Candy."

"CID is of course sanctioning this, are they not?"

Slattery interrupted. "I'm afraid not. For reasons best not known to you, it's important that only we know of this."

Candy was perplexed. "Highly irregular... How come the press has become involved in this? Sophie, why didn't you contact the police? You're needlessly risking your life."

Sergeant Jenson broke in. "What Vince says is true. Only we must know about this."

All eyes were on Candy as he squinted through the cloud of smoke. "Let me see if I've interpreted this correctly. For this to work, I must marry Sophie; am I correct in my assumption?"

"Yes, but..."

"Enough, Detective. As fond as I am of Sophie, I cannot violate my late wife's memory by marrying again. I vowed I would never marry and I intend to honour my obligation. I'm sorry."

Sophie intervened. "Okay, Maurice; so we'll have a bogus marriage."

"No. It's too risky," insisted Jenson.

Candy stubbed out his cigarette and took a long swallow of his pint. "Aah, I needed that… Sophie's right. I know a parish priest who'll no doubt cooperate if I make a small contribution to his church."

"A bent priest?" quizzed Slattery.

"Good gracious, no, nothing as dramatic as that. He's a good friend of mine, and I'm certain he'll oblige."

"He must not be told the reasons for the sham marriage."

Candy raised his hand in assurance. "Of course not, Sergeant. Naturally, our families and friends will not be too happy after all is revealed, but I suppose it's all in a good cause."

Jenson interrupted. "Families and friends are not to be told until after we have the killer in custody. Then we can hopefully rope in the rest of the conspirators."

"When's the big day?"

"We'll let you know, Maurice, but it has to be soon."

The wealthy man rose and put on his overcoat. "One more thing, Sergeant. How do we know when the killer is coming for me?"

For the first time, the detective seemed ill at ease. "That's just it, we don't."

Candy was unperturbed. "Oh, well, I expect to hear from you soon." He grasped Sophie's hand and his eyes watered. He kissed her hand and left the pub quickly.

******

"Nice putt, Matthew," grovelled Lance Tyreman, before he addressed his ball. "This is for a half."

A golf cart approached and the pony-tailed executive director tried to blank the intrusion from his mind. The ball trickled towards the hole and stopped on the edge. "Damn!"

"I believe that's another fifty pounds you owe me, Lance," grinned Torrance.

The driver of the golf cart was now visible. Ross Chivers applied the brake and scurried towards the two golfers.

"This had better be important, Chivers," growled Tyreman, who still seethed over his bad fortune.

"Oh, it is… Dr Fleming wants out."

"Sorry, I don't think I heard you," groaned Tyreman.

"I said, Dr Fleming wants out… He's had a visit from that meddling detective, Jenson.

"Fuck! You said he wasn't going to be a problem," cursed Torrance.

"I'll get onto Entwistle and find out what's going on."

Torrance was unsatisfied with the response. "He must be taken out, Lance, no ifs or buts. I want Jenson dead!"

Tyreman turned towards Chivers. "How much does Jenson know?"

"According to Dr Fleming, Jenson suspects he's working for us. He mentioned us all by name."

Torrance swung the golf club wildly and dislodged a large divot from the green. "Have you at least taken care of Bojangles?"

"No, Mr Torrance," said Chivers, "but I'm working on it… He's apparently murdered his landlady."

"What?"

"His landlady must have recognised him from his pictures, and so he topped her."

"This is such a fucking mess… Why haven't you hired someone to take Bojangles out?"

"It's not easy hiring a killer, Mr Torrance… There is someone I have in mind, but he's out of the country at the moment."

Torrance spoke into the ear of his nervous employee. "Listen to me, Chivers; contact Bojangles and tell him to hit Jenson and the good doctor. In fact, it may be a good idea to kill Dr Fleming first, before he shits his pants.

I'm not concerned if it looks like an accident or not; just no cock-ups this time."

"I don't contact Bojangles. He contacts me. That's the way he works."

"Jesus Christ. When is he to contact you?"

"Tomorrow. He calls me every Thursday."

Torrance replaced the divot. "Did you at least check out the girl?"

"Yes, she's clean. She's already met Candy, and he's rather fond of her."

"Well, that's something. Next time you contact me, I'll expect some good news."

Chapter Twenty Two

The unexpected knock on the door interrupted Slattery as he bathed. He cursed and wondered who could be calling at this late hour, for visitors recently had been scarce. He towelled himself and put on his bathrobe, before he descended the staircase. Inwardly, he wished the visitor was Cheryl, but there again; she would have let herself in. He missed his wife and children, and talked regularly on the telephone to them, but his stubborn nature prevented him from leaving the career that he loved.

He opened the door and Sophie faced him. She smiled and clutched a bottle of wine. Slattery looked the denim-clad girl up and down, his expression one of disdain.

"Shit, don't overdo the welcome, Vince, will you?"

"What do you want?"

"I thought I'd cheer you up and cook you something… When is the last time you ate a proper meal?"

"I had a Chinese last night."

"Well, aren't you going to invite me in?"

"I suppose so." He examined his colleague. "You haven't exactly pushed the boat out with your appearance have you?"

"Cheeky bugger. This is my casual look."

Sophie grimaced and she followed Slattery into the lounge. The carpet was in serious need of a vacuum, and a rancid odour lingered. "Bloody hell, not one for housework are we?"

"I didn't invite you here."

She sauntered into the kitchen to be faced with a mountain of washing up and an overflowing laundry basket. "Vince, why don't you hire some home help?"

"I'm not bloody Maurice Candy, you know; just a lowly underpaid journalist?"

He heard the water running and entered the kitchen. "What do you think you're doing?"

"What does it look like I'm doing? I'm washing up."

"I don't..."

"No arguments, Vince. Now go and get dressed before I have lustful thoughts... Nice legs by the way."

He blushed and relented. If marriage had taught him anything, it was never argue with a woman, as you always come off second best. He dressed casually in a tee shirt and jeans before he rejoined Sophie, who was almost finished the washing up. He opened the drawer, reached for the corkscrew and examined the wine.

"Don't worry, it's not cheap plonk," insisted Sophie. She opened the fridge-freezer and wrinkled her nose up at the contents. "Frigging hell; half of this stuff is alive."

She disposed of most of the foodstuff into the bin after reading the use by date.

Slattery watched her disapprovingly. "Hey, there's nothing wrong with those tomatoes!"

"If you want food poisoning, they're fine... Shit, there's nothing in here I can use. Looks like a takeaway."

"I'm not hungry," moaned Slattery. He proceeded to pour out two glasses of red wine.

They settled on the couch and talked until the early hours of the morning. After the wine, Slattery had produced a bottle of malt whisky, which they had almost finished.

Sophie's eyelids drooped and her words were slurred when she confided in Slattery. "I've always been unlucky in love, Vince. A good man is so bloody hard to get nowadays. The best ones are always taken. Take you for instance?"

Slattery looked into her eyes. "This is a side I've never seen in you, Sophie. Is this the drink talking?"

"No! I've always had a thing for you, Vince, but with you being married; you know how it is?"

He checked his wristwatch. "Jesus, look at the time. It's almost two-thirty."

Sophie hiccupped. "I suppose I'd better go then." She rose from the couch and removed her car keys from her pocket.

Slattery grasped her hands. "No way can you drive in that state."

He embarrassingly realised the contact and released her.

She counteracted by reaching for his. "What do you suggest, Vince?"

"You can sleep in my bed. I'll sleep on the couch."

"Are you s-sure?"

"No problem."

He showed her to the bedroom and faced her; the lingering essence that her body radiated stirred him. She looked so angelic. That perfect mouth demanded to be kissed, and those seductive brown eyes entranced him. "I'll be going then. Goodnight."

"Wait! Vince. The bed is so large and I feel put out, confining you to the couch."

"Sophie, you're drunk and there's no way I'm going to take advantage of the situation."

She giggled childishly. "You fool; I'm a grown woman and I know what I want, and it's standing in front of me."

Slattery hesitated. "You'll regret your actions in the morning."

She approached him and put her arms around his neck. *"Regrets, I've had a few but then again, too few to mention."*

Their lips met and Slattery's arms engulfed the girl. They shuffled over to the bed, their bodies embraced, and he lowered her onto the mattress. Sophie's breathing was rapid as they undressed one another and discarded the clothes onto the bedroom floor.

She gasped when Slattery entered her gently, his rhythm slow as she moved with him. Their lips met again and their tongues were entwined, their perspiring bodies as one. His mouth turned to Sophie's petite breasts. His tongue lapped at the erect nipples as she moaned in ecstasy, their bodies now building into a frenzy. Their rhythm increased and her legs held him like a vice when they climaxed together. Their breathing was heavy and they kissed passionately.

Sophie rolled her lover over and mounted him. Her hips grinded against him powerfully, as her head rocked from side to side. For two hours they made love, until they fell exhausted into each other's arms.

******

The dressing gown hung loosely on Sophie. She sat on Slattery's knee and kissed him, a piece of toast in one hand, a cup of tea in the other. The journalist's prediction that Sophie would regret their frolics was proved wrong. She had sobered up, a king size headache her reward for the consummation of too much alcohol.

"Sophie, we're going to be late if you don't hurry up and get dressed."

"No regrets?"

"No regrets," he echoed, and kissed her.

"So, Madison's agreed on another week, eh? What have you got on him, Vince?"

"Let's just say he owes me a favour or two. Hurry up or he may change his mind."

The front door swung open and Cheryl faced the couple. Sophie jumped up off her lover's lap.

Cheryl trembled and her eyes displayed disbelief. "Well, well, I was right after all. And you, I take it are the photographer that my husband is not interested in?"

"You're mistaken, Mrs..."

"Don't! You're wearing my husband's dressing gown and you're telling me I'm mistaken? Get out of my house, you slut!"

Slattery tried to console his livid wife. "Hold on, Chez, it was only the once."

"Ah! And that's supposed to make me feel better? All the supposed overtime. Now I know where you were."

"I'm telling you, last night was the first time."

Chery slumped into an armchair, her face ashen. "I've been talking to Roland Madison. He's worried about you. I inferred that the overtime was to blame in the break-up of our marriage, and do you know what he said? He said you haven't worked overtime for at least six months. You've lied to me and used me. You two deserve each other."

Her eyes filled with tears as she turned her back and departed. She shrugged away Slattery's efforts to restrain her. He returned to the lounge.

"I'm sorry," whispered Sophie.

"Story of my life. Bad timing."

"What did she mean about overtime? So where have you been?"

"It's a long story… Come on or we'll be late."

Chapter Twenty Three

Ross Chivers was a nervous man when he strolled alongside the Serpentine Lake in Hyde Park. He smoked profusely and dreaded his rendezvous with the crazed Mr Bojangles. The killer understandably was not too happy with the proposal that they meet up.

Chivers saw the lone figure sat on a park bench. He was immaculately attired as usual, and wore a large pair of sunglasses that concealed most of his face.

It was a glorious day and not a cloud could be seen. The roses and other exotic blooms made a wonderful floral exhibition, and the butterflies and bees vied for their individual preferences. The Houses of Parliament and Westminster Abbey were visible in the distance, which added to the magnificence of the picturesque park. All of these things of beauty seemed so much out of place in the presence of such a terminator of life.

The manager sat on the bench and sidled up to Bojangles, who checked the vicinity for any uninvited guests. He rose up and ordered Chivers to follow.

"Where are we going?"

"On a boat trip. You do like boats, don't you?"

"Not really."

"Too bad."

Bojangles paid the attendant and they stepped into the rowing boat. They disturbed a swan, which nestled in the shade of the vessel.

"Well, Chivers. Row towards the centre of the lake, that's a good chap."

"Me?"

"I can't see anyone else in the boat, can you?"

Chivers reluctantly gripped the oars and commenced rowing. He continually glanced at the intimidating killer, and a spark of recognition registered somewhere in his unconscious mind. He felt the eyes of Bojangles burn into him, which made him feel rather uncomfortable.

. "Okay, this will do. Now what is it you want?"

Chivers ceased his rowing. "I have a couple of assignments for you."

"Why didn't you contact me the usual way? You know I like to keep a low profile?"

"We had to meet. This is urgent." Chivers reached into his inside pocket and Bojangles flinched. His hand gripped his pistol that was nestled in his jacket.

"Relax, Charlie. It's just the envelopes containing the hits."

Bojangles scanned the contents of the first envelope. "A doctor, eh? His face looks familiar."

"It should do. He's the doctor that examined the bodies of Sherwood and Cochrane."

"So why have him killed?"

"Since when did you acquire scruples?"

Chivers felt a lump in his throat, and regretted his show of bravado.

Bojangles turned to the other envelope. "Our friend, the detective. He'll be difficult. He'll be expecting me this time."

"Make sure this time. No fucking slip-ups. My employers weren't too happy with your efforts last time."

"The copper was lucky… Do you want it to look like an accident?"

"It matters not. Just make sure there's no mistake this time."

Bojangles counted the money out. "What's this?"

"You've already been paid for Jenson, remember... Contact me by my mobile phone when the job's done… Oh, by the way. The doctor ought to be eliminated first."

"Consider it done."

Chivers saw his reflection in the sunglasses of the killer. "That landlady, Bojangles. What's the story behind her?"

"She recognised me from the newspaper photo-fit. It's becoming more difficult as the investigation against me gains momentum."

Chivers commenced rowing towards the shore. "I've seen that photo-fit and wouldn't pick you out from it. That landlady must have had some imagination."

"Nevertheless, I can't afford to take any chances… I'm thinking of skipping the country."

"After you've completed this task of course?"

"I'm not sure you're paying me enough."

"I don't think my employers will be too happy about that. Why the sudden change of heart?"

Bojangles ignored the question. "Fuck your employers. Get yourself another patsy."

"Two more hits, Charlie, two more."

"How soon do you want them dead?"

"I'd say as soon as you can... I'll ask my employers to see if they can increase your fee for them."

"Double."

"Be reasonable, man. They won't buy it."

"Well, it's double or nothing. I'm a sitting duck here. I need the cash to set me up abroad."

"Okay, I'll see what I can do."

******

The fresh-faced priest was on his knees, but not in prayer. Another batch of blooms was added to the impressive display in the cemetery of St Hilda's Anglican Church in Aylesbury. Reverend William Keller was thirty years of age and much loved by his congregation. It was not easy at first, as his unorthodox methods were not accepted. This rock-music-loving priest adored his alternate role as disc jockey in the village hall; his efforts to raise funds for local charities successful.

Seeing their Reverend haring along the roads of Aylesbury on his Suzuki 1000 was a common sight among the locals. The once ailing church was now filled to capacity, thanks to his hilarious sermons and unconventional rhythmical hymns, sometimes played with an electric guitar.

He struggled to his feet, peered over the stonewall and watched the limousine brake. He smiled gleefully when he saw Maurice Candy approach.

"A good morrow, you old fool. What brings you to my kingdom?"

"Billy, I see you haven't lost your charm."

"Cup of tea, Maurice, or something a little stronger perhaps?"

"A man of my own heart. A wee dram of whiskey wouldn't go amiss."

They embraced and walked towards the quaint cottage that adjoined the church.

"So how are you missing the big smoke, Billy?"

"Missing it, are you kidding? I love it here, Maurice. I can't thank you enough for everything you've done for me."

"Nonsense. Your destiny was always in your own hands. I was always confident you'd be accepted into the church. Your old man would have been proud of you."

Reverend Keller, once known as plain Billy Keller, had not always been so devoted to the church. After the death of his father, the best friend of Maurice, Billy had turned to drugs and crime. Maurice had tracked him down and placed him in a rehabilitation centre, where he gradually recovered. His introduction into the Church of England was also the old man's doing.

Billy passed a generous measure of whiskey to his friend, and for himself a glass of fresh goat's milk. "You're looking well. How are you?"

"As well as can be at my age… Listen, Billy; I want to ask a favour."

"Anything. Just name it."

"How would you feel about performing a sham marriage?"

"Sham? I don't follow."

"I need to get married, but to have the marriage annulled at a later date."

"You've lost me."

"Listen, Billy; I know this sounds insane, but I cannot relate to you my reasons for this. You have to trust me."

"Most peculiar. And how am I supposed to conduct this so-called sham wedding?"

"I thought you could help me there."

"Sorry, Maurice, no matter how much I owe you, and hell, I owe you a lot, but I can't perform such a ceremony."

"Can't or won't?"

"It can't be done. A marriage can only be annulled if you're either both related, you're found to be of the same sex, or the bride is under-age."

"Surely there's another way?"

"Is the bride an illegal immigrant?"

The old man almost choked on his whiskey. "Good god, no. My reasons are of a vital nature."

The reverend pondered. "If it transpires that I carry out any irregularity in the service, then I'll risk losing my standing in the church. I'm afraid I can't help you."

Maurice shook Billy's hand and gripped his shoulder. "Don't apologise, Billy; I'll find a way around this. Take care of yourself and get yourself a car instead of that death machine."

The reverend waved at his departing friend. "Wait!" He scurried towards the limousine. "There may be a way."

"I'm listening."

"I imagine you want someone to believe you're married, right?"

"That's about the gist of it, yes."

"Okay. Tell them you've been married... You wanted privacy and had a service that included only a select band of friends, or even just the witnesses. The person or persons you hope to fool are no doubt up to no good, and if they contact me, then I'll verify the wedding took place... There's only one problem though."

"Oh, what's that?"

"The marriage certificate. You must understand I cannot put myself at risk by indulging in a fraudulent ruse. You must acquire the certificate by other means. You tell me the names of the people you want me to authenticate the wedding to and it shall be done. In no circumstances will I lie to members of either of your families or friends."

"That's a generous proposition, Billy. I'll have to contact some people and get back to you on it. If it's the only way, then so be it. I'm certain they'll agree. No way will this reflect on your career. On that, you have my word."

They embraced and Billy swallowed the dregs of the whiskey from his friend's glass, before he watched him clamber into the limousine. A hint of a smile shrouded the face of the reverend, when he recalled the old days, when such an offer would have stimulated him. He owed Maurice Candy. He owed him so much.

Chapter Twenty Four

The gangly man who nibbled at his roasted pheasant with his protruding teeth, looked like he would have been more at home at the Mad Hatter's tea party than Innectos, a swish Italian restaurant in Baker Street. Dr Graham Fleming brushed away the quiff from his eyes and giggled hysterically at the comments of one of his colleagues, which was directed towards the slender Italian waiter. The five tipsy doctors had been extremely boorish and insulting the whole evening. Their merriment prompted the waiter to consider quitting his position.

The black and white woven, walnut strips on the ceiling and the tall amber glass doors were impressive features in the popular restaurant. The fine cuisine on offer also contributed to the reputation of the establishment.

One lone diner watched the boisterous behaviour of the medical men from the corner of the restaurant. His face was partly concealed by a large rubber plant, the placement intentional rather that coincidental.

"Luigi, fetch us another bottle of wine will you, old chap?" demanded a bearded doctor.

"If you ever get tired, just wave a white flag, you wop!" joked another.

Dr Fleming screwed his eyes up and peered through the smoke at the man who sat alone. The friendless customer sipped his brandy and stared towards him. The medical man wiped his mouth with his napkin and took in the indistinct features of the man. He was well dressed, possibly an Italian himself, which would explain his presence. Fleming turned away momentarily, and another look suggested he was not mistaken. He tossed the napkin onto the table and almost upset the table, before he staggered towards the man.

"I say, it's rather rude to stare. Have you a grievance or are you just ignorant?"

The cigar smoke cleared and Fleming began to have misgivings about his act of bravado. The man with the dark eyes sneered at him, a threatening look without words. None were needed.

"Do I know you?" asked the doctor.

Bojangles inhaled deeply on his cigar and blew the thick plume of smoke into the doctor's red face.

"Is there a problem, Graham?" asked his bearded associate, who looked Bojangles over.

"Forget it, Tim. My mistake."

They returned to their seats and Dr Fleming could not help but chance another peek. His relief was apparent in the absence of the dark stranger. The group hurled more insults at the waiter and finished another two bottles of wine. Needless to say, a tip was not forthcoming, and a middle finger was directed towards the doctors as they staggered towards the staircase. They never saw the gesture, but it made the waiter feel better all the same.

******

The doctors hailed taxis, all that is except Fleming. He headed for Baker Street tube station, and mumbled to himself as he progressed. The station was near deserted at this late hour. Only the late night revellers and a few vagrants were present. Fleming rummaged in his pocket for the appropriate change and purchased his ticket from the machine. He waited on the platform, leaned against the subway wall and squinted in his effort to see his wristwatch.

"Dirty bastards," he murmured, when he inhaled the stench of fresh urine.

He heard footsteps and looked along the platform. An old tramp was bedding down for the night, but the unfortunate soul was not what held his attention. A tall man, who wore a long, black, leather coat and matching gloves approached and stood a few feet away. Fleming turned his head steadily to his right and glared at the man, who munched on peanuts.

"Do you know what time the next train is due?" asked Fleming. He already knew the answer, but hoped to not confirm his suspicions.

Bojangles turned towards the frightened man. "To you it matters not, because you're not getting on the train."

"What do you mean? Hold on, I know your face. Who are you?"

"The grim reaper, my friend."

"You work for Chivers, don't you? Listen, I'll pay you." He fumbled for his wallet and dropped his credit cards onto the platform.

"It's a bit late for that, isn't it?" groaned Bojangles.

They heard the loud rumble of the approaching train.

Dr Fleming was now delirious. "Listen to me, god damn it! I'll pay you double... treble!"

"Mmm, a good offer. Let me think it over."

Fleming was now on his hands and knees to retrieve his credit cards.

Bojangles reached down and seized the doctor by his long nose.

"Aah! No, please!"

The hired killer walked briskly towards the edge of the platform and dragged the distraught doctor by his reddened nose. His futile efforts of restraint only caused him more pain.

"I've thought over your offer, Doctor, but no thanks. Happy landings, Doc!"

Bojangles jerked the nose violently and Fleming hurtled from the platform towards the railway track. He screamed and struggled to his feet, but the impact of the oncoming train crushed him as he disappeared beneath the wheels. The breaking of the bones was audible, a noise that was like music to the ears of Charlie Bojangles.

The train slowed and the killer crouched down to ensure his assignment was fulfilled. Only a pool of blood remained where the doctor had met his death. Dr Fleming had given out his last prescription.

******

The blazing sunshine had lured an abundance of tourists to Trafalgar

Square. The pleasant weather was a contrast to the last time Slattery and Jenson had met. There was an uncomfortable silence between the two journalistic employees of The Echo. Sophie was unsure of Slattery's feelings, after their jaunt together, two nights previous.

The journalist removed his spectacles and wiped his brow before he spoke. "About the other night, Sophie. It should never have happened."

"Hallelujah! He speaks."

Slattery responded. "Well, you haven't exactly been shooting the breeze have you?"

"That's because I don't know how to take you. One minute you're screwing me and whispering sweet nothings in my ear, and then you're giving me the silent treatment. Okay, so your wife caught us together, but just in case nobody's ever told you, Vince; life's a bitch."

"You sanctimonious cow. My marriage is in tatters because of you."

"Bullshit! Your marriage was already in tatters long before I appeared on the scene. I'm not the one who made up all the shit about working overtime. So whom exactly have you been screwing?"

Slattery raised his voice. "Drop it! The other night shouldn't have happened. I never told you to come around."

"And I suppose I raped you, did I? Funny, but I couldn't recall much resistance."

Slattery calmed down. "Listen, Sophie; I'd be lying if I said I didn't enjoy it; of course I did. I'm just confused. Sure, I have feelings for you, but it's not that simple. I have a family to consider."

"Ha! What happened the other night was sex and that's all. A one night stand, whatever you want to call it. In case you're stuck in a time warp, this is the twenty-first century. People sleep together for thrills, not for commitments. You were okay, but I'm not about to cut my wrists… Let's drop this and concentrate on what we're here for."

Sophie lit a cigarette and saw the tall, jacketless figure of Danny Jenson amble towards them. A flock of pigeons scattered as the big man's stride never faltered.

Sophie's words were directed at the journalist. "Incidentally, where were you last night? I called at your house, just to clear the air, you understand."

"Since when have you been my baby sitter?"

The detective sat between them on the bench and loosened his tie. He seemed to sense the tension. "You two okay?"

They nodded in unison.

"Hell, it's hotter than a scarecrows armpit," moaned Jenson.

"And I suppose you'd know," joked Sophie.

Slattery intervened. "Why the urgency, Danny?"

"Our good doctor died last night. Fell onto an incoming train at Baker Street. They're still scraping him up this morning."

"Was he murdered?"

"What do you think, Vince? At the moment, there's no evidence he was pushed and it's been classified as suicide. No witnesses, only an old tramp who was too stoned to know what he saw."

Sophie blew out a cloud of smoke. "Maybe it was suicide. The doc knew we were onto him. What exactly did you say to Dr Fleming, Danny?"

"Hang on a fucking minute. What are you trying to say, Lady bloody muck?"

"I'm just saying he may have opted to take his own life rather than face the consequences."

"Or maybe he opened his mouth, in which case you'll be in danger, Danny," added Slattery.

"I can take care of myself. I've given this a great deal of thought, and maybe we should tell Entwistle, or go over his head."

Slattery objected. "No way! Talk sense. If you report this, we have nothing, and all our work will have been pointless."

The detective was adamant. "Even if we catch Bojangles in the act, what proof will we have against Torrance and his cronies?"

Sophie coughed and tossed her cigarette butt to the ground. She watched as a hungry pigeon swooped for it. "A wire; it's the only way."

"Forget it. We've already been through this, Sophie," stated Slattery.

"Maybe she's right."

"Christ, not you as well, Danny. Chivers has already frisked her once."

"Exactly, but there are many places to conceal a wire."

"Can you acquire one?" asked Sophie.

"Maybe... Well, Vince; it's your call."

"I have to say no. I gave my word to Madison."

DS Jenson relented. "Okay, I appreciate that… Has Candy spoken to that priest yet?"

"Reverend, he's a reverend," insisted Sophie. "He won't marry us, but he will verify that we married on the quiet. A sort of private affair."

Jenson stamped his feet and scattered the pigeons. "Shit, you're playing with fire there, baby. Chivers is not stupid. He'll no doubt check out the wedding."

"And he'll discover that there were only two witnesses to the wedding; Joseph Granger a close friend of Maurice, and Clare, a friend of mine."

"Is that legal?" asked Jenson, as his suspicious eyes scanned the square.

"Yes. By law, a wedding in the Church of England requires only two witnesses."

"And what if they question this Granger and Clare?"

"Maurice insists he's a good man and will play along. As for Clare, she's a close friend of mine."

Jenson unwrapped a piece of chewing gum and inspected it before he dispatched it to his mouth. "I suggest we announce the marriage as soon as possible."

Slattery disagreed. "Slow down, Danny. They've only known each other a week."

"The quicker the better. We want Bojangles off the street. The media are putting pressure on us to catch him."

"We are the media, remember?" said Slattery.

"We should arrange a party to celebrate the wedding."

The two men scowled at Sophie.

Slattery was the first to speak. "Too risky, Sophie. That would mean inviting family."

The photographer continued. "Clare Dougal's mother died some four years ago in a road accident. Her father had a hard time after that and he's in a mental institute. Incidentally, Clare, who has volunteered to be my witness at the wedding, is to use another name of course."

Jenson stood up to stretch his legs. "Wait, maybe a party wouldn't be a bad idea. It's inconceivable that they wouldn't celebrate, even though they opted for no guests at their wedding. You could invite Chivers and we could wire the house."

Slattery nodded. "Maybe you have something there, Danny. He couldn't check for a wire; not in front of a houseful of guests."

The two journalists joined Jenson, who strolled towards the statue of Nelson.

The detective pondered. "Sophie would have to have guests, or it wouldn't look right. I don't want to put a dampener on this, but we can't afford to have one of her friends slip up by calling her by her real name."

"Clare will be my only guest, Danny. Don't forget, I've been working in Rome, or so Chivers thinks."

DS Jenson was unconvinced. "No way. We can't afford to take that chance."

A stray dog ran at the scattering pigeons and barked loudly in victory.

"Okay, let's say next Thursday for the wedding, and the party on Saturday. How does that sound?" asked Jenson.

"Aren't you going to kiss the bride, Vince?" joked Sophie, who puckered her lips.

"Don't push it girl. Don't push it."

Chapter Twenty Five

The wiggling finger of DCI Entwistle summoned DS Jenson to his office. DC Jamie Benton, who had a smug smile on his face, squatted on the cluttered desk and sipped his coffee. With his ridiculous perm, he resembled a lap poodle, and the chief inspector was his master.

"Have a seat, Danny," offered DCI Entwistle, as he scratched his baldhead. "I'm putting Jamie here on the case to assist you."

"No fucking way! I'm not working with that arse-wipe."

DC Benton made to protest, but was stopped by the senior detective. "You have no say in the matter… Now, have you made any progress finding Goldie or Brady?"

"Not a thing. I've checked their usual haunts, but nobody's seen them."

"It's looking more likely that Bojangles has topped them," suggested DCI Entwistle.

"I disagree," countered Jenson. "A contract killer would not bother with a tranny and a bum, even if they had stolen from him."

"A contract killer? He murdered Rosie Cochrane and Dorothy Parish."

"And Gus Sherwood, Ralph Cochrane, and Elizabeth Todd, along with Dr Graham Fleming; a friend of yours I believe, Chief Inspector."

"He told you I was a friend?"

"As a matter of fact he did."

"When did you speak to him?"

"Shortly before he died."

The chief inspector continued. "Didn't I tell you, Jamie? He's mad. Stark raving, fucking mad? Bojangles, if that's his real name is a psychopath. He kills for pleasure. Enough of this hit-man nonsense."

DC Benton sneered at the sergeant, then refrained, when the

threatening gaze was returned.

Jenson spoke up. "Have Special Branch made any inroads with the Lance Tyreman case?"

"Danny, Danny, that's confidential on a need to know basis, and you don't need to fucking know. Now, before you make me really angry, get your arse out on the streets and do some detecting. Find Mr bloody Bojangles. He's not the invisible man."

"And where do you suggest we start?"

"Do you want me to do your job for you? Out, and remove that bastard off my streets."

The two detectives strolled past their colleagues, and a chorus of wolf-whistles accompanied them on their way. It was well known that Jenson loathed Jamie Benton, and a posy of flowers tossed towards the couple enhanced their joke.

DS Jenson left the police station and breathed in the clean, fresh air. He could not help but laugh, as he noticed the array of tin cans tied to his rear bumper. "Bastards," he muttered.

"Danny, phone call for you."

Jenson tossed the car keys to Benton. "Warm up the car will you."

The smiles were still displayed on the faces of his colleagues when he answered the phone. "Detective Sergeant Jenson here."

"Mr Jenson, can I interest you in our range of lingerie for your new bride?"

"What the fuck?" Jenson slammed down the telephone and put up his middle finger to a laughing, red-faced detective, who peered through the glass partition.

A loud explosion shook the building. Jenson's face was ashen, and his pulse beat rapidly as he sprinted for the door. The black plume of smoke spiralled towards the blue sky, the stench of petrol strong. Dancing, orange flames engulfed his car; the trembling figure of Benton sat at the wheel, shrouded in black smoke.

Jenson sprinted for the car, amid the screams of some of the pedestrians, some of whom were lying on the pavement. He took off his jacket and covered himself, before he attempted to advance through the intense heat. He reached for the door handle and recoiled in agony when the heat burnt his flesh. He felt the hands encircle him and pull him away from the carnage, as the unmistakable odour of burning flesh accompanied the agonising screams of DC Benton.

Several detectives armed with fire extinguishers dashed towards the blazing vehicle, but their efforts were in vain. The faraway sound of sirens was audible above the fading scream. For Jamie Benton, it was too late.

Jenson stood transfixed and acknowledged that the burning man behind the wheel should have been him. A feeling of revulsion spread through his shaking body. Two men had died within twenty-four hours of each other. They had died because of him. Of that, he was certain.

******

Matthew Torrance sat at the head of the table. A sliver of chicken desecrated his normally immaculate beard. The similarity to Henry VIII was astonishing, thought Lance Tyreman, as he was fed a prawn by a busty, bikini-clad girl who sat on his lap. Tyreman liked to convey his apparent supremacy aboard his luxury craft, but everyone knew that Torrance was the real kingpin of the team. Tyreman loathed the big man, who was held in high esteem by the others, but Torrance, as far as he was concerned, was only keeping the throne warm for his imminent ascendancy.

Torrance wiped his slobbering mouth with his napkin and neglected the sliver of chicken, which irritated Tyreman. He half expected the bearded man to toss his chicken-bones to the ground, to be gobbled up by a pack of hungry hounds. Torrance clapped his hands and the scantily clad girls departed onto the sun-baked deck.

"Okay, let's begin… It appears that Bojangles, our bungling friend has botched up again. What happened, Chivers?"

"I'm not sure, Mr Torrance. I haven't been able to contact Bojangles, but it appears he wired Jenson's car, and one of his colleagues was killed."

"Fuck! Is Jenson going to be a problem?"

Tyreman tapped one of his diamond rings on the table. "Entwistle tells me he's getting touchy. Jenson knows about Bojangles being a contract killer."

"Well, at least he did dispose of the good doctor. Beneath a train, eh? I like his style."

There was a lull in proceedings whilst Torrance swallowed a mouthful of brandy. "How are the lovebirds doing?"

Chivers shifted uncomfortably in his chair. "Candy adores her. She tells me he'll propose soon, no problem."

"Just as long as she doesn't bonk him to death before the big day, eh?" joked Torrance. His booming laugh echoed around the room. "Anything on this reporter, Chivers?"

"I haven't been able to locate him, Mr Torrance."

"Why?"

"It's not easy. I can't just walk into the buildings of every newspaper in London and study the faces of the employees." The smirk was quickly vanquished from his face when he realised Torrance was not amused.

"What about this other man we talked about? The one who you said would sort our Bojangles problem?" asked Torrance, who expertly prodded his pearly-whites with a toothpick.

"You still want Bojangles eliminated?"

"Of course I still want him fucking eliminated! Are you a complete imbecile, or do you have to work at it?"

Chivers gulped. "I'll contact my source immediately. I believe he's back in the country."

"Good. Now, are there any more pressing matters? I'm due in Southampton tonight?"

"I have a question." All eyes turned to the worried-looking George Mikhos. "This girl, you did check her out didn't you, Ross?"

"I've told you, Mr Mikhos; the girl's clean. I even frisked her myself.

She almost snapped my hand off at my offer."

"Really?" quizzed Tyreman.

Torrance joined in. "This is what I want. Get your man to take out Bojangles, before or after he kills that meddling detective. It matters not. If it is before, then offer the contract to the new man, with the promise of two more big pay days. The usual terms apply of course. None of us present here will be exposed to the killer. That privilege will remain yours, Chivers. Keep me posted on the progress of this girl and Candy. The sooner they are married the better. Have a word with her; a few blow-jobs here and there, but nothing too strenuous. That should make up the old bastard's mind. Now, if there's nothing else, I'll bide you a good day, gentlemen."

******

One week had passed since the death of Jamie Benton. Tension ran high at Charing Cross police station, and pressure mounted to apprehend the bomber. DS Jenson had been questioned several times by various investigators, including Internal Affairs, who grilled him about his strained relationship with Benton. That Jenson had been a victim of a practical joke had saved his life and offered him an alibi.

Forensics had a major breakthrough, soon after the incident. A fragment from the explosive device, which turned out to be a pipe bomb, had a fingerprint on it. The conclusion was that the man who had planted the bomb was an amateur, and the clumsiness of the device bore this out. A statement from a bomb squad officer suggested that the killer was extremely fortunate not to have blown himself, up given the inapt structure of the bomb. How he had acquired the knowledge to make the bomb was in dispute. The suggestion that the devise was probably manufactured via the Internet was accepted.

A thorough investigation was underway to determine who would want to kill DC Jenson. A list of all the criminals he had arrested was compiled, but no obvious suspect was apparent. His senior officers had stressed that

Jenson was to have twenty-four hours protection, but the stubborn detective snubbed the request, and stated that he was an experienced detective and could take care of himself.

Jenson knew in his heart who was responsible for the attempt on his life, and the investigating officers had finally agreed that Bojangles was their prime suspect. It was still unclear why the killer had targeted Jenson, and the sergeant was most certainly not about to share his information on Cupid's Arrow, not just yet anyway. It was suggested that Bojangles might have watched Jenson when he questioned one of the witnesses, and had decided to make an example of the detective. It was assumed that Bojangles was indeed insane.

******

Before she entered the building, Sophie stared at the garish, pink structure with its window adorned by hearts. She told herself, whoever designed the exterior of the building was devoid of style. She straightened her blonde wig before she confronted Hilary, who was engrossed in a magazine.

"Oh, it's you."

"Is Ross in?"

"Yes, Mr Chivers is in. I'll check to see if he's free."

Sophie ignored the secretary and knocked on the office door before she entered. Chivers practiced his putting, and judging by his scowl, her intrusion was unwelcome.

He composed himself. "Ah, Clare, I'm so pleased to see you. Have a seat, my lovely."

"She just barged in, Mr Chivers. I tried to stop her."

"Hilary, Hilary, always one for red tape, aren't you? Relax; Clare is one of the family."

Chivers combed his ginger hair and Sophie noticed the ever-prominent sweat stains beneath his armpits.

"What can I offer you, tea, coffee?"

"Nothing for me… I just thought you'd like to know; we've done it."

The manager's face was impassive. "Done what exactly?"

"We've tied the knot. We're now married."

"Bloody hell, you're serious?"

"Of course. Here, take a gander at my wedding ring."

"Slow down, Clare. You mean to say, you married, just like that?"

"He proposed and I said yes. He suggested keeping it quiet. Maurice is a very private man, as I'm sure you're aware?"

"But, hell, I'm lost for words here. Why didn't you tell me you were getting married?"

"I thought I'd surprise you, Ross."

His expression was not one of ecstasy. "You certainly did that, girl. How? I mean, where did you marry?"

"St Hilda's Anglican Church in Aylesbury. It was wonderful."

Chivers was suspicious. "How could he arrange this wedding so quickly? I mean, what about the guests and the catering for instance? It takes time to arrange a wedding."

"No guests, just two witnesses. Maurice knew the reverend, and he did it as a favour."

Sophie felt uncomfortable. The only sound in the room was the whirring of the overhead fan and the fingers of Chivers drumming on the desk. She felt his eyes scrutinise her, and knew she had to convince him.

"We're holding a party tomorrow evening. You're invited if you fancy it."

"That wouldn't be a very good idea now, would it, Clare?"

"Why not? Maurice owes you a great deal. After all, you brought us together, didn't you? You're a bloody matchmaker, Ross, you old romantic."

"Clare, I wouldn't become too attached to Candy."

"But, he's a wonderful man, and he's as fit as a spring lamb. I don't know where you received your information from, but Maurice doesn't strike me as a man who's in the throes of death."

Chivers remained unsmiling. "He's dying, believe me. Of course, he's not going to reveal that to you, is he?"

Sophie enjoyed her role more by the minute. "But Maurice is so kind. There's no way he'd marry me if he knew he was going to die."

"What time does this party begin?"

"Eight 'o'clock. What do you say, Ross?"

"Perhaps I will attend. It'll be most interesting to hear how Mr Candy arranged this wedding. Incidentally, have you a marriage certificate?"

"Of course. Why do you ask?"

"It's nothing. I just want to make sure there are no complications when the old man dies."

"I'll be on my way then. See you tomorrow night, Ross."

She walked towards the door and the butterflies in her stomach faded.

"Oh, Clare."

She turned to face him.

"Nice ring."

Chapter Twenty Six

Reverend Billy Keller wiped his oily hands on a rag and slid out from below his Suzuki. He listened attentively above the twittering starlings to confirm that his telephone was ringing.

"Damn!" He cursed. He looked up to the blue heaven and put his hands together in mock prayer as a sign of apology. He jogged to the cottage and wiped his feet before he entered. He picked up the receiver. "Reverend Keller."

"Good afternoon, Reverend. I've just arrived back from Canada and am trying to trace a good friend of mine, Maurice Candy."

"Yes."

"Someone mentioned that you knew him, and I wonder if you could tell me where I could locate him?"

Keller pondered a moment before he answered. "Who is speaking please?"

"Finch, Daniel Finch."

"Mr Candy was married in my church yesterday."

"Really? What a coincidence. Looks like I was a day late, eh?"

"There were no guests present at the wedding. Mr Candy wanted a private wedding."

"He did? How could you arrange a wedding at such notice?"

The reverend smiled. He realised now that man on the other end of the telephone was the person Maurice wanted to trick. Billy had not mentioned that the wedding was arranged at such short notice. "Maurice is a very good friend of mine and I owe him a lot. I had no prior arrangements yesterday and so complied with his wishes."

"Thank you very much, Reverend. You've been most helpful."

Chivers replaced the receiver on the cradle and punched the air in delight. He had at last some inspiring news for Matthew Torrance.

******

The starry-eyed guests watched in awe when Candy and Sophie glided across the ballroom dance floor to the orchestra. Candy, attired in a tuxedo, and Sophie in her turquoise ball gown moved gracefully, and gratified their attentive audience. The music ceased and a smattering of applause rippled through the ranks. The orchestra resumed and the guests took to the floor.

The happy couple approached the bar and selected a glass of champagne to quench their thirst. Sophie noticed Chivers being escorted into the ballroom and waved to him. The ginger-haired manager looked out of place with his powder-blue suit and grey tie. The redness of his face testified to his embarrassment.

"Ross, glad you could make it. You know Maurice of course?"

"We've met once. Congratulations, Mr Candy on your marriage. Your taste is excellent."

"Why, thank you. Actually, I owe you a great deal. Where did you pluck this beautiful creature from?"

"Actually, she came to us."

"Like an angel sent from the gates of heaven, eh?"

"Right... Clare, why didn't you mention that it was a tuxedo function?"

"Oh, it completely slipped my mind. Relax, Ross, you look fine. I'd lose the tie if I were you though."

An elderly woman in white dress and pearl earrings approached and linked Maurice. "You saucy old devil you. And you, young lady, I've had my eye on this one for a long time and you come along and steal his heart. What does she have that I haven't, Maurice?" She winked at Sophie.

"It's called youth, Doris."

"Ah! Come and dance with me, you old fool."

Maurice shrugged his shoulders and was ushered towards the dance floor by his eager companion.

"This is certainly impressive, Clare," said Chivers, as he eyed up the crystal chandeliers. "Perhaps we undervalued old Maurice."

Sophie sighed. "That's what I wanted to talk to you about, Ross… Come on, let's talk somewhere more private."

They meandered through the jovial guests, who feasted on the marvellous buffet. Chivers strode after the long-loping woman. Her high heels made a din against the polished wooden floor of the corridor. She stopped at the study and beckoned for Chivers to enter.

"Wow! This is so…" He never finished his sentence. He sauntered slowly through the whiteness and took in the gilded statues and the green columns. "Magnificent."

"Yes, Maurice certainly has style; I'll give him that."

In the next room, DS Jenson, Slattery and a young-looking, bespectacled man who wore a *Queen* tee shirt, listened in to the conversation. The words were indistinct, and the young man fiddled with the controls until they were clear. Jenson gave him the thumbs up sign and fed another piece of gum into his mouth.

Sophie led the conversation. "As you hinted, perhaps you undervalued the wealth of Candy."

"What?"

"The house. When Maurice dies, who gets the house?"

"What are you talking about?"

"Am I speaking in Chinese? Who gets the fucking house, Ross?"

He stared at her suspiciously and scowled. Sophie's unblinking eyes were focused on the apparently nervous manager as he loosened his tie. He approached her and ran his hands down her body. She squirmed at his touch, as his fingers seemed to inspect every crevice of her body.

"What the fuck do you think you're doing?" she moaned.

He backed her up against the wall. "Just checking. You never can be careful can you?"

His hands were either side of her head and his sudden lunge was unexpected. He pressed his mouth firmly against hers, and his revolting tongue attempted to find her tonsils. She reached out, seized him by the genitals and squeezed powerfully, until he ceased his onslaught. He bent over double, and his hands gripped his nether region.

"You cow!"

"You ever try that again, Chivers and I'll kill you! Do you hear me?"

Chivers straightened up. "It's nothing different to what you've been getting all these years. You're nothing more than a whore and don't you forget it."

"Listen to me, you leech. You keep your filthy hands to yourself."

The look on the face of Chivers unsettled Sophie. "There's something not right here. How come you waited until now to ask about the house?"

"Because it's just entered my head... Now, are you going to answer my question? Who gets the house?"

"Come on. Come on," whispered Jenson.

Chivers opened his mouth to speak, when the study door opened. A group of guests were being given a guided tour of the house by Joseph Granger, Maurice's closest friend.

"Oh, I do hope we weren't interrupting anything? I'm just showing them around the house. This is my favourite room. Isn't it just splendid?"

"Shit!" moaned Slattery.

The young surveillance man shrugged his shoulders and took off the headphones.

"Come on, Clare; let's return to the ballroom before Maurice misses us," insisted Chivers.

They marched along the corridor in silence, until Chivers unexpectedly seized Sophie by the arm. "You sell the house and the proceeds go to us."

"Why didn't you mention this before?"

"Don't get greedy. You knew the terms we agreed on before you decided to marry Chivers. Take it or leave it, Clare?"

"I don't have any choice, do I?"

"No, I don't suppose you do."

The trio in the next room waited until Sophie and Chivers had left before they spoke.

"He's on to her, Vince," fretted Sergeant Jenson.

"You can't be sure."

"Christ! You heard what happened in there. He knows."

"He suspects maybe, but he has to take the risk that she's kosher. There's too much at stake."

Jenson considered his options. "It was too bloody obvious, Vince. She should have been more subtle with her approach." The detective patted the sound technician on the back. "Okay, thanks, Terry. You won't be needed you any longer. I guess it's back to the original plan. We wait for Bojangles to make his move."

"Can you get firearms, Danny?" quizzed Slattery.

"What do you think?"

******

Slattery sat behind a barrel, and his back leaned against the cold wall of the cellar. The cushion beneath him his was only solace. He gripped the pistol tightly. Every sound, no matter how insignificant was greeted with a jerk of the head. He fought the fatigue. His eyelids drooped and his mouth let out yet another yawn.

It was the third night since the party, and Jenson curled up on the sofa in the drawing room and waited for his turn to stand guard. The house in Belgravia had a high-tech security system, and nobody could enter the premises undetected without an alarm sounding. They came up with the idea between them, to leave the cellar trapdoors unlocked in the hope of luring Bojangles to them. That any intruder would have to climb down a stepladder to gain access to the cellar would work to their advantage. The cellar offered the only entry into the mansion; a spider's web waiting to catch the fly.

A squeak roused Slattery and he held the pistol nervously in his sweaty palm. Jenson had taken him to a private firing range to show him how to master the weapon. The squeak could have been the hinges of the cellar trapdoors, thought Slattery, as he tried to generate some spittle into his dry mouth.

The darkness played tricks with his night vision, and he pointed the weapon at a dark shape at the foot of the steps. He squinted, took aim, and his hands trembled with fear. It looked so easy on television, but to actually have the power to end someone's life was not something he cherished. He stopped breathing and held his position for what seemed like an eternity. The shape was static, so still. Slattery clambered to his feet and approached slowly. The wavering pistol homed in on its target. His smile was one of relief when the intruder turned out to be an old hat-stand. The thankful journalist returned to the safety of the barrel and slouched down on the pillow.

******

"For crying out loud, Vince, you were asleep."

Slattery opened one eye to see the shaft of sunlight across the cellar floor. The breeze from the open trapdoor tickled his face, as he glanced at the bare-chested detective.

"Why didn't you wake me?" quizzed DS Jenson.

"I must have nodded off," answered the journalist.

"Obviously. We can't afford to let..."

"The trapdoor, Danny."

"What?"

"The fucking trapdoor; it's open."

They looked to each other before they swiftly climbed the steps. They trotted down the corridor and shouted at the top of their voices.

Sophie emerged from her bedroom, still half-asleep. "What is it?"

They never answered and walked past her towards Maurice's bedroom.

DS Jenson entered the room. "Oh, my god! Keep her out of here, Vince."

"No, please no," screamed Sophie, as she tried to wriggle from the strong grasp of Slattery.

The detective had seen it all before; the pillow placed over the head and the bloodstained sheets. Splashes of blood stained the daffodil-coloured walls and the feathers were tainted by the bodily fluid.

Danny reached for the bedside telephone and dialled. "Guv, it's backfired. Maurice Candy is dead. Same method. There's no doubt it was Bojangles."

"Fuck! Where are you?"

"At his home in Belgravia."

"So tell me how come you just happened to be passing his home at this time of the morning?"

"I got an anonymous tip-off."

"Danny, if you're fucking with me."

Jenson hung up on the chief inspector and left the bedroom, to be confronted by Slattery, who attempted to console a tearful Sophie.

"I'm in deep shit here, Vince. You two get out of here. Entwistle is going to want to interview the widow. The media will be crawling all over here soon. It'll only be a matter of time before someone recognises you, Sophie and then you'll have the whole Cupid clan after you."

"You've got to tell Entwistle about her. If you don't, her life will be in danger," insisted Slattery.

"I suppose you're right, but I don't trust Entwistle... Apparently, he knew Dr Fleming. Go, before it's too late and I'll explain to Entwistle. It's imperative that Sophie's true identity isn't revealed."

Slattery sighed. "We're in a right fucking mess now, aren't we?"

Jenson looked across at his friend. "If it's any consolation, I know how you feel. I'm responsible for the death of Dr Fleming and Benton. Welcome to club reaper."

The journalist attempted a smile and patted his friend on the shoulder.

Sophie wiped the running mascara from her eyes and went to her bedroom to dress.

In the garage, Sophie opted for her red Mini, rather than one of the more elegant motors on offer.

Jenson watched them go and heard the sirens pierce the morning air. He had a lot of explaining to do.

Chapter Twenty Seven

Duncan Brady stood in the doorway of the pub, and a thin roll-up dangled from his lips. His unwashed hair and beard gave him the appearance of a tramp, and one old woman in passing actually handed him a handful of change, which he accepted without thanks. He peered through his milk-bottle spectacles at a teenage girl who passed, her skirt hinged on the verge of indecency.

"Who the fuck are you looking at, four-eyes?"

Brady grinned and shouted. "Get your tits out, luv."

"Fucking pervert!"

He looked up at the charcoal night sky. The drizzle eased off sufficiently for him to continue on his way. He spotted the bus, ran, and held out his hand.

"Where to, man?" asked the Jamaican bus driver, who tried not to inhale the fumes that Brady gave off.

Brady was thankful that the bus was empty. "Just give me all your money, Sambo"

"What? Is this a joke, man?"

Brady had his hand inside the pocket of his raincoat and he jerked it forward. "I'll shoot, believe me I will. Now hand over the money."

"Not a very good robber are you? You'll be lucky if I'm carrying twenty quid."

"Yeah, well, the banks are closed in case you haven't noticed."

"That's not a gun," suggested the brave driver.

"Wanna find out, do you?" yelled Brady, who again thrust his hand forward.

"Okay okay, you can have the money. I'm not risking getting shot for the peanuts they pay me."

A bag of change was handed over and Brady backed off the bus slowly. "Count to one hundred, Sambo. If you try to follow me, I'll blow your fucking head off."

Brady walked backwards, took the banana from his pocket and threw it at the bus. He laughed loudly, turned, and ran straight into a constable.

"Stop him, officer! He's robbed my bus."

Duncan Brady cursed his luck. He was set for another stint in the cells.

******

Detective Sergeant Jenson was sent home the morning Maurice Candy was murdered, and told to return to work the next day with a full explanation. He could not but help glance over to the empty desk of Jamie Benton, and felt a little remorse, even though he detested the man. Some of his colleagues were cold towards him, as if he was to blame for the death of the young detective. His greetings were returned by only a few of the detectives he passed on the way to Commander Sadler's office.

That such a senior officer was involved. spelt trouble for the sergeant. He took the chewing gum from his mouth and stuck it beneath a desk, before he approached the office. His knock was answered by a deep authoritative voice he never recognised.

"Enter!"

Jenson felt like a schoolchild about to be punished when he faced the three senior officers. Chief Inspector Entwistle sat and stroked his beard, a mere pawn compared to the uniformed officers that flanked him. Commander Sadler, he had always found to be fair, and his attendance did not worry him as much as the presence of the stern-faced man with the broken nose.

It was the stranger who spoke. "Good morning, Sergeant, do have a seat. My name is Chief Superintendent Hargreaves from Ealing. I'm here as an independent mediator to overlook proceedings. You see, this case has attracted so much attention, not only within the Met, but also in the media… There have been two attempts on your life, is that so?"

"Yes, sir."

"The last attempt ended with DC Benton losing his life. I've read the file and so have many of my colleagues, and I must say, I'm rather baffled with the contents. You're working on a murder enquiry, I gather. The slaying of Rosie Cochrane?"

"I was."

"Excuse me."

"I was taken off the case and later reinstated. It appears I've been taken off it once again."

"For your own safety, you understand," butted in DCI Entwistle.

Chief Superintendent Hargreaves continued. "This Bojangles, he's the prime suspect in this case, is he not?"

.   "He is, sir."

"And you think he's the man who's trying to kill you?"

Jenson nodded. "Yes, I do."

"And why do you think that, Sergeant?"

"Because, Cupid's Arrow have taken out a contract on me."

The chief superintendent frowned and Commander Sadler shrugged his shoulders.

"A contract? Are you suggesting this Bojangles is a hired killer?"

"Yes, I am."

"And who pray is Cupid's Arrow?"

"It's an escort agency. They hire girls to befriend wealthy, elderly men, and then to eventually marry them. Then..."

"Utter bloody nonsense," interrupted Inspector Entwistle. "Sergeant Jenson has this absurd notion that..."

"If you please, Chief Inspector, let the sergeant finish. Go on."

"The husbands die allegedly from a heart attack and then the girls are murdered."

"How extraordinary. The motive?"

"Money. The girls are paid a sum of money for their troubles, and they then invest a huge sum into a bogus company."

"Ha!" laughed DCI Entwistle.

The chief superintendent studied the face of Jenson. "This Bojangles. Didn't he murder his landlady?"

"Yes."

"Motive?"

"She recognised his picture from the newspaper."

Chief Superintendent Hargreaves studied his notes. "Apparently, according to this report, nobody at Gower Street actually identified Bojangles. In fact, the other lodgers have vanished too."

"That's correct, sir, but the bullets that killed Rosie Cochrane and Dorothy Parish came from the same gun."

"Indeed. This is an incredible story that you have told, Sergeant. Why didn't you relate all of this to Chief Inspector Entwistle?"

"I did, but he wouldn't listen."

The chief inspector shook his head. "Nonsense! He never ever mentioned anything of the kind."

"You're a liar, Entwistle and I can prove it!"

"Shut up!" demanded Commander Sadler. "Did anyone hear you mention this to the chief inspector, Sergeant?"

"Yes, DC Benton."

"Ah! How convenient," scoffed DCI Entwistle.

Jenson was now even more convinced that Entwistle was corrupt. "I have the names of the people involved in the conspiracy. One of them, Dr Graham Fleming, mentioned that he knew you, and now he's dead."

The senior policeman once more intervened. "Hold your tongue, Sergeant before you say something you'll regret... Dr Fleming, you say. I'm confused. Who's Dr Fleming?"

"He's the doctor who signed the death certificates of Ralph Cochrane and Gus Sherwood. He was about to talk, I know he was, so they murdered him."

The chief superintendent seemed genuinely concerned. "This list of conspirators you talk of. Did you give Chief Inspector Entwistle the names?"

"Yes, sir, that's when he took me off the case. He said that Special Branch was investigating two of the men on the list."

DCI Entwistle rose up and gripped the table. "Lies, lies, lies. Sergeant Jenson; I understand you've been going through a stressful and emotional roller coaster. The attempts on your life and then the death of DC Benton must have taken its toll, but I resent…"

Chief Superintendent Hargreaves butted in. "The murder of Maurice Candy yesterday. Can you tell me, Sergeant, how come you found the body?"

"Because, I was protecting him."

"Protecting him. So you knew an attempt would be made on his life?"

"Yes."

"His wife, Clare. Do you know of her whereabouts?"

DS Jenson hesitated. He realised if he disclosed the identity of Sophie, she was as good as dead. "No, I do not, sir."

The chief superintendent stroked his stubble. "This is most confusing. Why would she disappear, unless she was involved in the murder?"

Jenson could not hold back. "Would it be possible for Chief Inspector Entwistle to leave the room, sir?"

"A most irregular request that I must strongly decline… Again, why would Candy's wife disappear, unless she was guilty?"

Jenson hesitated. "Because, she doesn't wish to reveal her true identity, sir."

"Her true identity?"

"Yes. She infiltrated Cupid's Arrow and was assigned to marry Maurice Candy. We laid in wait for the killer, but he somehow slipped past us."

"We?" asked Commander Sadler, who filled his pipe.

"I'm afraid I can't say any more, sir."

"That's because you're lying," stated DCI Entwistle.

Chief Superintendent Hargreaves scratched his head. "Sergeant, we must know the names of your friends or your story is groundless. You must see the logic in that."

"If I tell you their names, then they'll both be dead within twenty-four hours, won't they Entwistle?"

The face of the chief inspector was red with rage. "This is an outrage! The man is obviously insane. I've given thirty-years to the Met and my record is flawless."

Commander Sadler sighed and shook his head. "Sergeant Jenson, you are hereby suspended from duty without pay. You're to go home and not to return to this station until called for. You will face an independent inquiry, led by Chief Superintendent Hargreaves. Do not attempt to contact anyone in this department and do not speak to anyone about this case, especially the press. Do I make myself clear, Sergeant?"

"Yes, sir."

"Have you any questions?"

"What's the point? You already have me hung drawn and quartered."

He noticed the wry smirk on Entwistle's face as he departed. Jenson realised, he may never see another dawn.

Chapter Twenty Eight

DCI Entwistle smiled at the sight of a young boy running, whose kite fluttered liberally in the morning breeze. His little sister sprinted after the boy and complained of his selfishness, but her ranting was ignored. Entwistle plunged his cold hands deeper into the pockets of his sheepskin coat. The cold park bench did not offer him much comfort. The inconsistency of the British weather prompted his warm clothing and the pork-pie hat that was perched on his head. He saw in the distance, a man head towards him.

The man was opulently attired in a Cashmere coat, the features obscured, due to the cigar smoke. Lance Tyreman looked over his shoulder and displayed all the symptoms of a nervous man. He sat apart from the inspector on the bench and tossed his cigar butt to the ground. "Well, Entwistle, this had better be good. I gave up a free lunch for this."

"There may be a problem, Tyreman." The seasoned detective showed no respect or fear towards his companion.

"Problem? Candy is dead, is he not?"

"Oh, he's dead all right, but Jenson knew in advance that Bojangles was coming for him. He and at least one other man were present in the house when Candy was murdered."

"Tell me you're joking?"

"Do I look like I'm joking?"

"How did he know?"

"The girl. She is not who she seems."

"Shit! So who is she?"

"I don't know… Jenson also has at least one more accomplice, but he won't divulge their names."

Tyreman was deep in thought. "Let me get this straight. Jenson put the girl up to this?"

"It looks that way… Listen, Jenson has talked. He gave the enquiry team, names, including yours. Don't worry, I've convinced them that Jenson is looney tunes for now, and he's been taken off the case."

"Shit! Will this team investigate me?"

"You, Torrance, and Mikhos."

"What a fucking mess. Let me think?"

"They have nothing without the girl," insisted the detective.

"We must find her. Do you know of any friends that Jenson has?"

DCI Entwistle pondered before he answered. "Not really. He keeps his social life outside of work. You must get to the girl, Tyreman or you're done for."

"We're done for, Inspector; we're done for... Okay, this is what we'll do. We'll put a tail on Jenson and hope he leads us to the girl and anyone else involved. I want them all eliminated from the equation."

"What about Bojangles?"

"Don't worry about him; he's history."

Entwistle contemplated. "If Jenson is murdered, suspicion will turn to us."

Tyreman rose from the bench and stared menacingly into the shorter man's eyes. "There's no other way. Jenson is too dangerous alive. We have to take a chance they haven't any taped or filmed evidence."

The sound of the detective's mobile phone disturbed the conversation. He reluctantly answered. "DCI Entwistle."

Tyreman took out a hip flask from the pocket of his Cashmere coat and swallowed a liberal mouthful. He noticed the pained expression on the inspector's face. "What is it?"

"Shhh!"

Another minute passed before the detective spoke again. "It's impossible. It can't be."

He listened intently to the voice on the other end of the phone. "I'll be there in ten minutes. Who's questioning him?"

DCI Entwistle replaced the mobile phone into his pocket and held out his hand for Tyreman's flask.

"So?"

"You're not going to believe this. Duncan Brady was arrested on Tuesday night for robbing a bus. He..."

"Hang fire. Who the hell is Duncan Brady?"

"The landlady that Bojangles topped; he was one of the tenants who disappeared."

"So?"

"His fingerprints; they match the ones found on the fragment of the pipe bomb."

They stared at each other in silence. The two laughing children ran passed them and attempted to keep their kite aloft.

"How can that be?" muttered Tyreman. "Bojangles planted the bomb."

"Did he, Lance, did he? I thought there was something funny about Brady. He had no credentials, no history, nothing. Come to think of it, neither did the transvestite."

"Transvestite?"

The chief inspector grinned, as the reality now sank in. "Bloody hell; they're a team."

"What on earth are you ranting on about, Entwistle?"

"They have to be a team… Brady must have helped Bojangles plant the bomb."

"Chivers said nothing to me about a team. He was dealing with one man, and one man only. Bojangles."

"So, how do you explain Brady's fingerprints on the bomb?"

Tyreman shrugged. "I don't, that's your job. Maybe Brady touched the pipe at another time?"

"Bit of a coincidence, don't you think? No, they're in this together."

"Nothing's changed. I want the girl and Jenson killed."

DCI Entwistle shook his head slowly. "Oh, but you're so wrong. Something has changed. If Brady is in cahoots with Bojangles, then what's to stop him talking? He no doubt knows of your little arrangement with

Bojangles."

"Bastard! What do you suggest?"

"I suggest, Lance, that you check your passport is up to date."

******

Jenson stepped into the telephone booth, and his trained eyes focused on the darkness of the shop doorway. He saw a flicker of a movement, but that was all it took. He picked up the receiver and tapped in the number. The familiar, educated voice on the other end greeted him.

"Hello. Hello, is that you, Vince?"

"It's Danny. Listen carefully, Sophie. I think my phone may be tapped, that's why I'm calling from a booth. I want you and Vince to meet me outside St Paul's in an hour's time."

"Danny, I don't know where Vince is. He hasn't turned up for work and he's not at home. I'm frightened."

"Don't be. If they'd discovered your identity, you wouldn't be there now. I think I'm being followed, Sophie, but I'll shake him off... Be there in one hour."

"Wait! We have to tell the police. It's our only chance."

"I am the police remember, or at least I was... I've been suspended. Entwistle is one of them and I don't know who to trust. If I reveal your identity, then I'll be putting your life in danger."

"Be careful, Danny. I'll be there."

Jenson's eyes never left the shop doorway, as his orbs adjusted to the night vision. He left the phone booth and walked briskly towards the main road, The colourful lights of Croydon offered the only illumination to this moonless night. Danny turned down a side street and stopped abruptly. He angled his head around the corner to see someone indeed appear from the doorway.

He was a tall, black man with a shaved head, his attire not that of a poor man. His full-length black leather coat and matching gloves, combined with his expensive shoes, were the luxuries of someone with style. He had an unusual swagger, as his pace increased. His arms appeared to be too long for his body, and swung liberally as he gained ground on his adversary.

Danny's walk developed into a trot. He jogged across the road and heard the clip-clop of the footsteps behind him. The pistol in his waistband was an option, but only if he was desperate.

"Want some business, honey?" Jenson ignored the request from the gum-chewing, peroxide blonde prostitute.

Danny increased his pace.

"Well, excuse me; that's no way to treat a lady," moaned the prostitute.

Danny was quick, but his pursuer was swifter. The detective's efforts would be rendered futile unless he found some cover. He held his side when he developed a stitch, and entered the smoky bingo hall. As he opened the main door, not a head turned. The congregation of eager bingo addicts kept their eyes firmly focused on their books.

Danny walked briskly, thankful for the dimmed lights. He selected a table in the centre of the hall, sat down, and received a curious stare from a toothless old woman in a headscarf. He picked up a used book from the table and placed it in front of him. Jenson removed a pen from his pocket and drooped his head towards the bingo book.

"You been running, sonny?" asked the woman. Her gaze never deviated from her books.

"Yes, listen. I'll give you ten pounds if you'll loan me your headscarf for a few minutes?"

The headscarf was promptly unravelled.

"Here, you're not one of those transparents, are you?"

"What? Transp… No, of course not."

"Well, I've nothing against them. Horses for courses, that's what I say."

"Shhh!" came the request from the next table.

The talkative woman continued. "Bloody Mary Howard, she's in here every night. No wonder her children are so..."

"Please," interrupted Jenson. "I'll give you another tenner if you shut up."

"My lips are sealed."

Jenson tied the headscarf and put his head down. His inquisitive eyes swiveled towards the entrance. The shaft of light told him someone had entered the room. The black man strolled through the room and took in each player, his eyes sharp and alert. He was a handsome man with perfect, pristine teeth. A bullet fashioned into an earring dangled from his lobe.

Jenson tried with a great degree of difficulty to control his breathing. With his head lowered, he awaited the approach of the dark stranger. The footsteps appeared closer, and the odour of expensive after-shave polluted the air. The detective shrunk further down into his seat, with one hand on his pistol.

His pursuer passed by and sat on a chair at the front of the hall, his back against the stage.

"Bingo!" Someone close to Jenson screamed and his heart skipped a beat. The joyous woman waved her winning book in the air and the lights were turned up. The black man looked towards Jenson, and screwed his eyes up to focus on the face behind the headscarf. Jenson realised he had been spotted and rose to his feet. He struggled through the ranks of the bingo players, their curses directed towards him.

The pursuer scrambled through the crowd, ignorant of the protesting folk. He knocked the woman who had been waving her books to the ground and a tirade of groans filled the bingo hall. A flat-capped pensioner barred the tall man's way. He held his liver-spotted fists up to challenge the intruder.

"Out of the way, Pops," said the pursuer in a deep voice, whilst he watched Jenson make his escape.

"I'll show you who's Pops. I never fought in the war for..."

The angry stranger pushed the old man to the ground and felt someone jump on his back. Another joined in, and a barrage of handbags rained down on him as he struggled towards the exit.

"Calm down, ladies and gentlemen," came the plea from the camp bingo-caller.

The intruder finally broke through and turned to face his attackers. He straightened up, removed his pistol from his holster and waved it about menacingly.

"Ahhhhhh!" He screamed at the top of his voice.

The startled crowd backed off.

"Wrinkly, decrepit bastards!"

The diversion gave Jenson the time he needed for his escape. He turned the corner and headed for his rendezvous with Sophie.

******

Jenson paid the taxi driver and walked towards St Paul's Cathedral, its imposing shape silhouetted against the night sky. The wind had died down and it was a pleasant evening. A small group of pilgrims bearing lit candles sang hymns as they sat and swayed on the steps.

Jenson spotted Sophie, even though she wore a baseball cap and sweatshirt in an attempt to disguise her gender. She sat alone on the steps, a worried look etched across her pretty features.

Jenson nodded at her and realised by her blackened eyes that she had been crying. He sat beside Sophier and placed a comforting arm around her, something completely out of character for the big man. Her face looked so innocent, devoid of the make-up. Sophie attempted to light a cigarette with trembling hands.

"Here, let me," offered Jenson. He held her lighter to the tip.

"Danny, I'm so bloody scared. Where is Vince?"

"When's the last time you saw him?"

"Tuesday morning. We left you and went back to work at The Echo. Madison wasn't too happy with us after the murder of Maurice, but he's not about to advertise the fact he sanctioned the scheme. He told us to cool it for a few days and see what developed. Vince went home, and I haven't seen him since that day."

"I don't think he's dead, Sophie."

She took a long draw on her cigarette. "What makes you think that?"

"They only know about me. Okay, they know Clare was an impostor, but don't actually know who you are. They know someone else helped me, but they can't have traced Vince. His name was never mentioned in any of this."

"Clare phoned me earlier today," said Sophie.

"Oh, what did she want?"

"The police have questioned her. Don't worry, she won't say anything. I warned her she might get a visit from them, and she was prepared. That Clare had the same first name as Maurice's widow is the only reason they questioned her. No doubt Cupid's Arrow will have erased all of Clare's details from their database. Apparently, Reverend Keller and Maurice's friend, the other sham witness to the wedding have talked. The police know about the wedding, but they apparently still don't know the reason for it. Luckily, Clare had alibis for the days she was supposed to be with Maurice."

Jenson chewed vigorously on his gum. "Entwistle may hold the key to all of this. If I can prove he knows Chivers or any of the others, then the enquiry team will have to believe me."

"So where does Duncan Brady fit into this, Danny?"

"Brady?"

"You did see the evening paper, didn't you?"

"No, what's happened?"

"He was picked up for robbing a bus, and it so happens that his dabs were the same as the ones on the bomb that killed DC Benton."

"What! It doesn't make sense. He stole money from Bojangles. Surely, they cannot be working together."

Sophie went on. "He's been transferred to a secure psychiatric ward in Broadmoor."

"Are you sure? They think he's insane?"

"What are we going to do, Danny?"

"Jesus, this could work in our favour."

"How, I don't understand?"

"If Brady talks, he could reveal that Bojangles was probably hired by Cupid's Arrow. Then hopefully, they'll collapse, just like a pack of cards."

"But, will he talk?"

"He might, if Bojangles doesn't get to him first… Broadmoor, eh?"

"What are you thinking?"

"Evil thoughts, Sophie, my princess. Evil thoughts."

Chapter Twenty Nine

Clare Dougal was about to indulge in her Friday evening treat, a chicken chow mien and a chilled bottle of chardonnay. Clare had a strict regime, which she occasionally wavered. She ate sparingly throughout the week, watched the scales in anticipation of any weight gain, and Fridays, she spoilt herself rotten. True, she no longer paraded the catwalks of Rome and Paris, but she still lived comfortably, and earned a generous salary by modelling for catalogues and magazines.

She settled down on her sofa and brought the television to life with a deft flick of the remote control. Her long legs were folded beneath her as she tucked into the chow mien, her eyes fixed on the screen. The fork stopped mid-flight on its journey to her mouth. Her instincts told her something was not right. Clare felt she was not alone in the room. No physical presence offered itself to the ex-model, but she sensed that someone was behind her. The reflection off her television captured a shape, a large shape, which caused the hairs to stand up on the back of her neck. She was paralysed with fear, unable to turn her head to confront the intruder.

She heard the breathing when he lowered his head close behind her. The reek of garlic and the warm breath on her neck eliminated any claims of a vivid imagination. The man paced slowly around the sofa and sat beside her.

Clare whimpered softly and managed to focus on the tall, black man in the leather coat. He smiled at her and took the fork from her trembling fingers. He selected a large portion of her chow mien and savoured it.

"Mmm, lovely. I don't like your taste in television though. What is this shit, you're watching?" The voice was deep, yet kind.

"B...Big Brother," she stuttered, and watched him as he helped himself to another mouthful of her supper.

"Ah, chardonnay if I'm not mistaken," he said. The intruder licked his lips and drank from Claire's glass.

"W-what do you want? Who are you?"

"Women, they always ask two questions at a time. Why do you think that is? What do I want? Just some information and then I'll let you get on with your life… Who am I? You don't expect me to answer that, now do you? Okay, this is how we'll play it. I'll ask you a question and you answer me. If I don't like the answer, then I'll hurt you. I'll hurt you real bad. Understand the rules?"

She nodded frantically and placed her meal on the coffee table.

"Good. What is your name?"

"Cl-Clare Dougal."

"Very good, you're getting the hang of this, Clare. Now, who's been using your name whilst working for Cupid's Arrow?"

She hesitated before she spoke. "I don't know what you're talking about."

The stranger shook his head and rubbed his gloved hands together. He lashed out with his fist and caught the startled girl flush in the mouth. She fell back onto the sofa and nursed her cut mouth.

"Wrong answer, white sweetmeat. You don't even resemble the girl working for Cupid's Arrow, so who's been using your name?" He nodded slowly, waved his hand, and encouraged the words from Clare's mouth. None came. He towered over the cowering girl and pointed a menacing finger at her. "Stay put, girl. Move from here and I'll feed your innards to those fish over there."

He strolled towards the kitchen and Clare contemplated a dash towards the door. His ominous threat persuaded her otherwise. He returned with a length of green cord that Clare had used as a washing line.

"Hands."

She hesitated again.

"Give me your fucking hands!"

He tied the cord around her hands and threw the other end over one of the beams in the ceiling. He jerked the line aggressively and Clare's hands shot to the ceiling. She screamed in pain as the large man pulled powerfully on the cord and forced Clare onto her tiptoes. A final tug had the frightened girl dangling in the air, her feet inches from the floor. He tethered the cord to the door handle and removed his jacket.

"P-please, don't hurt me?" she begged.

"Too late for that, baby, unless you want to tell me who the girl is?"

"I-I swear, I don't know."

He punched her forcefully in the stomach and she gasped for air. She choked back the tears.

"You swear! People nowadays have no scruples. I'm a deeply religious man and I look down in contempt at people who swear to save their skins. To swear is sacred, not something to use as an escape clause."

He placed his face close to hers and licked the blood from her lips. She tried to turn her head away, only for him to grasp her face with his large hand. He continued to lick her mouth, until the blood was erased. "One more chance, babe. Your friend, who is she?"

"Don't you think I'd tell you if I knew?" she sobbed.

The black man proceeded to take off his clothes, and folded them neatly into a pile on the sofa. He faced her and she closed her eyes. "What's the matter, white trash? Never seen a real man before?"

"Please, d-don't hurt me."

"Please don't hurt me," he mimicked in a high voice. He gripped her blouse, pulled vigorously, and dislodged the buttons. Again, he headed for the kitchen, and left Clare to dangle helplessly.

Her eyes bulged in terror when she eyed the shining object in his hand. He cut away her skirt, before he done the same to her bra. The knickers were torn from her, and she tried in vain to cross her legs in an attempt to retain her dignity.

"My, my, not a bad body if I say so myself. Perhaps I'll have some fun before I kill you."

She cried hysterically, the effort to hide her private parts aborted.

Clare's tormentor was naked, apart from his gloves. He cupped her full breasts and watched her reaction. "Have you ever had a black man,

Clare? No, I don't believe you have." His hand went between her legs and she grimaced as he laughed softly. He evidently enjoyed her discomfort.

"Well, I'm afraid I'm not going to give you the pleasure; you're just not my type."

He reached for the knife and ran it across her breasts slowly. The cold steel forced the girl to grimace. Without warning, he made a long cut mark across her stomach, just deep enough to cause pain.

"Ah! Please no."

"That's entirely up to you, girl."

Clare was silent, and he made another long incision.

"Oh dear, and you a model as well. Listen; let's stop fucking about. Enough of the bullshit. The next one will be across your kisser. What's it to be?"

"Y-you're making a big mistake. I-I don't know this girl."

He held the blade against her cheek. "Now, I have a decision to make. Are you telling the truth or not? Personally, I think you are telling the truth, but my employers need to know for certain."

The blade cut deeply into her face as the knife ran across her mouth, until it sliced the other cheek.

"See, you have a permanent smile now… I don't suppose you have anything to tell me, have you?"

She shook her head and the blood oozed down her tearful face.

Again, he headed for the kitchen. This time he returned with another implement of torture. He plugged the electric iron in and left it to heat up. She felt his warm, naked body against hers, as he took her face in his hand.

"My, my, what a mess. They do say that plastic surgery can do wonders nowadays though. This girl; she must mean a great deal to you… Hey, you're not a dyke are you?"

His erection pressed against her stomach. He kissed her on the mouth and she watched him lick the blood from his lips. His eyes were unblinking, such evil, intense eyes. She focused on his bullet earring and tried to blank the pain from her mind.

"Serious stuff now, baby. Come on, save yourself a lot of pain. Who is she?"

The television flickered in the dimness of the room. The fish tank gave off a friendly pretentious green glow, so out of place in this torture chamber.

Clare blanked out her emotions and crooned softly, some anonymous song in an unreal world. She would wake up any minute now; oh yes, and then she will laugh and be so relieved, as always. Clare had a built in mechanism in her system. She had the ability to terminate her nightmares.

The girl felt the searing pain on her stomach and realised this was no dream. She opened her mouth to scream, but there was only silence. Her torturer's face glistened with perspiration; the ecstasy on his coffee-coloured face, evidence of his enjoyment. He withdrew the iron and stooped over to inspect the wound.

"Shit! You can smell the flesh cooking. Awesome. Are you ready to talk now?"

Again, she shook her head. He held the iron inches from her face, and she gasped at the intensity of the heat.

"Well, it's your call, honey. You've got balls, I'll give you that. Not literally of course," he laughed. "Why are you protecting her? Do you honestly think she'd do the same for you? How old are you, twenty-eight, thirty? You have the rest of your life to live for. Tell me her name and I'll cut you down and walk out of your life forever. Your scars will heal and you'll not hear from me again… You tell the police I wore a mask of course."

"W-what about her? What will you do to her?"

His eyes lit up at the admission that she actually did know the girl. "I merely want to speak to her. I don't want to harm her."

"Y-you sick bastard! Do you expect me to believe that?"

"I've told you, I'm a religious man and I never break my word. I swear on the holy bible."

"Sophie Wilson," croaked Clare.

"What was that, babe?"

"S-Sophie Wilson…. Her name's Sophie Wilson."

"And where can I find this Sophie Wilson?"

"She works for The Echo. Sh-she's a photographer. Now cut me down."

"Cut you down?" The hired killer frowned at his distraught victim. "I'm sorry, darling, but I don't think that will be a good idea do you?"

"You swore! Y-you gave your word."

"So I did. Oh, well, I guess Satan will have a place for me when I'm ready."

He brought the iron onto her face and she attempted to scream, which prompted her attacker to cover her mouth with his hand. She blacked out and the dark stranger inspected his work, like an artist would his painting. He reached for the knife and brought it across her throat.

An advertisement appeared on the television and the naked man smiled and sang along with the ditty. He proceeded to dress before he swallowed the remainder of the chardonnay.

"A little dry for me, sweet cake."

Chapter Thirty

The same evening that Clare Dougal was viciously murdered, Detective Sergeant Jenson lurked in the shadows of a shop doorway and watched the boisterous group of revellers leave the wine bar in Kings Road. He was unshaved, and the bags beneath his eyes were evidence of the sleepless nights in his quest to evade detection. He had stayed at a small hotel in Paddington; the risk of him returning to his home too great.

One of the group waved to the others, walked in the opposite direction, and tried to hail a taxi. Jenson jogged across the road to confront the young detective. The face registered, but Danny Jenson was the last man Robbie Felgate expected to encounter that evening.

"Fucking hell, Danny, what are you doing here? Christ, you look like shit."

"Robbie, I need a favour from you."

Felgate looked around anxiously, to ensure they were alone. He edged into the darkness of a doorway for added security. "You're not supposed to make any contact with anyone from the station, you know that. My arse is on the line here."

Detective Constable Felgate had been with CID for two years. When Jenson took him under his wing, he had been as green as grass. Felgate was not a natural detective; in fact, he was downright awful. He had been coupled with Jenson for three months, and the older man had felt sorry for him, going as far as to let Felgate take credits for certain arrests, and even perjuring for him. Jenson was cashing his chips in.

"I need you to half inch my ID, Robbie."

"Shit, Danny. You know I can't do that."

"Can't or won't? I've bailed you out countless times."

"Yes, and I appreciate it, I really do, but this is different. I could lose my job over this."

"And I could have lost mine by perjuring myself for you. You beat Griffiths to a pulp, Robbie. The poor bastard wasn't even in the country when the robbery occurred."

"Okay, so I made a mistake, but Griffiths is pure evil anyway. Don't you ever make mistakes?"

"Oh yes, I make mistakes. I've made quite a few lately… Listen, Robbie; I wouldn't ask this if it wasn't important. I need the ID, just for a few hours. I'll return it to you and nobody will be the wiser."

"I don't know. Where's it kept?"

"In Entwistle's desk."

"Stone the fucking crows, Danny; are you serious?"

"Entwistle never arrives at the nick before eight 'o'clock. You get there early, before anyone else. It's that simple."

"And what if the desk's locked?"

"Entwistle doesn't lock his desk. He has nothing worth nicking, apart from his whiskey that is."

"I don't know." The fresh-faced detective held his head as he pondered.

"Okay, I'll try; but if there's any risk, then no deal."

"That's all I ask."

"I don't suppose you're going to tell me why you need it?"

Jenson detected the strong reek of alcohol on his young colleague's breath. "You don't want to know, mate… Meet me at nine-tomorrow morning in Store Street. I'll be inside the telephone box. As you approach, I'll push the door open slightly. Toss the ID inside."

Felgate checked the surroundings, before he departed into the darkness.

******

Jenson switched off his the engine and stared up at the imposing sight of Broadmoor psychiatric hospital, with its large archway and twin towers. Broadmoor houses some of the most dangerous criminals in the country, but reference to it as a prison is scorned upon by the officials there. The inmates are classed as patients, and they are there because of their mental illness.

Jenson slid down the seat of his newly purchased, second hand black Escort. Chief Superintendent Hargreaves and a younger man emerged from within the walls of the notorious hospital and headed for their car. Jenson waited until they had departed before he made his move.

The elderly prison warder challenged Jenson when he entered the archway.

"Yes, sir, can I help you?"

"Yes, I'm here to see Duncan Brady." Jenson displayed his ID.

"Are you expected, Sergeant?" asked the warder, who checked his book.

"My colleagues have just been to see him, but I've still a few loose ends to tie up."

The craggy-faced official picked up the telephone and waited. "Dr Bullock, there's another detective from CID here to see Duncan Brady. A Sergeant Jenson."

The warder nodded when the instructions were relayed to him. "Okay, Sergeant, Dr Bullock will be here shortly."

The large door was unlocked and a white-coated man, who looked no more than thirty years of age greeted him. He had a charming smile and shoulder length hair, his piercing grey eyes a most attractive feature. This was not a man who fitted the criteria of a psychiatric doctor. Someone with a beard and spectacles would have been more fitting.

"Sergeant Jenson, I'm Dr Bullock, the deputy head psychologist. I understand you wish to see Duncan Brady? Your colleagues have just left."

"Yes, I know, I've just been assigned to the case and need to question him. You can check with Charing Cross police station if you wish. Here, I'll give you the number."

"No, that won't be necessary, Sergeant. I have a busy schedule, but will accompany you."

They passed through another large gate and entered the warmth of the secure unit. The slamming of doors and the anonymous voices echoed around the ward.

"So why's Brady in a psychiatric ward, Doctor?"

"You don't know?"

"I've just arrived back from the Seychelles. I'm still to get acquainted with Brady."

"You don't seem to have acquired much of a tan… I'll keep you in suspense, Detective. I'm sure you'll be intrigued by what you're going to see. What do you know about Duncan Brady?"

They progressed down a long, bare corridor.

Jenson talked as they walked. "He was lodging at the same boarding house as a suspect in a murder case, until he disappeared. There appears to be no evidence of his existence whatsoever. His fingerprints were found on the fragment of the pipe bomb that was used in the murder of one of my colleagues. He was apparently picked up for attempting to rob a bus. Not a reason for being locked up in a secure psychiatric ward, surely?"

"All will be revealed, Sergeant… Dennis, open the door if you please?"

"Should I shackle him, Doctor?"

"Heavens no, that won't be necessary."

For a hospital, the room certainly resembled a prison cell. The cell stank of disinfectant, and the coldness bit into the bones of Jenson. Maybe it was just his imagination, but he had a feeling he had seen the pathetic figure of Brady before.

Brady huddled in the corner, clad in a blue gown. His long, blonde, greasy hair and wild beard remained unwashed, as he peered through his thick spectacles at his visitors. His hands were wrapped around his knees, as he rocked back and forth.

The doctor smiled at his patient. "Duncan, it is Duncan isn't it? Sorry to intrude, but you have another visitor. Sergeant Jenson is here to see you."

"Tell him to fuck off."

"Now, now, Duncan, don't be like that. Come on, sit at the table; it's much more comfortable than the cold floor."

He reluctantly rose to his feet. The burly prison warder watched alertly for any signs of aggression.

"That's better, Duncan. Now sit down please."

He obeyed the doctor and sat with his head bowed.

"The sergeant wants to ask you a few questions; is that okay, Duncan?"

"I want a tab."

Dr Bullock nodded to the warder, who placed a tobacco tin and a box of matches on the table. Brady looked up at his interrogator and expertly rolled a cigarette, without taking his eyes off Jenson. He lit the roll-up, smiled, and coughed when he blew out the smoke.

"Duncan, I can call you Duncan can't I?" asked Jenson. "Are you acquainted with your former lodger, Mr Bojangles?"

Brady slowly shook his head from side to side.

"Okay, can you tell me how your fingerprints came to be on the bomb that exploded outside Charing Cross police station, killing a police officer?"

A loud cough followed. "Excuse me! What is this you've given me? Camel shit?"

Jenson felt the blood drain from his face as he heard the feminine voice.

"My cigarillos. Where's my cigarillos?"

The doctor intervened. "Okay, Goldie, I'll fetch you some cigarillos… How are you today?"

"I want a mirror. How's a girl supposed to look her best without a mirror?"

Jenson went to speak, but a restraining hand from the doctor prevented him.

Dr Bullock continued. "You know that's not possible, Goldie. No sharp objects are allowed in your room."

"Room, you call this a room? Why am I here? You cannot hold me. I've done nothing wrong."

"But Duncan Brady has, Goldie. Mr Bojangles too."

DS Jenson looked on bewilderedly.

The patient raised his voice. "That bastard murdered Mrs Parish. I don't know why I'm here. I've already told you, I don't know the whereabouts of either Bojangles or Brady."

"Goldie, you're here for your own good. You're sick and we hope to cure you."

"I'm not sick. I'm a woman, I tell you! I'm a woman in the body of a man."

Goldie struggled to her feet. She touched her face and her eyes bulged wildly. "My face! What have you done to my face? You bastards, what is this?" She proceeded to claw at her own face.

The prison warder was joined by a colleague in their struggle to restrain Goldie. Her shrill screams could still be heard with the departure of Jenson and the doctor.

"What the hell is going on here, Doc?" quizzed the puzzled detective.

"Come on, I'll buy you a cup of coffee and explain."

The canteen was empty, apart from two other doctors at the far end of the room. Jenson settled opposite the doctor and eagerly awaited his explanation.

"Sergeant, Duncan Brady and Goldie Lamour, along with Mr Bojangles are the same person. The patient is suffering from Multiple Personality Syndrome, known today as Dissociate Identity Disorder."

"Split personality?"

"If you want to call it that, yes. This disorder is usually triggered off at a young age by some form of abuse, possible sexual or a trauma. A natural disaster perhaps, or having been a victim of torture. This disorder is extremely rare, and the child develops an effective means of escape by dissociating him or herself from terror, whenever they feel threatened. They develop what is known as alters, or other personalities. These alters have their own memories, and even though they know of each other's existence, they are unaware they are living in the same body… This disorder can lead to bouts of amnesia. It can also be a child's way of craving attention, something possibly lacking in their childhood."

Jenson listened with interest. "You're telling me these three alters live apparently normal lives?"

"Yes. A sufferer may encounter strange clothes or objects that they have no recollection of. Take Goldie there; she was confused when discovering she had hair on her face. Her natural reaction was to regard us with suspicion, hence her trying to tear the beard from her face. Whoever that man is, has at least three alters. Given that no records can be found of any of the three personalities, I'd hazard a guess that the secret of who this actually person is has not surfaced yet. He may have more alters, and he's being monitored twenty-four hours a day."

"Hold on," said Jenson. "So the beard is false?"

"The beard, the wig, it's all part of the alter of Duncan Brady."

"So why not remove them and we can see what he really looks like?"

"In time, Sergeant. We have to be patient here. This is a most delicate matter. The wig and beard have not been removed for a very good reason. When the actual host appears, I want to convince him of his illness, and what better way than to let him see for himself?"

Jenson countered. "Are you sure you're doing the correct thing? If we issue a picture of him, we can identify who he is."

"Why the hurry? He's not going anywhere, and after all; he's not actually guilty of murder. Bojangles is responsible for that."

The detective pondered. "At least that explains the fingerprints being the same... How can he live all these lives? Someone must be missing him. He lived at Gower Street, or at least his alters did. Why hasn't he been missed?"

The doctor blew on his hot coffee. "At this moment, we're unsure how long he remains as a respective alter. It could be minutes or it could be days. As I related to Chief Superintendent Hargreaves, someone may come forward, missing a husband or a son. It will be only a matter of time before he reveals his true self to us. Another theory is that perhaps his condition has deteriorated over the years. Maybe his real self is locked away, never to be released again. He is confused. First of all, you have Brady, an uncouth thief. Maybe this man had an inner obsession to steal. Goldie the transvestite. That is the insecure side of him coming out. He's questioning his own sexuality. Bojangles, now there's an interesting character. A cool, cold-hearted killer. The hatred in our friend has been released into this alter."

"Can he ever be cured?"

"In time he may recover. He will have no recollection of his alter egos. They'll be erased from his life."

Jenson was curious. "If Bojangles gave evidence in court, would he be classed as a credible witness?"

"No way. His testimony would be inadmissible on the grounds that he was mentally unfit to stand trial... Is that a problem?"

"I'm back to square one, Doc. Thanks anyway. You've been most helpful."

"Not at all. It's been my pleasure."

They shook hands and Dr Bullock escorted Jenson to the main gate. The troubled detective sat in his car and pondered for a few minutes. He digested all the facts of this astonishing turn of events. Cupid's Arrow was in the clear, and the funny thing about it was, they probably weren't even aware.

Chapter Thirty One

Saturday lunchtime and various journalists and office workers sat at the tables outside the Cat & Canary pub. Sophie sat alone and smoked She stared out over the river towards the Isle of Dogs, and her confused mind deliberated her destiny. Slattery had been missing for five days now and she had given up what faint hope she had of seeing him alive. Cheryl had called at the office that morning, no doubt to serve her husband divorce papers.

Sophie sipped her gin and tonic and mused. *Christ, I'm to be cited as the other woman.* She felt so alone, isolated in a corrupt world that wanted to claim her as its next victim.

The overcast sky threatened rain, but she needed the fresh air. She was smothered in her own ambiguity. She swayed towards going to the police; after all, surely they would protect her. To Slattery, it mattered not now, and Jenson, after all he had done for them deserved her support. Besides, Jenson had withheld her name in order to protect her.

As she weighed up the pros and cons of going to the police, a tall, black man in designer sunglasses confronted her. She looked up at this colossal of a man who was dressed in black. His kind smile made an impression on her.

"Excuse me. Is this seat taken?" he asked.

She shook her head without speaking and returned to her ponderous evaluation of her dilemma.

"More and more of them are appearing every day, eh?" said the stranger.

"What?" asked Sophie. She took another long drag on her cigarette.

"Cranes. The bloody wharf is covered in them. I remember when this dockland was waste ground."

"Really?" sighed Sophie, who wished she were alone.

"Jonah. Jonah Kumar," he said, and offered his manicured hand.

"Sophie Wilson."

"How about a drink, Sophie?"

"No thank you."

"Aw, come on. Your glass is almost empty?"

"I have to be back at the office in... Oh, go on then, but just the one," she relented, after she glanced at her wristwatch.

She ground out her cigarette and lit another with shaking hands. Sophie had been popping the pills recently in an attempt to combat her nerves. She realised she smoked too much and never ate enough recently, but her health was the last of her worries. The photographer jumped when the chimes of *You are my sunshine* escaped from her handbag. She received humorous stares from the other customers and reached for the offending mobile phone.

"Hello."

"Lucy, it's Danny. Where are you?"

"Having lunch at a pub on Canary Wharf. Any news on Vince?"

"Sophie, listen. Meet me in one hour's time at the same place as we met earlier. Don't go back to The Echo, and don't return home."

"What is it, Danny?"

"You haven't seen the lunchtime news, have you?"

"No, I'm outside."

"I don't know how to tell you this… Clare was found murdered in her home this morning."

"No, no, nooo! Why would they kill her?" She sobbed uncontrollably.

"I called a friend of mine at the station. She'd been tortured."

"Clare, oh, poor Clare. This is all my fault. I should never have involved her."

"Snap out of it, Sophie. We may have to change our strategy."

"Strategy, ah! Did we ever have any strategy?"

Several people stared at her curiously when she raised her voice.

"Bojangles is no longer a problem. He cannot testify, even if he wanted to."

"He's dead?"

There was a pause. "Bojangles, Duncan Brady and Goldie Lamour are the same person."

"You've lost me, Danny."

"I'll explain later… Listen; have you noticed anyone following you?"

"No, why should I have?"

"You have to face facts. Clare must have told her killer who you are. He's no doubt the same man who's been following me."

She watched nervously as her admirer approached, laden with fresh drinks. "What does this man look like?"

"He's black. Built like a brick shithouse."

She lowered her voice and her eyes regarded the stranger attentively. "Tell me he doesn't have a bullet for an earring?"

"Fuck! Sophie, what's…?"

She switched off the mobile phone.

Kumar placed her drink in front of her and noticed the phone in her hand. "Hell, baby, you are cold, aren't you? Maybe you want to go inside?"

"No! I'm just fine."

"Are you sure, honey? You're shaking like a rattlesnake on heat."

"I'm fine, thank you… Tell me, what do you do?"

He took a sip of his coca-cola. "What do I do?"

"Yes, your job, what is it?"

"Let's just say, I put things right."

"You put things right?"

"Hey girl, you are nervous. You've already got a ciggy on the go."

She returned the cigarette to the packet.

Kumar continued. "I sort of do odd jobs. You know; build a wall here, a conservatory there. You could say I'm a general dogsbody."

"I see."

"And you? What do you do?"

"I'm a photographer with The Echo."

"No! That mother of a newspaper over there? That's one mighty, glamorous job, baby."

"Not always."

His eyes devoured her. "Mmm, I took you as a model. You sure do have the looks."

Sophie looked into his eyes and realised he was toying with her. "Excuse me. I need the ladies room."

He politely rose from his seat, and towered above the denim-clad girl. Sophie offered a pretentious smile. She walked swiftly to the ladies room and once inside, she looked for a means of escape. The windows backed onto the river, and given that she could not swim, the escape route was not an option. She paced up and down and mused over her plan of action. She left the ladies room, walked to the bar, and ensured she was out of sight from Kumar.

"Macca, I need a favour."

The silver-haired landlord with numerous tattoos that covered his arms approached. "Sure, Sophie, just you name it."

"I'm sitting out there with this big, black guy. He's coming onto me real strong, Macca."

The landlord winked. "Nudge nudge, say no more. Don't worry about it, luv, I'll deal with him.

Sophie rejoined Kumar.

"You been sick or something, girl. You look awful."

"You ought to see me first thing in the morning."

"Is that an invitation? I might just take you up on that."

Sophie saw Macca approach out of the side of her eye.

"Excuse me, sir, can you please come inside?"

Kumar stared up at the landlord with steely eyes. "What's the problem, man?"

"I'd rather we go indoors."

"Yeah, well I'd rather we didn't. Now piss off while I enjoy my drink."

"Okay, if that's the way you want it. I'll call the police."

"What the fuck are you going on about, man?"

The chattering from the other tables ceased, as all eyes were on the confrontation.

Macca cleared his throat. "The twenty pound note you passed across the bar, sir. I'm afraid it's a forgery."

"Say what? I gave you a ten, man."

"I'm sorry, sir, but you definitely gave me twenty."

"Shit, you're teasing my black arse, right?"

"I'm afraid not. Either we can do this inside, in a civilised manner, or I can call the police. I accept that the note may have been passed onto you, but I'm afraid I can't take it."

"Okay, what if I just gave you another twenty right now?"

"I'm sorry. The reason I asked you to come inside was to save you any embarrassment. I must jot down the serial number, as well as your name and address."

"Well, do it here."

The landlord was adamant. "Inside, sir."

Kumar eyed Sophie suspiciously, and glanced to see the onlookers turn away one by one. "I know I gave you a ten, but let's get this over with."

Kumar followed Macca to the bar, and glanced over his shoulder to see Sophie caress her drink.

"I really didn't want to embarrass you, sir, that's why I asked you to come inside."

"Yeah, yeah, you've already told me. Enough shit, man, just give me the goddamn dodgy twenty back and I'll pay for the drinks."

The landlord opened the till and removed a large wad of notes.

"What gives?" moaned Kumar. "The dodgy note must be on the top, right?"

Macca held each note up to the light and inspected them individually.

"Are you fucking with me, whitey?"

"Funny, I can't seem to find it. Maybe it was genuine after all. I do apologise, sir. Accept the drinks on the house?"

"Fuck you and fuck your drinks!"

The irate man walked out into the open air to see a red mini speed away in the distance, the untouched drinks still on the table.

He turned to face the smiling landlord, who whistling away whilst he dried a glass. Kumar put up a threatening finger, before he conceded that he'd been tricked. He ran for his car and left behind a chorus of laughs.

Chapter Thirty Two

"Take her past Westminster again, Larry, that's a good chap."

Lance Tyreman's tanned face showed signs of anxiety. He leant on the railing of his cruiser and eyed the landmarks of London. Matthew Torrance joined him, his plate laden with food.

"This is such a fucking mess, Matthew."

"Will Brady talk?" asked the obese man.

"That's the million-dollar question. Why didn't Bojangles tell Chivers he had a partner? In fact, where is the son of a bitch?"

"Probably lying low, Lance, after all; his arse is up for grabs too with the arrest of Brady."

"This is shit. We might as well have hired *Inspector Clouseau* to do the job. This Kumar; he's no better than Bojangles."

"He did find out who the girl was."

"But what good did it do? It's only a matter of time before the law listens to her. And this bastard, Jenson; he's turning out to be a right pain in the arse."

"I think now would be a good time to take a holiday, Lance. It makes sense to be abroad when the shit hits the fan."

"Maybe you're right. I'll see to the transfer of my money, and I suggest you do the same."

"Can we get to Brady before he stands trial?" asked Torrance, who nibbled on a chicken leg."

"Not in bloody Broadmoor we can't. Mind you, he still has to appear at a hearing to arrange his trial date. Tuesday isn't it? Our favourite chief inspector hasn't been in touch for a while. I'll have a word with him and find out where the hearing is to take place. Also, he could fill us in about the security arrangements."

"That's a bit risky isn't it?"

Tyreman cupped his hands over his eyes and looked along the deck.

"Where's fucking Chivers? Chivers! Get your arse over here."

"Mr Tyreman."

"We have another job for your incompetent killer. Brady is to attend his hearing on Tuesday morning and I want your man to take him out."

"But..."

"Yes?"

"He'll be well guarded. How can...?"

"Offer your man treble money. I'll contact you with the security details.I don't care how, but get the job done."

"Yes, Mr Tyreman."

"Oh, and Chivers, be ready to leave for the continent at a moment's notice."

"The continent?"

"What do you think? Mexico sounds good. We're relying on Brady being eliminated, and if he's not, then *'we're all going on a summer holiday'*. A long, long holiday."

Tyreman lit a cigar. "Any idea yet who this other friend of Jenson's is?"

"No. We were hoping to get that information from this photographer tart," said Chivers.

Tyreman scowled at his employee. "We were until this bungling hitman of yours allowed her to escape. If he's the snooping reporter who arranged to have my photo took; you can bet he also works for The Echo. I'll do some checking."

"You do that, Ross, you do that. Okay, that concludes our business. Take in the marvellous sights, gentlemen. It may be the last time you do."

******

DCI Entwistle entered his office, tossed his pork pie hat towards the rack, and missed the hanger as usual. He cursed and stooped over to retrieve it. He realised he was not alone.

"Good afternoon, Chief Inspector. I'm sorry for this intrusion, but your office appears to be a little cooler."

The presence of Chief Superintendent Hargreaves was most unexpected. "That's perfectly alright, sir. What can I do for you?"

Hargreaves rose from the chief inspector's chair and invited him to sit in it. The grey-haired man walked to the window and looked out. "Chief Inspector, the girl who was murdered on Friday, Clare Dougal. What do you know about her?"

"Not a lot really. Model, twenty-seven years old."

"Didn't you question her shortly after the death of Maurice Candy?"

DCI Entwistle loosened his tie and poured himself a glass of water. "Yes, that's correct."

The chief superintendent noticed that his colleague perspired heavily. "In fact, Clare Dougal was the name of Candy's missing wife, was it not?"

"Yes, that's why we questioned her."

"And you thought it not important enough to report this to me?"

"With all due respect, sir, this has nothing to do with you."

"Oh, but it has, Chief Inspector, it bloody has. You see, I, as the investigating officer in this case require all the facts. Do I make myself clear?"

DCI Entwistle wiped his saturated face with his handkerchief. "The murder of Clare Dougal is unrelated to the case you're investigating, sir."

The chief superintendent scowled. "Give me some fucking credit here, Chief Inspector. If you cannot see the link, then maybe you're in the wrong job… There's an awful reek in this department, and I detest the smell of corruption."

"Are you accusing…?"

"Let me finish, man!" The chief superintendent leaned over the table, his rugged face and his large hands testified to his youthful days as a boxer. "I've done some checking into this case. Lance Tyreman, Matthew Torrance and George Mikhos all had a large sum of money transferred to their bank accounts shortly after the deaths of Rosie Cochrane and Elizabeth Todd. The accumulated amount is very close to that invested in the bogus companies. I've also checked the employees at Cupid's Arrow, past and present, and can find no evidence that these girls ever worked there; but there is something extraordinary about this escort agency. I questioned four of the girls, and amazingly, each one did not know a single other girl who worked there. They have been dissuaded from making contact with any of their colleagues. Don't you find this strange, Chief Inspector?"

"Strange?"

"Perhaps they didn't want anyone to know about Rosie and Elizabeth, because after they were murdered, they would not be missed. Something to think about, eh, Chief Inspector?"

DCI Entwistle took another sip of water. "What are you getting at?"

The senior officer thumped the desk. "Sir! What are you getting at, sir?.. I'll tell you what I'm getting at. Sergeant Jenson's story looks more credible, the more I look into it. I'm starting to believe that maybe he was telling the truth after all."

DCI Entwistle protested. "Jenson's a bad egg. Just ask anyone... sir!"

The chief superintendent stared intensely at his troubled colleague. "It transpires that DS Jenson has disappeared. His enquiry is to begin in one week, and personally, I don't think he'll show up, do you?"

"How should I know?"

"You still maintain you have never met Lance Tyreman, Matthew Torrance or George Mikhos?"

"Yes… This is absurd. Am I being investigated?"

"No, of course not, Chief Inspector; not someone with your impeccable record. I just thought I'd let you know that I've got your card marked."

"You've got this so wrong, sir."

"Have I? Have I really? I hope so for your sake, because you know what they do to ex-coppers inside, don't you?"

"Have you finished, sir?"

"Almost… When Bojangles talks, and I have no doubt he will, all will be revealed."

DCI Entwistle grinned. "He won't be allowed to stand trial, and you know it. He's criminally insane."

"Well, that's for his brief to prove, isn't it?"

DCI Entwistle swallowed another mouthful of water. "Bojangles doesn't exist, Chief Superintendent. He's a figment of his imagination."

"Oh, he exists all right. He's responsible for those murders. It will be most interesting when we discover the true identity of this man, don't you think."

"Now have you finished, sir? I have a heavy workload."

"Yes, I think so. Have a nice day, Chief Inspector… Oh, and by the way. Nice car. It must have cost you a packet."

Chapter Thirty Three

DCI Entwistle, Commander Sadler, Dr Bullock and solicitor, Jonathan Hall travelled in silence as they approached the imposing sight of the Central Criminal Court, more commonly known as the Old Bailey. They gazed through the rain dotted car windows at the hostile crowd, who were shepherded behind the barriers. Ahead of them was the prison van that contained the enigmatic killer, who had captured both media and public attention. The numerous flashes from the media cameras, merged with the blue rotating lights of the two accompanying police cars.

News had leaked out that Duncan Brady was in fact Charlie Bojangles. Dr Bullock had relented and taken away the disguise of Brady, due to the insistence of the murder enquiry team. Only the occupants of this car, and the two escorting prison officers had seen what the mysterious prisoner actually looked like. After the initial hearing in which the trial date was to be set, the prisoner's photograph was to be taken, and circulated nationwide in order to identify him.

It was Dr Bullock who broke the silence. "This is so wrong. This man is sick and not evil. That he has been brought here to this media circus is an outrage."

"Tell that to the families of Rosie Cochrane, Dorothy Parish and Jamie Benton, Doctor," moaned Commander Sadler.

The doctor ignored the comment. "I'm applying for an application to detain him in Broadmoor, Commander, on the grounds of his mental health. That man needs treatment, not punishment."

"Really? Are you certain that he's not faking in order to escape prison?"

"That is for the judge to decide, but in my professional opinion, there is no way that man is faking."

Above the din of the sirens and the baying pack, the loud engine of a motorcycle could be heard. The lone rider stopped abruptly and watched proceedings from afar. He lifted his visor when the handcuffed prisoner emerged from the prison van, his head shrouded by a blanket. Escorted by two prison officers, the manacled man stooped forward and loped swiftly.

DCI Entwistle and his entourage followed closely behind and walked the gauntlet of hate. Several of the spectators jeered and spat at the elusive figure. His rapid footsteps plodded through a shallow puddle.

The motorcycle engine sparked into life and the machine sped towards the crowd. The blasts of the horn caused all around to part like the Red Sea. The prisoner officers and the killer halted and turned to see what the commotion was.

The motorcycle skidded and threw up a torrent of spray, the pistol in the rider's hand clearly visible.

The impending panic was inevitable and the crowd scattered Some threw themselves onto the sodden ground and others fled for their lives, amid the hysterical screams.

Three dull cracks echoed along the Strand, as the bullets sped towards their target. The intended recipient of the missiles was fleet in his response. He grasped a startled prison officer and hurled him into the path of the bullets. The hot metal ripped into the prison officer's chest and spewed a warm pool of blood onto the cold, grey terrain.

The intended victim saw his opportunity amid the chaos and clambered over the barrier unchallenged. The frightened onlookers were more interested in their own welfare, and no attempt to apprehend the madman was made.

The escaping prisoner darted through the crowd, and knocked to the ground anyone who stood in his way.

DCI Entwistle crouched behind a police car and reached for the radio. "Victor Bravo, Victor Bravo, this is Delta Charlie. We have an officer down; I repeat, we have an officer down. Requesting an ambulance and the Armed Response Unit to the Old Bailey. Do you read me, over?"

"Delta Charlie, we read you, over. An ambulance is on its way. The Armed Response team have been notified, over."

Chief Inspector Entwistle cradled the young prison officer's head with his bloody hands and watched the crimson fluid pump out of his ravaged chest. Commander Sadler removed his jacket, and Dr Bullock held it against the wounds in an attempt to stem the flow of blood.

Several police officers sprinted towards the gunman, as he turned his motorcycle around. He put down his visor and screamed at the confused crowd when he applied the throttle. One woman was knocked to the ground in his haste to escape, but he managed to regain his balance. He raced rapidly down the Strand and found his way blocked by a bus. He manoeuvred around the bus and the motorcycle skidded and accelerated across the road into an oncoming taxi. The impact catapulted the rider through the windscreen of the cab; and the startled driver, blinded by the glass, drove his vehicle into a wall.

Frenzied screams pierced the streets of London, as the body of Jonah Kumar lay dying. His legs twitched and protruded from the windscreen. The taxi driver's bloodied head rested against his steering wheel, and the loud horn sounded, as if to announce their deaths.

Amid the bedlam, DCI Entwistle's eyes oscillated from Kumar towards the fleeing prisoner. "Get after him, do you hear? Get after him?"

The escapee ran awkwardly, his progress inhibited by his manacled hands. He looked back over his shoulder to see several police officers giving chase, but his rapid response had offered him an advantage. He turned into a department store and barged into an elderly woman. He fell to his knees, recovered and continued on his way, amid the stares of the shoppers. He emerged from the store and ran towards Smithfield Market, as the pedestrians watched him curiously.

One man emerged from a bank and tried to stop him. He received a smack to the jaw with the cuffed hands. The fleeing prisoner turned down an alleyway and prayed it was not a dead end.

DCI Entwistle caught up with the chasing officers and bent double, his hands on his knees. He fought for his breath, his red-face confirmation of his unfit state. "Where the fuck did he go?"

"I'm not sure, sir," answered the panting sergeant. "It's difficult, locating him in this crowd."

"You imbecile! You and your men were supposed to be guarding him."

"The gunman had to be apprehended, sir. The public was in danger."

DCI Entwistle barked out orders. "Get onto the station. He cannot get far. Issue his description. I want roadblocks set up, do you hear?"

"Y-yes, sir," stuttered the sergeant.

"The rest of you spread out and keep your bloody radios turned on."

The chief inspector watched as the uniformed policemen dispersed, before he closed his eyes. The escape of Charlie Bojangles had offered him a lifeline.

******

The fugitive squatted down in the alley and watched for his pursuers. His eyes were drawn towards a derelict building opposite. He entered the back yard and grimaced at the stench of the discarded rubbish. The door to the building was open and he proceeded with caution. The abandoned premises were dirty and damp, but that was the last of his problems. He moved to the dusty window that overlooked the High Street, before he slumped to the ground, his head rested between his hands.

"What's happening to me?" he asked himself.

He heard a sound and struggled to his feet. There was a movement and he looked around for a weapon. A discarded piece of piping was his choice, as he eyed the shadow in the doorway.

The figure that emerged was a tall, shabbily dressed man. The stranger wore a long trench coat that had definitely seen better days. A piece of string held up his tattered trousers. The narrow, unafraid eyes of the tramp focused on the mysterious intruder. The unfortunate man was almost bald, with a bushy black beard. His red eyes and the bottle of wine he clutched, verified he had been drinking heavily. The voice of the middle-aged man was pure cockney. "What the fuck do you want? This is my fucking squat."

The voice of Goldie answered. "You live in this hovel?"

The surprised tramp scowled. "What the fuck! Are you a queer or something?"

"Excuse me! I'm a lady… Goldie Lamour, future model and catwalk queen of Paris. My, you stink."

The tramp swigged his wine and eyed the stranger suspiciously. "Sure you are. What's with the cuffs?"

The sounds of police sirens were heard through the cracked windows. Goldie looked down at the manacles and wept.

The tramp moved closer. "Come on, there's no need for that. Are the coppers looking for you?"

"I don't know. I just don't know anymore."

"You don't know? You come in here wearing a set of handcuffs and you don't know? You're one fucking mixed up fruitcake, aren't you?"

The head rose rapidly and the eyes changed. "What's your problem, shithead?" The voice was that of Charlie Bojangles.

"Shit, you are a fruitcake. Why are the coppers looking for you?"

"You wouldn't want to know."

The tramp offered his bottle, but Bojangles declined.

"So what's with the tarts voice?"

"What?"

"Why were you talking like a tart just now?"

The vagrant realised he may have made a mistake, when Bojangles rose and approached him.

"A tart?"

"Yes, you were…Oh, it doesn't matter. Well, as I've already told you, this is my squat."

Bojangles inspected the surroundings. "Don't worry. I've no intention of staying here longer than I have to. I need you to help me."

"Help you? Why should I?"

"Because, I have money."

"Now you're talking. What sort of help?"

"First of all, I need to get these cuffs off."

The tramp scratched his head. "That, my friend could be a problem."

"Can you get your hands on a gun?"

The tramp stroked his beard before he took another swig of his wine. "Shouldn't think so. I do know a locksmith though."

"You know a locksmith?"

"I know a lot of people. I wasn't always an unfortunate victim of this unforgiving and cruel society you know."

"So what were you?"

He smiled proudly and straightened up. "I, my friend was once an artist."

"Piss off."

"No, really. Nothing special, but I made a few bob off my paintings. All of the homeless people you see on the streets; they were once someone. It just so happens one of the unfortunate ones used to be a locksmith."

"Can you contact him?"

"You said you had money?"

"Not on me. Listen, you have to trust me. I have money in my hotel room."

The tramp looked the stranger up and down. "You don't exactly look like you have money. Not in that garb."

Bojangles looked down and frowned, bemused to see that he indeed wore the unflattering clothes of Duncan Brady. "Listen, trust me. Get me out of these cuffs and I'll give you five hundred pounds."

"Ha! Christ you're serious aren't you, mister?"

"I'm always serious."

"Get the money first."

Bojangles held up his hands. "And how the fuck am I supposed to do that? I can't walk the streets in these, and I certainly can't return to my hotel wearing them."

The tramp drained the contents of his bottle and smashed it against the wall. He held it threateningly towards the face of Bojangles. "Okay, I'll help you, but if you're lying about the money, I'll cut your fucking throat."

"I'm not lying."

The sound of footsteps in the backyard interrupted their conversation. "I'll take a look in here, Sarge."

Bojangles moved towards the door and the tramp seized him by the arm.

"Long John Driscoll," he said, and offered his grubby hand.

"Charlie Bojangles."

"Come with me, Charlie."

Long John led him to a room filled with empty barrels. He pushed one out of the way and reached for the trapdoor in the floorboards.

"This, my friend used to be a pub. The Ditton Arms, a fine pub at that. Hide down there. You'll be safe."

Bojangles never argued, as he heard the approach of the footsteps. Long John replaced the barrel and turned to face the policeman.

"Well, well if it isn't Long John? How's it going, mate?"

"You know me, Alex. I get by."

"A little upmarket for you this place, isn't it?"

"Ah, ah. More privacy than cardboard city, Alex. What can I do for you?"

"Has anyone been here in the last half-hour?"

"Been here? Who are we talking about?"

"A dangerous prisoner did a runner from the Old Bailey. He's in this area."

The tramp shrugged his shoulders. "I've had no visitors… What's this bloke done anyway?"

He watched as the constable searched the barrels, removed the lid of each, and peered inside.

"He's a murderer, Long John. A right nasty piece of work. Are you sure you haven't seen him?"

The tramp hesitated before he smiled. "Positive. Now if you don't mind, it's time for my siesta?"

The policeman made his way towards the exit. "Hell, it stinks in here. If you do see anyone suspicious, get in touch with us. There may be a reward."

"A reward? How much?"

"I didn't say there was one, just that there may be one."

"I'll bear that in mind, Alex."

He waited until the constable had departed before he moved the barrel. He lifted the trapdoor slightly, which prevented Bojangles from exiting the cellar. "A killer, eh? Now, what's to stop you from murdering me once I've released you from those cuffs?"

"Trust, Long John. I don't break my promises."

"I don't know. I'm taking a big risk here. Maybe I'll just claim the reward."

"One thousand pounds. I'll give you one thousand pounds."

"Cash?"

"Cash."

The vagrant rubbed his hands together. "Here, let me give you a hand."

Chapter Thirty Four

The occupants of the Charing Cross incident room fell silent with the raised hand of DCI Entwistle. Chief Superintendent Hargreaves, arms folded, looked on from the rear of the room and awaited the briefing of the chief inspector. Commander Sadler stood alongside the chief inspector and leafed through some documents.

"Right, calm down. As you know, the prisoner was last seen heading towards Smithfield Market. We've placed the search on full alert, but so far he's managed to evade us. Our problem is his description. You see, he has a disorder, a multiple personality syndrome. In other words, unless he was faking, in which case he is very clever, then this man assumed at least four various characters. Duncan Brady a compulsive thief, Goldie Lamour a transvestite, and most worrying to us, Charlie Bojangles, a vicious murderer."

"Chief Inspector, you mentioned four," queried an Asian detective.

"Yes, that's correct. Our main problem is we don't know who this person actually is. We can say for certain that he is none of the three characters I mentioned. None of the three has records. They don't exist, only in the mind of the host. Dr Bullock, the Deputy Head Psychologist from Broadmoor claims this man has been living the lives of his three imaginary friends, and we do have proof of this. They all lived under the same roof, the guests of Dorothy Parish, who was murdered by Bojangles. Who is this man? That is what we're determined to find out?"

"When he assumes the guise of Brady or Goldie, is he harmless?" asked another detective.

"Not necessarily. We believe Duncan Brady was responsible for robbing a betting shop on Tottenham Court Road over a month ago. One of the shop assistants was viciously assaulted with a baseball bat. Someone answering his description was seen fleeing from the shop by a local taxi driver."

A burly detective spoke up. "So who is he, sir? Surely, his family or friends must miss him if he spends so much time assuming the role of these characters?"

"Precisely what I was thinking, George. Whilst he was in Broadmoor, Dr Bullock confirms that he only assumed the identity of these three. One theory is that he's confused and out of control, and perhaps he doesn't wish to exist. Brady, Goldie and Bojangles only appeared on the scene about three months ago. Where were they before they moved into Gower Street? Dr Bullock says it's possible that whoever this man is may have only been in this condition for three months, which would explain their non-existence before then. His reasoning is that he may be suffering from stress, which could be triggered from a number of things."

"So we do have a description of what he actually look like?" asked Chief Superintendent Hargreaves.

"Only a vague one, I'm afraid, sir. Dr Bullock insisted on him maintaining the guises of his alters, in order to convince him that he was sick when he assumed his true self. Only, he never assumed his true self. His wig and beard were only removed the morning he was taken to court. No photograph was taken of him, as we were going to go public after the trial."

"So we're back to square one then?"

"Not exactly, George. We at least know what names they use… I with six others have actually seen what he looks like without his disguise. Our artist is at work as we speak. Commander Sadler is to make a plea on national television tonight. We hope to have viable sketches of all three characters by then. Meanwhile, I want you all on the streets. I want this bastard found before he murders again. There are roadblocks set up on the outskirts of London, and all airports and train stations are being monitored. When he escaped, he was wearing handcuffs, so there's a chance he was seen, but as yet, nobody has reported any sighting of him."

Another detective spoke up. "This assassin, sir. Who was he?"

"Jonah Kumar. We've been after him for quite some time. He's suspected of being involved in a number of murders, none that we can prove.

He's usually careful and covers his tracks. The latest information suggests he hires himself out to everyone and anyone. Not only do we suspect him of murdering Clare Dougal; we also know he was after Bojangles... Who hired him and why? Put out the feelers. Who has he been associating with and where did he hang out? Okay, that's all, and remember, this bastard is dangerous."

The chattering detectives left the room. DCI Entwistle felt an encouraging pat on the back from the commander as he placed the papers into his briefcase.

Superintendent Hargreaves stood smiling at the back of the room.

"What's so funny, sir?" asked DCI Entwistle.

"Are you Irish, Inspector?"

"No, why?"

"Fucking lucky break for you wasn't it? You're off the hook again."

******

The murmuring that came from the lips of the disturbed man was a mixture of verbal ranting. He sat against the damp, bare cellar wall and held a conversation with himself. The man was confused, his words meaningless. His head shook from side to side as he tried to comprehend what was happening. He struggled to his feet and faced the wall. The steam off his urine rose and contaminated the already odorous cellar.

The faint footsteps from above alerted him, and his instinctive nature compelled him to step into the shadows. The trapdoor opened and a shaft of light invaded his tormented world.

"Charlie, Charlie, are you there?"

The inquisitive man was unresponsive. He listened to the whispers of the men above. Long John descended the ladder, followed by a small man with rat-like features. His nose twitched vigorously, as though he had picked up the scent of the stranger. They approached cautiously, and the rat-man cocked his head to view the man who hid in the shadows.

"What's up with him, Long John?"

The tramp ignored the question. "Charlie, are you okay? I've brought along Kelly the locksmith. He's here to unlock your handcuffs… Charlie, can you hear me, god damn it?"

"Who are you?" came the voice from the shadows.

"Just what are you playing at, Charlie? I do so hope you're not fucking with me?"

Long John approached cautiously, reached out and pulled the mysterious man towards him. His expression certainly had changed. Gone was the confident suave manner of Bojangles, to be replaced by the sneaky-looking Duncan Brady. His eyes went from one face to the other, as he curiously regarded his visitors.

Long John tried to reassure Brady. "Kelly's going to unlock you ,and then we're off to your hotel for the money, right?"

"Money, what money?"

The large hand of Long John encircled the frightened man's throat and pinned him against the wall.

Kelly's nose twitched with even more vigour, his rodent-like eyes fixed on the strange man. "Have you been wasting my time, Long John? You told me there's fifty pounds in it for me if I uncuffed him," said the small man in a broad Irish accent.

Long John slapped the face of Brady. "Listen to me, Charlie or whoever the fuck you are. Kelly's come a long way to help you. Now, are you prepared to pay or not?"

"I have no money. I don't know what you're talking about."

The powerful blow to his stomach caused him to double over. He coughed loudly when a kick was directed at his head and connected with his temple. Brady collapsed to the floor and curled up in a ball. The two vagrants stood menacingly over him, fists clenched.

Kelly snarled. "I thought you said he was a killer, Long John? He looks like a pussy to me."

"My head! What have you done to my beautiful head?" groaned the injured man.

"What the fuck!" yelled Kelly.

Long John grabbed Goldie by the hair and forcing her to look him in the eyes. "We're back with the tart are we? I don't know what sort of game you're playing, mister, but one thing's for certain. You'll not leave this building alive unless you cough up the money you promised me."

Goldie regarded the tramp repulsively. "Oh, it's you again. Still haven't managed to take a bath I see."

The slap across her face brought tears to her eyes.

"That's it, I'm off, Long John," insisted Kelly.

"No! This bastard's got money, I know he has." Long John stooped over Goldie, his alcohol breath repulsive to her nostrils. "You're a sick mother, aren't you? I want to speak to Charlie, do you hear? Bring out Charlie?"

"You're insane," said Goldie in a camp voice.

"What? I'm insane? For the last time, where's Charlie?"

"Charlie who?"

"Bojangles! Where's Charlie Bojangles, bitch?"

Another slap helped match the red handprint on the other side of her face. Goldie began to whimper.

"Frigging hell," moaned Kelly. "Can you tell me what's going on? Do you want me to release him... her. Well, do you?"

"A hefty kick was delivered between the legs of Goldie and she screamed out in pain, before she clutched at her aching crotch.

Long John gloated. "What do you feel, bitch? Not a pussy, but a dick. A big throbbing member."

The mocking of the distraught woman only fuelled to her emotional state.

"Charlie, Charlie, where art thou, Charlie?" cited Long John.

Kelly was impatient. "I've seen enough, I'm off. This sick bastard has no money."

Long John loped after the rodent and grasped him by the shoulders.

"You're going nowhere, Kelly. We'll just have to wait until Charlie makes an appearance, now won't we?"

"Have you two finished rabbiting? Get these fucking cuffs off me."

Their heads turned in unison towards the rising man.

"Charlie, you're back. It is you isn't it?" asked Long John, who stared into the eyes of the man who was rubbed his crutch.

Bojangles growled. "Well, what are you waiting for?"

"Kelly, take of the cuffs. You do recall our little deal don't you, Charlie?"

"Take these bracelets off and the grand is yours."

Kelly cocked an ear. "Grand! A fucking grand and you're paying me fifty sovs, you greedy bastard."

"I had to take all the risks, didn't I? It was me who hid him from the pigs and risked being arrested."

"Two hundred quid or I walk."

"Be reasonable, Kelly. One hundred?"

"Bollocks! One-fifty or nothing?"

"Will someone take these fucking things off me?" moaned Bojangles. Kelly stood with his implements in hand and awaited reply. "Well?"

Long John relented. "Okay, but you're a robber, Dermot Kelly."

Bojangles held out his hands and the rat-faced man went about his work with expertise. Within two minutes, the manacles lay on the ground. Bojangles rubbed his wrists vigorously in an attempt to circulate the blood.

Long John rubbed his hands together. "Now how far is this hotel, Charlie?"

The killer's hand darted out rapidly, and his two fingers located the eyes of the big man. Long John sunk to his knees, the fingers of Bojangles still bored into his sockets. The ear-splitting screams echoed around the musty cellar. Kelly whimpered, whilst he attempted to ascend the ladder.

Bojangles response was swift. He gripped the foot of the ladders, lifted them off the ground, and pulled them towards him. Kelly gasped when his back slammed against the wall, which caused him to fall to the ground.

He held his hands up in his defence and tried to crawl away into the dark corners of the cellar. Bojangles picked up the discarded handcuffs and walked slowly towards the cowering figure. He brought the manacles down on the locksmith's head repeatedly. The blood splayed against the cold walls of the cellar.

The moaning of Long John, who lay on the dusty ground and held his eyes, aroused Bojangles. He removed the bottle of wine from the tramp's pocket and poured it over him, before he rummaged through the pockets of his tattered trench coat. A box of matches was produced and the deranged killer struck one and held it over the wounded man.

"Did you honestly think you could outwit Charlie Bojangles; and you, a festering shit of the earth tramp? Long John, I send you to a better place. Burn in hell, you bastard!"

The match ignited the tramp's clothing and he rolled around screaming. Bojangles backed off and admired his work. The odour of burning flesh polluted the air. The assassin climbed the ladders, replaced the trapdoor, and wondered why his crotch ached so badly. He was glad of the fresh air. He was back in the real world, his world. The world of Charlie Bojangles.

Chapter Thirty Five

The orange evening sky promised another fine day tomorrow. Sophie marvelled at the beautiful setting, before the matter close at hand trespassed her thoughts. She had been careful and had left her easily recognisable red Mini at her abandoned home. She preferred instead to take the tube. Sophie had not been into the office for almost two weeks. The impending danger was obvious. Her decision to stay with her cousin Donna, was only reached because of her desperation.

She recalled the telephone conversation; the pleading voice of Slattery, who requested that she meets him at his house. Though relieved he was alive, her nerves had suffered, as every shadow and every unfamiliar face was viewed upon with suspicion. Although Jonah Kumar was killed during the attempted assassination of the man he believed to be Duncan Brady; Sophie's confidence was still unstable. At least she had known what her stalker had looked like before. No doubt the Cupid's Arrow organisation would have hired another killer to take his place.

Sophie approached the familiar house and flicked her cigarette butt into the gutter. Her drawn face, devoid of make-up, and her uncombed hair, was the result of her stressful predicament. Sleep no longer came easy to her.

She decided not to ring the doorbell. The longer she exposed herself to the outside world, the greater danger she was in. The door was unlocked and she entered the lounge. The haunting music of *Madam Butterfly* played on the CD player. The room was tidy, as though a special effort to cleanse the house for her visit had been made. She wrinkled her nose up and took in the odour of cigarette smoke.

Sophie approached the dining room cautiously, with the knowledge that Slattery loathed smoking. Either someone else was in the house, or had been. An opened bottle of red wine sat on the mahogany dining table, along with a wineglass, tarnished by the smear of red lipstick. In the centre of the table, lay a saucer filled with cigarillo butts.

"Vince," she called out, just loud enough to be heard above the music. "Where are you, Vince?" She heard a thud from upstairs and froze, paralysed by fear. Something was not right.

"Vince," she shouted, a little louder, as she looked towards the staircase.

Curiosity conquered her fear and she made her way slowly to the summit of the staircase, the music now only a hushed lullaby. The cigarette smoke was not a figment of her imagination. She checked two of the bedrooms before she pushed open the door of the third.

Sophie stood transfixed. She stared at the back of a blonde woman, attired in a pink, silk dressing gown. She sat at a dressing table and applied her make-up. The woman ceased with the lip-gloss and stared through the mirror at the unexpected intruder.

"Who are you and what do you want?" she asked in a husky voice, before she ground out her cigarillo.

"I could ask you the same question… Where's Vince?"

"Who?"

"Vince Slattery. He owns this house. He phoned me earlier asking me to meet him here."

The blonde swivelled on her stool and her eyes examined her inquisitor. "I think you're mistaken, luv. You have the wrong house."

"I don't think so. I know this..."

The reality hit Sophie like a slap in the face. She recalled the newspaper reports that confirmed that Bojangles, Brady and a transvestite by the name of Goldie were in fact one person. "I'm sorry, perhaps you're right and I do have the wrong house after all."

Goldie hurried towards the door to block Sophie's departure. "No damage done. Stay and have a drink. God, I could do with the company after what I've been through."

It was more a demand than a request. Sophie nodded and decided to delay her escape. She followed Goldie down the staircase, and her fear prohibited her from pushing the transvestite.

"I just love opera, don't you?" asked Goldie, who replayed the CD. "What is your name by the way?"

"Sophie. And yours?"

"Goldie. I'm going to be a model you know. Do pour yourself a glass of wine, luv."

Sophie obeyed the transvestite. "How long have you lived here, Goldie?"

"Only a couple of days... Actually, I don't own the house. I'm renting it, along with two other people. The house owner is away on holiday, jammy bastard."

"Really? Where are your two friends?"

"Friends? I certainly wouldn't call them that. In fact, I loathe them."

"So, why don't you leave them?"

Sophie noticed Goldie's eyes narrow. Her face was ashen, as though she was about to vomit.

"What did you say?"

"I said, why don't you leave them?"

"I only wish I could, dear."

The transvestite knocked over her glass of wine and held her head.

"Are you okay?"

"Yes, I'll be fine, dear. Do me a favour, sweetie and clean up the wine while I go to the ladies room."

Goldie walked unsteadily to the front door and Sophie heard the click of the lock. Goldie proceeded to climb the staircase, and one hand massaged her head.

When out of sight, Sophie ran for the door to discover it was indeed locked. The other two exits were also locked, along with all the windows.

Sophie's breath was laboured. She considered smashing a window with one of the chairs. Instead, she searched downstairs, looked in every closet and room, and expected to find the corpse of Slattery. She picked up the telephone to find there was no dialling tone. In her frantic state, she reached into her handbag for her mobile phone and prayed that Danny had his with him.

Sophie waited at the foot of the staircase and prepared for the re-emergence of Goldie. "Come on, come on," she pleaded, as she held the phone to her ear.

"Detective Sergeant Jenson."

"Danny! It's Sophie. Listen, I'm at Vince's house. He's here, Danny, he's here."

"Vince is there?"

"No, not Vince, the killer. I've just been talking to..."

The appearance of the olive-skinned man at the summit of the staircase struck the photographer dumb. The man who wore an Italian tailored, blue suit, descended the flight of stairs and adjusted the rings on his fingers.

Sophie backed off into the lounge, and the steely black eyes of Bojangles seemingly penetrated her.

"And you are?" he asked.

"Sophie Wilson. I'm a friend of Goldie."

"Who were you phoning?"

"My mother."

He snatched the mobile phone from her grasp and pushed the redial button.

"Jenson. Hello, is that you, Sophie?"

Bojangles smirked. "Hello, Detective. Your nine lives are running out."

"Who is this? Put Sophie..."

Bojangles switched off the phone and smiled at Sophie. "Well, well. Detective Sergeant Jenson, if I'm not mistaken. I've some unfinished business with him... So what are you really doing here?"

"I've told you. I'm a friend of Goldie."

He seized her by the wrists. "Don't lie to me. That woman has no friends. Tell me why you're really here?"

"Okay, this house belongs to Vince Slattery, a colleague of mine.

What have you done to him?"

"What have I done to him? You're in no position to ask me questions. What I require from you is to sit quiet while I wait for your boyfriend to appear."

Sophie was no longer afraid. "You're Charlie Bojangles, aren't you?"

The cocky man removed his pistol from his jacket and fitted the silencer. "My picture doesn't do me justice, do you not agree?"

Sophie ignored the question. "You're history, Charlie. They don't care about you. Why did they send Jonah Kumar to kill me? Why not send you?"

"Shut up! I don't know, and don't wish to listen to your pathetic pleas to save your arse. In fact, you could be a bonus for me. If indeed they do want you killed, then maybe I'll cash in my chips."

"Listen, Charlie; the man who tried to kill you is the same man who was hired to kill me. They want to keep you quiet, can't you understand that?"

"You're testing my patience, lady."

Sophie laughed. "Ah! The great Charlie Bojangles, hunted by the very people who hired him. They don't trust you. They want to eliminate you so you don't talk."

"Shut the fuck up, bitch! I won't tell you again," he yelled, whilst he held the pistol against Sophie's forehead. "Do as I say and you may just walk out of this alive... Does your boyfriend possess a gun?"

"You really are pathetic, aren't you, Charlie? Do you know, I once feared you, but now I realise you're a penny short of a shilling. Think about it. Why did that man try to kill you outside the Old Bailey?"

"I was never outside the Old Bailey."

"Oh, Christ, Charlie, you were, or at least Duncan Brady was. They wanted him dead before he gave you away."

"Shut up! You're confusing me, lady."

"Charlie, you're sick. You are Duncan Brady and Goldie Lamour. You don't realise..."

"Right, I've had enough of this." Bojangles dragged Sophie towards a closet and slapped her in order to calm her down. "Maybe I will kill you after all."

He slammed the closet shut, locked the door and checked his weapon for ammunition. He settled in the armchair and awaited the arrival of Jenson, his mark.

The deranged man mumbled to himself. "Charlie Bojangles hasn't flunked a job in his life. No, I've been paid and will deliver." He fidgeted and he pondered what Sophie had said. *True, Chivers had not contacted him in a while, and how come he had ended up in Broadmoor?* The more he thought of it, the more sense it made. *Chivers had hired another man to take him out. Bastard! They had the audacity to think that Charlie Bojangles would inform.*

The confused man looked towards the closet and tapped his pistol on his knee. He sprung up from the armchair and advanced towards the front door. He cursed, as it was locked. He fired three shots at the lock and the door opened. He replaced his weapon in his shoulder holster and walked into the coolness of the night, revenge uppermost in his warped mind.

******

Sophie cowered in the shadows of the closet. The opening of the door startled her. She saw the weapon pointed at her, closed her eyes, and prayed that her death would be swift.

"Miss, are you okay? It's safe to come out now."

She hesitated before doing so, and only the caring smile of the armed policeman persuaded her. She looked past her rescuer and ran into the arms of Jenson.

"Danny, Danny, thank God."

"What happened, Sophie?" he asked, as he hugged the distraught girl.

"Bojangles was here… He said he was going to kill you."

"Don't worry, Miss Wilson. He's not here now."

"Sophie, this is Chief Superintendent Hargreaves. I phoned him right away, as soon as you contacted me. The chief superintendent then notified the Armed Response Unit."

"Miss Wilson. Did Bojangles say where he was going?"

"No, but I think I may have convinced him that his employers were trying to kill him."

"What was his mental state?" asked the senior policeman.

"He was calm at first when he was Goldie, but as Bojangles he's a psycho. He was willing to kill me."

A constable joined them. "Sir, we found a blonde wig and women's clothing in the bedroom."

"It appears you're telling the truth," admitted Chief Superintendent Hargreaves.

"Of course I'm telling the truth," she barked.

The senior officer addressed Jenson. "Danny, can I have a word in private?"

They strolled into the kitchen and the older man faced Jenson. "DCI Entwistle has been arrested on suspicion of receiving illegal funds, paid to him for providing information in this case. We checked with his bank and discovered that large payments had been credited to his account. I believe I owe you an apology."

"Will Entwistle testify against Tyreman and the others?"

"At the moment, we still have no evidence linking Entwistle with Tyreman or any of the others in the ring, but with a bit of bargaining power, who knows? In my experience, I'd say there's a good chance he'll talk."

DS Jenson sighed. "It may be too late. Bojangles may be meting out his own justice."

"I'll send out teams to watch the suspects' houses. With a bit of luck, we may be too late and they'll get what they deserve."

"And what happens to me?"

"Your hearing goes ahead as scheduled on Monday, Danny, but I don't reckon you have anything to worry about. Sophie will no doubt substantiate your story, now that she's revealed herself… Incidentally, who is the other person who helped you infiltrate Cupid's Arrow?"

"Vince Slattery, a journalist for The Echo. He hasn't been seen for over two weeks."

"Do you think they got to him?"

"Vince is alive!" came a voice from behind.

They turned to face Sophie, who cradled a cup of tea in her hands.

"How do you know he's alive?" asked Hargreaves.

"Because he phoned me earlier this evening and told me to meet him here."

"Are you sure it was him?"

"Of course I am."

"So, where is he now?"

"I wish I knew. I only know that it was definitely Vince on the other end of the line."

Chief Superintendent Hargreaves walked to the window and stared out into the darkness. "How come the killer was here? Did he know Slattery?"

"No, Vince had never met the killer, as far as I know."

"Are you sure, Danny?"

Sophie interrupted. "Goldie told me they'd rented the house off someone who was abroad on holiday."

The chief superintendent mused. "Yes, perhaps that is what she thought, but what about Bojangles? He must have somehow traced Slattery, after receiving instructions from Cupid's Arrow. It appears Slattery might have been exposed and may be on their hit list."

Sophie put down her teacup. "Vince did come into contact with one of them."

"Who?"

"Ross Chivers, the manager of the agency. He tried to pass himself off as a potential client and even asked about Elizabeth Todd. Chivers promptly dismissed him, but Vince returned, and we took a photograph of

Chivers."

DS Jenson nodded. "That explains it… There is one other possibility though. Clare may have told her killer who Vince was."

"No, Danny," protested Sophie. "Clare knew nothing about Vince."

Chief Superintendent Hargreaves pondered. "Okay, Clare obviously gave her killer, who we can assume was Kumar, your name. They'd have no trouble finding out where you worked, and maybe Chivers traced Slattery, owing to your work relationship with him."

"But, that still doesn't answer the question. Where is Vince?"

"Mmm, I can't understand why he would phone Sophie and tell her to meet him here, unless he was forced to," added the chief superintendent.

Jenson offered another theory. "Or perhaps Bojangles murdered him and was unaware of the phone call. That would make sense, as he wouldn't be expecting Sophie to turn up here, sir."

"But if that was true, where is the body?"

They were interrupted by a sergeant, who held a radio. "Sir, all units report that the premises of all four of the suspects are empty. Torrance, Tyreman, Mikhos and Chivers are not at work or at home."

"What? Maybe they're out together. Keep surveillance on their homes and inform me as soon as one of them is sighted."

"Yes, sir."

"So now what do we do?" asked Jenson.

Chief Superintendent Hargreaves responded. "Me, I wait until Bojangles makes his move on one of the suspects. You, Sergeant, you go home and take Sophie with you. If she has persuaded Bojangles that he's been betrayed, then you may be out of danger. Besides, Sergeant, you're still suspended. I'll keep you informed of any progress."

******

The area surrounding Cupid's Arrow escort agency was cordoned off with yellow tape. The inquisitive crowd, including several journalists jostled for position. Their cameras clicked with every appearance of a new face to the scene.

Chief Superintendent Hargreaves stepped from his vehicle, accompanied by DCI Yates, newly drafted in as a replacement for DCI Entwistle. Yates was a veteran in CID; a real pain in the arse as his colleagues called him. Jimmy Yates was a hard man and liked to use his own methods to procure an arrest, something that did not go down too kindly with his superiors. Yates was fifty years of age, and given his thirty years of service, he ought to have made a superintendent at the least, but his unorthodox methods and his ignorance of discipline excluded him from such a post.

White-clothed members of the forensic team scoured the reception area for any piece of fibre or fingerprints. The two policemen were handed overshoes and plastic gloves, a pointless exercise as far as Chief Superintendent Hargreaves was concerned.

Hilary, the receptionist sat in her chair, her head in position as if nothing had happened; but something had happened. A single red hole was prominent on her forehead, and on her desk was an upturned bottle of red nail varnish.

Chief Superintendent Hargreaves and DCI Yates entered the office of Chivers, to see the manager slumped on the floor, surrounded by his golf balls.

The seasoned detective bent down and inspected his injuries.

"Shot to each kneecap, sir," offered one of the forensics team. "He's been tortured."

"I can see that, Johnny. Took a couple in the guts, eh?"

The forensics man nodded. "See this pencil? His killer used it to poke the wounds in the kneecap."

"How do you know that, Johnny?"

"The pencil was protruding from his knee when we found him."

"Oh, that's sick."

"We found a bullet beside the body. It's been taken to the lab, sir"

DCI Yates was unmoved. "What for? We know who done this? Poor bastard must have suffered before he died."

"So why torture him?" asked Chief Superintendent Hargreaves. He straightened up. "We've fucked up, Jimmy. While we were watching the houses of the suspects, he comes here and blows Chivers away. What does that tell you?"

"Chivers was his contact?"

"You're not just a pretty face, Jimmy are you? It could mean that Bojangles does not know the people who employed him. Chivers is just small fish, and he knows it."

"So do you reckon Chivers talked, sir?" asked DCI Yates, who already suspected the answer.

"Look at his face. What do you think?" Chief Superintendent Hargreaves looked past Yates, towards a stocky looking detective. "Larry, have we located any of the other suspects yet?"

"Negative, sir. We've been watching their homes since last night, but none of them have returned yet."

"Bastards are probably having a party somewhere. Tyreman, he owns a cruiser, doesn't he?"

"Yes, sir."

"Find out where it's moored, Larry. Also, check with their family and friends. I want them located as soon as possible, before Bojangles finds them."

"Sir, some geezer from Frazer's Security claims he's seen Bojangles," interrupted a redheaded, female detective.

"When? Where?"

"Thursday afternoon, sir. He said he was watching television with his wife last night and recognised the mug shot of Bojangles. He apparently has a postal deposit box with the firm."

"Shit, Becky. Check it out will you? Maybe that's where he kept his gun."

"Will do, sir."

"Come on, Jimmy," urged Chief Superintendent Hargreaves. "I want to be there when we take this bastard."

"Where to, sir?"

"Tyreman's place. It's as good a starting point as any."

Chapter Thirty Six

Jenson rolled over and kissed Sophie on the lips. She smiled without opening her eyes and snuggled up to the detective. That they had decided to move in with each other seemed the natural thing to do. A mutual bond formed between the two, from tokens of affection to mutual love. Jenson was reinstated as a detective, and Sophie had returned to her job as a photographer for The Echo.

Jenson turned on the radio full blast and disturbed the beauty sleep of his partner, who covered her head with a pillow. "No, Danny, let me sleep."

"You'll be late for work. Come on, I'll make you breakfast."

The unmoving girl felt her feet being tickled, and giggled as she kicked out playfully at her tormentor. "Bastard! Okay, I'm getting up."

The naked photographer sat up in bed and rubbed her eyes. "What time is it?"

"Almost seven."

Her mind wandered. "You know, they say crime doesn't pay, but it did for those three, didn't it?"

"I'm not so sure, kitten. Okay, so they're lying on a beach in Acapulco, but they'll never ever be able to return to England."

"I think I could live with that, Danny."

"So what do you want me to do, rob a bank?" joked Jenson.

"Now that you put it that way. Would you?"

He hit her flush in the face with his pillow, and they wrestled on the bed before they kissed.

"No, I must get up. There'll be time for that later," insisted the detective.

They sat at the breakfast table and read the morning newspapers. Bojangles was forgotten, his disappearance almost a month ago a mystery. The case only took up a small space on page six, such as the wane of public interest.

The premises that had once housed Cupid's Arrow were boarded up, and the homes of the three instigators of the crime had been left fully furnished. They had collected their visas at the passport office, prior to their arranged flight to Mexico. They had fled well in advance of them being detained. The evidence against them was conclusive. DCI Entwistle had indeed sung like a canary, but to no avail. Tyreman, Torrance and Mikhos would not stand trial, as they had no intention of returning to England. The corrupt detective was being held at her Majesty's convenience, awaiting sentencing. The body of Vince Slattery had never been found.

Sophie kissed her lover and headed for her beloved Mini, a piece of toast held between her fingers. She heard the telephone ring and dashed back inside to see Jenson's worried face turn a shade of white.

"Who is it, Danny?"

"Shh!" Jenson held the receiver against his ear and listened carefully before he responded. "What the hell are you playing at, Vince?"

"Vince!" yelled Sophie.

"He wants to speak to you."

She snatched the receiver off him and spoke. "Vince, where are you? We thought you were dead"

"I'm in Mexico, Sophie."

"What? Are you serious?"

"Listen, I know where Tyreman and his pals are staying. I've been watching them for a week."

"It doesn't matter. There's nothing you can do. The Mexican authorities are not about to extradite them… Where have you been?"

"There's something I have to tell you. Bojangles is here in Mexico."

"What, but how? I mean, how do you know?"

"Because, I'm here to witness the execution of Tyreman, Torrance and Mikhos. I tracked Bojangles down."

A worried look appeared on the face of Sophie. "You have to contact the authorities, Vince. Bojangles is a psycho."

"Bojangles?" quizzed Jenson, who seized the telephone from Sophie's grasp. "What do you know about Bojangles?"

"How are you doing, Danny? Not too bad it seems, and in Sophie's house too."

"Where are you?"

"Acapulco. I'm about to get the scoop of a lifetime."

"I don't know what your intentions are, but don't fuck with Bojangles. Do you know he has multiple personalities?"

"*Of* course I do. I spoke with him only an hour ago."

"You spoke with him?"

"Put Sophie back on please?"

The detective reluctantly passed the receiver to his lover and added another piece of chewing gum to his mouth. He passed one to Sophie, a substitute for the cigarettes she had promised to give up.

"Vince."

"Listen, Sophie; I want you to come out to Acapulco."

"You're crazy. If Bojangles is over there, then no way. I don't particularly wish to be on the same planet as that wacko, never mind the in same country."

"Llisten to me. Bojangles has agreed to let us cover his story. This guy is a celebrity and he wants to give us an exclusive."

"Shit, you are crazy."

"No, this is a chance of a lifetime, don't you understand that? This could win us the Pulitzer Prize, pumpkin."

"Is that where you've been all of this time; tracking that monster?"

"Yes. You do understand don't you?"

Sophie was livid. "You insensitive bastard. Why didn't you contact me before now? We thought you were dead. You could have at least let your wife and children know you were alive. Can you imagine what they must be going through?"

"It's complicated, Sophie."

"That night you told me to come to your house. Where were you?"

"What are you talking about?"

"The night Bojangles was at your house. You told me to meet you there."

*"*No, Sophie, you're wrong."

"It wasn't you? It had to be you."

"No. Do you think I'd place you in danger?"

"Goodbye, Vince."

"Wait! What about Clare? Those cold-hearted bastards hired Kumar to kill her. He tortured her, Sophie, and they paid him to do it."

"And?"

"Come to Mexico. Let Bojangles have his revenge… your revenge. You get to take the photographs, and we make a killing off the story."

"And you think Bojangles or Brady, or whoever he just happens to be that day, is going to let you walk away after you've witnessed him murdering those three men? Come down from planet Ga-Ga, Vince."

"But that's what he wants. If Bojangles were any vainer, he'd walk around with a mirror on his shoulders. This man is in love with himself. To see his story in print would be like a gigantic fix for him."

"This is not right."

"There's a ticket waiting for you at Gatwick Airport information desk, along with your tourist card. A visa isn't necessary, unless you're staying for more than ninety days. The flight's at six-fifteen tomorrow evening. I'll be waiting at Acapulco Airport for you, Sophie, and bring your camera."

Sophie focused on Jenson. "You really think I'll be there, don't you?"

"If not for yourself, then for Clare. You owe her, Sophie."

The line went dead and Jenson took the receiver from her. "Well?"

"He wants me to go to Acapulco."

"And you of course refused?"

She stared into Jenson's eyes, a stare that told him of her decision.

Chapter Thirty Seven

Acapulco.

The luxurious villa was perched on the cliff top and overlooked the spectacular bay of Acapulco. The villa was smothered in rich vegetation, and the umpteen palm trees concealed the plush haven from unwelcome visitors.

The large man who sported a flowered shirt and long white shorts had a Cuban cigar clamped between his teeth. He reached out and fondled the breast of the Mexican girl. Matthew Torrance, his face reddened by the burning sun, drooled when the topless beauty fed him yet another grape.

The sound of laughter interrupted them. Lance Tyreman held the side of the large swimming pool, a glass of tequila in his hand. He smiled contently, as a young girl pleasured him beneath the blue water. She lifted her head up for breath, only for the pony-tailed man to push it back towards his groin.

"This is the life, eh, Lance?" came the shout from Torrance.

"Beats bleeding London... Where's that miserable Greek sod?"

"Inside. He doesn't like the sun."

"He doesn't like the sun? He's bloody Greek isn't he?"

Tyreman tapped the girl on the head and climbed out of the pool. He towelled himself down and selected a cigar from the poolside table. "I'm thinking of making the owner of this place an offer, Matthew. What do you think?"

"I think he's happy renting it out to us. He's a bigger robber than you."

"No, I could go for this. A paradise in Acapulco."

"Don't you miss London?"

Tyreman poured himself a glass of cold beer and frowned at the big man. "Are you kidding or what? We haven't been here a month yet."

"Will they come looking for us?" quizzed Torrance.

"Relax, Matthew, the Mexicans don't give a shit about extradite laws; and besides, we're contributing generously to their economy aren't we?"

George Mikhos emerged from the villa. He wore Hawaiian shirt and long shorts. He adjusted his designer sunglasses.

"Book him, Danno," laughed Torrance.

Tyreman joined in with the mirth.

"Any news yet?" asked the worried Greek, insensitive to the mocking from his companions.

Tyreman shook his head. "Relax, George. Nobody's going to come here looking for us, and even if they did, what are they going to do?"

Mikhos was unsatisfied. He pushed away one of the topless girls. "I don't feel comfortable here. The police know we're here, even if they can't touch us."

"Well, nobody's stopping you from moving on, Zorba," moaned Torrance.

"Maybe I'll do that... It's all right for you two. I have a wife."

"She's in bloody Athens. Why not tell her to fly over here, George?" suggested Tyreman.

The three men looked towards the gate to see a man in a white shirt and beige trousers, his jacket slung over his shoulder. The man was dark, his eyes hidden by his sunglasses. He approached, and Torrance reached beneath his sun bed for his pistol. He tucked it in the back of his shorts and awaited the stranger.

"Hello, do you speak English?" asked the dark man.

"This is private property," insisted Mikhos. "How did you get in? The gate was locked."

"Apparently not," responded the stranger.

Tyreman stepped forward. "Where's your manners, George. An Englishman abroad, eh?"

"I'm sorry. I'm sort of lost. I'm looking for the El Mendoza Hotel."

"The El Mendoza? That's a fair way off if you're walking," said Tyreman.

"I have a car."

"You just follow the road towards the bay and take a right at the diving school."

The man nodded. "Thank you... You're English aren't you?"

The three men eyed the stranger with suspicion.

Torrance's stubby fingers fondled his weapon in anticipation. "Yes, we are. Are you here on holiday?"

"No, business. I arrived here this morning."

Tyreman, unseen by their guest, shook his head slowly at Torrance. "What sort of business?"

"I'm an architect."

Torrance slapped him on the back. "Splendid. Why don't you join us for a drink?"

"I thought you'd never ask. A beer would be fine, thank you."

He was invited to sit down, and could not but help notice the three topless girls, who offered their services to the three men.

"Cigar?"

"No thanks, I'm fine."

Torrance relaxed his grip on his pistol and selected a ripe banana from the fruit bowl. "So, what is your name?"

"Charlie."

"Charlie? The obese man's frightened eyes almost popped out of their sockets. "Charlie what?"

"Morgan. Charlie Morgan."

The three comrades smiled, more out of relief than amusement.

Torrance saw the funny side of the situation, especially the look of horror on the face of Mikhos. "Well, Charlie, welcome to Mexico."

"What do you three do?"

Tyreman passed his cigar to a dark-haired beauty, who puffed vigorously on it, before she passed it back to its owner. "We're in the escort agency business. Or should I say, we were?"

"Really? I didn't realise it paid so well?"

"Oh, it pays well," laughed Tyreman.

The stranger finished his beer and clambered to his feet. "Well, I thank you for your hospitality. I must go or my colleagues will think I've missed the flight."

Torrance offered his hand. "Enjoy your stay and I hope we'll meet again sometime."

"Oh, we will. No doubt we will," said the dark man, with his back turned to them.

The three companions looked to one another as Morgan departed.

"Shit, he had me going there," sighed Torrance, who wiped his perspiring brow with a towel. "When he said Charlie, I thought he..."

"Relax, Matthew; besides, Bojangles work for us doesn't he?" stated Tyreman.

Mikhos spoke up. "He sure does look like the man in the newspapers."

Tyreman grabbed one of the girls by the waist and kissed her. "Are you two paranoid or what?"

Charlie Bojangles reached the gate and looked back at his three ex-employers. At least Chivers had told the truth, but there again, who would not with a pencil gouging your bullet wound? Bojangles strolled towards his jeep. He had surveyed his killing field.

Chapter Thirty Eight

Acapulco.

Sophie resembled, and felt like a zombie as she waited at the luggage carousel. Her craving for a cigarette was only slightly lessened by her nicotine patch. It had been a long flight; eleven and a half-hours in all, and that coupled with the delay, left her feeling disorientated. Forty-five minutes she had been waiting for her luggage. She leaned heavily on her trolley and stifled a yawn, the jet lag taking effect. Her new white trouser suit was creased and her feet were swollen, as they always did whenever she flew. She checked her wristwatch and adjusted it, with one eye on the large wall clock.

It was now two-fifteen in the morning and Sophie desperately needed some sleep, and not the irritating piped Mexican music that escaped from the speakers. The airport was cool, owing to the air conditioning, the temperature outside the airport humid.

Sophie felt the presence of someone looking over her shoulder, and the reek of chilli suggested he was a native of this country. She glanced at him and her suspicions were confirmed. The tall, wild-haired man with the droopy moustache and permanent smile nodded at her. He wore an outrageous purple suit, complete with a red, flowered shirt. A large medallion lay against his hairy chest.

Sophie's suitcase made an appearance at last, or at least it looked like hers. She edged up to the carousel and received an unwelcome scowl from a tiny, grey-haired man. The suitcase advanced towards her and she steadied herself. She fumbled with the label and attempted to read it. She gripped the handle, only for it to be snatched away from her. She turned around to face medallion man, who had placed her suitcase on the luggage trolley.

"Thank you," smiled Sophie.

"It is nothing," beamed the Mexican.

Sophie pushed her trolley and headed for the concourse.

The Mexican loped after her. "Wait, Senora! You cannot leave me without telling me your name."

"Sophie. Pleased to meet you." She offered her hand.

"Miguel. I see you've travelled alone."

"I'm meeting someone. My husband," she lied, in an attempt to dissuade the gigolo.

The disappointment on the charmer's face was apparent. "You win some, you lose some, eh? It's been a pleasure meeting you, Sophie. Enjoy your stay in Acapulco."

She sighed heavily, more out of relief than fatigue. The Romeo returned to collect his luggage. She trundled through the nothing to declare door and only attracted a half glance from the official, who was more interested in the two young girls who, seemed to be exhibiting their beachwear a little prematurely.

Sophie passed several people that held up cardboard notices with anonymous names. She exited the terminal and grimaced at the humidity. Three taxi drivers bartered for her service, but she dismissed them politely. Her eyes scanned the surroundings. Loved ones embraced, and tour reps escorted the holidaymakers to their coaches, but there was no sign of Slattery.

She felt clammy, the unpleasant heat and the fragrance of the local plant life were not to her liking. She slumped against the wall of the airport, as the jet lag now took maximum effect.

"It's you again. Where is your husband?"

Sophie swivelled her eyes towards the garishly dressed Mexican. "He'll be here just now, I'm sure."

"I'm going along the Costera. Perhaps I can offer you a lift in my taxi?"

"No thank you. I'll wait."

One hour passed, and Sophie was roused from her sleep by an intruding hand that shook her by the shoulder.

"Senora, you cannot stay here."

She opened one eye and focused on a pock-faced policeman, who sipped from a bottle of coca-cola.

"I'm waiting for someone."

"You're blocking the way. You must move. Who are you waiting for?"

"My boyfriend. He was supposed to be waiting for me when I landed."

"American?"

"English."

The policeman seemed concerned. "You've come a long way to be disappointed, Senora. Do you know your boyfriend's address?"

"No, he doesn't live here."

"Too bad… Was your flight delayed?"

"Yes, as a matter of fact it was."

"Well, maybe he's been and gone."

Sophie disagreed. "He's not stupid. He'd check the monitor to see if there were any delays."

The policeman continued to probe. "You have a cell phone I take it?"

"Yes."

"So why hasn't your boyfriend called you?"

Sophie shrugged her shoulders. The same notion had occurred to her.

"You look really tired, Senora. Why don't you check in at a hotel and return tomorrow? I'm sure he'll have left word by then. If he hasn't, I'll give you my phone number, and I promise we'll trace him. How does that sound?"

"That sounds fine. This is most kind of you. Do you know of any cheap hotels nearby?"

"Hop in, Senora. I know just the place."

******

Sophie's body was drenched in perspiration when she stirred from her sleep. The hotel the policeman had recommended was indeed cheap, and it did not take a philosopher to see why. The tacky décor she could tolerate, but the lack of air conditioning was most unpleasant. She puckered her lips when another fly crawled across her mouth, and blew at the offending insect. The knock at the door brought her back into the real world. Her eyes took in the unfamiliar surroundings, the ghastly orange painted walls and the off-white ceiling with the unmoving fan.

This time there was no mistaking, the knock was real. Sophie almost fell out of bed, before she slipped into her trousers and blouse in an effort to retain her decency. Her bare feet were no longer swollen, but the feel of the broken hot tiles was unpleasant.

"Who is it?"

"It's Vince."

She opened the door and fell into his arms. "Vince, you bastard. You were supposed to meet me at the airport."

"I was there, but there was a mix up with the times. The lady at the information desk was unaware of the delay, and to be quite honest, I never expected you to turn up."

"How did you find me?"

"I did a bit of detective work. First of all, I rang your mobile phone, but it appears you either have it switched off or you've left it at home."

Sophie foraged through her handbag as Slattery continued.

"I then rang Danny, who told me you had flown out against his will. I went back to the airport and checked at the information desk to see if there were any messages. Apparently, some policeman left a message, saying he had dropped an English girl off at this hotel. An English girl who was waiting for her boyfriend."

Sophie located her phone to see that that it was indeed dead. "Do you know what it's like to be left alone in a foreign country?"

He cuddled her and kissed her on the top of her head. "I'm so sorry, Sophie. Well, you're here now and that's the main thing... Christ, this room stinks."

"You didn't have to sleep in it. I'm sure that bed is alive."

"Come on," suggested Slattery. "Let's get out of here. You can shower at my hotel."

As they passed the dishevelled desk clerk, Sophie could not help but pass comment. "I think I'll skip breakfast, Senor."

******

Sophie welcomed the breeze that wafted through the window of Slattery's rented Dodge Neon. The air conditioning cooled her saturated body as she sang along to the music of *Meat Loaf.*

"Like a bat out of hell I'll be gone when the morning comes."

Slattery looked across at Sophie. "You sure have livened up."

"I'll be okay once I've recovered from this bloody jet lag. This is beautiful, Vince. What do they call those mountains?"

"They, my sweet petal are the mountains of the Sierra Madre."

She took in the sights of the Costera, the main road that runs through the Bay of Acapulco. She eyed the natural horseshoe bay, with the clear blue waters and pristine white sands that accommodated the swaying palm trees.

Slattery was reluctant to ask the next question. "Are you and Danny an item?"

"Does it bother you?"

"I'd be lying if I said it did not. These last few weeks, I just haven't stopped thinking about you."

"What about your wife, Vince?"

"We have no future; she's made that obvious to me... I thought you detested Danny?"

"Detested is a bit strong a word, don't you think? Disliked maybe, but I never detested him. Funny, how tragic circumstances can bring two so different people together. There's something mutual about our relationship. Danny was there for me when I needed him."

The journalist raised his voice. "Damn it! I had a good reason for my absence, and you know it?"

"Do I, Vince. Do I?"

"This story is going to make us famous, Sophie. Not forgetting the fortune we'll make from the book."

"Book? What book?"

"Bojangles has agreed to let me write his story."

"He's a crazy mother. He can't be trusted."

"He's eccentric, I'll give him that, but he's not as bad as all that."

Sophie protested, her craving for a cigarette great. "He's a psycho. I've met him already, remember?"

"Oh yes, he did mention your meeting. He owes you a favour it seems. You see, you were the one who put him onto Tyreman and his pals."

"Vince, what's happened to you? Charlie Bojangles is a sick, bloodthirsty killer."

"But interesting, don't you think? He is an extraordinary man."

"Who is? Bojangles, Brady or Goldie?"

"We're witnessing someone special here, Sophie; someone who lives at least three separate lives. Aren't you in the slightest bit curious as to whom this man really is?"

"Not really. He ought to be in Broadmoor, receiving treatment… Has he revealed his true identity to you?"

"No, that's the funny thing. Every time I've met him, he's been one of the three personalities. I think his condition is deteriorating. The personality changes are becoming more frequent. Only yesterday in the hotel bar, I was talking to Bojangles one minute and then Brady the next."

"Did Brady know who you were?"

"No, I don't think so. He left the hotel, confused and in a rage."

"Hold on a minute. He was at your hotel, Vince?"

"Yes, in fact he's staying there."

"Shit you're winding me up, right?"

"No, he's in the room next to us."

"Us?"

"Yes, I thought I'd book a double room. I hope you don't mind?"

Sophie rolled her eyes. "A bit presumptuous, aren't you?"

"Don't worry. I'll sleep on the couch. I wouldn't want good old Danny thinking I'm boning his bird now, would I?"

"Grow up, Vince... Incidentally, how did Bojangles get a passport?"

"You can acquire a number of things in Soho if you have the right contacts and money... I want you to meet Bojangles this evening; a sort of icebreaker you might say."

"I don't know about that. He won't be holding a ice pick will he?"

Slattery was amused. "Ha,ha. Bojangles doesn't wish to hurt you, Sophie. If he did, he'd have killed you at my home, wouldn't he?"

"Great party this will be. Should we invite *Charles Manson* and *Hannibal the Cannibal* too?"

The car pulled into the El Mendoza hotel, which was situated at the bottom of the cliff. Sophie removed her sunglasses and placed a stick of chewing gum into her mouth.

"I see you've even acquired Danny's habits, eh?" moaned Slattery.

"Vince, in case you haven't noticed, I'm trying to give up the weed? Nicotine patches, nicotine gum. Shit, is it worth it?"

They parked the Dodge Neon and entered the luxurious hotel. The exterior was certainly impressive, with tall palm trees, a waterfall, and a fountain. Inside, the green, marble tiled floor gave the lobby a tropical look.

Sophie scrutinised every person inside the lobby, relieved that Bojangles or Goldie were nowhere to be seen. Brady, she had not met, and had no desire to do so.

"Come on, Sophie, you need a shower."

Chapter Thirty Nine

The tropical foliage and fresh ripe fruit trees flourished in the serene area around the pool. Sophie relaxed on her sun lounger, read her novel, and habitually reached for her non-existent cigarettes. The prickly pear margarita was a suitable substitute, as the alcohol almost diminished her craving for tobacco.

Slattery had suggested that she lounged around the pool that afternoon, to get over her jet lag. His parting words as he departed for the bank were, "I shouldn't be too long."

She reached for the sun lotion and dabbed it on her red arms. She then looked up to see the reason for the eclipse of the sun. Goldie stood before her in a yellow bathing costume, a broad, matching hat on her head. In one hand was a pink coloured cocktail, in the other a cigarillo. She raised her sunglasses and pouted at the bikini-clad photographer.

"Well, I never. Isn't it a small world?"

"Goldie, you look..."

"Ravishing? Yes, I know. See those two hunks over there. They can hardly keep their eyes off me? So what brings you to Acapulco, dear?"

"Sun, sea and sex."

"Oh, you naughty girl. Do you mind if I join you?"

Goldie pulled up a sun bed, planted herself on it, and faced the two men who paid her a little too much attention. Little did Goldie know that they mocked her, and not admired her. She took a drag of her cigarillo and the smoke drifted into Sophie's face. It tested her powers of resistance.

"Are you on your own, Goldie?"

"I wish. Those two pathetic excuses for men are somewhere around. Brady has made an effort with his appearance, but he still stinks... Do you know, I don't think he's taken a shower since he arrived here?"

Sophie looked sincerely into Goldie's eyes and noticed the obvious resemblance to Bojangles; something she had never perceived before. *What goes on in that tortured mind?* Sophie wanted to ask, but resisted.

Goldie ambled over to an orange tree and ensured she wiggled her butt sexily, desperate to entertain her watching audience. She was so camp, it was obvious to all around the pool that this was a man.

Sophie could not feel hatred for this mixed-up person, only pity. She found it hard to comprehend that at any given time, this friendly likable transvestite could turn into a vicious, bloodthirsty killer.

Goldie returned with her prize and proceeded to peel it in a provocative way. She noticed that the two giggling Adonis's watched, and wiggled her tongue at them. They gave her the middle finger and shouted something unintelligible, before they departed.

"Goldie, have you a family?" probed Sophie.

The transvestite remained silent and sucked on her orange.

"Goldie, did you..?"

"Yes, I heard you. Why do you ask?"

"I'm just curious."

Goldie pushed her sunglasses to the top of her head. "You know, it's funny? I cannot recall my family at all. I try, you understand, but I just cannot... Does that seem strange to you."

"Is it because you don't want to remember them?"

"Honey, I wish I knew."

They watched a small, thin man approach. He had a pencil moustache and wore the red jacket of a hotel employee. His emotions displayed embarrassment. He cleared his throat before he spoke to Goldie. "I'm sorry, er, Senora, but I've had several complaints from the guests."

Goldie fluttered her long eyelashes. "Complaints? Come on, man, spit it out. Complaints about what exactly?"

"Well, I don't know how to put this."

"Try, Manuel."

The hotel clerk rubbed his chin before he continued, his awkwardness apparent. "Well, Senora, you are a man, are you not?"

Goldie, open-mouthed looked towards Sophie. The photographer could not help but to chuckle."

"Prove it!" barked Goldie.

"Excuse me?"

"You say I'm a man, so prove it."

"Senora… Senor, you are being most uncooperative and place me in a very difficult position. I must ask you to please leave the pool area?"

"I will not! I'm a woman and until you can prove otherwise, you can piss off, Speedy Gonzales."

"You leave me no choice but to call the police."

"There's no need for that," said Sophie. "Come on, Goldie; let's go to your room."

"I've never been so insulted in my life," complained Goldie.

"That's another thing," uttered the hotel employee, who felt brave now that he had emerged as the victor. "What room are you in? I don't seem to recall you checking in."

Goldie pouted. "I'm staying with friends."

"Oh, really? Well that is strictly not allowed. I'm calling the police right now."

"You do that and I'll stick your dego head that far up your arse, that you'll shit blood for a week."

The voice was not Goldie's, neither was it Bojangles. Duncan Brady had emerged. The look on the clerk's face was one of confusion and terror.

Sophie could not but help being amused at his predicament.

"I beg your pardon?"

"You heard, now fuck off."

"Right, I'm calling the police."

"Wait, we're going," yelled Sophie.

"Who the hell are you, lady?" asked Brady, as he studied the face of Sophie.

Sophie was unsure how to react. The scenario of a tough-talking, streetwise thug, speaking through the mouth of Goldie would have been funny, if she did not realise whom this man was.

Brady seized the small Mexican by his lapels and pushed him forcefully towards the pool. With one immense shove, the clerk plunged into the depths of the pool. Brady now stood on the edge of the pool and watched the frightened man doing the breaststroke, towards the safety of the other side. The thief looked into the rippling blue water, until it was still. He gasped when he saw his reflection. The peroxide wig was torn from his head and tossed into the pool. His hands groped at his beautified face. He looked down and realised he was wearing a bathing costume.

"What is this?" he screamed. "Are you laughing at me? Are you?" He pointed a threatening finger at one startled man, who shook his head briskly.

Brady turned to say something to Sophie and thought better of it, and instead sprinted into the hotel foyer.

"Call the police! Somebody call the police," yelled the clerk when he climbed out of the pool.

Sophie replaced her sunglasses and returned to her novel.

Chapter Forty

London.

Jenson rubbed his aching eyes. The last four hours browsing his computer had taken its toll. He scrolled down the last page of his list and was joined by DCI Yates.

"Any luck, Danny?"

"Not yet. I've been through almost all of the passengers who have flown to Acapulco from London since 20th July, the last time Bojangles was seen. All the people so far are legitimate, so how did he slip through the net?"

"You've checked all these people out?"

"Yes, with the help of Larry and Becky. Like I said, I still have a dozen or so people to check up on."

"Why go to all this bother?"

"Because, if he used a false passport to fly to Mexico, I want to know who supplied him with it. Someone gave him the false documents, and I want the bastard locked up."

"Maybe he never flew from London."

"Oh, he flew from London all right. It wouldn't make sense him flying from another city, and I think we can safely rule out him sailing there."

DCI Yates was curious. "This Wilson girl. What's in this for her?"

"Slattery's convinced her that Bojangles wants to give them an exclusive. Bojangles aims to kill Tyreman, Torrance and Mikhos, and Slattery wants Sophie to take pictures of the event."

"Is Slattery that desperate?"

"Apparently so, guv. He's become unnaturally absorbed in this case. In fact, you could say he's infatuated."

The chief inspector glanced at a sheet of paper. "The authorities in Mexico have been informed about Bojangles, but they can find no record of anyone by that name staying in the country. No Duncan Brady and no Goldie Lamour either. They've checked all the hotels and come up with nothing."

DS Jenson turned his back on his computer and sipped his cold coffee. "What about Tyreman and co? Tell the Mexican authorities they're in danger, and that Bojangles will eventually find them."

"I've already done this, Danny, and they're not interested. As far as they're concerned, no crime has actually taken place in their country as yet."

"Vince and Sophie could find themselves in an embarrassing position, guv."

"Why's that?"

"If they are aware that Bojangles is going to kill the three suspects, then they could be charged with withholding evidence or even worse, aiding and abetting. A Mexican prison is not a pleasant place to be."

"How do you know?" quizzed the chief inspector.

"I've seen the *Magnificent Seven.*"

DCI Yates checked his wristwatch. "It's late. It's time you were going home."

"You go, guv. I want to check out the rest of these names. It shouldn't take me too long."

"Bloody workaholics. Goodnight, Danny, I'll see you in the morning."

"Goodnight, guv."

Jenson checked his diary and tapped in the number on the telephone. Something Dr Bullock had said had compelled him to make the call. He heard the garbled voice on the other end of the line.

"Hello, who is this?"

******

Acapulco.

Slattery and Sophie waited in the Dodge Neon and their eyes watched the villa for any sign of the three men. The tall palm trees obstructed their view, and Sophie's patience was spent. She left the vehicle and walked away from the villa towards the cliff edge, her camera dangling from her slender neck. Slattery cursed beneath his breath and scrambled after her. When he caught up with her, she snapped away at the picturesque view of the harbour and the magnificent passenger ship, which set sail for faraway waters.

"What are you doing?"

"What does it look like I'm doing?"

"Sophie, you're supposed to be taking pictures of those three."

"What three? We're unable to see them from outside, and you're telling me it's too dangerous to go near the gate. What do you want me to do? Climb a bloody tree?"

"Do you think you could?"

"Piss off, Vince. That's not even funny."

Slattery pondered. "There must be a way we can take their pictures without them suspecting."

"Why is it so important to take their pictures," asked Sophie. "We know what they look like?"

"It will add authenticity to the book, to show them actually living in Mexico."

"Well, there's no way I can do this without revealing myself to them."

Slattery smiled. "Maybe there is."

"I don't think I'm going to like this."

"Come on back to the car."

"What for?"

"We wait… Wait until they leave the villa and then we follow them. We take each other's photograph, only we capture them in the background. They'll naturally think we're holidaymakers."

"And what if they know who I am?"

"Sophie, even if Chivers showed them your photograph when you worked for Cupid's Arrow, you were wearing a blonde wig, right?"

"I don't know."

"It's the only way, Sophie."

******

It was just after three 'o'clock in the afternoon when they heard the gate open. Slattery wakened Sophie from her slumber and they slouched down low. They watched the red Ferrari exit the grounds of the villa. George Mikhos was in the driving seat and beside him sat a black girl, dressed in a tee shirt and shorts. Seated behind them, the corpulent, bearded figure of Matthew Torrance was being entertained by a giggling, redheaded Mexican girl.

Slattery had trouble-keeping pace with the Ferrari when it sped westward along the coast road. Sophie clicked away whenever they closed on the Ferrari in traffic, only for it to accelerate away again.

"Why do you think Bojangles never showed last night, Vince?"

"After what happened yesterday afternoon, it would make sense for Brady to leave."

Sophie recalled the confrontation at the pool. "That manager. He took some convincing that I didn't know Goldie."

"I don't think the police were too concerned, Sophie. Probably thought it was just some transvestite catching a few hours in the sun."

There was a carnival atmosphere in La Quebrada. The colourful costumes and Mexican music contributed towards the occasion. Torrance was the first to leave the car. He shook hands with the doorman of the exquisite hotel. Mikhos parked the car and followed with the two girls. The manager of the hotel greeted the four guests and they followed him into the lift.

Slattery and Sophie entered the hotel and watched the lights when the lift ascended. Behind them, three guitar-playing men who wore sombreros, and a maracas shaking girl entertained the residents of the hotel. The lift stopped on the sixth floor and the two journalists entered another of the lifts.

Sophie unwrapped a piece of chewing gum. "What is this place, Vince?

"La Quebrada. Surely, you've heard of it?"

Sophie adjusted her baseball cap and removed her sunglasses. "Sorry, but geography wasn't my strong point at school."

"The cliff diving. Does that ring a bell?"

"Oh, that… So what are we supposed to do when we get to the sixth floor?"

"Beats me."

The lift door opened and the manager stood inside a large glass door that led onto an outside terrace. An attendant led Torrance and his party down a flight of stone steps, towards a set of balconies that were built into the cliff face.

The manager, with his greasy hair plastered to his head turned to confront the undesirable couple. His face registered disgust when he looked them over.

Sophie sported denim cut-offs and an Arsenal football top; Slattery, a granddad shirt and baggy green shorts.

The manager approached purposely, his hands behind his back, like a schoolmaster about to scold his pupils. "I'm sorry. You must be in the wrong place. How did you get in here?"

"We walked," sneered Sophie.

"I'm afraid all the balconies are fully booked, and in any case, we have a strict dress code at our hotel."

"So what about those two then?" asked Sophie, who pointed to the two girls that accompanied Torrance and Mikhos.

"As I've already said, Senora, we're fully booked."

Slattery removed his wallet and thumbed through his wad of money. Sophie looked to the heavens and shook her head.

"Surely, you could find us a balcony close to those four," pleaded Slattery.

The manager looked around to see if he was being observed. He took the wad of money and shouted towards the young attendant, who came running. "Emilio, show these people to their balcony please. Number twelve will be fine."

"Number twelve it is, Senor Rodriguez."

Several of the spectators gave the couple looks of contempt when they headed down the stone steps towards their balcony. Emilio showed them to their table, smiled broadly and coughed. Sophie nudged Slattery. He placed a handful of coins in the usher's hand.

"Thank you, Senor. Ten pesos. What a difference that will make to my life," mocked Emilio.

Slattery addressed the young man. "A couple of drinks, Ramiro. A beer for me and..."

"A tequila sunrise will be fine thank you," added Sophie.

"One beer and one tequila sunrise coming up, and my name is Emilio, not Ramiro."

Sophie laughed and linked her colleague. "You skinflint. Do you know how much ten pesos is?"

"About seventy pence isn't it? That bandit Rodriguez almost cleaned me out."

Torrance and the black girl occupied the adjoining balcony. They turned towards the new arrivals and nodded. The blonde girl muzzled Mikhos's neck, an action that clearly irritated him.

Slattery whispered. "Okay, Sophie, take a few shots when the divers are ready, only don't let them see you."

The applause echoed when the line of divers took their positions on the cliff top and prepared for their plunge, one hundred and thirty six feet into just eleven feet of water. The custom was for their dive to coincide with the incoming waves, hence cushioning the impact.

Sophie made her way to the front of the balcony, and with her fingers inside her mouth, whistled loudly. Mikhos stared at her and shook his head at her antics. She removed her camera from around her neck, fired off a roll of film, and occasionally turned the camera on her unsuspecting victims.

Mikhos turned unexpectedly and looked directly into the camera. "What are you playing at, lady?"

"Pardon me."

"You took my photograph."

"Bullshit! Why would I want a picture of you?"

Torrance put down his drink and walked over to the adjoining wall between the balconies. "Forgive my friend; he's paranoid. He's got a thing about cameras."

"Of course," accepted Sophie.

Sophie felt uncomfortable. There was something in the way Torrance eyed her. Something that told her she had been detected.

Slattery, who sipped his beer joined her. "I told you to be careful," he whispered.

The whistles and screams were deafening, as the diver plummeted from the rocky cliff into the crashing surf. Mikhos and Torrance were deep in conversation, and glanced occasionally at the photographer and her partner.

Thirty minutes passed and the divers took a break. Torrance lifted his huge frame from his seat and went indoors, escorted by the redhead. The delicious buffet no doubt tempted him. Mikhos snubbed the attention of the black girl and again glanced at Sophie.

She ignored the attention and turned to Slattery. "Where's that waiter, Vince. I'm thirsty?"

"I'll go to the bar. Tequila sunrise?"

"You got it."

The black girl sulked, her head rested on her fists. The object of her attention obviously pined for his wife.

Sophie sat down and put on her sunglasses and baseball cap to protect her from the scorching hot sun. Her eyes focused on the figure on the next balcony, who stood behind Mikhos.

Bojangles, as usual was dressed immaculately. He looked towards Sophie, and even though his sunglasses hid his eyes, she knew what he was there for. She left her seat, and with trembling hands, brought the camera to her eyes, ready to snap the inevitable. Mikhos grimaced when he noticed the camera directed towards him. "You've been fucking warned, lady!"

"That's no way to speak to a lady," came the voice from behind.

Before Mikhos could turn around, Bojangles seized the startled Greek's arm and ran with him towards the balcony edge. With all of his might, Bojangles hauled the screaming man over the precipice. The Greek's hands clawed the air and attempted to cling onto a non-existent ledge.

The black girl screamed hysterically, as Bojangles peered down at his handiwork. He watched the waves crash against Mikhos's battered and broken body. The surf turned red, and the spectators from the balconies below howled and turned their heads upwards to see who was responsible.

Bojangles turned towards Sophie and said, "Did you get that?"

She nodded, and he walked casually towards the exit, unchallenged.

The black girl wept when the returning Torrance embraced her. Her frightened eyes stared into the large brown orbs of Sophie.

Chapter Forty One

Matthew Torrance perspired profusely and dabbed his face with his handkerchief. Across the table from him sat a thin man with tinted spectacles and sporting a handlebar moustache. The detective, dressed in a white ill-fitting suit, blew cigar smoke into the face of Torrance. A single fan hummed loudly as it rotated, the only relief from the sweltering heat in the depressing room.

"Senor Torrance, I have a file on you as tall as this table."

"I cannot think why."

The detective continued. "You see, we received a telephone call from England about a fortnight ago. CID and Special Branch were adamant that an attempt on your lives would be forthcoming, and it appears they were correct in their assumption. It seems you and your two friends committed a very serious crime in your country, and that is the reason you came to Mexico."

"I do object," protested Torrance. "I'm a highly-respected businessman and I have opted to see out my retirement in your country."

The police captain sucked his teeth before he continued. "If I had my way, Senor Torrance, you would be deported immediately, but my government do not agree with me. Not all laws are judicious; however, they are there to be complied with. It was a mistake to come here, Senor Torrance, a big mistake. It appears you've been followed by a fellow compatriot of yours, who appears to be a sadistic killer. I doubt you'll tell me why this man seeks retribution, and to be honest, I expect nothing more... You claim you did not see the man who threw George Mikhos to his death this afternoon?"

"That's correct. I was at the bar. Rosa saw him though."

"Ah yes, the delectable Rosa. Our paths have crossed over the years. I remember when she was picked up for blowing her first client."

"What is your point, Captain?"

"My point? My point, Senor Torrance is this. Tell me who this man is and I may be able to help you, otherwise; well, you would be foolish not to cooperate. After all, this man got to your friend did he not?"

Torrance loosened his tie. "His name's Charlie Bojangles and he's insane."

"Bojangles? Like the song?"

"Yes, like the song. Listen, Captain, I've told you all I know. May I go now? It's hotter than a whore's crutch in here."

"And you would know, wouldn't you?"

"I resent that comment, Captain. I demand to see your superior officer!"

"You demand, Senor? You do not demand anything. This is Mexico, not good old England with your drug pushers and your rock and roll. No, Senor, you demand nothing." He took a long draw on his cigar and watched as a fly swarmed around the obese, sweltering man. "Why does this man want to kill you and your friends?"

"Because, he's insane. He believes we tried to have him killed."

"And did you?"

"Of course not. Now can I go?"

"Do you think I should let him go, Sergio?" asked the captain. The question was directed to the long-faced detective who sat next to him.

Sergio shrugged his shoulders.

The detective continued his interrogation. "You do realise that failure to cooperate with us would render us powerless to offer you protection?"

Torrance brought his fist down onto the table. "This is an outrage! I demand protection. If need be, I'll contact the British Embassy."

The captain's face assumed a sterner look. "And they'll welcome you with open arms and say, Senor Torrance, our fine upstanding citizen, what is it you want? We will do everything we can to help you… I don't think so. You apparently are an embarrassment to your government, and I'm certain that if you went to them, they would lock you up and throw away the key. You and your friends are believed to have been responsible for the deaths of several people, and for what? So you can live the rest of your life out in a cosy villa in Acapulco. You make me sick! Do you know how much I earn a year?"

"No, and I don't want to know."

"Get out! Get out of my office and watch your back, Mr Torrance. Watch your back very, very carefully."

"Will you give me protection?"

"I'm obliged to, Senor Torrance. I'm obliged to."

The detectives watched Torrance leave. This prompted the captain to nod to his partner, who in turn flicked the switch for the air conditioning.

"Did you see him, Sergio, sweating like a pig?"

"Are you going to give him protection?"

"What do you think?"

******

The orange sun was low in the sky and the darkness descended on this paradise, which conflicted with the vibrant colours of the city. The aroma of the barbecue hung in the air and nullified the citric scent of the fruit trees that were abundant around the villa. The trees were still, and the absence of a breeze added discomfort to this already humid evening.

Charlie Bojangles, his black sweatshirt and trousers merging with the ever-darkening landscape, focused his binoculars on the stern-faced man who stood inside the gates of the illuminated villa. No weapon was evident, but Bojangles was aware that the hired security man was armed. From a branch of the tree, the killer could survey his quarry in the knowledge he was unlikely to be detected.

His eyes swept the grounds of the villa, until he located another man, who was dressed in a black suit and tie. The man had one eye on the perimeter wall, the other on the topless girls.

The inadequacy and sheer lack of manpower angered Bojangles. Only two guards, as far as he could tell. They had grossly underestimated their opponent. He attached the silencer to the pistol that he had acquired from a shady character in a sleazy nightclub, before he took aim. At fifty metres, his aim had to be true. He checked to see that the other guard had his head turned towards the girls, and watched them engage in a game of water volleyball with Torrance and Tyreman.

Bojangles held his breath and prayed the weapon was as good as what the undesirable Mexican had said it was. He squeezed the trigger and a red blotch appeared on the startled guard's shirt, the bullet having pierced his heart.

Bojangles climbed down from his perch and decided to enter the grounds from elsewhere, as no expense had been spared with the newly installed security system. He ensured he was out of range of the cameras, jogged through the undergrowth, and dropped to one knee when he reached his destination. He looked up at the eight-foot wall that was covered with razor wire, took a step back, and surveyed the trees around him. As agile as a chimpanzee, he scaled the tree until he was above the fence. Holding onto a limb, he edged along a branch, until he was two feet short of the fence.

Fortune favoured Bojangles, as the amplified music of *Pavarotti* blared from the speakers. Without hesitation, he leapt from the branch and cleared the fence with ease. He landed heavily and rolled over into the cover of a bush. A chorus of disturbed grasshoppers accompanied the haunting lyrics of *Nessun Dorma.*

Bojangles massaged his sprained ankle and cursed his clumsiness. He began to mumble gibberish, and odd phrases passed his lips, phrases uttered by Goldie and Brady. Goldie stared at the weapon in her hands and tossed it into the bush, before she grimaced in pain.

"Oh, my poor foot," she said, and stared down at the unfamiliar black boots and trousers. She struggled to her feet, limped towards the source of the music, and took in the strange surroundings.

Torrance saw the limping figure first, and took his eye off the ball as it soared over his head. He motioned to the armed guard. "Felix, shoot him! Shoot him!"

"Shoot who, Senor?"

"Bojangles. It's fucking Bojangles!"

The buck-toothed, bald Mexican withdrew his pistol and stared, eyes squinting at the limping man who headed towards him. He held up one hand to shield the bright spotlight, before he reached for his radio. "Javier, Javier, can you hear me? Get your arse over to the pool now. We have company." There was no response, as the radio lay next to the dead body of Javier, the message unheard.

"Stop there or I'll shoot!" threatened Felix.

"Help me. Help me please," came the plea of Goldie. "I've sprained my ankle."

"Who are you and how did you get in here?"

"Don't listen to him, Felix, shoot him," ordered Tyreman.

"Are you sure, Senor Tyreman? I mean, this is surely not your killer?"

"Of course, I'm fucking sure. Where did you get this clown, Matthew?"

The perspiring security man pressed the muzzle against the forehead of Goldie and stared into the feminine eyes.

"Please don't listen to him. I'm but a defenceless woman."

"You sure don't look like a woman. Sorry, but orders are orders."

The eyes of Goldie changed dramatically and the gunman never expected or saw the punch to his windpipe. He fell to his knees, dropped his weapon and clutched his throat. Bojangles picked up the pistol and shot Felix between the eyes.

The four occupants of the pool swam for their lives in an attempt to reach the other side. A shot rang out, audible above the loud music. A small pool of blood converged around Torrance, as he gripped his shoulder and groaned loudly.

"Anyone attempting to leave the pool will be shot. Now swim back to the centre of the pool," ordered Bojangles, as he motioned towards the deep end.

Torrance groaned. "How can I? I'm wounded."

"You, Tyreman, help him."

Between the two of them, they managed to swim towards the centre of the pool. Bojangles pointed the pistol at the redheaded girl and ordered her to leave the pool. He limped to where she stood. "Do as I say and you and your friend will live. Okay?"

She nodded rapidly, and her body trembled

"I want you to go to the garage and bring me two cans of petrol. If you disobey me and attempt to escape, I'll shoot your friend and you'll be responsible for her death. Understand?"

Again, she nodded before she bounded off to the garage.

Tyreman and the black girl, Rosa, struggledto keep the big man afloat, and treaded water jadedly.

"Okay, how much do you want Bojangles?" asked Torrance, who bled profusely.

"Imbecile! Do you think you can still buy me with your blood money?"

"Why are you doing this?"

"I've always honoured my contract, carrying out my task in full. Did you think you could kill me off so easily?"

"No, you've got it wrong," insisted Torrance.

"Have I? I know you hired that man to kill me. You insulted me by not trusting me. Even when threatened with prison, I would not have talked."

"One million pounds in cash," offered Torrance, who struggled and swallowed a mouthful of water.

The redhead returned with the two petrol cans.

Bojangles pointed towards the black girl. "You, out of the pool," ordered the disturbed man.

Rosa swam towards the steps wearily. She left the pool and hurried towards Bojangles.

"I can't hold him up much longer," moaned Tyreman.

"Shut up!" Bojangles addressed the two frightened girls. "You two, pour the petrol around the perimeter of the water."

They did as they were told, amid the protests of the struggling swimmers, who decided to make for the steps.

Bojangles took aim and the bullet buried itself in the shoulder of Tyreman. He let out a loud scream.

"Back to the centre of the pool or I swear the next one will be between the eyes."

"The two distraught men had no choice but to obey the madman. They treaded water sluggishly and their limbs ached with fatigue. A pool of crimson blood surrounded them.

Tyreman breathed heavily. "Okay, what exactly do you want?"

"A match," demanded Bojangles, as he looked towards Rosa. "Run along girls, this will not be pleasant."

Bojangles smiled and witnessed the two men swallow their own blood, as they sank lower into the depths of the pool.

"Anything, Bojangles! Name your price," yelled Tyreman.

Bojangles struck the match and stared at the flickering flame smouldered between his fingers. The faces of Tyreman and Torrance registered horror when they watched the match ignite the petrol. A ring of fire enveloped the pool; the screams of the helpless men unnecessary, as nobody was there to hear them. Tyreman released his obese partner and swam slowly and tediously towards the steps, ignorant of the screaming pleas behind him.

Torrance's head was now below the water, his stubby fingers waving for help, help that would never come.

The agonising screams coming from the mouth of Tyreman when the flames ignited his tired body, even shocked Bojangles. He raised his pistol at Tyreman and watched the pony-tailed man plead with his eyes for him to pull the trigger and end his agony. Bojangles laughed loudly, a bellowing insane laugh that drowned out the music. He lowered his weapon and watched the orange flames eat away at the body of Tyreman. The burning flesh mingled in the air with the cooked meat of the barbecue.

Bojangles cocked his head to one side and the smile was gone.

Duncan Brady stared at the carnage, open-mouthed. He shrugged his shoulders and rifled through the wallets of the discarded clothes, before he limped towards the gates. What exactly had happened, he neither knew nor cared, but what he did know, was that he was a lot richer for it.

Chapter Forty Two

The hotel bar was hectic, the guests obviously all opting for aperitifs before they toured downtown Acapulco. Sophie and Slattery had seen on TV the events that had occurred the previous night at the villa. A translator was not necessary, as the graphic images of the body- bags being carried away and the mention of the victim's names were enough. The two frightened girls gave their accounts of what happened in Spanish, and gestured with their hands to describe the flames.

Sophie stared at Slattery, who seemed distant. Since she had arrived in Mexico, she had noticed a change in him. This was not the man she once harboured fond feelings for. His obsession with Bojangles had brought out the venom in the journalist. She sipped her Pina Colada conservatively and reminded herself that tonight she needed a clear head. She checked her wristwatch and noticed that Slattery grinned at her.

"Relax, there's nothing to be worried about," he suggested.

Sophie looked around and ensured she was out of earshot before she spoke. "How can I relax when I'm going to be sitting not two-feet from a mass murderer, who has just made a toasted teacake of one of his victims?"

"It's over, Sophie. A series of interviews with Bojangles and we'll be home within a week. I must say though, I'm disappointed we didn't get the pictures of the executions, like he promised."

"How can you be sure he'll turn up, Vince? How can he make an appointment when he doesn't even know who he'll be at nine 'o'clock?"

"Then we'll wait until he does arrive... Bojangles appears to be the dominant personality and maybe he can exercise more control than we believe. You have plenty of film I gather? In fact, it'll be a bonus if Goldie or Brady make an appearance."

"This is morally wrong, Vince. I feel like a conspirator."

"Bullshit! Someone has to tell the story, so why not us? We've been involved from the beginning, and don't forget, nobody believed us about

Cupid's Arrow. Let's just say it's payback. Do you know how much money we can make from this?"

Sophie was unable to feel much enthusiasm. "What happened to the Vince Slattery I thought I knew, or was it all an act to lure me into your bed?"

"Don't flatter yourself, Sophie. Yes, I fancied you, but I have my principles… Why are you so concerned about me; you have a new boyfriend after all?"

I'm not concerned about you, and to be quite honest, I'm past caring. I pity you." There was a prolonged silence before Sophie continued. "What happens after we've interviewed Bojangles? Do we just walk away?"

"That's exactly what we do. Have you any suggestions?"

Sophie frowned. "Yes, as a matter of fact I have… We hand him over to the local police after we conclude the interviews."

"Are you mad?"

"Am I mad? This psychopath isn't going to stop killing. He has to be stopped."

"Forget it, Sophie. I gave him my word."

"You gave your word to a killer? I'm sure St Peter will still admit you into the gates of heaven after telling that white lie."

"Bojangles walks. That's the deal."

Sophie headed for the bar and returned with a pack of cigarettes.

"I thought you'd given them up?" enquired Slattery.

"Emergency rations. My nerves are shattered."

"Okay, I'll check to see if he's in his room, and if he is, we'll get started. It'll be worth it, Sophie, believe me."

Sophie waited ten minutes, and felt most uncomfortable sat on her own. She approached the bar and pulled up a stool. The short, chubby barman with the thick moustache mixed a cocktail expertly, tossed the bottles into the air and caught them.

"Tom Cruise, eat your heart out," he winked.

Sophie lit a cigarette.

"What can I get you, my English rose?"

"A Pina Colada will be fine, Jorge."

"You should be out enjoying yourself, not moping in here. Where's your boyfriend?"

"Oh, he'll be back shortly."

The barman noticed that the English girl was flustered. "Your hands are shaking. Too much sun, eh?"

"Something like that," she answered, and blew a plume of smoke out of the side of her mouth.

"Your boyfriend, he suffers too, eh?"

"In what way, Jorge? What do you mean?"

"I don't want to sound insulting, but he ought to see a doctor."

Sophie narrowed her eyes. "Come again, Jorge, you've lost me."

"You must know. You're his girlfriend, are you not?"

He placed the cocktail on the bar.

"Sort of."

The barman reluctantly continued. "He talks to himself. Does this ring any bells?"

"Talks to himself? No, I don't think so."

"Yes, yes, I've seen him twice… Two or three nights ago, he was sitting where you are. I've never ever seen anything like it in my life. He was holding a conversation with himself. In fact, it was more like an argument."

"There must be some mistake. Are you sure?"

"Of course. Others saw him too."

"You say he was arguing. What sort of things was he saying?"

Jorge leant closer. "He was most loud. I had to tell him to keep his voice down. I put it down to too much drink, but if he was indeed drunk, he never purchased the booze from here."

Sophie felt a lump in her throat. "These voices. What were they saying?"

"Cow! Stay out of my life, and things like that… Then something amazing happened. He spoke in a woman's voice."

Sophie dropped her drink and it smashed on the floor.

"Are you okay?"

She stared ahead and her breathing was labored. Her big, brown eyes watered. "A woman's voice?"

"Yes, I'm sure you have nothing to worry about. Sun stroke perhaps. The sun and too much drink can do funny things to a person."

Sophie jumped when the telephone rang. Jorge answered and looked towards the disorientated girl. "Is your name Sophie?"

She nodded and he handed her the receiver.

"Sophie, he's here waiting. Hurry and bring your camera."

"Vince, I..."

"What is it?"

"Nothing." She hung up.

"Are you sure you're okay?"

"Yes, thank you, Jorge, I'll be fine."

******

She hesitated outside the door. Her mouth was dry and her stomach felt as if she had devoured a thousand Mexican jumping beans. There had to be an explanation. Her bravado, more down to curiosity than heroism prompted her to go ahead with the rendezvous. She knocked on the door and there was no immediate response. Her clammy hand gripped the handle, and she half-hoped that the door was locked, in order to prevent her illogical inquisitiveness. It was not.

The whiff of cigarillo smoke was evidence that Goldie was or had been in the room. Sophie advanced vigilantly and saw the reflection of Goldie in the full-size mirror. A feeling of relief swept through Sophie. Goldie had never been violent towards her before.

The transvestite faced her, a strange gaze in her eyes. Sophie frowned. Something was wrong. Goldie's eyes were grey and not blue. Her make-up looked as if it had been applied with a trowel. The demented smile offered no comfort to Sophie.

Goldie opened up. "Hello, did you want to see me?"

"It depends who you are," replied Sophie.

"Who do you think I am?"

Sophie looked down to see Goldie wore black loafers beneath her orange-flowered dressing gown. "I'm not sure if it's Goldie Lamour, Duncan Brady or Charlie Bojangles. Or maybe it's Vince Slattery?"

The lop-sided grin never wavered.

"Who?"

"It's beginning to make sense now. Vince, listen to me. Fight this. Show yourself. Do you hear me? Show yourself?"

Goldie's grin vanished, to be replaced by a look of sheer hate. "You! Where is Slattery?"

"Ah, Charlie Bojangles. I could ask you the same question… Fight it, Vince; don't let this monster take you over."

The slap was powerful, knocked her backward against a table, and forced her to drop her camera.

Bojangles closed in. "Don't fuck with me, lady. Slattery was supposed to meet me here. Perhaps we should start without him?"

"Listen to me, Vince. You're in there somewhere. Speak to me. Remember your wife, Cheryl and your daughters, Mandy and Debbie? Free yourself from this evil."

Another slap sent her reeling. Bojangles reached out and seized her by the throat, his manic eyes full of anger. He forced her head down onto the table and placed the muzzle of his pistol against her forehead.

She could sense his excitement building up inside him, as the adrenalin flowed. His pupils dilated and his teeth were clenched.

"You think you can play games with me?" he growled. "We had an agreement, but I don't see Slattery anywhere. One thing I detest is dishonour and unpunctuality. You see, your word is sacred, an oath to God. Without Slattery, I'm afraid I have no use for you, and of course I have to think of my own well being."

Sophie tried to raise her head, but her attacker was too strong. "Listen to me! You are Vince Slattery and you're sick. Charlie Bojangles does not exist. Do you hear me? Bojangles, Brady and Goldie are figments of your imagination."

"You stupid bitch! I exist and this gun against your head exists. Prepare to meet your maker."

The door imploded and DS Jenson appeared. He stood in front of four armed policemen, their weapons pointed at the blonde-wigged Bojangles. Jenson held up his hand. "No, Charlie, don't do it!"

"Tell them to drop their weapons or I'll blow her away. You know I will."

Jenson nodded towards the police captain, who had entered the room. "Do as he says, Captain."

"Sorry, Sergeant, I'm in charge here. We will not surrender our weapons. He, or is it she, doesn't look so tough to me?"

Jenson raised his voice. "Listen, do as he says or he'll kill her, and you'll have to face the consequences of your actions, Captain."

The thin, bespectacled detective wiped his brow and weighed up his options. "Okay, men; place your weapons on the ground."

The armed policemen obeyed.

"Now kick them over to me." ordered Bojangles.

There was near silence for a minute, the only sound being the whirr of the overhead fan.

"Charlie. It is Charlie isn't it?" asked DS Jenson. "I want to speak to Vince."

Sophie scowled, surprised that Jenson knew about Slattery.

Bojangles grinned manically. "You pathetic man. I should have finished you off in London."

"Clumsy work for a pro, Charlie," countered Jenson. "No wonder Tyreman wanted you killed. You murdered an innocent man with your so-called bomb."

"Maybe I'll just finish you off now."

"I had a talk with your mother, Vince."

"Don't call me that!"

Jenson continued. "You see, I couldn't fathom out how you got a passport, and then it clicked. Vince Slattery used his passport under the impression that he was to meet Bojangles to write his story."

"Don't tempt me, Jenson."

"Your mother told me all about it, Vince. How your father caught you with your mother's underwear and wearing her make-up. Sixteen years old and insecure about your sexuality. It can't have been easy for you."

Sophie grimaced as the angry gunman squeezed her throat firmly, and pushed the muzzle even more forcefully against her head.

"Shut up, do you hear? It's lies, all lies."

Jenson was relentless. "I had an interesting chat with Dr Bullock. You remember him don't you, Vince? He reckons that your relationship with your father deteriorated and you were not allowed any money. You were bitter, and who wouldn't be? You were prevented from dressing as a woman and were without money; not easy for a teenager growing up in Croydon. The bitterness turned to hate, and you immersed yourself into your own private world. You created the fantasy characters. Goldie, someone you longed to be for obvious reasons. Brady, to steal the money you never had; and Bojangles, to vent your hatred and anger on the society that failed you."

"Have you finished?" asked Bojangles, whose eyes filled with tears.

"Over the years, your condition worsened, until the characters appeared more regularly and with more impact. Your wife leaving you pushed you over the edge, Vince. It was you that asked Sophie to come to your home, only you couldn't recall it. Vince Slattery, the real Vince Slattery is slowly losing his mind. Bouts of amnesia that Dr Bullock mentioned would explain a lot."

Bojangles loosened his grip on Sophie's throat and she inhaled liberally. Bojangles wept and the voice changed. The voice was that of Slattery. "My father hated me. He called me a Nancy boy and beat me... Do you know that when he died of cancer, I went to the cemetery and danced on his grave? I was free. Free at last."

"Give me the gun, Vince. You're going home," uttered Jenson, who held out his hand.

Slattery wept openly. "Why did Cheryl and the children leave me? I was a good father, wasn't I?"

"Vince, you are sick. Cheryl will understand. Hand me the gun."

The sobbing man looked up and held out the gun. Jenson saw the red spot settle on the side of Slattery's head and looked past him, through the balcony doors. The police marksman laid on the hotel roof opposite, his rifle sight homed in on his target.

Jenson held his hands up in a futile attempt to stop the sniper. The explosion of glass caused the occupants of the room to dive for cover, all except Jenson, who was covered with the blood and mucus from Slattery's head when it disintegrated.

Sophie screamed and had to be consoled by the startled detective.

The Mexican captain lit a cigar and bent down to inspect the corpse of Vince Slattery. "You see, Sergeant; we do things different in this country. Now go back to your drug-infested country and take this lesson with you."

"H-he was about to hand me his pistol," stuttered Jenson.

The captain shrugged. "Maybe he was and maybe he was not. It makes no difference. The world is a better place for the death of this animal."

Sophie escaped from the clutches of Jenson and faced the smirking captain. She spit in his face.

Jenson walked over to the dressing table and inspected the contents that were neatly laid out. The make-up, the fake tan lotion, black hair dye and the wig of Brady lay on the surface. Inside the drawers were an assortment of coloured contact lenses, a pair of spectacles, and the false beards of Brady and Bojangles. The detective reached into the corner of the drawer and withdrew a photograph; a memory from happier days of Slattery posing with his family. Jenson's eyes took in the sad sight of Sophie, who was covered in blood. She sobbed loudly as she embraced the body of the deceased.

Jenson's eyes focused on the ravaged, blood-covered, blonde wig that lay on the ground. He wept unashamedly, and recalled their childhood days together.

Epilogue

Danny Jenson lurked in the shadow of the bare chestnut tree and watched the two young girls feed the ducks. Their mother sat on a park bench, in conflict with a crossword puzzle. He composed himself and advanced towards the fatherless family, unsure of his strategy. This for him was the worst part of his job; to inform loved ones of the death of their child, or in this case her husband. Jenson had in fact volunteered to be the bearer of the tragic news. It was only fitting, and Vince would want it no other way.

How Slattery had managed to avoid detection from his family and close friends was credited to his obsessive manipulation of the characters. The various disguises had been enough to hoodwink people who had grown to like and love him. The insertion of the coloured contact lenses, the wigs and beards, were all props in his great deception, but it was the mannerisms of the characters that had diverted suspicion from the host. The campness of Goldie, the vulgarity of Brady, and the cool demeanour of Charlie Bojangles.

It was little wonder that stress contributed towards Slattery's deteriorating condition. To live out the lives of four totally different characters had taken its toll. The enormous debt Slattery had amassed had only just been revealed after his death. Did his money pay for the rents of his three characters, which would mean that he was actually aware of his condition and predicament? This is something only Slattery knew. The irony of it all was that Bojangles had amassed a sizeable amount of money. His blood money could have prevented the debt, which led the police to believe that the journalist was unaware he was actually the host. The enigmatic man had managed to fool them all, and his numerous absences now made sense.

On the cliffs of La Quebrada, Slattery had returned to the rented car and transformed himself into Bojangles, before he hurled the luckless Mikhos to his death. Slattery, in his advanced mental state of mind had offered his services as a professional hit man, and Chivers was only too willing to accommodate him.

In total, sixteen people had died, eight murdered due to the greed of Tyreman, Torrance, and Mikhos. Thirteen had died at the hands of Charlie Bojangles, including the three conspirators.

There were other victims of the Cupid's Arrow conspiracy. DCI Entwisle for one. He was sentenced to serve ten years in HMS prison.

Jenson now approached another of Slattery's victims.

Cheryl looked up from her book and Jenson's sad eyes told her that this was not a social visit. The children chased the ducks and giggled, unaware of their father's demise. Vince Slattery had left more than a widow and two fatherless children. So much more.

More books by Anthony Hulse

Insanity Never Sleeps
Insanity Never Sleeps II (The Resurrection)
The Eternal Chain
This Blood Red Sea
Nurtured Evil
The Orphans of Dachau
Forever and Ever
The Culling
The Cruise
Comrades of Deceit
The Abduction of Grace
Cries from the Deep

E-Books

Insanity Never Sleeps
Insanity Never Sleeps II (The Resurrection)
The Eternal Chain
The Culling
This Blood Red Sea
Forever and Ever
Cries from the Deep
The Orphans of Dachau

Blood Money
Comrades of Deceit

Available from http://www.lulu.com/spotlight/HULSEY
and www. Amazon.com

My Website:
http://anthonyhulse.angelfire.com/index.htm.lhome.html